D0018520

The Build Up deals with topics some readers may find difficult, including fatphobia, colorism, sexual harassment, alcoholism and the death of a parent (off page).

THE BUILD UP

Tati Richardson

carina
press

Recycling programs
for this product may
not exist in your area.

carina
press®

ISBN-13: 978-1-335-62193-1

The Build Up

Copyright © 2023 by Tatianna Mathews Richardson

For questions and comments about the quality of this book, please contact us at CustomerService@Harlequin.com.

Carina Press
22 Adelaide St. West, 41st Floor
Toronto, Ontario M5H 4E3, Canada
www.CarinaPress.com

Printed in U.S.A.

To Mama: A piece of you
will always be between the lines.

THE BUILD UP

Chapter One

Ari

"Dear Sweet Baby Jesus!"

The middle-aged receptionist, with her short natural graying near the temples, looked me up and down over her wire-rimmed glasses, her eyes eventually landing on the massive brown stain on my shirt. After a pit stop in the bathroom and an unsuccessful attempt at making myself appear decent, I had made it to the front desk.

She put down her pencil, refocusing her attention on my face. "Can I help you, miss?"

I get it, lady. I look like crap. Trust me, Crappy Chic wasn't the look I was going for on my first day at a new job.

I cleared my throat and attempted to stand up straight, projecting what little confidence I had left. "Hello. I'm Ari James. Here to see Porter Harrison. I'm the new junior associate."

The beginning of my epically disastrous morning began when the only thing I could find in my closet that fit was a basic ivory blouse and a black skirt that was so tight that it was riding up my ass. To make matters worse, the radiator in my nearly twenty-five-year-old Honda, affectionately named Honey, blew on the hottest day in August to which my neatly blown out hair responded by slowly reverting into a Lady of Rage level afro-puff. Honey's infirmity forced me to run to the West End MARTA station at breakneck speed, the morning's soundtrack provided by my Spanx mimicking a Girl Scout attempting to start a campfire. My heel got caught in a subway grate and broke. I squeezed into a seat on the nation's worst public transportation system, while barely holding a cup of cappuccino (which wasn't what I ordered at all) and an annoyingly large architectural portfolio that snagged on my last decent pair of pantyhose. I had a run as long as the Chattahoochee River that extended all the way to my big toe. But the cherry on top of an already shitty sundae was the teacup Pomeranian who poked its head out of its owner's Birkin and licked the rim of my coffee cup, causing my hand to jerk wildly. Before I knew it, a massive, lukewarm, brown splash of sugary liquid landed on my ivory blouse. After hobbling two blocks down Peachtree Street to the office building and a last-ditch effort in the bathroom to blot the stain away on my blouse, I gave up.

Shitty Day: 3, Ari's attempt to make a great first impression: 0.

After I introduced myself, the woman smiled, wide and warm, kindness reaching to her eyes. "Oh, Ms. James! Good to meet you, dear. We've been expecting you!" She came from behind the desk. Dressed in a lightweight knit twin set and slacks, the receptionist was shorter than me, with a behind wider than mine. I found that strangely comforting. At every job, I was always the biggest woman in the room. I mean, in all units of measurement, I was still bigger than this woman, but I appreciated another woman with ample hips like myself.

"I'm Gayle Jones, office manager. Everyone calls me Ms. Gayle." She extended her hand, and we shook firmly. Immediately, the tension I didn't realize I was holding in my shoulders released. Maybe that was a good sign.

"I'm sorry, Ms. James. It seems that Port… Mr. Harrison is still on a call. Why don't I take you to your office instead of waiting in here in the lobby, getting gawked at like you're on display in a museum!"

I widened my eyes. "Do I have an office? I just assumed I'd be out in a cubicle or something."

Ms. Gayle smiled. "If Mr. Riddle wants to give you an office, take the office. Most junior associates don't get one. And trust me, you don't want to be out there in the cubes with that lot. Follow me."

I stood up and hobbled on my broken heel after her with my portfolio in front of me, trying to hide the increasingly large run in my pantyhose. Ms. Gayle looked at me, hobbling at her side like a church usher at a second service. "Miss James, do you need some help with that shoe? I can try to locate some glue."

I felt my ears grow hot with embarrassment and forced a smile. I didn't enjoy asking for help. I was a "grin and bear it" type of girl. "I'll be okay," I assured her.

As we made our way down the hall, the people we walked past stopped talking and stared. I noticed everyone was Black. That differed vastly from my previous firm. At least I wouldn't have to deal with bullshit microaggressions. My eyes roamed from the cubicles, down the hall, and into other offices. Everyone was male. Yet again, I'd be the only female architect here. That was utterly disappointing. As we rounded another corner, a guy walked toward us, holding a well-worn Harvard mug that clearly needed replacing and sporting a goatee that seemed a little too dark and perfect. I gave my warmest nonthreatening smile in his direction. He responded by staring curiously for a beat and frowning. *Well, isn't he delightful?*

Ms. Gayle opened the door to my office, which was spacious, albeit basic with light gray walls and no windows. I sighed.

"Everything okay?" asked Ms. Gayle. I hadn't realized I'd been standing as still as a statue in the doorway.

"It's fine. I just need to put up some photos. You know?" I lied. The bareness of the office was another reminder that I was starting over. In Chicago, I had windows that overlooked downtown and the river. I had worked hard for that office, busting my ass quarter after quarter only for my life to be blown to smithereens.

Ms. Gayle raised a brow with concern. "Are you sure there isn't anything I can do for you, Ms. James? I can send your blouse out for dry cleaning. Or get a courier to get you something brand-new. Whatever you need. We ladies need to have each other's backs here and make the best impression." She gave me a wink.

Embarrassed, I bit the corner of my lips. She was right: Ladies needed to look out for each other. I had to learn to let my guard down. *She's just being nice, Ari. Everyone isn't out to get you or hurt you.* I finally agreed. "Ms. Gayle, is there any way you can get a courier to get me a pair of size 8.5 black heels? Something sensible like Nine West or Cole Haan. Nothing over three inches if possible."

"No Jimmy Choo?" chuckled Ms. Gayle.

"Ah no," I laughed. "Just a simple pair of black heels. And a plain white blouse. A size 2X? No, a 3X, maybe. I want to be comfortable."

Ms. Gayle clapped her hands with delight. "Great! I'll get on that right away. You just make yourself comfortable in here. I wrote your computer log-in right there on the sticky note on the monitor and put anything else you need in the desk drawers. I'm sure Porter will be ending his call soon. He's right across the hall. Oh, you're going to love him! He's the best. A real standup guy and the nicest associate I've ever worked with!"

I gave Ms. Gayle a wry smile. I highly doubted that I'd love this guy. I didn't know that much about him. After weeks of internet sleuthing, I couldn't find a decent photo of Porter. Despite being one of the senior most architects at the firm, there were no updated photos of him on the Riddle and Robinson website. Coupled with his sparse social media pages, filled with covers of vinyl jazz records and artsy shots of food—so many shots of food—I figured either the guy was trying to keep a low profile, or he hated taking photographs. The only thing that I knew for sure about Porter Harrison was that he attended undergrad at Hampton, like I had. He apparently had a keen eye for design; the guy had won a few awards over the years. So had I. Mr. Riddle said he'd hope that we could "cultivate a great working relationship" based on those commonalities alone. I wasn't sure how easy it would be. I had hardly been the social butterfly at Hampton. I didn't know many people. I'd kept a relatively low public profile within our industry, refusing to mingle outside of work. Besides, I wasn't here to make friends and get close to anyone. I'd made that mistake once before.

I was just trying to repair the damage and get back to the job I loved. After months of being rejected by every other architectural firm in town, this opportunity with

Riddle and Robinson was more than a job. It was an answered prayer.

Ms. Gayle made her way toward the door, but quickly pivoted on her heels. "You know, with a name like Ari, I thought you'd be a guy. Or Jewish. Well…you could still be Jewish. I'm not one to pry about religion. Either way, it's nice having another woman around here." With that, she closed the door behind her.

I sat in my sterile office, tapping my fingers on the table and occasionally glancing at the time on my watch. After logging onto the computer and putting away my things, I glanced across the hall. Squinting, I could only see the back of Porter Harrison's head through the partially opened blinds of his office door. Dude was really taking his sweet ass time. Was he the prince of the firm or something? If there was one thing I hated more than being late, it was being entitled. I couldn't and wouldn't work with another entitled jerk.

Twenty minutes later, an out-of-breath bike courier carrying a bag from a high-end department store knocked on the door. The tall, skinny white guy with black skater hair that peeked from underneath his helmet warily gave me a smile. He gripped the items with his fingerless gloves as if his life depended on it.

"Ms. James. Here are the things you requested. Are these sufficient?" He stood pensively, waiting for me to inspect it.

I opened the luxury shopping bag and peered inside. I was confused. Had they switched my bag with someone else's? I was sure I had not requested Tamara Mellon pumps. These shoes were at least $250. The blouse was a plain white button-down in my requested size. It, too, was perfect. *Wait? This blouse was a $300 Eileen*

Fisher. Good lord. I gulped, thinking about how that was going to come out of my first check.

"It's great. What do I owe you?" I asked as I went to my desk to pull out my Mastercard. Between this and the renovations to my house, I was going to eat ramen for the next month.

"No need for payment, Ms. James. It's been taken care of. As well as the tip." The courier exited my office as swiftly as he had appeared.

That's weird. Architectural firms had personal shoppers and *accounts for associates?* I had really come up in the world.

I quickly tossed my heels in the trash, ripped off my torn pantyhose, and slipped on the new heels. They were the perfect fit. I eased off my dirty shirt and tossed it into my tote bag, stuffing it all back into the large industrial bureau behind my desk. Just as I was buttoning the fresh shirt, relishing the feel of the material against my skin, my door flung open without warning.

A male voice boomed. "Ms. James. I'm so sorry for being late this morning. I..."

I turned around....

God must be auditioning for Def Comedy Jam.

Ms. Gayle's "You're going to love him" was a gross understatement, which included no mention of how handsome this man was. Christ! She could have warned me that Porter Harrison looked like the missing brother in a Michael Ealy/Jesse Williams doppelgänger set of triplets. He had sparkling green eyes, and a chiseled jawline framed by a faded beard hid a slight dimple that framed his wide, inviting, bright smile.

Or maybe I imagined that. I couldn't be sure. Having

someone walk in on you in a state of undress makes one disoriented.

I hurried and covered myself, holding my shirt together so tight I feared I'd rip off a button.

"Oh, dear God! I'm so sorry!" Porter squinted, closing his eyes tightly, unsure of where to look while his face was turning a bright shade of apricot.

"Well, can you turn around, please? So, I can finish changing my shirt."

"Oh sure. Do your thing!"

Porter turned quickly to face the corner of the office while I quickly buttoned my shirt and tucked it into my skirt in record time. I prayed the zipper would hold under the increasing pressure building up in my midsection. I could see why the man didn't have a photo on the company website or social media. He was too fine for public consumption.

I inhaled a deep breath before responding in my most professional voice. "Mr. Harrison. You may turn around now."

My mouth went dry as I took in his alarmingly good looks. It was a face that I would steer clear of under all circumstances. There was no way that this man was real, standing in front of me. Dude had the looks of an Instagram model. An impeccably dressed man, Porter wore a tailored gray suit and maroon tie. Too focused on his eyes, I almost missed when Porter extended his hand to me. I wiped my sweaty, quivering hand on my skirt and extended it toward him.

Porter, realizing that he was still holding my hand a beat too long, finally let go. "Wow…you're here. I mean. Sorry. Don't get up. I'm so sorry for the wait. I was on a call and I couldn't get them off the phone. Forgive me, Ms. James. Let's sit."

I slid back down in the chair nearest to me, unsure if I was melting or just obeying. "Ari. Ari is fine," I stammered. His voice had a twang that reminded me of candy-coated paint jobs, bayous, and Texas heat. *A sweet, sticky heat.*

Porter smiled a smile that was toothpaste-commercial ready. "Ari it is. Just call me Porter."

He sat down in the chair next to me. My skirt was so tight that I knew crossing my legs would cut off circulation and lead to my death. A death witnessed by this handsome man in the well-tailored suit.

Porter continued. "Mr. Riddle has told me such great things about you. Your work is top-notch."

My eyes darted away from the intensity of his gaze. "Seems that I can say the same about you."

Porter's lips curled up into a shy smile as he smoothed his tie. "I'm excited to work with you on our upcoming projects. The Serrano Group soccer stadium is going to be big for the firm. The crown jewel. Are these some of your conceptual designs?" He pointed to the black portfolio on the table.

As I watched him slide the portfolio toward his side of the table, the hair in my now frizzy kitchen stood on end.

Porter's fingers flipped through my designs with a slow sensualness. "Your résumé is impressive. Northeastern for graduate school. Hampton for undergrad. Which is crazy because I also went to Hampton. When did you graduate?"

"2001."

"Wow, I graduated in 1999. Funny. I wonder why we never ran into each other. Our department was so small, it's a miracle we never had a class together. Everyone knew everyone."

I swallowed. "Apparen ly not everyone." There was no way a man this fine would have been in any circle I was in. The extent of my collegiate life was the library, architectural studio, watching Anime, and singing in the Gospel choir. I was semi-reclusive.

Porter looked up. "Guess not. Do you attend homecoming? I mean, I would have remembered running into you there."

"I haven't been to homecoming in a while," I confessed. "Major projects have kept me busy these past years." I realized Riddle's emphasis on commonalities was something Porter had taken to heart. Hampton homecoming was legendary, but there was no way he'd recognize me in a sea of thousands.

"Did you pledge anything?" Porter asked. "A sorority, that is."

"No," I said flatly. Now, it seemed, he was grasping at straws. I hoped he wasn't one of those snobby, entitled, party-all-weekend frat boys I used to see running around campus. Porter looked like the type of dude on campus who went to all the frat parties, was on the sailing team, summered in Martha's Vineyard, went horseback riding, and had a ton of well-connected, old-money friends. Guys like that were not checking for me back then.

Porter folded his arms. "Oh…it's just so weird we've never run into each other. Not in the department. At an alumni event. Nothing. I feel like… Never mind."

What was this dude getting at? I watched as Porter continued to peruse my designs with his rather large and capable hands. Great, now I wondered how he looked holding well-worn leather reins.

"I was in Gospel Choir," I blurted out, trying not to think about...horseback riding.

Porter scratched his temple. "Oh. Okay. I didn't know anyone in choir. Partying on Saturday night with my frat brothers kind of took precedence over the Lord. You know how it is!" He let out a little chortle.

Well, he was indeed a frat boy. But the snorting? A pleasantly awkward, adorable surprise that came from a devilishly handsome face. The jury was still out on the "snobby and entitled" part.

I forced a smile on my face and Porter, following my lead, did the same. The difference was that his smile was genuine and reached his eyes. It was an incredibly gorgeous fucking smile, making me clench my abs.

"Anyway," Porter continued, closing my portfolio. "We have all the time in the world to get to know each other better. I'll let you get settled. Welcome home... I mean...well... You know what I mean."

He scratched his head of low curls sheepishly. Cute, humble, and awkward, but with the face of an Adonis? Talk about rare.

"My office is across the hall, so holler if you need me, fellow Pirate." Porter put his hand on my shoulder, then quickly removed it. "I'm going to go. I have another call in a minute. So...let's meet back up after that? Say thirty minutes?"

I nodded, with a dumb smile plastered on my face, completely transfixed, and trying hard not to look at Porter's butt as he left my office. It was so perfect that I'm convinced that if you bounced a quarter off it, you'd get five nickels.

I looked at the sticky note and quickly dialed up Ms. Gayle.

"Yes, Ms. James? Those things brought by the courier working out for you?"

"Yes, they are." I looked across the hall at Porter, who gave me a wave. And…was that a wink? I smiled, then turned my back. Nope. This will not work. Not if I have to work with…*all of that*. I have too much riding on this.

"Ms. Gayle. Is there any way I can get some blinds on my door? I'd appreciate it."

"Sure thing, Ms. James."

Chapter Two

Porter

I stood at the bathroom sink, splashing cold water on my face for the tenth time, replaying everything that just happened—Spike Lee style.

Heat pricked the tips of my ears.

Shit, shit, shit.

She was here.

The girl from the train.

My God, she was gorgeous. Thick legs adorned with modest heels and a fitted (no, tight) black skirt. I'd seen her tug at it this morning, trying to hide the run in her stockings, which had to suck. I didn't understand how women could wear pantyhose in this heat. All I had to worry about was picking out the right suit and maybe color coordinate my socks. She'd pulled her look together with an ivory shirt that was working overtime to hide an ample bust. The fabric clung to her nipple, which had hardened and was peeking out a bit from under the stain. I'd had to reposition myself in my seat as I felt myself growing wildly uncomfortable in the crotch. She wore her makeup light and beautifully natural, enhancing the deep caramel undertones of her skin.

And Jesus, those lips. The bottom lip was fuller than
the top. At least, I think it was. She was nervously biting her bottom lip. This unbearable heat was making
her thick hair frizzy. I couldn't stop staring. I couldn't
stop thinking about running my fingers through her hair.
I had to get a hold of myself. But it was proving to be
impossible. I never saw women that fine on the train in
Atlanta.

Up close, here, in *my office*, Ari was a magnificent
beauty to behold. A thing of movement, magic, and
brown-skinned wonderment.

The slamming of the bathroom door snapped me out
of my daydream, replaced with the sound of one associate making a loud delivery at the urinal.

I wiped my face with a paper towel and exited the
bathroom, passing by the receptionist desk. I leaned over
and picked up a few pieces of peppermint out of Ms.
Gayle's candy dish.

Like an annoyed mom, Ms. Gayle slapped my hand,
placing a solitary piece of peppermint in my hand. "Take
one, Porter! And again, that was real sweet what you
did for Ms. James. I tell you; the girl was a wreck. Hobbling on a broken heel. And that awful spill on her shirt.
Poor thing."

When Ms. Gayle had come into my office and whispered that the new junior associate had shown up looking
like she'd been in a losing fight with a mud wrestler, I'd
simply reached into my wallet and pulled out my black
AmEx. Holding the receiver of the phone, I whispered,
"Get her whatever she needs."

Ms. Gayle smiled. "Porter, you're the sweetest. Do I
have a limit?"

I'd raised a brow. "Ms. Gayle, I mean, be reasonable."

I was sweet, but I wasn't that six-hundred-dollar shoes sweet. Then again, I had no idea how much women's clothing cost.

Ms. Gayle walked out, chuckling, and waving the credit card in the air, declaring "Prada it is!"

Before I could object, she was already on her cell phone with someone to get the replacements for Ms. James. *Fine as hell, Ms. James.*

Ms. Gayle snapped her fingers. "Porter? Did you hear me? Don't keep Riddle waiting."

I blinked. The call. Shit. I had totally forgotten about the call to Madrid. "Damn. I told Ari, I mean Ms. James we'd meet again in thirty minutes. The call shouldn't take too long."

Ms. Gayle tossed me another mint for the road. "I'll buzz Ms. James and let her know you're running behind. Go do your thing, Porter."

As I was heading into my office, Darius Greer blocked my path. The dude made me uncomfortable. One of those smug bastards who looked down on HBCU-educated folks and thought his membership in Skull and Bones was far superior to any Black frat, Greer stood sipping coffee from his Harvard mug. The scholarships to boarding school and going on ski trips with his friends where he was the only brown face had done a number on him. The irony was that he grew up in the tough neighborhood of Compton and tried his best to forget that life ever existed for him. I never understood why he wanted to work at a firm that was Black-owned and led. The only thing that came to mind was that he figured the path to partnership would be easier at Riddle and Robinson. I was standing in the way of that.

"Greer? What can I do for you this fine morning?"

I said in my most sarcastic tone, preparing myself for some version of the same tired conversation.

"Harrison. Late isn't on time," quipped Greer. "Then again, CP time is kind of your thing." His eyes looked me up and down. "And you look paler than usual, like you've seen a ghost or something."

I rolled my eyes. "Yeah, well, I'm just in a rush. It's been a hell of a morning. I got held up on the train. My car is in the shop. And—"

"Oh, I forgot," Greer interrupted. "You're taking dirty transportation because your Porsche got repossessed or something."

"Repo...what? My car did not get repossessed, Greer."

"Whatever. By the way, I passed the new associate in the hallway. She was not what I expected."

I folded my arms across my chest. "What is that supposed to mean?"

"Man... I wasn't expecting her to be so..."

"So what?"

"You know...*big.* How big do you think she is? Like 225? 250?"

And there it was. Day 19563849 of Greer being an asshole.

I pinched the bridge of my nose. "You realize you're violating like several HR and EEOC rules, right?"

Greer took a sip of his coffee and shrugged. "Whatever. Her size doesn't matter. She's cute for a big girl I suppose. I mean, you won't have to worry about me trying to bang her is all."

I clapped my hands sarcastically. "Well, we can thank God for sparing her from two weak pumps from you." Michelle Obama wants us to go high, but in a verbal sparring match with Greer, the only option is going to hell.

"So, are you going to have time to onboard the new associate? Or do you need me to do it, Trust Fund? I know you're both... Hamptonites, Hampers, or whatever it's called."

Greer knew what alum were called. Asshole. "I'll have time to show her around. After my Madrid call." I didn't bother to let Greer know I'd already met Ari. *And busted in on her like a pervert.*

"I heard she's good as hell. Great designs. Maybe even better than yours. Thank God she's here to save your ass. You've been missing the mark lately, buddy."

We were far from buddies. "We'll see. One thing's for sure: I'm sure anything she or I come up with will be ten times better than anything you've done, Darius." I turned, walked into my office, and slammed the door. Every day, Greer gave me a reason to put rat poison in his coffee. He wasn't worth the energy or an attempted murder charge.

Darius Greer was hungry and just as determined as I was to make partner. We'd both started as interns at Riddle and Robinson, each of us being mentored by one of the founding partners. Initially, I'd really admired his drive and determination. He was young and scrappy, always feeling the need to claw his way to the top. He had a passion for design that I only occasionally could muster. He was talented as he was conniving—stealing clients, plagiarizing designs, and resorting to lying had often been his M.O. That's when I realized he'd probably sell out his own mother to get ahead, closing the book on any potential friendship we could have had. Despite growing up in different parts of the country, we had shared similar experiences. Private schools, ski trips, and being in spaces where sometimes you were the only

Black face… I knew that reality all too well. Finally, another brother I could commiserate with. But I don't think Greer ever saw it that way. Greer's resentment had everything to do with my family name. I was a Harrison, a member of a political dynasty of powerful men going all the way back to Reconstruction. Greer claimed to anyone within earshot that the only reason I was here was because Riddle was a friend of my grandfather, not because I had any talent. For that reason, he'd given me the nickname Trust Fund and I hated every time he said it. Fifteen years of the same shit, and it still annoyed me like a pebble in my shoe.

I looked at the clock. I was super late. I quickly connected to the video conference in Madrid.

"Porter. You're late," admonished Mr. Riddle. He was my mentor and like a second father to me. Third, counting my stepfather. "And I see you skipped the razor this morning."

I rubbed my chin. Ugh, I probably should have shaved before meeting Ari. "So sorry, Mr. Riddle. I was in a rush this morning. What are the Serranos saying? Do they have any idea what direction they'd like to go in?" I had been anxiously awaiting to hear all week from Riddle about the initial conceptual meeting with the client.

"Honestly, they aren't quite sure. I'm hoping you and Ari can work together on some stellar ideas. I think this stadium project needs some warmth."

I smirked. "I can do warmth."

"I doubt that. Warmth isn't your strong suit. Hence, hiring a woman. Another subject that you aren't well-versed in."

I scoffed. "Tsk. I know women!"

Mr. Riddle pulled his glasses off and looked at me directly. "Son, if you knew women, you would have one."

I frowned. True, I didn't know women. If I did, I wouldn't be such a colossal fuck-up in relationships. I'd ended my last relationship six months ago. We simply filled a void in each other's lives, taking up space where loneliness had been. It wasn't healthy. It was a colossal waste of two years with a woman who I didn't see a future with.

"Porter? Porter? Did we get disconnected? I think you're frozen."

Riddle's words snapped me back to reality. "Sorry, yeah. Just trying to figure out how quickly I can get Ms. James up to speed on the project. I already introduced myself this morning." *And probably saw a good bit of her tits, twice, but who's counting.*

"Excellent! Well, I'm glad you've introduced yourself to Ms. James. She's bright and the opportunity to hire someone of her caliber that used to work at Leland, Stokes and Brandies was heaven-sent. Make a good impression and please, don't be all awkward because she's our latest female hire. We can't have any more…situations."

"That means keep her away from Greer," I said, half joking, then cleared my throat. Besides being a colossal dick, Greer also ran off all the female architects we'd hired by either undermining their work or trying to lure them into bed. If it wasn't for his talent and his unapologetic ass-kissing, Greer would have been out of a job a long time ago.

Mr. Riddle's laugh was interrupted by a cough. "I'm glad you caught my drift. See you back in Atlanta by the end of the week. After you give us a design that'll

knock their socks off, we'll start the request for tender
for construction firms. You'll have at least a year to get
it done. Good day, Porter."

I ended my call and looked at the computer screen.
Pfft. I knew women. I mean…at least I think I did. Now
wasn't the time for a new relationship unless God and
the Pope himself intervened. Right now, the focus was
designing a world-class stadium and getting my name
on the building as partner.

But Ari? Was seeing her twice in one day divine intervention?

I shook the thought out of my head as I looked at
myself in the mirror, adjusted my tie and smoothed my
jacket. I checked my breath and popped one of Ms. Gayle's mints into my mouth, trying not to look nervous.
This was my first time having a co-designer on a project of this magnitude. I couldn't get distracted. I made
it a rule to never date coworkers. Since I worked mostly
with men, it was a rule I never had to employ. *Until now.*

I opened my door and paused before walking across
the hall. Ari's door was closed, but she was sitting at
her desk, typing away on her computer, diving headfirst
into work. I studied her profile; the curve of her jaw, the
fullness of her cheeks, how her hair was sticking to the
nape of her neck. She was, in a word, stunning. *Rules,
Porter. You have rules.*

Realizing I'd been standing there looking like a creep,
I nervously rapped my knuckles softly against her door.

Looking up from her computer, Ari smiled, her lips
mouthing "come in." My body involuntarily shivered.

"Hi," I said, sheepishly. A beautiful bouquet was on her
desk. I hadn't noticed those earlier. Had they been there
earlier? Then again, my eyes may have been elsewhere.

"Hi," Ari said, smiling widely. I'd never tell a woman she should smile more, but Ari's smile was too incredible not to want to see every minute of every hour. I made a mental note to get her to smile at me more.

I finally noticed Ari's new blouse. It fit her beautifully, hugging every curve tastefully. Ms. Gayle had evidently spared no expense. I was in for a surprise next month on my credit card bill.

I diverted my eyes to the fragrant bouquet nearby. "Lovely flowers. Someone must really be excited about your first day here."

Were they from a boyfriend? Girlfriend? I wasn't exactly subtle with my fishing expedition. Women as fine as Ari usually aren't single. And if they were, they wouldn't remain single for long.

Ari smiled as she nodded toward the flowers. "Oh. Thanks. These are from my mom. She sends me flowers anytime I start a new job."

I relaxed my shoulders. So, not from a partner. That's good. I mean, not good. It was just…surprising.

I eased myself closer to her desk, sitting in the chair next to desk. "So, how about you show me more designs for the new soccer stadium? I only saw a few in your portfolio. I know you have more."

Ari's right brow rose. "And what makes you think that?"

I leaned back in the chair. "Because you seem like a woman who comes to the job prepared. Even doing her homework ahead of time. Am I right?"

Ari laughed. "You may be right, Mr. Har… Porter."

"Cool! Maybe I can show you what I have been working on. I'm doing some 3D renderings."

She perked up at her desk. "That would be totally

cool. I mean, I'd love to see what you've done so far."
The excitement about the project in her voice was palpable. I appreciated her enthusiasm. It felt like Riddle partnered me with the right person for a change. Maybe he knew what he was doing.

"Why don't we work in my office? I have a large drafting table. We can spread out."

As soon as the words *spread out* were uttered from my lips, an image of Ari, legs spread open across my drafting desk, popped into my head. The image solicited a twitch in my slacks. *Settle down, fella.* I clasped my hands in front of myself, reminding my penis to act like it had a reasonable amount of fucking sense.

"Sure thing! Let me gather my stuff." Ari stood up, picking up her portfolio. I got a better look at those black pumps I'd paid for. They looked amazing and made her legs—supple, shapely legs—look even sexier. That skirt, which was tight in all the right places, failed to conceal what Senior would call "baby-making hips." I resisted the old-Uncle-at-a-cookout-urge to bite my lip and say "lord, have mercy!" *Thank God she couldn't hear what I was thinking.*

"After you, Ms. James," I said, trying my best to focus on anything other than Ari's ass. *It was a very nice ass, though.*

"Like I said, it's Ari…" she said, looking back at me with that smile again. Seems like my goal of getting her to smile more at me was on target.

"Right! Ari… Let's get to work, partner-in-design!" *Wow, Porter, real smooth, brother.*

Ari laughed. "Partner-in-design. That's funny! Are you always this funny?"

I shrugged, embarrassed. "Not always." Funny isn't a

word people would associate with me. But a woman who laughed at my jokes, despite them being corny? Be still my beating heart…

I watched as Ari walked across the hall into my office and began laying her designs on my drafting table.

Porter, you don't date coworkers. You don't date coworkers. You want to be partner. You don't date coworkers, Porter.

I closed the door to my office. We had work to do.

Chapter Three

Ari

Porter Harrison's office was meticulous. With its leather couches and gorgeous, industrial art pieces, his space was very modern. His Hampton and NYU diplomas hung on the steely gray walls. On a shelf was a photo of people that I presume were his family. Next to it was a portrait of a man in a military uniform who was the spitting image of Porter. Next to what I guessed was his father's photo was a photo of an older, near-identical man, shaking hands with former President Carter. His grandfather, I presumed. Along the shelves behind his mahogany desk were a plethora of vinyl records. His Instagram was spot-on. He could open a record store with the number of albums he owned.

Along the far side of the wall was a large drafting desk and stool, along with a nice, bright lamp. Above the drafting desk were several paintings that were very modern and abstract. The paintings were a lot like Porter: a mix of old and new, with an expert eye for design. I liked it.

I bent over the drafting desk and spread out all my designs. I turned to address Porter, but he was right there next to me. Startled, I jumped, and papers flew across the desk. We both reached for the papers, attempting to put them in order.

"Sorry," Porter said. "I was just eager to see...everything."

There was something about the way he said "everything" that made me hot between my newly pantyhoseless thighs. His voice was like butter on a hot pan.

"Here are my designs. I was thinking of a retractable roof. I was looking at some old designs of the Rio Olympics soccer stadium by Claudio Velez and I wanted to play on that. The south is a new market for soccer, so we should give them elements that work with the climate since we usually have glorious weather during soccer season."

Porter nodded and pointed at another design. "And this one?" he said flatly.

Oh Jesus, maybe he hated it. So much for me trying to be innovative.

"Well, are you familiar with where the Toronto Blue Jays play?"

"The Rogers Centre. Sure," he said, smiling. "Do you like baseball?"

I smiled. "I love baseball. Ever since the Braves went to their first World Series in 1991. I was twelve and crazy about David Justice."

He laughed. "That's pretty dope... I mean... That's interesting." He folded his arms and inched closer to me. He smelled amazing. At that moment, I was also glad that I put on extra deodorant because I could feel sweat percolating under my pits.

"Well, um. This design plays off the existing design of Rogers and its retractable roof, but see here, there is some extra room here for the dimensions of the soccer field and an interactive area here for the fans and soccer clubs, so they can feel close to the game."

Porter looked closely and then nodded. "I like it, but… it feels a bit cramped. Like right here." He pointed, and the sleeve of his arm inched up to reveal a vintage diamond-encrusted Chopard watch that had to cost a fortune. My daddy used to say you can tell a lot by a man and his watch. And this man had exquisite taste.

"But I do like where you're going. It's a good start, Ari," Porter continued. "Better than what I had. They hated my initial ideas. But you've really done your homework."

"Thanks. I've studied the aesthetics of the firm. I wanted to be in line with what you all do. But…"

"You also have to be yourself. Put a bit of you in every design that you do, right?" he said, nearly completing my thought, eyes twinkling. *Green eyes on Black men must be the Lord's way of making people even more jealous of their handsomeness.*

"Yeah. My thoughts exactly." My heart was beating a millisecond too fast.

"Can I show you my ideas?" He walked over to his desk and typed away on his iMac. I sat in the chair directly in front of his desk.

"Why are you over there?" he asked as he looked at me seated in front of him.

"Oh, I was just…waiting until you pulled everything up." There was absolutely no way I would stand next to him for fear that I'd faint. I didn't need to add that to my catalog of embarrassments today.

"I see. You can come over, Ari. I won't bite."

Listen, with those perfect teeth, I wish you would take

a bite out of me. I clenched my thighs so hard that I was sure I heard a seam burst in my skirt.

I looked around, realizing that neither his desk nor my thighs would allow for me to move the chair to his side of the desk to view the screen. Standing next to him and bending over, I was more worried about my skirt ripping or my boobs hitting him in the face. I took a deep breath, barely smiling. *Dear God, Allah, and Buddha, don't let me make a fool of myself or have my tits go tumbling out of this blouse.*

I stood next to him. His renderings were pretty good but not great. I bent over to get a closer look. I could feel his breath, a low whirling heat, on my neck and had to reposition myself as to not get lost in the feeling. It was warm and smelled familiar, like sweet peppermint from your grandma's candy dish. *Perfect teeth. Intoxicating eyes. And fresh breath? Well, that's just not fair.*

"These are pretty good," I declared, trying to distract myself from everything about this man.

Porter smiled, a little. "I started with hand-drawn drafts, then REVIT."

He moved the mouse around so I could get a 360° view, and then an interior view of the stadium. Everything was so detailed, down to the shape of the seats. His eyes caught mine, waiting for me to say something. I had to think of a question fast.

"I, uh, was just wondering. Why didn't you open it up more on the left for more natural light? Instead of closing this off for this large scoreboard?"

He looked puzzled, leaned back, and scratched the stubble along his chiseled jawline. I wanted to take my index finger and trace along its ridges. Feel the roughness against my skin. *Dammit. Focus, Ari. Focus!*

"Oh, I didn't really think about that. Maybe for our next design, we can try that. I'll make a note of it."

I smiled and moved back around to the other side of the desk. I had to sit down. The cologne, the peppermint-smelling breath, the stubble—I felt light-headed. Maybe I needed something to eat. I had nothing but cappuccino in my stomach. Did the dudes here even eat, or did they go to the gym on lunch breaks? The guys I'd passed in the hallway were ripped. Including Porter. Not that I'd noticed.

"Lunch?" asked Porter.

Was he reading my mind? "Huh?"

"I asked, would you like to go to lunch? My treat. There is a great sushi spot around the corner. It stays packed but I know a guy who can get me a reservation. Actually, it's not that close. We'd have to drive. The body shop just brought my car to the garage. I'm sure you're hungry by now." Porter paused. Instantly, his face turned red. *Dude, it's okay. People think I'm always hungry.* This time, I actually was starving.

"Sure. That'll be great." I smiled, assuring him he hadn't committed a social faux pas. His eyes twinkled with so much delight that I didn't have the heart to tell him I couldn't stand sushi. I liked my fish fried with hot sauce.

"Okay, I'll meet you in the lobby. Give me like five minutes."

I got up and walked toward the door. I looked both ways down the hall in confusion.

I looked back and Porter smiled as he pointed a finger left. "The lobby's that way, Ari."

Maybe the day was looking up.

Chapter Four

Porter

Ari sat across from me in a half booth at Tomo. She shifted uncomfortably, which made me second-guess sitting here. She tapped her fingers on the table, the same way she did in the office.

"Nervous habit?" I asked as I opened my chopsticks to pick up some edamame. I was picking up on all her quirks.

"I guess you can say that." She looked around the restaurant. It was crazy busy even though we'd arrived during the beginning of lunch. Ari looked down at the menu, her nose scrunched up, blinking a few times. She would be a terrible poker player. Her tells were obvious.

"Do you want to change tables? We can get an open table," I said, concerned about her comfort.

"Oh no. I'm good. There is room," she said with a slight smile.

"Do you like sushi?" Great, now it probably seemed like I was second-guessing the entire lunch. But I just wanted her to be happy, this woman I just met four hours ago.

"Oh no. This is fine. I love sushi." She bit the corner of her lip. I laughed. She was cute even when caught in a lie.

I put my hand on my chin, smiling. "Anyone ever tell you that you have a terrible poker face?"

"So, sushi isn't my favorite, but luckily, they have other stuff on the menu," Ari confessed with a smile. "I didn't want to offend you on my first day."

"You wouldn't have offended me by suggesting another spot. Remember, I'm treating you to lunch. But I'll say, the udon noodles are amazing. That's a safe bet."

"Thanks for the suggestion." She smiled widely at me, then with a chuckle asked, "How'd you know I was terrible at poker?"

I smirked. "Call it a hunch." *More like me noticing every movement, cataloging every detail, because I can't get enough of looking at you.*

The waitress walked over with a bowl of edamame, hips twisting with fury. She wore a long, jet-Black weave, a tight black minidress and fishnets with combat boots. She flashed a seductive smile at me, standing so close to me she obscured my view of Ari.

"I'm Tara. And what can I get you, sir?" she crooned.

Upon further inspection, her weave wasn't that great. Not that I was a weave expert, but I had paid for my fair share of hair extensions for girlfriends over the years. "I'll take the rainbow roll."

Cheap Weave then turned toward Ari, not directly looking at her, and said, "And what will your…guest be having?"

Ari frowned, cocking her head to the side. I didn't know what was going on, but I was picking up a very weird vibe.

I intervened. "My date will have the udon noodles with…" *Fuck. I said "date."* I mean, technically, she was my date. My lunch date. This wasn't a "date" date.

"Tempura shrimp," Ari interjected, the smile slightly returning to her face.

"Yes. With the shrimp. Thanks. That'll be all."

The waitress then said, "Let me know if you need… anything." The way she said "anything" was as though a side of sex was also on the menu.

"I think we'll be fine," I said with enough conviction in my voice that I hoped she got the hint that I wasn't interested.

The waitress walked off, and I turned my attention back to Ari. She had gone quiet. Her head was slightly down as she scrolled on her phone. I reached out and touched her free hand across the table. *Why can't I stop touching her? Good grief. It was like I had an addiction.*

"You good?" I asked, pulling my hand back swiftly.

Ari quickly looked up from her phone. "Yeah, of course!" She quickly turned her phone over. "I'm sure you get that a lot."

"Get what a lot?" *Now I was the one playing dumb.*

"Servers throwing themselves at you," Ari laughed, her lips curling into a tight smirk. "Hilarious. I think she thought we were on a date."

"Right."

Internally, I winced. I'd had the same thought, but hearing Ari say it out loud was like a stepping on a LEGO brick.

"It's not cool. This chick is mad rude. And for the record, I don't get servers throwing themselves at me on the regular." I watched as Ari delicately put the napkin on her lap and opened her chopsticks, that smirk still across her face. She didn't believe me. The goal was to get to know Ari, not talk about women and dates. That was making me uncomfortable.

"So...baseball, huh? Got any favorite current players?" I asked, changing the subject. I didn't know a damn thing about baseball beyond home runs and grand slams. I'd grown up playing basketball with my brother.

Ari sat up a bit, the smirk turning into a warm smile. "I dig Mike Trout. Hell of an outfielder. Pretty speedy too for his position."

"Wait? So, baseball players don't like to run? Isn't the point to run the bases?"

"I hate to sound biased but..."

We both laughed. Ari laughed so hard that her eyes were glistening, deep amber pools of light, reminding me of the changing leaves of fall. In that moment, I didn't think she could be any more beautiful.

"You know, my love of baseball got me into architecture," Ari said as she slid her chopsticks around the bowl of edamame.

"How so?"

"My dad. He loved baseball. The summer before I began college, my parents bought me a new car. My dad and I went on a tour of all of the major league baseball stadiums. We would have little adventures all the time. Just the two of us. That was the last solo trip that I took with him. He said it was my last trip as daddy's little girl because I was officially an adult. I think I've seen every stadium in the league, well, at least before many of the old ones were demolished. I studied the construction. What made each one special. We had a blast."

"Are you a daddy's girl?" I asked, sheepishly. I didn't have sisters and only a few female cousins. But I knew girls and their fathers usually had a special relationship.

"I was..."

Her voice trailed off, but the twinkle in her eye remained. I knew that look. I wasn't a daddy's boy, but I certainly had my fair share of memories with my dad.

Finally, she smiled, a faint, sweet smile. "He's gone now but I'm still a daddy's girl." She brushed her hands away in a feeble attempt not to cry. I could see the tears pooling at the corners of her eyes before she quickly dotted them away with her napkin. I knew that pain all too well.

"I get it. I lost my dad too. Years ago, but I get it."

"Oh, yeah?"

"Yeah. Time can't heal every wound."

"Right. Well." Ari shook her head, blinking away her tears. "That's why this soccer stadium is so exciting! I get to help design a state-of-the-art stadium. Something my dad would have loved. How dope is that?"

The server brought our food, rolling her eyes as she slid our plates in front of us. Out of the corner of my eye, I could see Ari bite her lower lip, trying to suppress a laugh.

Over lunch, I learned so much about Ari. After Hampton, she graduated top of her class at Northwestern, earning a prestigious internship in Florence, and lived in London for a few years before returning to the States. She worked at one of the big three firms in Chicago before returning to Atlanta shortly after her father passed away. When her dad died, it was her sign to leave and be closer to her mother.

In between bites, I tried to get insight to her time in Chicago. "So, is that why you left such a big firm like Leland, Stokes, and Brandies? Because your dad died?"

Ari's eyes avoided mine as she stirred her noodles. "Part of the reason," she answered somberly.

A tension seemed to radiate in her body language, sadness now in her eyes at the mention of Chicago. There was a story there. I didn't want to ruin lunch by pressing the issue further, so I didn't.

The lunch wasn't all somber topics and talking about work. I learned she was DC over Marvel, with Shuri being the exception. Ari was a native of Atlanta and loved all the home teams, which made me playfully groan because I was a devoted Saints fan. I didn't disclose that yet because I still wanted her to like me. I made a mental note that our next lunch should be Mexican because that was her absolute favorite food. Tacos, according to Ari, were their own food group.

"Did you ever take Mr. Garnett's class? Global theory?" I asked, looking over my water glass at her.

Ari laughed, covering her mouth between bites of her udon. "Oh, my god! Yes, that class was so tough! And he would always say…"

"You're shaping the landscape of the world!" We both said in unison, laughing. It had been so long since I had laughed with a woman. Hell, with anyone. It felt good.

I looked at the time on my watch. An hour had gone by fast. *Fuck! Two hours!* "Shit! Robinson is going to kill us. And Greer is a snitch, so we better get back."

"Who's Greer?" Ari asked, genuinely puzzled. I guess she hadn't realized that Greer had already peeped her in the hallway. *Thank God he hadn't said anything to her!* I'd hate for Greer to be her first impression of the associates at the firm.

"That would take another two hours. I'll give you the abbreviated low-down on the ride back to the office. We better go."

Ms. Gayle raised an eyebrow. The consummate mother hen, she looked at her watch and tapped it.

"Two hours? Porter, you know better! Mr. Robinson is looking for the two of you," said Ms. Gayle. "He looks like he can smell blood in the water."

I looked at Ari in horror. Mr. Robinson, the other half of Riddle & Robinson, was nothing like Mr. Riddle. Robinson, to be frank, was a bit of a dick, which was why he and Greer got along so well. Coming back from lunch after two hours wouldn't be a good first impression for Ari. But I'd take the heat. It was my fault.

"Listen, let's meet back in my office," I suggested. Ari nodded. We both swiftly walked down the hall, the whispers of other guys in the office clearly audible. I walked past the cubicles and then past Greer's office. He stood in the doorway, shaking his head.

"What?" I asked. I had no time for his bullshit. Not with a potentially pissed-off Robinson headed our way.

"What took so long? You take her to a buffet?" he whispered, then laughed like Muttley from Hanna-Barbera. If anyone ever wanted to torture me, they could play a loop of Greer laughing.

I rolled my eyes. "They must teach Being an Asshole 101 at Harvard."

"Don't be mad at me because you're late," Greer chastised. "Hope Robinson doesn't chew you guys out. I'd hate for ol' girl to get fired on her first day." Before I could respond, he slammed his door in my face. What a dick.

Ari was at my door, waiting with her tablet and pen in hand. She looked nervous. After ushering her into my office, I opened my computer and beckoned her to put her sketches on the larger table.

"Porter, this is my first day. This isn't the best example of what I can do. I know it."

"I think they're great. Let Robinson judge for himself."

Suddenly, we heard a knock at my door. Before I could answer, Earnest Robinson let himself in. He was in a fitted, pinstriped navy suit, his severely receding hairline framed by wire-rimmed eyeglasses. Ms. Gayle joked Robinson wouldn't go bald because then his hot, new wife would realize how old he truly was.

"Hi, sir, I'm Ari James, your newest junior associate." Ari extended her hand. Mr. Robinson looked at her, then her hand. Ari pulled back her hand and looked at me. I gave her a sympathetic look. Like I said, a dick.

"Where were the two of you?" Robinson barked.

"That was my fault, sir. We just got caught up talking about…the possibilities of this stadium project and what the client wants." Before I could say any more, Robinson was looking at Ari's sketches on the larger drafting table. We stood in silence as he looked on.

"You did these, Ms. James?" he asked, looking over his glasses and showing no emotion. Typical Robinson.

"Yes," said Ari. "I'm really trying to…"

Robinson held up his hand. Ari looked at him with a "who does this dude think he is" face. I pursed my lips and blew out a worried breath. Ari took a deep breath too and kept her cool.

"These are decent. They show promise but some seem a little…dated. I thought you were more innovative than that, Ms. James. At least that's what Riddle tells me."

Robinson then walked around to my computer. Without asking, he turned the screen of my computer to face him. I rolled up my sleeves, bracing myself for Robinson's criticism. You would think after fifteen years of working here I'd be used to his antics. But his brand of abrasiveness could be a lot for anyone to digest.

"You did these, Harrison?" he asked. He always called me by my last name. I hated it.

"Yes, Mr. Robinson. I'm just trying to experiment with some designs that could be LEED certified." I looked over at Ari, who looked a bit defeated. "But I think Ari, I mean, Ms. James, and I could come up with something spectacular. Something the city wouldn't even expect for the soccer team. Maybe something rivaling the Mercedes Benz stadium. As you can see, she really has a good eye."

Ari smiled. Robinson looked at both of us, his eyes darting back and forth. We probably looked like fools grinning nervously at each other. I snapped out of it and looked at Robinson as he moved toward the door.

"I see. Well, the next time the two of you decide to take two hours for lunch, it better be because you're celebrating finishing this project and the client is paying. Until then, curb the long lunches, Harrison. We have work to do." Robinson nodded and let himself out of my office.

I looked at Ari gripping the back of the chair. It looked as if she had been holding her breath the entire time.

"You can breathe now, Ari. He's just trying to flex his muscle as a partner. He's harmless. All talk and no bite."

Ari nervously chuckled and sat in the armchair nearest my desk. She put her hands on her forehead, with her elbows resting on her knees.

"He hates me. He hates my work," she said, sounding utterly defeated. "I mean, Riddle told me Robinson could be tough, but I didn't expect a total shredding of my work on the first day. I've had some tough critics but not like this. Dated? Really?"

I sat down next to her. "Don't take it personally, Ari. He's like this with everyone. He just expects perfection."

"I understand. I can produce perfection."

I bet you can. I smiled, watching her mood perk up a bit. "You will, Ari," I said, tempering my response.

Ari walked over to the desk, gathering all her drawings. She placed them gently in her portfolio.

"I'm going back to my office. There's some research I want to do."

"Of course, I totally understand. I've got some work to do as well. If I come up with any ideas, I can hit you on the office instant messenger."

"People still use instant messenger?" Ari asked.

I laughed. "It's not AOL, Ari. It's integrated into the video teleconferencing. It works well in this office. No one ever wants to get up from their desks if they're in a real groove."

Ari playfully tilted her head. "So, you're not going to ask my A/S/L?"

Woman, you have no idea what I really want to ask...

I scratched my head. "That's a throwback for real! I don't think I'll need your age, sex, or location. So, I think we're good there."

With a chuckle, Ari made her way toward my door. "Well, if I need you, I can just walk across the hall. I'd rather do that. I hope you don't mind."

I leaned against the doorframe. "I definitely don't mind." *Good lord, that sounded thirsty, borderline dehydrated.*

"Great."

With a smile, Ari nodded her goodbye.

Chapter Five

Ari

I walked out of Porter's office, feeling as if my architecture degree was worth toilet paper after Robinson ripped us to shreds. Thank God for Porter. I didn't need him to come to my defense, but it was nice to be supported. I appreciated having a real teammate in Porter. I looked back to say just that, but he'd already closed the door to his office and was working diligently on his computer.

As I was opening the door to my office, the rude guy from earlier that morning was approaching me, shaking his head with a smirk on his face. I froze with my hand on the doorknob.

"Hi. Can I help you?" I asked, defensively folding my arms across my chest. I got a bad vibe from him. Dude seemed slick, like a can of bacon grease. I recalled Porter's conversation with me on the ride back to the office. *Tall, arrogant, mouthy...with a face you want to punch.*

"It's Greer, right?"

Greer's eyes roamed the length of my body. "Yeah. Darius Greer. Everyone calls me Greer. Just thought I'd come over and introduce myself. Hope you're settled. Getting the lay of the land. Just so you know, we have snacks in the break room. You know, in case…"

Then the funky bastard looked directly at my boobs. Yep, punchable face, for sure.

He leaned against the wall, invading what little personal space I had. Frowning, I backed up a couple of inches. "I'm good, Greer."

"I heard Robinson ripped you a new one. Too bad. It being your first day and all. Don't take the criticism personally."

I looked directly at Greer, who was just a little above eye level with me with my heels on. His smug face with his shellacked goatee didn't scare me. He took a step back.

"I never take things personally, Greer. Now, if you'll excuse me, I have a stadium to design."

I turned on my heels, slamming the door in Greer's face. What a complete asshole! He reminded me of… I shuddered at the thought. I didn't have time to think about that. Dudes like Greer didn't matter. Partners like Robinson did. He was the paradigm of ruthless C-suite executive, which was certainly downplaying things. The ding of an instant message tone interrupted my thoughts.

P. Harrison: A/S/L?

I snorted. This dude was as corny as he was fine.

A. James: That may be an HR violation, sir.

P. Harrison: You're right. My bad. Anyway, did you just slam the door?

A. James: Yes. In Greer's face. That's his name, right?

P. Harrison: Was it a dude with a Bigen-dyed goatee?

A. James: Guilty. Sorry. I know that wasn't a good look.

P. Harrison: Don't sweat it. You know how many times I've slammed the door in his face? Trust me, I know he probably deserved it.

A. James: :) Indeed, he did. Also, he's not fooling anyone with the Just for Men dyed beard.

P. Harrison: Don't get too close. You'll have to get another blouse.

I laughed loudly, the sound echoing off my bare walls. I liked this dude. *No, Ari. Don't...* But liking him was good. At least I knew I could work with him. Anything beyond that... I wouldn't dare consider.

I shook all thoughts of Porter, Robinson, and Greer out of my mind and got back to work researching more on our client. The Serrano brothers were a pair of suave Spanish olive oil and wine producing billionaires with money to burn. They were also the new owners of Atlanta's latest powerhouse soccer team and wanted a state-of-the-art soccer stadium to rival any in the league. Although incredibly posh, the Serranos were also huge environmentalists, touting sustainability within all their business ventures. I tapped my pencil against my chin as I stared at the computer. They deserved a stadium for a team that was the same and set the tone for what they wanted to bring to the soccer league: style and sophistication all while being sustainable.

I wanted to ping Porter back, bounce some ideas off

him, but I left him alone. I could figure things out on my own. But part of me just wanted to talk to him. I enjoyed talking to him. I tapped my fingers on my desk. I wasn't here to make friends. I wasn't here to get close to anyone, even if we could laugh together. I was here to rebuild my résumé. Work truly should come first.

After what seemed like forever, I looked up at the clock. It was five minutes until six. I had spent the last four hours drafting and researching and I'd lost track of time. I peeked out my door and looked across the hall. Porter was standing at his desk, putting things into a messenger bag. *Fuck it. You can at least say good night. That's just being polite.*

A. James: Packing it up for the night?

P. Harrison: Yeah. Got to head out of here ASAP.

A. James: Hot date?

The chat messenger showed he was typing, then paused. I looked out my door and saw Porter, scratching his head. Finally, after what seemed like an eternity, Porter responded.

P. Harrison: I'll TTYL. Get home safe.

A. James: Sure. Thx. See you tomorrow.

Crap.

I stared at the screen, my eyes avoiding the hallway as I heard his office door close. Did I say something wrong? Was I getting too personal? His personal life was absolutely none of my business. I had slipped into getting my old habits of getting too comfortable, too familiar.

One thing was for certain, I damn sure didn't have a date.

The train ride home didn't take nearly as long as I thought it would, considering that MARTA never runs on time after rush hour. I had to call the mechanic as soon as possible to get my car fixed.

I walked the two blocks from the station to my little 1940s West End bungalow. Walking in heels from the station was for the birds. As soon as I got inside, I kicked off my heels, threw my portfolio down near the coatrack, tossed my keys in a bowl on the buffet next to the door. I took a moment to just take in my house and all the work I'd been putting into it for the past few months. It was all coming together.

This house had been my childhood home and my mother's childhood home. After my father died, my mom decided it was too hard to stay in the house. "Too many memories," she declared. She bought a condo in Vinings, close to active seniors, our church, and some of her friends to start a new life. So, when I moved back home to Atlanta, I knew I'd want to move into the family home and remodel it. I had made sketches of what I wanted to do. Over the past months, I was making strides in making the home more modern. *To make it my own.* I was finally settling down somewhere for a while. It was the least I could do with money that felt dirty.

I was most proud of the kitchen. It was sleek and modern, with cool, contemporary stainless-steel appliances and a massive island for entertaining that also housed a wine cooler. My mother had laughed and said, "A fridge just for wine? That is some bourgeois Black people's shit." Yet, she had been the first person to bring over a nice bottle of champagne to "test it out." The kitchen was a far cry from the outdated flowered wallpaper that had turned yellow from smoke, grease, and years of cooking. I smiled, thinking about how my father almost burned the house down trying to fry chicken. It had been painful for me to tear down that wall that had the last traces of my father. Once completed, Mama smiled and said I had brought new life to the place. But I couldn't cook in it yet. Not before she burned sage and removed the "negative energy of Uncle Cecil's wife's potato salad" which was the last thing we ate in the old kitchen at Daddy's repast. It had craisins in it. It was a family scandal.

In the living room, I had re-tiled the fireplace myself, in cool blue, gray, and green tile. Blue was my dad's favorite color. I knew it would be the perfect color scheme for the fireplace, and Mama agreed.

Despite the extensive renovations, plastic still lined the walls in the master bath. I had an ongoing dispute with George Flores, my lovely contractor, about what to do in the master bathroom. He said it would be more elegant with a detached claw-foot tub and a smaller walk-in shower. I told him I didn't want a tub at all, desiring a twelve-foot-long glass encased shower with imported tile and two waterfall showerheads instead. Mr. George, as he preferred to be called, was a lovely man and one of the best contractors in the city and knew his stuff. He thought that my idea was a waste of space and would bring the value of the house down. I didn't want a damn tub. I wanted the shower of my dreams because, to be frank, I wanted to have sex in a shower that would accommodate me and my eventual partner. Of course, that was none of Mr. George's business. I just let him think it was purely for "design aesthetics." I was an architect, after all. So, we were at an impasse.

From the color of the exterior painted brick to the renovated back deck, the months I'd spent working on the house were an ongoing labor of love. It felt like the famed Winchester Mansion, with my never-ending expansions and plans. I figured this would keep me busy on my days off. It's not like I was dating anyone I could meet for happy hour. *Was Porter meeting someone for happy hour? Did he even do happy hour?* Fuck. I had no business thinking about stuff like that.

Too lazy to walk back to my bedroom, I stripped off my skirt and shirt at the front door. One of the amazing benefits of being single and childless was being able to walk around half-naked. I went to the kitchen, feeling the coolness from the hardwood floors on my feet, and opened the wine cooler. After picking a nice bottle of pinot grigio, I grabbed a glass and settled in for the night on my couch. I placed an order for Greek food through a food courier app. This was going to be the perfect meal to destress after my first day at work.

As soon as I began flipping through the TV channels, I got a text message. I knew it wasn't my mom because she was on a bus heading to the casino in Tunica with her girlfriend, Carol. Besides, she hated texting. She was far too long-winded. Part of me hoped it was Bella, my best friend, inquiring about my day. We hadn't spoken all day and needed to debrief. Disappointingly, it wasn't Bella. Perhaps it was someone with potential to help me destress after work.

Korny: Hey stranger. I'm back in town.

I was wrong.

I cocked my head to the side, looking at the message as if it was hieroglyphics. Korey aka "Korny" in my contact list, was a guy that had been nothing more than one of many friends-with-benefits I'd accumulated since moving back to Atlanta. After Maurice, whose sex was so good that it clouded my judgement, I was over dating and sex that made me think I was in love. All of Maurice's lies about loving me and wanting to be in a relationship were his way to derail and eventually torpedo my professional life to elevate his own. For that reason, I had sworn me off relationships, especially those that distracted me from my job. Sex I could do. As cold as it sounded, men were just here to service me when I wanted sex that scratched that need-an-orgasm-filled itch.

Korey wanted to be the one to scratch that itch tonight, despite not hearing from him in forever. I preferred to be the one making the sex appointments. Korey was an absolute bore. He talked endlessly about his job as an associate professor of sociology at Emory. And as much as I loved sociological issues, I didn't want to talk about them on a date as the precursor to foreplay. I texted him back.

Hey. Kind of busy right now. Can we chat later?

Korny: Sure. Just wanted to see how you are. Maybe see if you wanted company. Celebrate your first day.

Christ. While I appreciated him remembering that it was my first day at R&R, this dude couldn't take a hint. I tapped the phone against my chin, contemplating if sex with Korey was worth suffering through the latest rambling about prison pipelines or school push-out. I mean, not that those issues weren't important. They just didn't make my pussy wet.

Fuck that. I wasn't about to suffer through foreplay that Henry Louis Gates could have written.

I texted back:

Thanks for remembering but truly, I'm kind of beat. New job stuff. New routine. Had to walk to the train station. TTYL.

I'm not even sure why I told Korey all of that. He would simply disregard my life and just start discussing his own.

Korey: That sucks. Just went to a conference in DC and I talked to Dr. Cornel West. It was amazing. I thought you'd like to hear about the talk I presented on Black male teacher retention in public schools.

Ugh. My pussy was officially the Sahara. I didn't bother to respond.

As soon as I closed the message, I felt a twinge of regret. Korey was boring, but the sex was decent. *Okay, more like reliable.* On a scale of 1 to 10, with 10 being amazing, Korey was like a 7.5. I'd probably achieve an orgasm, but not one good enough to put up with the boringness that came with it. After sex, he'd talk endlessly, and I'd usually fall asleep to the sound of his monotonous chatter. He was the human version of a sleep app.

It had been well over a month since I had some type of sexual anything, not counting solo trips around home base. But to break a month-long drought with Korey would be a waste. I'd rather watch *Holmes on Homes* find asbestos in the basement of a haunted house. On second thought, I'd rather watch paint dry. Come to think of it, one time while Korey and I were having sex, I looked at the walls and wondered to myself, "Hmm… I wonder how they would look in a smoky, navy color." I ended up calling Mr. George the next day to get a navy accent wall in the bedroom.

Okay, so maybe 7.5 was pushing it. He's really a 6. Or a strong 5.5.

As I sipped my wine and waited for my takeout, a thought ran through my mind. One month of no contact. No calls. No texts. And he hits me up for some coochie? Korey thinks I'm one of "those" fat girls: desperate and lonely.

A lot of folks think fat girls sit at home because no one wants to date us. Not true. Most of us sit home because we *choose* to. In my case, I was alone but not lonely. I had a phone full of the numbers of men who wanted to not only sleep with me but date me. Many accomplished, professional men from all walks of life. From construction workers to CEOs, I had my pick. This big girl wasn't pressed to just go out for the sake of going out. No free meal was that good to entice me out of the comfort of my home just to waste my time. All fat women are not sitting home sad, depressed, stuffing our face with cookies, and waiting on Prince (or Princess) Charming. Korey, in all his arrogance, probably hit me up because he thinks an over-40-year-old, single fat Black woman is grateful for attention, any attention, from a man. Hell, from anyone. If only he knew. One phone call and my drought would be over. No, sir, I was home now, enjoying my wine, waiting on my takeout, by choice. Besides, most of the guys whose numbers were in my phone just didn't do it for me anymore. I realized they all lacked joy. I didn't laugh with any of them. Not like I had laughed with Porter today. He made what started out a colossally shitty first day at work alright in the end. I appreciated that. I don't think any of the men in my current roster did that for me.

I wrapped myself in my throw blanket and settled into the comfort of my couch. I looked over at my phone and bit my lip. *But it has been a month...*

Ugh, no, Ari! Sex with a walking TedTalk is not worth the time.

I turned the TV to the home improvement network just as Bob Vila was fixing the porch of an eighteenth-century New England colonial. He was bent over in his overalls looking at an original wood-burning stove, explaining the gorgeousness of the patina of the copper.

Now this was sexy.

Chapter Six

Porter

In the weeks leading up to our first major presentation to the partners, Ari and I had been busting our ass. I didn't think I'd like working with someone, but I really did. It was nice to just pop over to her office to run an idea by her or talk over ideas at lunch. Lunch was my favorite part. In these weeks, we'd tried everything from tacos al pastor at Krog Market to slap-your-mama, finger-licking ribs at Sweet Auburn Barbeque. Besides being smart and talented, Ari was easy to talk to and funny as hell. I hadn't laughed that hard with anyone in the office in forever.

Ari and I worked late into the evenings, tweaking, and going over renderings for our end-of-the-week meeting with the partners and senior staff. We ordered takeout and debated the merits of one idea over another. In the end, her ideas were always better. These late nights, long lunches, and laughter was making it really difficult for me not to break my rule. I really wanted to ask her out on a real date.

When our workday was over, the temptation to ask her to happy hour or something was overwhelming. I just wanted to spend more time with her. Despite me feeling like our meeting was kismet, or fate, or something divine, I couldn't bring myself to do anything to jeopardize things. We had a stadium to build. I had a partnership to secure. I didn't date coworkers, I had to stick to that rule. Most of all, I wasn't trying to be another Greer by getting in her pants and running her off. (Even if those pants were on some thick, sexy thighs.) We worked great together. Why risk it?

Yet, Ari was all I could think about when I got home after work. I memorized the cadence of her laughter and played it on a mental loop. The thought of her delicate perfume drove me crazy. I would stand close to her so I could torture myself with her smell. I'd practice which way to position myself to feel the heat radiating from her body. Each time she leaned over the desk or reached for a pencil; I'd feel regret that her hand never grazed mine. It was a vicious cycle that repeated day after day. The good Catholic boy in me felt so guilty. Lusting like this wasn't healthy. What was I doing? *And why did I just not give a fuck?*

Our meeting to present our designs before Riddle, Robinson, and the senior associates was Friday afternoon in the large boardroom. Ari was nervous. She paced in my office so much that I was dizzy watching her. After we finished going over concepts, she paced more in her office, which now she had decorated with photographs of her parents, prints by Kara Walker, and a shit-ton of plants. She also made it a point to have copies of her diplomas and professional memberships on the wall just in case "dicks like Greer wanted to step to her crazy." I totally respected that. It was something I, as a man, took for granted.

"What if they hate this?" asked Ari, as she paced. I was worried she was going to put a hole in the carpet and that would piss off Ms. Gayle because we just replaced it. Gently, I put my hands on her shoulders and stood in front of her. I prayed I wasn't being too forward but calming her down was important. As I looked into her eyes, I felt her shoulders relax and a smile slowly formed at the corner of her lips.

"Ari, breathe. Things are going to go well. This is just our first run. They'll give feedback. No one will outright say they hate it…except maybe Greer. Because he hates everyone's work except his own."

Ari chuckled as she twirled her necklace around her neck. I hadn't noticed how she did this too when she was nervous. *Another quirk to add to the list. I liked quirky.*

Ms. Gayle knocked on the door of Ari's office.

"They're ready for you two." She gave us a thumbs-up.

I grabbed the jump drive, and we both walked down the hall to the larger boardroom.

Riddle and Robinson sat near the head of the table. Taking notes on her iPad was a representative for the Serrano brothers. Mr. Riddle gave us a slight smile while, naturally, Mr. Robinson gave us no expression at all. Greer sat to the left of Mr. Robinson like his little pet. As I looked around, I realized I'd never noticed how much of a guys' club this was. I'm sure this wasn't exactly the warmest environment for Ari, but I watched as she stood there, her back erect, handing out notes to the associates and partners, ready to get the entire presentation started. She was confident, way more than I had ever been for any presentation. I admired that a ton. I nodded to Ari, and we proceeded.

Our design was amazing. It called for a retractable

roof with a walkable green space in the nosebleeds for fans which doubled as a fully functional garden to grow herbs and vegetables for the restaurant concepts. There was an amazing beer and wine bar that overlooked the home team locker rooms. All the club level seats would recline, making room for the massive fan clubs that soccer attracted. It was literally the best of European and American styles. Above all else, it would be LEED certified as well, something the Serranos would appreciate. After our presentation, we got a few applauses, with Greer not reacting at all.

Finally, we opened the floor for questions. Naturally, Greer was first.

"Well, I found the style a bit…hectic," said Greer.

"Is there a question in that?" asked Ari. Damn, she came out the gate hitting dude in the balls. I smirked.

"No. Just felt like it needs to be said," Greer retorted.

Robinson nodded. "I'm inclined to agree with Greer. I think there needs to be a 'less is more' approach here."

I sighed. Of course, Robinson would agree with Greer. Greer was his pick for partner. He would do anything to make that happen. Including, undermining a perfectly logical design.

Riddle, trying to cut the tension, interjected. "Well, you two, this is a splendid start I think, but yes, it may be a bit much for our clients."

"They're Spanish. This shouldn't look like a Dominican bodega," said Greer.

The rest of the senior associates chuckled. Riddle gave Greer a pointed look, and he stopped laughing and cleared his throat. I looked over at Ari, her head held high. In the weeks since working here, her confidence soared. I had to admit that it was rubbing off on me.

"I hear what you're saying but… I think if we just present it to them with some minor tweaks…they'll appreciate it," I said.

"And it will only need minor tweaks. I promise our next showing will be stronger," said Ari.

Robinson looked at the notes and wrote some things down, finally saying, "I hope so. As you know, the Serrano Group will need to see progress toward an outstanding design during this concept phase. I'd hate to see them dissatisfied."

"Over my dead body," mumbled Ari. I stifled my laughter. I liked this woman. She was tough as nails.

"That would be a lot of body," Greer, seated to my immediate left, said under his breath. A few of the associates laughed. Riddle and Robinson didn't hear, as they were having their own discussion with the Serrano representative. I hoped Ari didn't hear him.

"What was that, Greer?" asked Ari.

Oh. Shit.

The associates went silent. "Oh…nothing. It was nothing," said Greer. I could see him getting hot under the collar. I was sure his painted goatee would melt off his face like a Dali clock.

"Let's try to keep it professional," I said, speaking directly to Greer and out of earshot of the partners. "The firm is a team, man. A win for one is a win for all."

"Well, since you brought up teams, I'd like to make a proposal," blurted out Greer, looking over to the partners to get their approval to continue. Both Riddle and Robinson nodded.

Ari looked at me wide-eyed. I shrugged, not sure what was going on. Our meetings weren't like this usually. Greer was trying to throw a monkey wrench in it.

Greer continued. "If I may. This stadium is a big deal for this firm. I mean, really. We're the first African American lead architectural firm in the nation to build something of this magnitude. For something with so many stakeholders, I think maybe we should get some… alternative concepts for the Serrano Group. Porter and Ari, what you've presented was…interesting. But I think the Serranos deserve to see what the best of this firm has to offer. That includes perspectives from, well, the best."

Ari's jaw went slack. Before she could say anything that started with a "mother" and ended with a "fucker," I held up my hand. "You mean yourself?"

Greer shrugged, nonchalantly. "I mean, now that you've mentioned it, Jacobi and I have been mulling around some ideas. I mean, we would have brought them to you guys but you appeared as if you had a handle on things. But it seems, I was wrong. This is a daunting task. We're more than willing to present what we have. If the partners and Serrano Group are interested."

Ari scoffed. "So, you're trying to make this some sort of competition?"

Greer let out a breath and adjusted his cuff links. "Oh, Ms. James, it's not a competition. That's so juvenile. We're beyond that. It's just about…options. Everyone likes options. Especially when the options are exceptional rather than just acceptable."

My nostrils flared. This weasel. Of course, Greer and his stool pigeon Jacobi would conspire to come up with a design of their own. I looked over at Ari who was totally dumbfounded. We both watched as Riddle and Robinson whispered to each other, and then to the Serrano Group representative. I looked at Greer out the corner of my eye. He sat there, beaming as if he'd won a prize at a state fair. I wanted to knock that smug grin off his face.

Riddle cleared his throat. "Well, what Greer has proposed is highly unorthodox. And yes, we aren't competitive at this firm. But he's right. We need to give the Serrano Group as many options as possible. But what you presented was good."

Robinson nodded. "Yes. It was good. But we want great. You two seem to enjoy being creative. The design reflected out of the box thinking. Impressive. But there also must be an element of practicality. That wasn't clear in the design you presented today. The two of you seem to make an incredible team. We know you can give us something better. So go back to the drawing board. I look forward to seeing more from you all. In the meantime, we will field other designs from Greer and Jacobi at these meetings as well. We've got plenty of time to get this right."

I watched as Ari's body language went from stark-raving mad to defeated. I had to get this meeting back on track. "Mr. Robinson, I can assure you, Ms. James and I can handle unorthodox. This is our project." Ari tapped her foot violently as she sat next to me. She had gone from defeated to pissed off. Eventually, she rubbed her hands down the side of her pencil skirt a few times, settling her restlessness.

Riddle and Robinson got up from their chairs. As they passed us, Riddle stopped to pat me on the back. "Good start, you two. Let's reconvene in about two weeks. Greer and Jacobi, I'll be expecting us to see these ideas you've been working on."

"Yes," stated the representative for the Serranos. "I'll

be letting the Serranos know the firm is off to a good start and going to present plenty of options. Well done."

Everyone dispersed. I watched as the representative for the Serranos gave us a courteous nod while exiting. I swallowed; thankful we hadn't fucked up royally. I let out a breath.

Greer walked past me, bumping into my shoulder. I stopped him. He looked down at my hand on his shoulder with a snarl.

"You're a fucking snake," I whispered. "Don't think for one second your name is going to be anywhere near this stadium."

Greer jerked his shoulder away from my hand, stepping close to my face. "And what are you going to do, Harrison? I guarantee it won't be creating a better design. You're coming up short, as usual. This won't be any different. Senator Harrison can't bribe anyone this time to get you what you want."

The veins in my neck pulsated. I wanted to curse him out, but he was lucky that Ari was there, stepping between us.

"Porter. I'd like to have a word, in private," Ari said, putting a gentle hand on my shoulder, coming between Greer who eventually left without another word.

"I'm sorry, Ari. I did not know Greer would pull a stunt like that. And in front of the partners and client no less."

Ari rolled her eyes, chuckling. "If I'm being honest, I should have seen this a mile away. I could tell he was a little jealous that he wasn't in on this. You need to study your enemy better, Harrison. Give me better intel." She bumped me slightly with her shoulder, winking at me.

Slowly, I felt the tension in my jaw slowly dissipate.

"You sound like you have experience in the art of office politics. I need your CliffsNotes because obviously I suck."

Ari leaned against the table. "Man, you have no idea. Guys like him…" Her voice trailed off, her eyes looking far off into some distant memory. "I've worked with my fair share of Greers in my career. The way to beat a guy like Greer is to be three steps ahead. Beat them at their own game. And next time, he won't catch us slipping. That's the only way that he'll respect you. We will have a design so amazing; he'll have to bow down."

I smiled, throwing up my hands in faux shock. "You're gangster, Ari. Let me not mess with you!"

Ari put up her fists in her best Evander Holyfield stance. "I'm from the West Side. Zone 4. You better act like you know!"

We both laughed, then stared at each other for a few beats. I followed her cola-colored eyes until we both looked away.

I blinked, then cleared my throat. "We better get our stuff and head out of here. It's getting late. I don't want to hold you up."

"You're not." Ari turned her back to me, fighting with the cord that connected her laptop.

We moved in silence for a few minutes, gathering our presentation materials. I ran my hands through my hair. *I'm about to go against all my rules. But what the hell…*

"What are you doing tonight? After work?" I asked, my eyes still pretending to examine random papers on the boardroom table.

"Why? No hot date tonight, Porter?"

I folded my arms and leaned against the table, shaking

my head. "Now, what makes you think I have a hot date. Maybe you're the one with the hot date?"

Ari made a "hmph" face with down-turned lips. "Didn't your mama teach you that making assumptions makes an ass out of you and me?"

I leaned in closer, speaking in a low voice to evade eavesdroppers. "Well, since neither one of us has a hot date, I'm asking you, Ms. Ari James, to go have a drink with me. We must celebrate the minor victories. Blow off some steam. Aside from Greer's shenanigans, this was a good start. Besides, it's almost the close of your first month here. Or do you have something better to do on a Friday night?"

Ari leaned against the table just a few inches apart from me. She looked up at the ceiling and tapped her chin as if she was thinking. Even when she was being funny, it was very sexy.

"Hmmm. Idris Elba is out of town. So, I'll hang out with you. But…only if you promise me one thing, Mr. Harrison?"

Girl, I'd promise you the world. I needed to rein it in because I was sounding like a seventies R&B crooner. "Absolutely. I always keep my promises."

She turned to me with a mischievous grin. "As long as wherever we go has a great burger to go along with that drink, then I'm game."

I laughed. "That's easy! I have the perfect place for that. I know a guy."

Chapter Seven

Ari

I should kick my ass because I suck at taking my own advice. Yet here I was, on a date with Porter Harrison. Okay, so, maybe calling it a "date" was a bit of a stretch. It was an innocent drink with my colleague to blow off some steam. That's the point of happy hour, right?

So why was I so damn nervous?

As we drove down the highway toward Decatur, I glanced occasionally at Porter. He looked relaxed in his rolled-up shirtsleeves and slacks, a far cry from all those fancy Italian suits he wore. His hazel-green eyes glistened in the setting sun. As Porter gripped the wheel of his car, I noticed the fine light brown hairs on his arm, wispy like dandelion fluff. His skin was flawless, not a pimple or scratch in sight. Geesh. I wondered if this man ever had an acne breakout as a teenager. He also really liked Jay-Z. I think I heard the entire catalog on the drive. I didn't want to break his heart and tell him I wasn't that big of a fan. But for the sake of our budding friendship and work relationship, I'd keep that piece of info to myself. I was more of a Nas fan. Who can deny the genius of a classic battle rap like "Ether"?

Porter parked the car. I was about to open my door, but he hurriedly came around to the passenger side. He waited as I adjusted my dress, then opened the door.

"What a gentleman," I said in an overly Southern accent.

"Hey, my mama raised me right," Porter said as he held open the door. "Automatic locks or not, I'm opening your door."

We walked up the narrow sidewalk to the pub, dodging kids on scooters and middle-aged retirees walking their dogs. Porter opened the door of the pub. A shiver went down my spine as his hand, once again, found the small of my back, guiding me inside. *My god. This man had absolutely no business touching me, a touch-starved woman.* As his hand lingered, enjoying the warmth of his palm at the small of my back felt so good. And safe.

Plastered on the wall of Hemingway's were pages from the author's books, like *The Old Man and the Sea.* There was an extensive number of dartboards, pool tables, and old-fashioned pinball machines in the dark, hazy pub. It was the perfect hipster hideaway. I'm surprised I had never been here before. This was right up my alley. Porter assured me that besides having the best craft beer in the city, that they also made a mean burger. He actually "chef kissed" his fingers to emphasize and said it was "heavenly." When anyone describes a burger that way, you know they aren't lying.

We sat in a booth near the pool tables. A lumberjack-sized waiter with a dashing blond ZZ Top-style beard, wearing a knit cap and flannel in mid-August, strode over to us. I looked around the pub and saw a ton of guys dressed this way. Clearly, it was the hipster uniform du jour. "Hey, guys, what's up? What can I get you?" he asked, pulling a pencil from behind his ear.

I looked down at the menu and could feel my nose scrunching up. Everything looked so good. There were so many choices on the burger menu alone that I could not decide. With food, I was usually good at deciding on just about everything fairly quickly but tonight, I was overwhelmed by everything, including the menu.

"Would you like me to pick something from their brewery list, Ari? I'm great at making drink choices for people," asked Porter. His eyes twinkled in the dim lighting. Somehow, this soft, hazy, slightly dingy pub made this man look irresistible. Damn. How could a man look good in any lighting? I needed a lot of concealer and highlighter to make that happen.

"Yes please," I said, my eyes not moving from his.

With his megawatt smile, Porter turned to our waiter. "She'll have the summer pale ale. I'll have the vanilla black stout. And can I get some chili cheese fries? I think a large order will do. Extra queso."

Did he just order chili cheese fries? Extra queso? Sir, just marry me.

A couple of minutes later, the waiter brought over the beers. Porter held up his beer and motioned for me to hold up mine for a toast.

"You did well today, James," he said. "And this is one small step in the design process. So…cheers. Oh. And fuck Greer!" We clinked our cold glasses, and I took a sip. Damn. Porter *was* good at picking out drinks. I'm much more of a wine than beer kind of girl. A man I can trust with my drink order and a chili cheese fry lover. He was really ticking all the boxes. *All the boxes for what? I didn't know.*

"Hmm," I moaned as the smooth, crisp beer hit my tongue. "Excellent choice, Porter."

He smiled, then took a sip of his stout. "Good. I told you. I'm very good at picking out drinks for people. It's a gift."

I nodded. *I wonder what other gifts he had. Nope. Ari. Don't think about sex at happy hour. Focus on the fries, girl. There's extra queso.*

In a matter of minutes, the waiter brought over two plates and a large basket of chili cheese fries, drenched in toppings. Porter ordered two more of the same beers.

"Ladies first," motioned Porter as he handed me a fork. I stabbed the massive mound of fries and took a bite. It was glorious. I wasn't exaggerating their taste just because I was starving. They were gourmet chili cheese fries. The homemade queso that topped fresh cut fries was spicy and smoky and the bison chili was equally amazing. It was the fanciest order of chili cheese fries I had ever had.

"I thought you said this was a bar," I scoffed at Porter, mouth full of fries. Clearly, I'd lost my home training. "These fries look and taste like Wolfgang Puck made them. For the Oscars."

Porter laughed. "Yeah… I forgot to tell you. The guy who owns this spot is like a Le Cordon Bleu trained chef. Friend of a friend."

"Another guy you know?" I asked, putting more fries on my plate.

Porter laughed, taking a sip of his beer. "You always have to know a guy that knows a guy. Comes in handy. Especially when you're a foodie."

Porter was a foodie. A real deal foodie. It dawned on me: He didn't take me to these amazing restaurants like this place or the sushi spot because I was a size 22 and looked like I loved food. He took me to fancy spots because he was trying to *impress* me. And dammit, it was working. I got another forkful of fries and put them on the plate. Porter looked on with delight as I took another bite. I was in heaven, or at least on the way to a chili-cheese-fry coma.

"Goodness! These fries are better than sex." *So much for not thinking about sex.* I swallowed my fries that now were forming a cold lump in my throat.

A cough strangled Porter's laugh as he rested his hand on his chin. "Better than sex, huh? I mean, they're good, Ari, but if they're better than sex, then you've had some terrible sex."

I gulped, moving the lump of fries finally, and averting my eyes from his piercing gaze. Was I drooling? I wiped the corners of my mouth. *Please let this be a reaction to these bomb ass fries and not this man.* I had to get out of this somehow.

"Do you play pool?" I asked, standing up and maneuvering out of our booth before he could answer. Luckily, he followed my lead.

"I sure do. My daddy was a pool shark," Porter said, his face serious.

I raised my eyebrow. "Really? Like Minnesota Fats?"

Porter bit his lip, trying to contain his laughter. "Okay, I'm lying. But I'm good."

"Well, we will see about that!" I said, egging him on. I walked toward the concierge desk, paid for a couple of games, and collected a rack of balls from the attendant.

"I could have paid for that, Ari," said Porter, annoyed.

"No. You get the food. I get the games," I said. "You've earned my trust with your taste in food."

Porter shook his head and took a sip of his beer that he was holding. He sat the frosty glass on the edge of the pool table, grabbed a pool cue, and began chalking it up with such a sensual motion that in that moment, I wished that the pool stick was my clit.

"Come on, Grandpa! You done babysitting that stick? Let's play!" I yelled over the raspy vocals of Eddie Vedder that were pleasantly assaulting my ears in the pub.

Porter raised a brow. "Grandpa? Oh, I got your grandpa. I'm going to make sure you eat those words, Ari James. Rack them."

"Already done. We're playing 10 ball." I positioned the balls in the middle of the table. I stood back, admiring my handiwork. I motioned to Porter to take a shot.

"Ladies first," Porter smirked, throwing up his hands.

I bent over the table with my cue to break. I looked over at Porter, who was slyly looking at me, then looked away. Suddenly, I wished I had taken his lead and worn slacks to work because I'm sure my ass was looking like two baked hams leaning over this table. But I didn't mind. Besides, ham is delicious. Porter looked like a man who appreciated both ham and ass. And I had a nice ass.

"Six ball, corner pocket," I said after I had already released my stick and hit it perfectly.

"Damn," said Porter in disbelief.

My game was going well as just about everything I called made it in. I even did one trick shot behind the back. To which Porter said, "Okay, now you're just showing off!" I laughed. After we both took our shots, we were in the last round. All that was left were the 10 and the 9 balls.

I stood up to assess my strategy. Just then, I felt the

warmth of spicy, vanilla-tinged breath on my neck and the hairs of my nape stood at attention.

"You know, if you just ease into it, you can get the 9 ball...left corner pocket."

His voice was low and gruff, like the cloth on the pool table. I felt my breath quicken, then settle in my chest. I tried to make my shot...and scratched. Porter broke out into riotous laughter.

"Oh, so you did that on purpose?" I pouted playfully, putting down my pool stick. I didn't enjoy losing. But this time, I'd make an exception.

"Hey, what can I say? I like to win and sometimes you got to get dirty," he said as he retrieved the balls for a new game.

The bar was getting crowded. It was a mixed crowd of young and old, Black and White. Atlanta still partied like it was the fifties on most weekends, with everything being segregated. But in Hemingway's, it looked like a little post-racial utopia. I sipped a freshly poured beer and watched Porter play. His muscular forearms rippled with every shot. He had a real command of the table. I thought about pulling a stunt on him like he did to me, but I was too busy looking at his arms, his thick thighs, and most of all, that ass. I think my earlier hypothesis about the quarters and nickels was right.

As we were about to head back to our table for more beer, fries, and the burgers, a group of brothers came into the pub. They wore casual clothes that were a bit too "young" for their age. If you're over forty, skinny jeans are not the move. One guy, wearing a Hampton Alumni shirt, recognized Porter, and walked over.

"Oh snap! It's PJ! What it do, man!" said the guy. He was a handsome guy, shorter than Porter with a close-cut fade, and gorgeous chocolate skin. He gave Porter what I noticed was a long and ceremonious handshake.

"Good seeing you, Frat!" said Porter.

Just as I suspected, Frat boys. *Groan.*

The guy turned and looked at me, then looked at Porter with a raised brow. "Yo, Frat, this you?"

I knew that question was every elder millennial Black man's way of asking a man if he and his date were a couple. I looked at Porter, who was both flush from the beer and being put on the spot. He put his beer down immediately.

"Jamal, this is my...coworker Ari James. Ari, this is my frat brother, Jamal Faulk. Oh, and Ari went to Hampton too."

"Oh, word?" said Jamal, turning to me, and slightly blocking Porter out. "What year were you?"

"2001." I tried to signal our ZZ Top waiter for another beer, but nearby patrons swamped him with orders. Fuck. I guess I was going to have to suffer this interaction sober.

Jamal looked at me hard, squinting his eyes behind his designer eyeglasses. "Hmm...you look mad familiar. I graduated in 2000. Porter, with his old ass, was my Dean of Pledges." Then he snapped his fingers. "I got it! I just remembered where I recognized you from. Weren't you roommates with Isabella Pierce? Bella? Short girl from Louisville with the Toni Braxton haircut? I used to stay sneaking into McGrew Towers to lay my mack down on the upper-class chicks, including Bella but she wasn't feeling me."

Weak game aside, it pleasantly surprised me that Jamal remembered me. "Wow! McGrew! That's taking it way back. Yeah, I was, well am still friends with

Bella. And she's Bella La Croix now." Hampton wasn't a huge university by most standards, so students formed close-knit circles. All I had was choir and Bella. Who would have thought someone other than my fellow His Chosen Sounds choir alumni would recognize me? I had to have been at least forty pounds lighter. Still a fluffy, plush girl, but certainly not my current size. I also wore the worst bob haircut on the planet. It looked like Edward Scissorhands did it. Such is the life of a broke college student who had to do her own hair. I'm not proud of that moment in my life.

"I knew you looked familiar! You were in Gospel Choir with her too, right?"

I shouted over the speakers, which were now blasting Nirvana. "Yeah, I was. We were. Bella and I are still close. She's in Atlanta now. Married with two kids. Twins."

"Man, the whole Gospel choir was fine as hell. And could blow! Porter wouldn't know that. He never made it to chapel. Too hung over from the night before! Right, P?" Jamal nudged Porter, who wasn't the least bit amused. He simply grunted something inaudible and took another sip of his beer.

Jamal laughed, as he rubbed his chin. "Man, I had a serious crush on Bella. She was so fine."

I playfully swatted Jamal's arm. "Hey, who didn't! She's still fine, but don't talk about my friend like she's a piece of meat!"

"Oh! So, she's a MILF!"

We both laughed. I looked over at Porter, whose annoyance at Jamal interloping on our "date" seemed to grow. In all fairness, didn't he say it wasn't a date and I wasn't his girl? With that, Jamal assumed it was fair game to talk to me. I already had peeped that. Trust me, if he asked me out, I was going to say no. I can't deal with the Jamals of the world. The combination of loud, brash, cocky, and handsome was something I'd had enough of. Porter's obvious annoyance at the possibility that I'd entertain Jamal's flirting was cute.

Before Jamal could continue going down Hampton memory lane, Porter interrupted. "Yeah, man, we were just about to finish up. Go order some burgers. So…" He hooked a thumb toward our booth.

I looked at Porter and then Jamal, who looked at Porter, then back at me. Jamal nodded and smiled, finally getting the hint that he'd overstayed his welcome.

"Oh, my bad! Don't want to hold y'all up. Good to see you, Frat. And good seeing you again, Ari. Tell Bella I said what's up. I'll find you on the socials. If you ever need a house, I'm your guy. The market is hot right now." Jamal slid us both business cards before rejoining a group of friends at the skee-ball machine.

I slid the sleek black card in my dress pocket and turned back to look at Porter, whose nostrils were flaring. *I should fuck with him.*

"Small world. He seems like a nice guy," I said as nonchalantly as possible. "Want to play another round of pool?" I looked toward Jamal and his crew. "Maybe some skee-ball?"

Porter rolled his eyes and grabbed the rest of his beer with force off the edge of the pool table. I watched as the foam sloshed onto the floor like a tidal wave. Porter drained his glass of beer, sitting it down on a nearby table with a loud thud.

"Come on. Let's get those burgers I promised you."

Chapter Eight

Porter

Once seated at our table, I signaled the grizzly waiter for a pitcher of beer and glanced down at the menu, occasionally looking up to see if Ari was doing the same. Once the beer arrived, I downed a glass quickly, trying to cool off. Jamal was just being Jamal. I should have known as soon as I introduced Ari as my coworker and nothing more, Jamal would try to go in for the kill. Did he really remember Ari? Maybe it was a lucky guess. But I get it. Ari is beautiful and I would have been pulling out all the stops, too. But Jamal? He was a dog. I wouldn't hook my sister up with him if I had sisters. Not that I looked at Ari like a sister. Not in the least. But Ari deserved better than a dude who'd sexed an entire floor of a dorm and a few TAs.

But the truth of the matter was, Ari was not my girlfriend. I had no right to be territorial.

So why was I acting like a jealous boyfriend?

Just then, my cell phone buzzed. It was a text. From Jamal. *This motherfucker.*

"Sorry, Ari it's…my mom," I lied. I was a terrible liar, but I was hoping Ari wouldn't catch on.

"Oh sure. It's cool," she said as she continued to peruse the burger selections.

I read Jamal's text.

Jamal: My bad, frat. I ain't know you was trying to tap that. Trust, she's had a major glow up. She's a baddie, now.

Furiously, my fingers flew across the screen:

I'm not trying to tap anyone. But I knew what you were trying to do. And trust me, she's not your type. You know you ain't shit, Jamal.

Jamal wrote back: LOL You're right, Frat. I ain't shit. She fine though, man. Thicker than cold grits. If you don't smash those cakes, you a punk ass b…

I forcefully swiped the screen and closed my texts before I could even read the rest. I picked up my menu and looked over it at Ari. She was staring at me with gentle, concerned eyes.

"You okay?"

"Oh yeah. It's all good. Wh…why do you ask?"

"Because you were texting like you were cursing out your mama," she said as a grin curled around her lips.

I laughed. "No. Just was trying to get her off the phone. You know how parents are. Old people and technology."

She laughed. "Yeah, luckily for me, my mama hates texting. Don't you hate that someone taught old folks how to text?" As we laughed, a calm washed over me. I was glad Jamal hadn't derailed our time—*my time*—together.

The waiter came back with pen and paper in hand. "You two lovebirds decide on a burger yet?"

"Which burger looks good to you?" I asked, feeling a prickly heat of embarrassment at being mistaken for "love-birds." "If you need help to decide...you know I got you."

Ari scrunched up her cute, upturned nose, examining the menu like a mad scientist. "Hmm...this one with bleu cheese and bacon seems good."

I frowned. "Bleu cheese is kind of funky, right?"

Ari rolled those big, beautiful brown eyes. "Hey! I like it. Besides, I'm not getting in anyone's face tonight. I'm just with you, Porter."

Ouch. The "just with you" stung. I had that coming. It was no better than me saying "just my coworker, Ari." The term *coworker* didn't encompass what Ari and I were to each other. It was safe to say we were, at the very least, becoming friends.

"Well, then bleu cheese and bacon it is," I stated to the waiter, who was scribbling. "I'll take the sunny side up burger."

"Yuck! Eggs on a burger? Is it breakfast or a burger?" Ari quipped.

"Why can't it be both?"

The waiter laughed and shook his head, leaving us to go put in our order.

"So," she started. "I told you about my dad. Tell me about your mama other than she is long-winded on text."

I smirked. "My mama, her name is Eloise, is a sweet woman from a tiny town in west Texas. And she's a die-hard Cowboys fan."

Ari turned up her nose. "I don't think Mrs. Harrison and I can be friends. Good or bad, I'm a Falcons fan."

I laughed. "It's Dr. Harrison, actually. Even though she hates anyone to call her that. I think she'd like you despite your affiliation. But you may hate me."

Ari's brows knit in genuine concern. "Why?"

I leaned in close, pretending to look remorseful. "I'm sorry but… I'm a Saints fan."

Ari feigned disgust, placing her hand over her chest. "I don't know if I should leave this table or what!"

"Before you get the burger?" I teased, sipping the cold stout.

Ari's lips quirked up. "You're right. I guess I'll wait for the burger. In the meantime, I guess I'll sit here and talk to you, a Saints fan. So, you're from New Orleans?"

"I was born in Virginia. But my dad's side of the family has deep roots in New Orleans." I paused a second to scan her face for some type of recognition of the Harrison name.

Relieved, I continued. "They stationed my dad all over the world. Being a military brat, it's hard to say where you're from, you know? I spent most of my childhood summers shuffling between my family in New Orleans or Armonia, my mom's hometown in west Texas. They were worlds apart from each other, but both feel like home. The best were summers with my grandparents in New Orleans. My grandfather, he would…" I got quiet as I thought about all the summers as a kid, all the hugs goodbye from my parents, and the last time I was in New Orleans in the summer. Standing in the humidity as Marines draped a flag over my father's shiny gold casket. Reporters clamoring to capture a photo of the prominent Senator Armand Pierre Honoré Harrison burying his only son. I could still feel his hand gripping into my shoulder as he stoically tried not to cry. I sipped my now warm beer. I couldn't talk about that. Not now.

Ari nodded as she swirled her glass of beer. "Ah, hence the accent."

"You think I have an accent? I've never heard that before."

"Totally. It's a mash-up of a lot of things. I like it."

My stomach weirdly flipped at the compliment. "Thanks."

Ari took another sip of her beer. "So, your mom…"

"Right! My mom. Mama was the first one in her family to go to college on a track scholarship. It was a big deal in Armonia. She had dreams of going to the Olympics. She and my dad met at Hampton, back when it was Hampton Institute. But she got pregnant with me in college, got married. Now, she's the principal of the Shabazz Charter School for Girls in Kirkwood. She refuses to retire because 'those girls need me.' Her words."

Ari's eyes widened in surprise. "Wow, son of a military man, an educator, and Hampton legacy. Impressive."

"It's not a big deal." To anyone else it probably would be a big deal. I was pretty sure my grandparents had something named after them there. A dorm. A boat. Some scholarship or endowment. I didn't care about stuff like that. Neither did my dad.

Ari eyed me with a little suspiciousness. "It's nice to carry on tradition. I'm sure your dad would be proud of you!"

"I hope he is."

Ari reached toward me, placing a warm, soft hand on top of mine. "Trust me, he would be."

The music faded away as I relaxed and leaned into her touch.

"Thanks. My dad was amazing. Luckily, Mom remarried about ten years ago to a guy named Desmond. Good dude. Total opposite of my dad. My dad was conservative and buttoned up. A tough love kind of guy.

Didn't express his feelings but you felt his love. Des is really laid-back, carefree, and very animated. He's a well-known visual artist from Anguilla and met my mom when her girlfriends convinced her to go to one of his gallery showings. If it isn't about soccer, soca, or cricket, he's not interested. But we get along great because he treats me and my brother Todd like his own sons but isn't trying to replace my dad. Todd, he's indifferent to Desmond, but usually respectful. I'm just glad that Des makes my mom happy and is an awesome grandfather to my niece and nephew."

"So, did your stepfather paint the paintings in your office?" asked Ari. "The ones above your drafting table."

I smiled, a little taken aback that she even noticed. "Actually, no. I did those."

"Wow!" Ari exclaimed with a smile. "An architect. A painter. Just an overall Renaissance man. So why didn't you pursue art?"

I felt myself blushing. "Thanks. Painting is just a hobby. I thought about being a fine artist. I can still hear my grandfather saying, 'Junior, that isn't a wise or lucrative profession.' I think it would have embarrassed him just to tell his snooty friends that I was a painter. But my stepdad Desmond thinks I'm wasting my gifts on this 'blasted building ting.'"

We both started laughing at my piss-poor rendition of Des's West Indian accent. Why was I telling her all of this? I never opened up to women like this. I felt so comfortable and at ease with Ari.

"Can I ask you something?" Ari asked before taking a slow, languid sip of her beer. She frowned a bit at this stout, which was a lot hoppier than what I picked before.

I could tell this beer wasn't up her alley, but like a good sport, she tried it anyway.

I motioned for her to continue. "Anything." She could have asked me to break-dance on this slightly greasy pub floor and I would have.

"Is it weird working so closely with me? I mean, a woman. I hear the other female architects in the office haven't lasted long."

I took a big gulp of my beer and shook my head. "Not at all. I'm trying my best not to be awkward around you because you have some serious cred in our industry. The other female architects left for good reason. Totally nothing to do with their work or anything."

Ari nodded slowly. "I see…"

I gestured my dismissal of her thoughts. "Pfft. Please! You have nothing to worry about. At the end of the day, I've enjoyed working with you on this stadium. It's been amazing. An honor that I don't take lightly."

Ari touched the top of my hand. My body felt like it was melting into a pool of mush. If she kept touching me, we were going to have to find a dark corner in this bar. Fast.

"Thank you, Porter. You have no idea how much your words mean to me. I totally understand the magnitude of this project, Porter. We got this!"

She reached her closed fist across the table, and I returned a fist bump back to her.

"You're right, Ari. We got this. We make a hell of a team."

"Good," she said, her face lighting up with a smile. "Glad you recognize that!" God, I had known her such a short time and every time she smiled at me, it felt as if her smile was the light showing me the way out of the dark.

My muddled brain tried to refocus. "Speaking of work…got any ideas about what direction you want to go next?" Just as Ari was about to answer, the waiter brought our burgers. The smell was intoxicating. We both stared at them and practically drooled in silence.

"Ugh, Porter. I don't want to think about that until Monday. Let me enjoy this very sexy-looking burger," Ari said. She picked it up with two hands and bit into it. I watched as she chewed slowly, eyes closed. I'd gone out with my share of women, but none made eating a burger sexy like Ari did. Hell, none would dare order a burger. I appreciated that Ari wasn't trying to be cute with a knife and fork. She was going to enjoy that sloppy burger fully, juices running down her arm and all. My foodie heart had found its soul mate.

"So how…" I began, trying not to show my pleasure at her enjoying these burgers. I'd hit it out of the park with my choice of happy hour spot, damn proud of myself for taking a chance at asking her to join me tonight.

Ari held up a finger to silence me. "Nope…you will not ruin this for me." Then, she took another hearty bite, eyes closed, and moaned. Watching her sent tingles down my toes and elicited a smile that was tinged with too much horniness across my face.

Ari opened her eyes to find me staring right at her. She bit her lip, a little embarrassed, then dabbed the corners of her mouth with a napkin before speaking.

"From now on, I trust you to make all food-related decisions when we hang out. Porter, this is fucking amazing!"

Yes. It was.

Chapter Nine

Ari

It was the best non-date date that I'd ever had.

We finished those amazing burgers and talked all night about everything. I looked at my watch. Shit, it was ridiculously late. The pub was clearing out slowly as the hipsters were being replaced by an annoying, rowdy college crowd. I looked across at Porter who was looking satiated from the food and beers. His eyes followed mine. I swallowed. If he looked at me one more time like that, I'd be in trouble.

"Are you ready to leave?" asked Porter. He signaled the waiter for the check, looking a little disappointed that our night was ending.

I hesitated. Honestly, I didn't want to go. We were having such a good time. I wanted to stay there all night, maybe play a few more games of pool. Maybe talk some more. I felt like I was just scratching the surface of this handsome, sweet guy with a fascinating backstory. But I knew better than to extend happy hour into a nightcap. That had gotten me in trouble before. *Coworkers and friends. That's it. That is all we could be.*

I folded my napkin on the table and reached for my

tote. "Yeah. I shouldn't have stayed out so late. And I live all the way in West End. I've got to head to church for choir practice with my mom in the morning. You've been drinking. I can take an Uber back home."

Porter narrowed his eyes. "An Uber? Hell no, girl. It is too late. I live downtown. West End isn't out of the way."

"You sure you haven't had too much to drink?" His cheeks were ruddy, but his eyes were clear.

Porter smiled. "I sobered up like 3 hours ago. Little-known fact: I have a high alcohol tolerance. Well, at least now I do. I blame Des for that. Him and his damn Pyrat rum."

I laughed and grabbed my tote. Porter paid the tab, including a hefty cash tip on the table. I smiled. He may be a "trust fund" kid as Greer often reminded us, but Porter was certainly thoughtful in everything he did.

We navigated through the crowd that was gathering near the entrance. Porter said the crowd was for the pub's famous late-night secret menu, so everyone was vying for one of the best tables near the kitchen. I felt Porter's hand again on the small of my back, his body closing the gap, guiding me out the door and through the crowd that was getting increasingly rowdy. His hand felt comforting and natural. With him next to me I felt safe. Protected. I couldn't remember the last time I'd felt that way with a man.

We stepped back onto the sidewalk. Gone were the retirees and their dogs and hipsters and their scooters. It was just me and Porter, walking along the quiet streets of downtown Decatur, heading back to his car. He maneuvered himself so that he was on the street side of the sidewalk. But his hand never left the small of my back. He opened my door, waiting for me to get inside before entering the car. A gentleman who opens doors and walks on the proper side of the sidewalk? They don't make those kinds of guys anymore. Now, it's all "let's go half on everything" and "what do you bring to the table" conversations on shitty podcasts.

"Where to, ma'am?" Porter asked as he pulled up his navigation on his console. I gave him my address as he eased out of the congested parking lot.

"Your turn to be the deejay. What do you like to listen to?" Porter asked as he searched his streaming apps on his phone. "I'm sure you're tired of listening to Jay-Z."

I laughed. "I ain't wanna say nothing but yeah." I thought about tonight. Me in Porter's car. The moonlight outside. The way he had touched me. It felt like one of those golden age of Black romantic comedy dates. Minus the slam poetry, naturally.

I swayed to the imaginary melodies in my head. "I'm a big fan of '90s, early '00s R&B. You got anything?"

Porter smiled, as if he knew that my heart was thumping its own soundtrack. "I have the perfect playlist for that."

From his car speakers came the booming bass of the intro to "So Anxious" by Ginuwine. *Dear God, I lost my virginity to this song. Freshman year. And on a trip with the Gospel choir, no less.* I giggled.

"What?" asked Porter. "Not a Ginuwine fan?"

"Nothing. I just…yeah, this just really reminds me of well… Gospel Choir."

"Gospel Choir? Oh, there is a story there," said Porter. "Spill it." Even in the car's dimness, I could see his gorgeous smile.

I wagged my finger. "I'm totally not revealing that

story. I mean, we're cool and all, but I don't know you like that."

"After we just spent eight hours baring our souls to each other over burgers? That's cold." He laughed. "You're going to tell me one day. I'm going to hold you to it."

We listened to a '90s slow jams playlist all the way to my house. I leaned back, closing my eyes, and swaying to the beat. I hummed along in time.

"You have a lovely humming voice," Porter quipped.

"Wait until you hear me sing," I replied. "Not to brag, but I have the voice of an angel."

"Are you inviting me to church to hear you sing? We sing very little in Catholic mass. Not soulful stuff anyway."

"I don't know, Porter. I'm AME and church services last far longer than mass."

Porter groaned. "Do I have to wear a suit?"

"Yep. The flashier, the better. Also, make sure it has hella buttons."

Porter snorted. "A Steve Harvey special. I'll keep that in mind."

As we headed onto 285, Porter's playlist had moved on to Jodeci's greatest hits.

"I love the '90s R&B. People really sang songs that had feeling back then," I said, bobbing my head to the well-produced beats.

"Yeah, I have to agree with you. Songs meant something. When Jodeci said, 'My heart belongs to you,' they totally meant it."

"I agree. Even though I'm sure their hearts belonged to groupies back then."

Porter laughed. "True, but we didn't know that. There was no social media all in celebrity business."

There was a glimmer in his eye as he laughed. Had I done that? I didn't know why but I wanted to keep making him smile until his cheeks hurt and his eyes sparkled. I knew I shouldn't feel that way. The job. The project. Rebuilding my life. Those are the things I should focus on, not this man.

"Not to sound like an old lady," I began, looking out of my window. "But why is it that every male singer these days sounds like a whiny, horny teenager?"

"Yep, and you can't tell them apart. Nothing about them sounds special. Back in the day, you could tell your D'Angelo from your Maxwell."

I shook my head in resounding agreement. "Yep. And producers created well-crafted songs. I mean, there was innuendo. Nothing too overt."

Porter scratched his beard as he thought. "Hmm. I don't know, Ari. Don't you think the lyrics to 'Freek'n You' are overt?" It was playing on the radio at that very moment. We went quiet and listened to K-Ci croon his heart out.

As soon as it got to the chorus, we broke out into a fit of laughter. Without thinking, I slapped my hand gently on his thigh. Realizing I was about three inches from his penis, I quickly pulled my hand back into my lap. I felt my cheeks heat with embarrassment.

"Oh. Sorry," I said, twisting to look out the window. "I didn't mean to…you know."

"It's fine. Really, Ari." We rode down the highway in silence for several minutes until Porter cleared his throat.

"Remember when guys would give girls mixtapes or CDs to tell them how they feel?"

I felt a sour expression making its way across my

face. "I wouldn't know because I never received a mix-tape from anyone."

Porter's eyes widened. "Really? Not one mixtape? That's hard to believe. If I liked a girl, if I wanted her attention, I spent all my allowance on blank CDs or cassettes. I gave a mixtape to a girl to ask her to prom. I recorded all these mushy songs, and the last track was me asking the girl to the prom. Man, was that cheesy! But at least she said yes. A girl like you, Ari. You should have had a stack of mixtapes from guys. Just collecting dust in an old CD case."

A girl like you.

Heat rose in my chest as I registered the last part of his sentence. I stared at the lights on I-20, trying to shake the feeling. "Mixtapes to ask a girl to the prom? Nah, I wouldn't know about any of that. I didn't go to prom, either."

Porter shook his head slowly in disbelief. "You're kidding! Seventeen-year-old me? I would have asked you to prom. With the mushiest mixtape ever. In a heartbeat."

In the moonlight, I could feel my toes curling as heat rose from the depths of my chest to the top of my head. I never knew a woman my shade of brown could blush as much as Porter made me blush tonight. He really knew how to make a woman feel like she had his undivided attention. It wasn't well-crafted game from years of play-boy behavior to seduce women. It was genuine to a fault. This was Porter being Porter.

By the time we pulled up onto the quiet streets of my neighborhood, the opening chords of Silk's "Meeting in My Bedroom" reverberated through the speakers. *Really? This song. This playlist wasn't playing fair at all. Fuck.*

"I think my fraternity brothers and I performed this at

the spring step show in '99," laughed Porter. "The things we did to win that show. I'm not proud."

"I think I remember that show. It was my sophomore year and oiled up guys in towels make a big impression on a young, innocent girl."

Porter laughed, lowering his head in shame. "Wow, you remember that? Yeah, that wasn't my finest moment. But I'd do it again…you know, for charity and stuff. Service to All Mankind. But I assure you, my stripper days are behind me."

I felt myself getting flush at the thought of Porter as an amateur stripper. His skin glistening behind a crisp, white towel. A happy trail inviting eyes lower. Gyrating to a syncopated beat. I snapped out of it as I felt the car slow to a halt in front of my house. I'd obviously seen *Magic Mike* far too many times.

"Is this you?" asked Porter, turning off the engine, parking under an amber streetlight. "I can't make out the number on the mailbox."

I nodded, snapping out of my thoughts of Porter and body rolls. "Yep. This is me." The warmth of the streetlights seemed to engulf his normally green eyes, making them shine with reflections of hazel. His skin was luminescent. I wondered if he knew how beautiful he was. I wished I could tell him.

"Wow, I know it's late, but from what I can see from the street, the house is beautiful. Original brick?" Porter asked, his eyes peering to get a better view and sounding like the architect I met nearly a month ago.

"Yes, but we just repainted it. I also updated some of the stained-glass paneling," I said, beaming with joy. I really was proud of how the renovations were going.

"Wow…how did you happen to snag a house in the

West End? It is so hard to get into this neighborhood these days."

"Trust me, I know. Luckily, this was my family's home. My grandparents bought it in the fifties. Saved every dime they had to get that house. They were one of the first Black families on the block. It's mine now. I'm not selling. The gentrifiers will have to wait until I die. Or my kids die. Restoring it has been a labor of love. An expensive labor of love but I've enjoyed renovating it."

"I'd love to see what you've done with the place," said Porter, softly.

Was he inviting himself into my house? Listen, I wasn't trying to have an actual "meeting in my bedroom" tonight. But dammit, Porter was making it very difficult for me to resist inviting him in. In the month I'd known him, Porter had proven to himself to be an upstanding guy. A gentleman. *But they all start out as gentlemen, Ari. And in the end, even so-called gentlemen can gut you like a fish, roll you up in newspaper, and toss you out like trash. Remember?*

"Oh…maybe someday soon," I said, forcing a smile on my face and burying my thoughts. "Right now, it's a mess. I want it to be perfect before I have guests. You're an architect. You understand?"

I prayed that would give him the hint that I wasn't trying to have him in any room of my house, let alone my bedroom. Or on top of my new kitchen counters. *Fuck. Great. Now that thought was in my head.*

"Ari, I'm not trying to come in this time of night. We're coworkers and that would be highly unprofessional," said Porter, sounding a little rehearsed. My radar must have been off track because I swore there was a vibe going on. Maybe he didn't see me that way. That was somewhat of a relief. At least now I knew, without a doubt, that nothing could ever happen between us.

So why was I disappointed?

"Right! Highly unprofessional!" I said with an uncomfortable laugh, trying to dismiss the thought (well, thoughts) I had of him doing God knows what to me across my couch. *And my kitchen island. And my...*

"Can I at least walk you to the door? Make sure you get in safely? I mean, this is still the West Side. At 2 a.m. Gentrified or not."

"Sure."

Porter opened the auto locks of the door and came around to open my door.

"Again, automatic locks or not, Eloise would kill me if I didn't open your door." He smiled. I slid across the seat as Porter extended his hand to help me out of the car.

I tried to focus on the chirping crickets, the stillness of the night, anything to get my mind out of its lust-filled haze. We walked up my driveway, along the cobblestone steps to my house. The porch lights came on. It cast a glow on Porter that made it look like he was on a Broadway stage.

"They're on a sensor," I said, my voice unrecognizable.

Porter looked around, taking in the porch renovations. "You have a swing, too. That's really cool. My grandparents had one in New Orleans. We used to watch the Mardi Gras parade from the porch."

I looked at the swing and smiled. "Yeah, I've always wanted one. As a kid, my dad promised he would put one up and never got around to it. So, I did."

I was babbling nervously. I turned my back to Porter and reached inside my tote to get my keys. My hands were shaking as I fumbled to put the key in the lock. I had to get inside this house before I did anything stupid. When I turned around, Porter was barely a foot from me. My heart pounded, mimicking the electric bass thump of damn near every song on that infernal playlist.

I took a step back, my back within centimeters of touching my front door. "Well, thanks for tonight, Porter. It was fun." I squeaked the sentence out of my throat as fast as I could.

"I had fun too, Ari," Porter said, softly. I watched as his eyes roamed the canvas of my face, finally landing on my lips. *Oh God.*

I couldn't look at him anymore. I turned to put my key in the door, nose nearly touching the peephole. My palms were sweaty, shaky, and suddenly I'd forgotten which key was the right one.

"Ari?"

"Yes?" I said, my voice barely above a whisper. I continued fumbling with my keys, refusing to turn around. I could feel the soft breeze of his steady breathing on my neck. It was so warm. *Fuck.*

I turned around to face Porter who was now mere inches from me. I took in a gasping breath of air to steady myself.

Porter licked his lips, a flash of pink tongue darting out. "Ari, I really want to kiss you. But that would be…"

"Unprofessional," I whispered, completing his sentence. I could smell his cologne mixed with the heady scent of beer. Its distinctly masculine scent turned me on, the wetness pooling between my legs signaling my appreciation. I wanted to kiss him. I needed to kiss him. I *had* to kiss this man before we both exploded. Instantly, I regretted ordering bleu cheese. *Fuck, I really wish I was the girl who ordered salads on dates.*

Porter came close, looking down at me. Drinking me in like I was that stout. I could feel my chest rise, my breath ragged. The '90s playlist from the car was still playing in a loop in my head. I could hear Blackstreet's "Before I Let You Go" as clear as a bell.

"Very unprofessional," Porter whispered as his lips ghosted over mine.

I felt a bead of cold sweat run down my neck and into my cleavage. I shivered.

"Very," I whispered. This was torture. Delicious torture. I was down bad.

I was a millimeter from his lips, lips that were plump, peachy, perfectly placed yet simultaneously inappropriate on his very distinguished face. I felt my pussy doing Kegels like push-ups before a championship bout.

This was a bad sign.

Porter eased toward me as my back pressed against the door. "Ari? Can I kiss you? I want to kiss you, Ari. Would you…if it wasn't unprofessional?"

I licked my lips and swallowed. "I would kiss you… but you know…professionalism…and something else you said." My brain had officially short-circuited.

Porter smiled, biting his bottom lip with those perfect teeth, and leaned in, pressing his lips firmly against mine. With a loud thud, I dropped my tote bag, still holding on to my keys. I wrapped my arms around his neck and fully caught up in the rapture of his kiss. His tongue found mine and after a few awkward starts, we found our rhythm. He gently bit the bottom of my lip and I moaned into his mouth. I felt his hands in my hair, gently pulling me deeper into his kiss.

"Ari," he moaned. The way he said my name was like a song he wrote just for me.

My hands moved down and gripped his muscular back. God, he felt so incredible. Better than any daydream I'd had about him over these past weeks. This was no longer fantasy. This was very real. *And very good. So good.* And it had to stop. I pulled away, trying to catch my breath and regain my composure.

"I… I should go in, Porter. Choir practice and… I… Good night." I turned to open the door.

"Ari, wait…"

Without looking at him, I quickly closed the door in Porter's face. My legs were like jelly as I slid down the length of the door, collapsing like a pile of wet towels on the floor. I heard him whisper my name again in that sexy, melodious way of his. He softly tapped a few times as he waited for a response. Frozen, I couldn't speak. I squeezed my eyes shut, trying to tune it all out. When I heard the purr of his car engine, I finally rose from the floor and turned on my living room lights.

Oh God. OhGodOhGodOhGod.

Shit. Shit.

I threw my tote bag and kicked off my heels. With my buzz long gone, I went into the kitchen and poured a glass of Shiraz. I downed the first glass, followed by another. I left the glass on the counter, opting to bring the entire bottle into the bedroom. I put the bottle on the nightstand, opening the bottom drawer of the nightstand, frantically searching for my main man, Big Papi. Yes, my vibrator named is after a big, Afro-Dominican, major league heavy hitter. One look at it and you'd realize why it was the most appropriate name.

I turned him on. *C'mon and give me grand slam.*

I needed something, anything, to stop me from picking up the phone, telling Porter to turn around and come finish what he started.

Chapter Ten

Ari

The thud of the wine bottle crashing to my floor jolted me out of the bed. I had hit the alarm on my phone several times and slept half the day away. Between the wine and a few rounds with Big Papi, there was no way that I could be singing about the Lord this morning. I sat on the edge of the bed, and I looked at my cell phone. I had a half-dozen missed calls, most of them from my mom and Bella. And there was one missed call from Porter.

Oh God...last night.

I rubbed my throbbing temples as thoughts of last night replayed in my mind. What on earth was I thinking? What were *we* thinking? I rubbed the pad of my thumb against my lips, remembering the feel of Porter's lips on my own. Once we caught our groove, our tongues and lips met, touching, moving, and teasing as if they'd known each other's landscapes for years. Decades even. A kiss like that, where two people melt into each other, isn't just happenstance. I'm not one to believe in soul mates, destiny, and all that nonsense. Well, not anymore. History has proven that a kiss that good, that amazing, could only bring me heartache in the end.

I threw myself back onto the bed and felt something poking me in my back. Remembering, I threw Big Papi on the floor. I sat up, my head now ringing like a cathedral bell. *You're no longer twenty-one, Ari.* I needed coffee. An IV of it preferably.

As I staggered around the kitchen, the chime of the doorbell startled me, nearly sending my coffee cup flying. Who on earth could it be this time of…? I looked at the time on the coffeemaker. It was nearing early afternoon. I was so hungover from liquor and orgasms that my agenda was escaping me. I wasn't expecting anyone, was I? What if it was Porter? What if he wanted to finish what he started? My heart began to pound as loudly as my head, both sounds melding into a syncopated thump.

I walked to the front door and looked out the peephole. It was Mr. George, my lovely contractor, holding some blueprints and what looked like wood. *Thank God!* I looked at myself in the mirror next to the door. I tightened my fluffy robe around my waist, brushed my hair back and flicked the crusty boogers out of the corners of my eyes.

"Hey, Mr. George…did we have a meeting today?" I asked as I opened the door.

Mr. George walked in and politely put on his boot covers. "Yes, Ms. Ari. We did. Remember? I wanted to show you some more ideas for the master bath and some wood samples. Just got in some nice ones for the laundry room cabinets."

I slapped my hand to my head, signaling my forgetfulness. I was supposed to meet him after choir practice. I ushered Mr. George into the kitchen and offered him a seat at the island. Mr. George was a short, graying-at-the-temples, man from Ecuador who had come to this country with five dollars and a dream, eventually building a multimillion-dollar renovation business alongside his wife. He was so well-known that the popular home improvement television networks had offered him a show. But, as he always recalled when telling the story, he turned them down because he's about the work, not the fame. Network show or not, Flores Construction and Renovation was still famous in the city for their beautiful restoration work of craftsman style homes like mine. Now that he was a widower, Mr. George put all his energy into work. Sometimes, I would catch him looking at a photo of his wife on his cell phone and my heart would ache. Maybe someday someone would look at an old photo of me that way.

Sitting at the island that Mr. George had beautifully crafted, we both smelled the coffee that was finally finished brewing and smiled at each other. Without a word, I took down a cup for Mr. George, pouring him a generous amount. He hummed, "Hmmm… Café Bustelo?" I nodded, knowing that it was his favorite and mine too. I went to the fridge, retrieved the half-and-half, and pulled the raw cane sugar out of the pantry. Along with a spoon and napkin, I sat all of this on the island in front of George, who looked up from his iPad with concern.

"Rough morning, Ms. Ari?" he asked as he poured a little cream into his coffee and stirred. I noticed that he always made his coffee the exact shade of his forearm.

"More like rough night," I answered as I poured too much cream and spooned an unhealthy amount of sugar into my cup. Clearly, I looked crazy; I hadn't bothered to run a brush through my hair, I was in an old, fuzzy robe, and raccoon rings of mascara were around my eyes. My stomach rumbled with discomfort, signaling I needed to consume a little more than overly sweetened caffeine. I went to the bread box on the counter and selected two slices of raisin bread, placing them in the toaster. I leaned against the counter to wait.

"Well, I won't be long, Ms. Ari." George rolled out the blueprints and pulled out his iPad. "Listen, I know you're sure of what you want. But I think we can do a tub *and* the shower you want in the master."

I raised an eyebrow. "Okay, what would I have to lose to get this, Mr. George?"

The handsome gentleman gave me a sly smile. "Just a little closet space."

I shook my head. "No way, Mr. George. I need the extra closet space. Have you seen all my shoes? You know better than to ask a woman to give up closet space."

We both laughed, taking sips of coffee between chuckles. His laughter reminded me of my dad, big and boisterous. I looked away, trying to focus on something else. Three years and the pain was still there like a picked-at scab.

"Yes, my daughters would kill me if I took their closet space. Okay. We'll think of something else. Speaking of ladies, how is Señora James?"

I smirked. *Real smooth, Mr. George.* "Mama's good. She told me to tell you hello."

Mr. George, with his deep, sun-worn complexion, blushed. "Si. Yes, tell her hello as well. The scones were wonderful last week."

"I will." I nodded with a knowing grin. Old people flirting was so stinking cute.

"Anyway, back to this bathroom."

I bit my dry toast and watched as Mr. George scratched his temple with a pencil. "I don't know. But I really don't want you to lose the space with just a big shower. Plus, the classic tubs in these homes. Very popular for resale. You're an architect. You know these things."

When George mentioned the shower, my mind wandered. Images of Porter, naked with me in my imagined huge walk-in shower with the dual rainfall showerheads. *Our bodies all slick with soap. Porter, standing behind me, moaning my name like he did last night. My body up against the wetness of the glass and his hands going down my...*

"Ms. Ari?" said George, interrupting me from my very erotic daydream.

I blinked. "Okay. Mr. George. I hear you. But... I really want the shower."

Mr. George pulled out his pencil and pad to make some notes. "Okay, Ms. Ari. But I'm telling you, a nice, traditional claw-foot tub would be so elegant."

I frowned. Clearly an old-fashioned claw-foot tub would be too small for me, let alone me and another person. Clearly, we were still at an impasse. "Let's table it. In the meantime, can you just look at the tile I brought back from Italy for the bathroom? I just took it out of storage. We can at least get started on tiling near the vanity."

Mr. George shrugged, closing his iPad. "If you say so. Now...about these doors in the laundry room..."

Mr. George continued to speak about the plans for the house, his voice eventually sounding like white noise. I needed to get rid of these thoughts of Porter. He would not consume me for the rest of the weekend. No fucking way. As Mr. George walked into the laundry area to take measurements, I pulled my cell phone out of my robe and texted Bella.

Me: Bella, are you free? Too much to text. Brunch later? Technically, it's a late lunch/early dinner. Pick a spot.

I expected Bella to take the requisite twenty minutes to text me back, but she responded in seconds.

Bella: Bitch, where were you last night? Better yet, with who? I almost called Doris because I thought you had been kidnapped or something. Anyway, I'm down for some adult time. I'm starving. Leaving the girls with Zach. I'll txt you the addy.

I snorted. I could always count on Bella to be there for two things in this world: food and me.

I watched as Mr. George opened the box of tiles. He hummed his approval as he carefully examined each piece of tile out of the neatly wrapped box, holding them up in the soft light of the bathroom. It was a smoky blue and pure white color in a baroque pattern. I had purchased them on a whim in Florence. They sat in my storage unit in Chicago for years with the hope that I'd use them to build my house with my future husband. When that idea crashed and burned, I tucked those tiles away and let them collect dust until I decided to move back home. Finally, I'd have a use for them. Those tiles deserve to be used and admired. Husband or not.

Mr. George looked up from the box, adjusting the pieces neatly back in place. "No worries, Ms. Ari. I'll handle the tile with care. It's beautiful. Very romantic, si?"

Still in a daze, I nodded my head, grabbing the collar of my robe. "I thought that."

That and a hell of a lot more.

* * *

"Hey, go easy on the brakes. She sputters but she still runs, okay?"

The valet at Dunn's River Café frowned as I tossed him the keys to Honey, who was totally out of place in the parking lot of the city's hottest new gathering spot. I'd been so happy to have my girl back I'd donned my bright yellow sundress and matching block-heeled sandals, and my halo of coils was pushed back with a yellow Ankara scarf. I felt like the goddess Oshun. It is an unmitigated fact that Black women of all shades look good in yellow. Melanin rich skin needed to be adorned by Mother Nature's brightest color. Who was I to argue with Mother Nature?

As I walked into the restaurant, a classic Cutty Ranks jam was blasting through the speakers. I moved my shoulders to the beat as I looked at all the glamorous, chic, and upwardly mobile folks. Of course, Bella would pick this place. It had just the right amount of pretentiousness mixed with ratchetness that Bella loved.

I spotted Bella in a back booth near the long marble bar, looking amazingly chic as ever in a Carolina blue top and white skinny jeans, her hair in a sleek, low ponytail. Bella giddily waved me over. I looked around the restaurant. Only a few tables, all occupied. I groaned, anticipating the rather tight squeeze, boobs and gut smashed against the table, and the potential for a wrinkled dress. As I approached, I could see Bella downing the second glass of what appeared to be something fruity.

"So, you already got started, huh?" I asked with a teasing smile.

"Well, as soon as you said let's do late lunch, I knew I didn't have time to bullshit. I just threw this outfit on and grabbed my purse. Didn't even say bye to the kids! I was pushing 80 on the highway. So, hell yeah, I started with drinks!"

I laughed as I looked her up and down. "Just threw that on, huh?" I slid into the tight-fitting booth as Bella signaled for the waiter. A tall, deep mahogany man with dreadlocks approached. The stark white of his uniform enhanced his skin. I immediately wondered how he kept his clothes so clean, surrounded by rich sauces and drinks. The man must have had an endless supply of bleach at home.

"Hello, miss, what can I get for you? Perhaps one of our famous rum runners to start?" he said with a slight accent from an island I couldn't guess if I tried.

"Sure, I'll have a rum runner," I said, taking him up on the suggestion.

"Okay, gorgeous. I'll get that going and come back for your order." He smiled and looked me up and down like I was on the menu. After searing a hole through my dress with his dark brown eyes, the waiter quickly left to put in our drink orders. If I wasn't swearing off all men, trying to focus on myself, then perhaps I would have taken the bait.

Bella raised her eyebrows, observing the exchange.

"You know island men like them some thick women, honey! You should get his number. Let someone rub up on that juicy, homegrown booty of yours. It's been months."

"One, that's a stereotype. Two, it hasn't been months!" I dramatically flipped open the menu, irritated. It *had* been months, and I didn't want to think about it. Bella meant well, but I just wanted this lunch to be about eating some bomb curry shrimp and laughing with my girl.

Unlike most of the women in this place, all scantily clad, I didn't come here to find a date or hook a baller. I was too old for that. Besides, I didn't want to add this waiter to my roster only to get bored a few weeks later.

"Bella, I'm not thinking about men. I just want to hang out. I rarely see you these days. Me with the new job. You with the kids."

Bella sighed, slowly stirring the straw in her drink. "I know." She grabbed my hand and dramatically held it against her cheek. "If you would just get a car that worked, we could see each other more often. Now, why didn't you answer my texts last night?" She always had a flair for the dramatic. Everything was an event. Her new job suited her personality to the tee.

I playfully slapped her hand away. "I went out with my coworker after work and ran into Jamal Faulk from Hampton. Remember him? He asked about you. I'm shocked he remembered me, but of course, it was only because of you. He had a crush on you."

Bella rolled her eyes as she downed the last sip of her drink. "Jamal was such a player. I think he screwed half the cheerleading squad and a couple of my line sisters. But…is he still fine though?"

"Unfortunately," I said. "He's still fine as hell."

"Damn! I should have let him tap it before Zach locked it down."

We both let out a hysterical laugh as the waiter brought over the drinks. Luckily for me, he got distracted by a customer and didn't get a chance to eyeball my boobs a second time.

"So, did you get his number because I'm sure he was trying to get at you too," said Bella.

"No, because…"

I hesitated. *No because I was with a seemingly jealous Porter, with whom just a few hours later, I was locking lips. And I'm trying my darndest not to think about him so please don't ask.*

"No, because… I don't want a guy who just wants to bone! Not anymore. I'm on a man fast."

Bella cocked her head to the side in disbelief. "Man fast? Now that just sounds stupid. Come on, Ari! You're too gorgeous to be home drinking wine and watching old white men make cabinets, or worse, dubbed-over Japanese cartoons, like you used to in college. We're grown!"

Damn. Was I that predictable? Had my life not changed in almost twenty years? That's pathetic.

As the music continued to thump, I moved uncomfortably in my seat, my body pushing up against the table. Bella put her hands on her chin, waiting for a response. I felt stuck in more ways than one. I took a sip of my rum runner and folded my hands in my lap.

"Is my life that pathetic, Bella?" I asked quietly. "Has it always been pathetic? Is that why Maurice…" I nervously fidgeted with my hands in my lap as the question still swirled in my head. Bella reached across the table and motioned for my hand. Reluctantly, I removed one hand from my lap and placed it on the table. Bella put her perfectly manicured hand on top of mine, her wedding ring looking like a meteor against her slender, deep brown fingers.

"Of course not, Ari. Maurice was a dick. But it's time you found someone to be with. Give you some steady orgasms. Or babies. Or both. Not just someone you call when you have an itch. Someone to spend quality time with you. Have fun with! You don't need to spend your weekends sitting in your gorgeous house doing renovations with an old but sweet Ecuadorian man as your only male company. And don't think I didn't hear you say you went out with a coworker? That Porter guy, I presume?"

I sighed and rolled my eyes. "Yes. Just to celebrate my time there. He's my partner on the stadium project."

"Hmpf," said Bella with skepticism laced in her voice. She could always read me like a book.

The waiter came back to take our food order. He turned to Bella first, but kept his eye contact with me, mostly.

"For you, miss?"

"I'll have the jerk pork," said Bella.

He then turned to me, all bright white Colgate smile against that rich skin. "And what are you having, beautiful?"

"I'll take the curry shrimp," I said, not bothering to see how spicy it was. According to my mother, it was the perfect cure for a hangover and horniness.

"Dat all ya want, dahlin?" he asked with a raised brow. I looked at him, puzzled. Defensiveness shouldn't be my go-to response, but I absolutely hated the assumption that, because I was a large woman, that I was going to eat myself into a food coma.

"Yes, I'm sure that's enough," I said, slamming the menu on the table. Bella's eyes grew wide as she sipped her drink.

Instead of snapping back at me like I anticipated, the waiter leaned down, his locs grazing my shoulder, tickling the strap of my sundress. He whispered in my ear in a panty-dropping tone. "Because I get off in 'bout an hour."

I felt an uncomfortable heat making me hot in places that I shouldn't and a heartbeat thump down in my coochie. I looked at Bella as she continued sipping her drink with wide-eyed fervor. I looked down at his starched white shirt and found his name tag. Nigel. *Great. Even his name was sexy.*

"I'm good… Nigel. Really," I said, backing away from the melting tones of his voice.

"If you change your mind…" Nigel said as he winked, sliding a piece of paper with a number on it. "I can give you something more filling than some shrimp." Then walked off to put in our food order.

"Well, damn," said Bella, fanning herself with the wine menu like a genteel Southern lady. "That was hot! Girl, call him!"

"Girl, I'm not entertaining this waiter," I declared as I balled up his number and put it in my purse. "Look at this place. How many women has he picked up in here? Probably dozens. It's literally a sea of beautiful women here every weekend."

"Who cares!" shot back Bella, raising her brows playfully. "The man wants you!"

"Oh my God, you married women are all the same! You want to live vicariously through us single women, getting us to live out your sexy fantasies so you can get off on it!"

Bella snickered. "Yeah, Ari, you might be right. Married ladies get stuck with the same dick for eternity, doing the same five positions, and you all are out here living the life. So yes, maybe we're trying to hear about hot, new, and nasty sex."

My eyes bulged in surprise. "Sex that bad with Zach?"

Bella rolled her eyes, then sighed. "I don't get it enough to complain about if it's bad or not. We've got the twins, starting my new business, and Zach's residency.

Maybe if I was a patient in need of a facial reconstruction, he'd pay me more attention."

"Now you know you don't need a face-lift!"

Bella smiled, throwing her fake ponytail over her
shoulder. "Yeah, you're right. My face is flawless. We
look better than any of these twenty-two-year-old chicas
in this place trying to find themselves a sugar daddy!"

We both laughed and gave each other a high five.

"But seriously," said Bella. "You're too amazing to
be alone! Plus, you need to celebrate this job with a cel-
ebratory screw. Why not start with the Mr. Bombastic
until you get the real thing!"

I smiled at Bella's relentless pursuit to knock the dust
off my nether regions. Bella was one of my best friends.
We were opposites but bonded instantly when we were
paired as roommates in college. Bella was a gregarious
girl with a killer body and killer face, yet down-to-earth,
supportive, and most of all, kind. Folks always knew me
as "Bella's friend, you know, the big girl with the cute
face." On the rare occasions that I felt bad about my
weight, Bella was always there to brush the negativity
away. "You're perfection!" she would say. "If this was
the 19th century, you'd be a masterpiece." If that kiss
with Mary Turner in ninth grade hadn't sealed the deal
in my firm heterosexuality, I'd marry her.

"Actually, Bella, there is something I wanted to talk
to you about…"

"Oh!" Bella perked up in her seat, adjusting her perfect ponytail and letting her bangles hit the table with
a resounding thud of anticipation. "I'm tipsy enough to
receive the tea. So go ahead…"

I twirled a finger around an errant curl, winding it

tightly around my finger. "Well, there is this situation…
I did something I shouldn't have. And…"

Just as I was about to spill my guts about last night, I
heard someone call my name above the bumping bass of
the Damian Marley's "Welcome to Jam Rock."

Standing in front of me, in simple khaki shorts and short-
sleeved palm-tree printed shirt, was the most delicious
thing that wasn't on the menu. His eyes, the exact color
of the trees on his shirt, danced as faint smile lines appeared at their corners.

"Porter?"

Chapter Eleven

Porter

"Porter?" Ari questioned, staring at me with a look I could only describe as horrified.

Her friend looked at me curiously and smiled, then looked back at Ari with a raised brow. I couldn't tell if something amused or aggravated her.

"Hey, I just saw you over here. I was at the bar with my brother," I said. I extended my hand to her lunch guest, who I noticed wore an obnoxiously large, but gorgeous, wedding ring. "Hi. I'm Porter."

The friend smiled and shook my hand. "Oh, I know who you are. I'm Bella La Croix. Best friend. Confidant. Alibi if need be."

I smiled. So, this was the infamous Bella that Jamal was reminiscing about. I could see why. She was a beauty, but the real stunner at the table was Ari. I watched as she adjusted herself in the booth, her jaw tight with nervousness.

"Ah, Bella. I've heard so much about you," I said, trying to cut the awkward tension I felt. I really didn't know anything about Bella, but I was trying to be overly polite.

It wasn't clear if my usual dose of charm was working. Bella looked puzzled and then looked at Ari.

"Right!" Bella looked at Ari with a very quizzical look. Their looks, a secret language, told me that maybe I'd interrupted something.

"I'll let you all enjoy your lunch. I just wanted to say hello. Ari, you look…beautiful, by the way. See you Monday."

Before she could reply, I turned quickly and went back to the bar where my brother was standing, looking utterly confused.

"Dude, you left me to go talk to a girl! Devin's got our table ready. I'm hungry as shit!" Todd playfully nudged me as we walked toward our table.

"I was just saying hello to my coworker, Ari."

Todd peered over my shoulders, sipping on his rum and coke. "Oh, yeah. Ari is the chick you all just hired, right? She's fine…you know I like them slenderoni." Todd was looking directly at Bella, giving her a thorough inspection.

"No, Todd… That's her friend Bella. It was the other girl. In the yellow."

Todd looked again, craning his neck. "Oh." And then he fell silent as he continued to sip his drink.

"What does that mean? *Oh*?" I asked. I knew what that meant. Todd was being Todd—a judgmental asshole.

"When you said your coworker was cute, she's not what I was expecting. That's all," said Todd. "I mean she's cute. But not what I expected."

"I didn't say she was cute. I didn't say anything."

"Saying nothing meant she was cute, and you didn't want to confirm it."

I looked back over at Ari, who was now looking at me.

I mouthed "Sorry." And she mouthed back "It's okay," her face a bit flush. I smiled. She was cute when embarrassed. I kind of liked it.

"Fuck, I think I ruined her lunch with her girl," I said woefully. I stared at Ari. She looked over at me and smiled. Dressed in yellow, Ari reminded me of a Starburst. In fact, Ari's kisses tasted just as sweet and were just as juicy.

Out of the corner of my eye, I could feel Todd looking at me and then back at Ari, a smug look coming over his face.

"Whatever you have to say, Todd, just say it!"

"Holy shit! Did you fuck her? Your…um…coworker," Todd yelled. A couple of drinks in, he was getting wound up. Even over the seductive thump of Sean Paul's "I'm Still in Love," I could hear Todd's voice. "Damn, dude! You didn't waste no time getting in the drawers!"

A table of older women looked over at my brother, mortified. I grabbed his arm and led him toward our empty private chef's table in a back corner of the restaurant.

"Pipe down, Todd!" I put my fingers on my collar, feeling beads of sweat forming despite the air conditioner blasting full tilt. "Nothing happened. Well, not nothing…"

Todd narrowed his eyes. "What do you mean 'not nothing'?"

Before I could explain, Devin, Dunn's River head chef, came out to greet us at the table. Dressed in a gray chef coat with a Jamaican flag on it, he and Todd exchanged a bear hug.

"Yo, Devin. This is my brother, Porter. He's cool, but forgive him, he went to Hampton," said Todd. I knew it was coming and laughed. Todd and Devin attended Howard, the other HU, unfortunately.

"Oh, so your brother ain't shit then, huh?" said Devin. "Just kidding. Nice to meet you, man. Todd talks about you all the time."

I laughed and gave Devin a handshake. "You too! And it's all good. We all make mistakes. We will see who is talking that smack come football season."

"I don't care about none of that," said Todd, waving his hand. "I just want some oxtails, dude!"

Devin shook his head. "Always greedy, Todd! Be glad I saved the last of them for you. Just give me a minute. As you can see, it is packed. Before you all ask, this on the house, T!"

I smiled and looked at Todd, who was itching to brag about something. "I did the contract for this spot. He owes me one! Alright, time to get drunk." He flagged down a waitress and ordered two more drinks. When Todd asked what I wanted, I opted to order a ginger ale.

"So, this new hire at work. Ari. Tell me about her?" asked Todd. "I'm glad to see Riddle and Robinson remember that it's the twenty-first century and hired a woman. I'm shocked she took the job, given what happened to the last woman there. That place is a meat factory!"

I winced, thinking about Greer's past actions. "Exactly. I'd imagine for a woman; it would be especially tough. But it's been almost a month. She hasn't run for the hills yet."

"Okay. But are you all vibing? Getting along?"

I put my hands behind my head, leaning back against the wall. "We get along great. Her design skills are amazing. Crazy skilled. Smart. She's so easy to bounce ideas off. Not to mention…" My voice trailed off. *An amazing*

*kisser. The softest lips on the planet. Killer curves. Juici-
est thighs this side of the Mississippi...* "I mean. She's
quirky. A little guarded but opening up to me. At least
I think she was."

"What do you mean you think she was?"

I didn't respond. Just shrugged and sipped on my ginger ale.

Todd cleared his throat, interrupting my thoughts.
"But you like her? As in more than a coworker?"

With a sigh, I confessed. "I kissed her last night."

Todd's eye widened. "You kissed her? Damn. So, was
it a good kiss?"

"It was alright." *I was lying through my damn teeth.*

"So, you had one kiss! What's the big deal? You two
are grown. It doesn't matter what you do."

I looked at Todd, confused. "Shouldn't it matter? I
don't date coworkers and you know that."

Todd laughed until he damn near choked. "You don't
date coworkers because you've never had one fine enough
to date! You like her. Admit it! Otherwise, you wouldn't
have stomped your narrow behind across a crowded restaurant, past a slew of fine women drooling at you, to
say hello to someone you can see on Monday. You never
could lie worth a shit!"

Todd reached across the table and slapped my shoulder, hard. "Look. I'm sorry. Explain everything to me,
from the beginning. And how you two ended up kissing? Didn't you all meet just a week ago?"

"It's been almost a month. Have you heard a word I
said?"

He threw his hands up in protest. "My bad, PJ! I'm
just saying, how'd you make a move on the girl so fast.
She hasn't even had time to get used to the firm."

I put my hands on my head, rubbing my forehead. I was sure I was getting a migraine.

The waiter brought over the rum and cokes. Todd stirred the rocks glass and then slammed it on the table. "Alright. Now tell me about you and this kiss with Ari…" Todd had drained his first glass so fast that the glass was still cold to the touch.

"Nah, man. She's… I'm not thinking about her like that. I just… The kiss was a mistake. Plus, I'm up for partner." I was lying again. The only regret I had was not kissing her longer.

Todd raised a brow. "Right. Partner. So, you being into Ari doesn't really seem to align with your brand. Got it."

My eye twitched with annoyance. "My brand? What the fuck does that mean? I don't have a brand."

Todd waved his hands dismissively. "Yes, you do. The Harrison Brand. You know what I mean. The right school. The right job. And the right woman. Everything's got to be perfect for you. This girl is not on brand. God, what would Grandpa Senator say about his favorite grandson?" mocked Todd.

"Todd, you know that isn't true. I'm simply not trying to fuck up my professional life. What does Grandpa have to do with anything?"

Todd drained the last of his second glass. "Because ever since Daddy's death, Grandpa is the one you've been so eager to please. For what reason, I have no clue. The man is mean as fuck, but you wouldn't know that because you're his favorite. Look at how he treated Mama."

I bristled at the mention of Grandpa and our mom. It was true. Grandpa Senator was never nice to our mother. Our Grand-Mere was even worse. When our father died, it gave them more of a reason to pretend Mom never existed. In the end, I think guilt weighed on his conscience which was why he bent over backward for Todd and me. He paid our college tuition. He quietly set up trust funds and rewrote his will to have Todd and I inherit all of the family property and money upon his death. We didn't have to work. We were set for life.

Todd folded his arms across his chest. "Who got you into Hampton because we all know your grades were mediocre? Grandpa Senator. Who made a call and got you the internship that landed you the job at Riddle and Robinson? Grandpa Senator. Maybe kissing this girl was your way of blowing up your own career? Because it's not the career you really wanted in the first place."

I wasn't sure what they put in those drinks, but they must have given Todd liquid courage to be an even bigger asshole.

I leaned across the table. "C'mon, Todd! You and I both know I got into Hampton on my own. Listen, I've been there damn near fifteen years. I've more than proven myself as a damn good architect. I love what I do."

Todd rolled his eyes with a groan. "Be real with yourself, PJ. Do you really want to make partner at that firm? What are you trying to prove? That you aren't some entitled kid? You don't even *like* being an architect. You picked that major because Grandpa was going to cut you off if you stuck with fine art. Your paintings were so good, and you loved it. One thing Des and I can agree on is that you could have been the next Basquiat or something. But no! Listening to that mean old man, you're stuck doing some shit you're lukewarm about because you didn't want to be a disappointment."

"Uhm, I don't recall you turning down any money Grandpa gave you!"

Todd laughed. "The money? That was the least he and Grand-Mere could have done for me. God, don't get me started on that old hag." Todd mimicked our grandmother's accent. "'Stay out the sun, Todd, or you'll get darker, Cher. Put on a different color, Todd, that doesn't suit your complexion. Toddrick would be so handsome if he was just a touch lighter.' Crazy, colorist shit! Always pitting us against each other. You were the handsome one. I was *lucky* that I was the smart one, the next great Harrison politician. Fucking ridiculous. I damn sure wasn't going to do what *they* wanted me to do. I didn't want to be the next Senator Harrison. Fuck that."

I watched Todd's face contort at the memories. "I know. I'm sorry. I was a kid back then. I couldn't do anything about it, and I didn't realize how that hurt you. I would have if I could. But trust me, it has never been a competition between us."

Todd waved off my apology. "Whatever. I'm over it."

I knew deep down that he wasn't. It was why he drove himself to become a partner at his law firm before thirty-five. It was why he married and had kids first. It was why every conversation between us usually imploded into Todd airing his grievances. Todd was light-years ahead of me. Not much of a competition. If he could get his head out of the bottom of a glass of rum, maybe he could see that.

We sat in silence for several minutes, avoiding each other's heated glares until Todd's head was unsteadily nodding. *Yep, he was officially drunk.* I was never sure which Todd I was going to get when we went out. Baby brother with the sage advice or the heated, inebriated one who liked to dredge up old stuff and reopen wounds. I guess today I was getting heated, inebriated Todd.

I let out a sigh, running a hand over my head. "Todd, I didn't come here to argue with you. I just... I just wanted to talk to you. Get your advice."

"Why? Why do you care what I think?"

I laughed uncomfortably. "Because despite your bullshit, I love you. And when you're not two sheets to the wind, you give good advice."

Todd mumbled *"whatever"* under his breath, then got up from the table, wobbly but still standing. "I'm going to go to the bathroom...no...the bar. Maybe they have something stronger than this weak-ass rum."

I slid his keys off the table into my pocket. No way was he driving home.

Chapter Twelve

Porter

"What about this elevation?"

"No. That doesn't make sense."

"Then give me a better solution because nothing you're suggesting is working."

Ari and I had been going at it like this for days. Our kiss was the elephant in the room, making our work dynamic weird, and running into her at Dunn's River Café had only compounded the tension. The vibe I had bragged about to my brother was clearly off.

I stared at Ari, raking my hand over my head. Her eyes darted away from me, choosing to stare out the window. "Porter, we've been at this for hours. I need a break."

I shrugged, loosening my tie. "Sure. Whatever you need."

Ari nodded with a tight smile that didn't reach her eyes. I watched as she made her way toward the door. I took off my glasses and rubbed the bridge of my nose. I couldn't sit here and say nothing. We could either dance around what happened or address it head-on.

After a few minutes, I made my way toward the break

room. In the cramped space, we did an uncoordinated two-step toward the coffee machine, trying to keep a respectable distance between us.

"Sorry," I said as we simultaneously reached for the last espresso coffee pod.

"It's okay. You can take it," insisted Ari, pulling her hand back.

"No. It's all yours." I watched as she did her morning ritual of way too much sugar and cream in her coffee cup, her head straight ahead avoiding me.

"Where's the coffee to go with that sugar?" I quipped, hoping to elicit at least a chuckle out of her. I reached for one of the tea pods, opting for Earl Grey. Not my favorite but it would have to do.

Ari shrugged. "Sugar helps me focus." She stirred her coffee slowly and turned to face me, looking directly at me for the first time in hours.

"Ari, we need to talk about…"

She held up a hand. "We really don't. What we need to do is focus on our presentation."

"That's the thing, Ari. We aren't focused." I glanced into the hallway to make sure no one was approaching before closing the sliding glass door for privacy. "Everything's been off since our kiss. Really since I ran into you at Dunn's last week. Your emails are short. You scurry back to your office after we have a meeting. Ari, you won't even go to lunch with me. I…" *I miss us*. I stopped myself before I could say that out loud.

I hated every moment of this. This wasn't the woman I was enjoying getting to know just a week ago or the coworker with the brilliant ideas who understood my ideas. It sure as hell wasn't the passionate, sexy as fuck Ari that I'd kissed on her porch. We felt like strangers.

After taking a sip of her coffee, Ari took a breath. "Porter, it was just a kiss. We'd been drinking. We just got caught up in the moment and the vibe. Right now, I really want to focus on our presentation at the end of the week. That's what's important right now."

I threw up my hands. "Fine. But for the record, I wasn't caught up in the moment. This wasn't about the drinks or the vibe. I was fully present. That wasn't just a moment for me, Ari."

I examined the now pained look on Ari's face as her fingers tightly gripped her coffee cup. She drew in her lips tightly and sighed. "Porter, I think I'll work in my office for the rest of the day. If you need me, just ping me online."

"Ari..."

She didn't turn around. I headed back to my office, respecting her not-so-subtle request for space.

We pushed through the week, sticking to our schedule of meetings while also respecting each other's space. As promised, we didn't talk about our kiss. By Friday, Ari and I had managed to put together a decent presentation. *Decent* being the operative word. I internally groaned as I glanced over this recent design. It felt cobbled together and, dare I say, a little lackluster. *Was our kiss going to not only make things weird between us but also tank our project?* I would be lying if I didn't admit I was worried more about the latter. I didn't want the partners, or Ari, to lose faith in us as a team. Most of all, I didn't want to give Greer any opportunity to swoop in like some savior. I had to salvage this project and repair things with Ari at all costs.

In the boardroom, Ari sat directly across from Greer instead of her usual seat across from me. Out of the corner of my eye, I noticed Greer looking back and forth between us. He leaned over and nudged me.

"Say, did you piss off Big Mama?" He attempted to stifle a laughter through his poor attempt at whispering. Ari looked up from her notes and stared, then looked back down with an annoyed smirk.

I turned to face Greer, lowering my voice. "You never waste an opportunity to be a repugnant fuckwad. Seems like Harvard taught you everything but class."

"You're always so sensitive, Harrison," Greer remarked, turning to talk to Jacobi. I looked over at Ari, whose eyes quickly darted to the paper in front of her.

Our presentation wasn't a disaster, but it wasn't good either. If there was a level just below decent but above shit show, that was where we would land. We stumbled through questions from our colleagues and partners. In the end, our new concept received a lukewarm response from the room.

"What *was* that?" asked Riddle, confused. "This seems…disjointed. You all seemed to be much more in tune a couple of weeks ago. I mean, it wasn't perfect, but it was better than this."

There was a low rumbling in the boardroom. Ari shifted uncomfortably, avoiding eye contact with me. Greer smirked and nodded toward Jacobi as if he knew this fuckup would be the nail in the coffin. I rolled my eyes.

Robinson looked over his glasses. "I concur. This is… I don't know. It's acceptable, but there is no harmony. What happened to the green space, Ms. James? Granted, I didn't like what you did last time but the idea of functional green space is very desirable to the client."

Ari looked over at me and I looked at her blankly, then

looked away. We had forgotten all about it. Neither one of us had an answer for the omission, at least, not one we could disclose to the room.

"We will work this out. Omitting the green space was an oversight, right, Mr. Harrison?" said Ari.

So, we're back to being formal.

"Right," I said. "Ms. James and I need to better communicate our collective vision right now. I think we just missed some cues."

Robinson looked over at Riddle, who leaned in to whisper something. Robinson made a face which read annoyed, nodded, and sighed. This wasn't a good sign.

"Listen, you two," started Riddle. "You two are some of the most talented architects I've seen in the past twenty years. Ms. James, you worked for a top firm in Chicago so you're no stranger to big projects. You studied in Florence, for God's sake. Bring some of that experience, that European flair, to this project. Work this out. You have a week. Let's take a thirty-minute break. Greer and Jacobi, you're up next." Both partners got up from the table.

As the rest of the associates filed out, Greer stopped between Ari and me. He buttoned his jacket and shook his head. "You two aren't ready for the big time. When you fuck this up, which I know you will, I'll come in and save the day. Ari, you're in the big leagues now. I don't think you're ready. Not even Porter, the golden child of this firm, can help you."

Greer adjusted his tie and smoothed out his jacket, bumping slightly into me as he exited. I stood frozen. I didn't have the energy to fight with Greer, especially when he was right.

Once Greer exited, Ari and I were alone in the boardroom with only the whir of the central air as noise. She leaned against the table and looked down at her feet, slightly tapping her nervous fingers against the table. I smiled. I had missed her quirks, wanting to intertwine my fingers within hers. I resisted the urge; instead, I leaned against the table next to her, making sure there was ample room between us.

"We fucked up," Ari admitted.

"Yep," I agreed. "We were off this week."

"I know why we're off. I guess we should talk about our kiss," Ari said in a low voice.

I moved from the table and sat in the chair next to her, staring straight ahead. "I tried. But you didn't want to hear me out."

"I know."

"Ari, do you think us kissing was wrong? Because I don't. Do you—"

"It wasn't wrong," said Ari, cutting me off. "It was amazing. Mind-blowing. I can't stop thinking about it. But it can't happen again. For several reasons."

"Several reasons? Like what? Also, don't think I'm going to skip over the fact that you said our kiss was mind-blowing." I smirked, trying to contain my pride in my kissing abilities. "What's wrong with that?"

"Porter, be serious." Ari turned to look down at me with soft, rueful brown eyes. "We need to keep things professional. We work great together. Do you really want the office gossip to be that you're banging the new girl?"

I laughed. "Who's going to gossip? Ms. Gayle? I don't care about office gossip, Ari. That's silly. We're adults."

Ari's face grew serious. "It isn't silly. Gossip can kill any chance of you becoming partner or me having a career here. You have no idea! It's happened once, it can happen again!"

Again?

I needed an explanation. "Ari, what are you talking about?"

Ari took a seat next to me. "Porter, we need to talk."

The seriousness in her voice made me reach out for Ari's hand. She pulled her hand back, looking into my eyes. She looked afraid, damn near terrified.

"Be real with me. Is it me? Am I being an asshole about all of this?"

"No, Porter. That's not it," she assured me. "Remember how I said I hated Chicago, and I had to leave?"

"Yeah, because your dad died. Right?"

"Yes, but that's not entirely true."

Confused, I leaned against the arm of my chair. "It's not?"

Ari took a deep breath. "No. It's not. Chicago was… tough."

She rubbed her hands against the fabric of her slacks, rough and unsteady. I placed my hand on top of hers. "Ari? Talk to me. What happened in Chicago?"

I could see the tears well up in her eyes as she searched for the words to say. *Fuck.* Had she screwed up an account? Forgot something major in a design? Whatever it was, it was a memory bad enough to elicit tears.

Ari cleared her throat, her voice shaky. "I had been at Leland for four years. I was killing it. I'd gotten some extensive projects under my belt. The respect of the old boys' club in the firm. I really felt like my star was on the rise."

She stopped to look at me. I searched her eyes, and silently urged her to continue. "Well, in my fifth year, they tasked me with mentoring a new hire. Maurice. I was so excited because in that whitewashed sea, here was another Black person. He was smart, creative, had a real intelligent way of using space in his designs. We worked well together. And eventually, we got close…"

"Oh," I exclaimed. "Close as in?"

Ari nodded. "Close, as in *that* kind of close. We started seeing each other. We kept it on the low for months. I really liked him, and I thought he liked me too. He kept saying when the time was right, we'd go to HR and do the right thing. He told me he loved me, that he thought the world of me. That is, until the firm was chosen for an enormous project, and they wanted me to lead it. It was a game changer. A state-of-the-art high-rise that would be on Lakeshore Drive. A Black architect with a building there would have catapulted them to stardom. Name in the papers. Maybe even a feature in *Architectural Digest*. Or the *Tribune*. All that jazz."

Ari wiped the tears pooling in the corner of her eyes. I handed her my pocket square. I smiled reassuringly as Ari carefully dabbed her eyes, trying to avoid getting mascara on the silk fabric. I didn't care. She could ruin all my handkerchiefs if she wanted to.

Ari folded the silken square in her lap. "My design was amazing. I mean, if you think what I'm doing with the stadium is dope, that high-rise would have made you jealous. Well, the day of my presentation, my thumb drive wouldn't work. It was corrupted. I was like, well, that's cool. I had backed it up on the office cloud. I always backed my stuff up on the cloud. But it wasn't there either. I searched high and low, trying to see if I had copies of anything. It was as if it had vanished. Months of work gone."

"Damn…" Inside, I was seething. This dude Maurice was a piece of work. He reminded me a lot of Greer, but even Greer wouldn't go that low.

"It royally embarrassed me in front of the partners and client. I went back to the drawing board, but nothing I did was as good as that initial design. At the next meeting, Maurice wants to present his design. The higher-ups were impressed that a junior associate had taken some initiative. They let him present. As he pulled his designs up, I nearly screamed. It was my design. From start to finish. Every damn detail, down to window placement showcasing Lake Michigan. Maurice had taken my work, claimed it as his own. At least he was smart enough to cover his tracks with erasing the cloud."

My eyes widened as I sat in stunned silence. After a few minutes, I was able to compose myself. "So did you tell the partners?"

Ari nodded fervently. "Of course, I went to the partners. I told them Maurice was a liar and a thief. I said it was my design that somehow magically disappeared everywhere. They asked me how I could prove it and I said I knew he did because he knew my password. We worked closely together. Maurice said I was the liar, and that I was being vindictive because we had been in a sexual relationship and, for the greater good of our working relationship, he had broken it off. He said I was now hurling accusations of theft and that I was sexually harassing him because, and I quote, 'Ari's insecure and desperate for attention. Just look at her.'"

Now I was percolating with hate for a dude I didn't even know, but whose ass I wanted to kick. "Insecure? You? What a fucking asshole!"

Ari laughed. "Right! When have I ever been insecure? I may be a lot of things, but insecure isn't one of them."

"Oh, I know you're not. You're one of the most confident folks I know." I paused as she smiled, appreciating the compliment. "So, what happened?"

I felt a twinge of dread asking her to explain what was sure to be the worst part of her ordeal in Chicago.

Ari deadpanned. "What do you think happens when the only woman in a firm stands up to a man? They said I can either resign quietly, giving me a handsome severance package, sign an NDA, and provide recommendations with no mention of the incident. Leland, Stokes, and Brandies are well-respected and powerful in our industry. They could blackball me from every firm in America. During the mediations with LSB, my dad died. That was my sign. So, I resigned, took the money, came back home to Atlanta. I took part of the generous severance package to fix up my childhood home. After a few months home, I got a call from Mr. Riddle to recruit me for this project. That's the story."

I looked at Ari with all the sympathy I could muster. "I see."

"Porter, I hope you understand now why kissing you was a mistake. I don't want to risk my reputation at yet another firm. Then what? I'd be out on my ass with nothing. Hell, I'm taking a risk just telling you this."

I leaned in closer. "Ari, first, what you've said to me, stays between us. Secondly, I'd never do what Maurice did. Never! I respect you. I respect your talent. Your worth." I pressed her hand with a light, reassuring squeeze. "Trust me, I'd never do what that coward did. I'd never hurt you that way. I truly value our partnership."

Ari smiled. "I appreciate that, Porter. But do you understand where I'm coming from?"

I chewed the inside of my jaw. "You're right. We can't jeopardize our jobs here. I take full responsibility for my part in things. I just don't want any personal issues between us to show in our work. It's obvious to everyone that something is wrong."

"Yeah. Well. I get it. We have to work closely. But that doesn't mean we need to be *that* close. Let's just keep it friendly."

"Agreed. Before we do that, let's just state some facts."

Ari folded her arms. "I love facts. What facts would those be?"

"There is an attraction between us. An undeniably, strong attraction."

Ari let out a bit of a guffaw. "Well, aren't you blunt? And presumptuous."

I moved my chair closer. I was inches from her thighs and could feel the heat radiating from her body. The feeling brought me back to the night of our kiss.

"Presumptuous? Woman, I'm not a man who presumes. This is a fact: There is an attraction between us."

My eyes went to her thighs pressed together as Ari shifted uncomfortably in her seat.

"So, what if there is? It doesn't matter."

"We are and it does. Now that we've acknowledged it, we can move forward and start over."

"Okay. Let's start over." Ari stood up from her chair, extending her hand to me for a shake. I stood from my seat, looked her in the eye, and shook her hand firmly.

"Hi. I'm Porter. I love a good scotch and jazz on vinyl. I'm your partner on this project. I don't date coworkers

and I won't kiss you again," I said with all the seriousness I could muster.

Ari smiled that wide, gorgeous smile of hers, her hand
still in mine. "Nice to meet you. I'm Ari. I love baseball
and tacos al pastor. I too don't date coworkers. I also
don't want to kiss you again."

We laughed as we let go of each other's hands, staring at each other for a few seconds. Ari turned, breaking
the stillness, and began gathering her iPad and notes. I
watched her and my heart stilled. I knew I was fooling
myself. Despite everything that she'd just told me, I knew
it was too late. *How could I not want Ari when just one
look from her turned my world on its axis?*

"Well, let's get back cracking on this thing, partner,"
I said.

"Right. Let's work in the smaller boardroom. Meet
there in twenty minutes?"

"Got it." I nodded as we both gathered the rest of our
things. I watched her walk out of the boardroom. Her
hips in her slacks were doing this magical sway that had
me under their spell. I couldn't budge; my body was feeling the beginnings of a very awkward erection.

Friends. Professionals, Porter. I looked down at my
crotch. Now, if only the rest of me could get that message.

Chapter Thirteen

Ari

Telling Porter about the drama surrounding my departure from Leland, Stokes, and Brandies felt like a weight lifted off my shoulders. I could finally breathe. Most importantly, Porter and I could get the thought of our kiss behind us. Our rhythm wouldn't be off like it had been for days. We could move past it for what it was—a moment of weakness where we let emotions get the best of us.

That wasn't just a moment for me, Ari.

I shook my head at memory of Porter's words and decided to throw myself into developing fresh ideas for the stadium. Our presentation had been a bust and we had to redeem ourselves. Looking over at Greer, I could see he had the look in his eye that we'd opened the door just enough to plant a seed of doubt that we could present something amazing. Right now, we were barely in the conceptual phase; however, the Serrano Group could decide on a design anytime they wanted. That gave Porter and I the urgency to get our shit together and knock it out the park. *If only we could think of something amazing.*

The office phone rang, jolting me out of my thoughts.

"Ms. Gayle, I said I didn't want to put in on the office lotto pool," I said without looking at the caller ID.

"And why not? I played my birthday straight box and won 80 bucks. You could break me off a few million bucks," laughed my mother, Doris. I could hear the familiar clanking of her spoon against her coffee cup. I shut my eyes tight and slapped my forehead. *Shit.*

"Oh, hi, Mama. I'm sorry. I've been so busy these past few weeks. Sorry I haven't been keeping our daily call. I promise I'll be at choir practice tonight."

"Don't 'hi Mama' me! I know you've been busy but missing choir practice is unacceptable. You better come to choir practice tonight. No exceptions. Otherwise, they're going to give the Christmas pageant solo to Deacon Jordan's niece, Shawna. You know she sounds like a drowning cat, Ari! Talking about she used to tour with U2. Yeah, right! What I should have said was 'U2 is a damn lie!'"

I choked out a laugh. "Mama. That is so cruel. She isn't that bad. Is she?"

My mama huffed. "Like hell she ain't! The last time she sang a solo, we had the lowest collection ever in the church's history! The Holy Spirit didn't move folks to give. Probably because that girl's screeching voice made them shut their pocketbooks. Anyway, that ain't the only reason I called. So, I ran into your friend Bella and her beautiful twins at the farmer's market. And you know what she told me?"

I sat up straight, feeling a dry, gravelly lump in my throat. Somewhere between the collard greens and bok choy, Bella would have spilled the beans about Porter to my mom. I had been avoiding telling my mother about any of it, especially about the kiss. I wasn't ready for the inquisition of Doris James.

With hesitation, I responded as I nervously tapped my fingers on my desk. "Oh yeah? What did she say?"

"Bella told me you all had brunch a few weeks ago and your coworker just so happened to be there too. His name is Porter, right? She said the man was fine as hell. So…when am I going to meet him? Is he future son-in-law material?" Doris said in her usual, quick cadence.

"Mama, we're just coworkers. Nothing more. I can't and won't date any more coworkers. We know how that turned out."

My mother took a lengthy sip of coffee. "Well, that was then. Every situation is different. I said the same thing. Swore up and down I'd never date a coworker and ended up marrying your father. Honey, anything is possible. I just want you to be open to that possibility. It's been such a long time since you had a nice man around. When's the last time you've had a date?"

"I date. Remember Korey? He's a nice boy that I have around sometimes," I said, finally admitting that Korey was basically a booty call. "Besides, I don't need a relationship to make me happy. I have my job and need to focus on that." My mother's meddling in my love life was a nuisance but came from a good place. I didn't need a man to make me happy. *Even if that potential for happiness had dazzling green eyes, a kilowatt smile, and kissed me like I was water, and he was on fire.*

"Ari, dear, that's a load of crap and you know it. Either shit or get off the pot! One minute you want to be in a relationship, the next you want to be like those girls on that show. What's the show? Where those tired, but well-dressed white women just have a bunch of boy-friends and work all the time?"

"*Sex and the City.*"

"Yes! *Sex and the City*! You want to be a Samantha!"

I frowned. I always thought I was more like Carrie. But knowing my mother, she probably had the names and characters all mixed up. If it wasn't reruns of *In the Heat of the Night* or *Law and Order: SVU*, Mama had no clue about popular television shows. *Even if they'd been off the air for almost twenty years*.

"Anyway," my mother continued. "Bella said you got all weird when he came to your table. You like him, don't you?"

I turned my chair to get a look across the hall at Por-ter's office door. He wasn't at his desk.

"I don't know about that, Mama." I held the phone, trying hard not think about it. *It was a moment. A moment that we'd vowed not to have again.*

"Just be open to whatever happens. Everyone could use a little romance in their life. And by the way, I can hear you frowning through the phone, Ari! You'll give yourself wrinkles."

Dammit! I swear, there was no hiding anything from her. "I wasn't frowning. I swear."

"Sure, dear. Well, I got to go, sweetheart. I'm meeting Connie, Delores, and the girls at the mall. We're shop-ping for our fiftieth high school reunion. Maybe I'll con-vince Delores to invest in a girdle. Or what's it called? Spanx? I'll call you when I get back. If not, I'll just see you at choir practice tonight. Love you, daughter."

I shook my head, laughing, then an idea came to me. *Everyone could use a little romance in their life.* The conversation with my mother had given me a jolt of inspiration. I put on my headphones, deleted my last de-signs in REVIT, and did a rough hand-drawn draft of some ideas for the fan experience. Something that would mimic a night in the Serrano vineyards combined with the greens at Wimbledon. *Something romantic that could be enjoyed by everyone, every day.* After twenty min-utes of designing, I'd had something rough around the edges, but I was excited to show Porter.

I jumped out my chair, grabbed my tablet, and headed across the hall. Beaming, I flung the door open to Por-ter's office, taking a quick look over my notes. "Hey, Porter, sorry I took so long, I was just finishing up a call with my mom. But she…" When I looked up from my tablet, it took a few seconds to adjust to the sight of Porter in the arms of a woman who looked as if she'd stepped off the pages of Italian *Vogue*.

I held my tablet firmly with one hand, clutching it against my chest, its weight as heavy as a ton of bricks. "Sorry. I didn't know you were occupied. I can come back." The woman was a bronzed slender beauty, tall, with hair up in a topknot, a Louis Vuitton satchel slung on her arm, and designer shades perched on her head. *Who was this woman?*

"Oh gosh, Porter!" said the woman, playfully tapping Porter's shoulder. "Is this another one of your secretar-ies? My God, are they rude! Can't they see you're in-disposed? Listen, why don't you be a darling and come back in a few minutes. Or at least bring back a coffee. Black is how you like it, right, Porter?" She then shook her hand dismissively at me.

I know she didn't! I frowned, putting my free hand on my hip.

"Miss?" I asked, glancing at Porter. Before Porter could respond, the clone of Iman introduced herself.

"No need for Miss, dear. It's Kai. Kai Mengestu." Kai stood with one hand perched on the desk, the other still on Porter's chest. She was so unnaturally contorted that it looked like she was one of those department store mannequins.

I responded calmly. "Well. Ms. Mengestu. I'm not a secretary. I'm a junior associate here, and Porter's partner on the Serrano stadium project."

"Oh!" said Kai, shocked. She quickly removed her hand from his chest, smoothing an errant strand of hair out her face. I smirked.

Porter leaned back against the chair in front of his desk. "Kai, this is Ari James. My partner, as she stated, on the Serrano stadium. Ari, this is…"

"Kai!" Kai repeated as she extended her limp hand for a handshake as if she was the Queen. I gave her the quickest of shakes.

"Porter's partner? Well, isn't that nice!" said Kai, who looked at me suspiciously.

"Porter, we can pick this up when you're free. Nice to meet you, Ms. Mengestu."

"A pleasure," Kai said in a half-earnest tone.

"Ari, wait…" Porter spoke.

My hand was already on the doorknob when I turned to face him. "Porter, it can wait. Really."

Annoyed, Porter shoved his hands in his pockets. "Are you sure? Because Kai was just leaving. Right, Kai?" Kai continued scrolling on her phone as if she hadn't heard a word Porter had said.

I nodded, reassuringly. "Yeah. I'm sure. We'll catch up when you're done."

But not before I set this broad straight.

"Ms. Mengestu. There is free coffee in the lobby. But by the looks of those Gucci shades, I can tell it wouldn't be up to your standards. Luckily for you, there is a Starbucks on the main floor. By the way, Porter likes his coffee with one cream and one Splenda. Don't forget to validate."

Kai audibly gasped, her jaw slack.

Before she could respond, I gave her my most charming of smiles and walked out the door.

Bitch.

Chapter Fourteen

Ari

I stepped off the elevator Monday morning at Riddle and Robinson to see Ms. Gayle, who smiled at me like one of those creepy ventriloquist dolls. It was unsettling.

"Good morning, Ms. Gayle. You must have had an enjoyable weekend," I said, curious about the unnatural smile plastered on her face.

"Oh, I had a wonderful weekend. But you, my dear, are about to have an incredible morning," she said, waving me away from the front desk.

"Uhm. Okay?" I frowned, confused. *Was it a raise? Did the partners want to give me an office with a window and better ventilation?*

I turned down the hall, running into Mr. Robinson, who gave me a slight smile and said, "Ms. James." I nearly froze in horror. Maybe I was in a parallel universe. That had to be the explanation because Mr. Robinson barely acknowledged me, let alone formed his lips into something that resembled a smile.

I walked cautiously toward my office, and much to my dismay, ran into Greer. He was stirring his coffee-filled Harvard mug in his usual, obnoxiously slow way.

I tried to step aside but he deliberately impeded my way. Resisting the urge to knee him in the balls, I faced him. I wasn't over how snide he continued to be in our weekly meetings, finding reasons to undermine the progress of the stadium design at each step. With each presentation Greer did, he found a reason to sabotage our design. From the placement of seats to the field measurements, he was constantly looking for cracks in our design, and damn if we hadn't opened the door with that last presentation.

"Morning, Greer," I groaned, attempting to sidestep him. He followed my steps. I'm sure we resembled a pair of contestants on *Dancing with the Stars*.

"Hey, James, didn't know you had a boyfriend. You must have really put it on a brother. Not that I care."

I folded my arms. "What on earth are you talking about, Greer?" *Also, put it on a brother?* Greer never ceased to find new ways of making my skin crawl. It was the unexpected gift that kept on giving. Like a cold sore.

"Whatever. Play coy if you must. I was just trying to make polite conversation for a change," Greer retorted, finally slithering past me down the hall.

Before I opened my office door, I looked across the hall into Porter's office. I waved and smiled, but he quickly turned his back to me. *Now Porter was being weird? What the hell had gotten into everyone?* Strange couldn't begin to describe the start of my morning.

When I turned on the lights in my office, I nearly passed out, dropping my tote and portfolio on the floor. There were dozens of roses in a variety of shades in my office. I stopped counting after twenty dozen bouquets. *Who could have sent these?* Was it my mother? No way.

She would have sent my favorite flower, stargazer lilies, and she only sends flowers on special occasions. She'd rather spend her cash at the casino. Was it Korey? I hadn't spoken to him in weeks. He was at a conference in Seattle with Malcolm Gladwell per his social media. Not to mention, he was too self-absorbed to do something this thoughtful.

I closed my eyes, inhaling the smell of each vase full of flowers, marveling at the fact that my office now resembled a palatial garden. I looked for a card from the sender on each bouquet. I had all but given up until I looked at the bouquet of white roses on my desk. A small gold card peeked out between the flowers and baby's breath. Carefully, I removed it from the bouquet and read it.

"It's not a mixtape. But I hope these will do."

I looked up from reading the card. Porter was standing in my doorway, looking sinfully delicious as he wore the coyest of smiles.

"I might have gone a little overboard. I didn't know your favorite color, so I got them all," said Porter, as he leaned against the doorframe. "At least all the ones that were available at my florist."

Placing the card on my desk, I walked toward Porter, pulling him inside, and closed the blinds on my door. I stared at him, unable to say anything. A hiccup halted the tears that were threatening to crash down my cheeks.

Porter's eyes searched my face for a response. "Do you hate it? Fuck. You hate it, don't you? It's corny, right? I…"

I waved the card around. "What is all of this about?"

"Ari, Kai's not my girlfriend."

"Wha…what? I…"

Porter shook his head. "I said Kai's not my girlfriend. I broke up with her months ago."

With wide eyes and with a desert-dry throat, all I could muster was a pathetic "Oh."

"After Kai left, I went by your office to explain. But you'd hightailed it out of the building. I got the impression that you thought Kai and I were together."

"Porter, you don't have to explain."

"Yes, I do." Porter motioned for us to take a seat at the small table in my office. "We broke up almost seven months ago. I'd been dodging her calls for months, so she showed up at the job. Flew right past the front desk. Do you know she had Ms. Gayle chasing her down the hall like Gail Devers? The woman is in her sixties, for God's sake."

I tried not to laugh at the image. "That's not cool but I'm surprised that she made it past Ms. Gayle at all. The woman treats the reception area like Fort Knox."

Porter smiled. "Right! Anyway, what Kai wanted was for me to help her find a real estate agent. She figured since I'm here and I know a lot of people, I could help her. She's pressed for time because her place is in escrow. So, I gave her the info of the best but most annoying, pain-in-the-ass real estate agent I know."

"Jamal," we both said with a laugh.

"What you saw was her hugging me goodbye. Kai can be a bit rude. Faking like she was my woman was taking crazy to the next level."

Fine as you are, you'd drive any woman a little crazy, I thought.

I looked around my office, still amazed. "So, you sent me a shit ton of flowers to make your point?"

"Something like that." Porter folded his arms across his broad chest as he eased closer to me. I smelled the heady scent of his aftershave the closer he came to me. Combined with the scent of the roses, it all made me delightfully dizzy. "I don't kiss other women if I'm in a relationship. I wouldn't play those types of games with your heart. Especially after what you told me about Maurice. I wouldn't play with a woman who remembers my coffee order. Seems dangerous."

I tried to hide my smile. It was sweet of him. A bit much but sweet. "So, you spent a mint on flowers!"

Porter shrugged. "It's just money. And it was worth every dime to see the look on your face."

Geesh. Maybe this dude really was as loaded as Greer claimed he was. Not that it mattered.

"But, Porter, I thought we talked about this. I…*we*… we can't be together. Not like…three-hundred-dozen-roses level together."

"Actually, it was twenty dozen. I was going to send you thirty-five dozen. For every day you've been here. For every day I've been lucky enough to know you."

I bit my bottom lip as the tears I'd been holding back finally came. "Shit. You're good."

With a smile, Porter gently took the pad of his thumb and wiped a tear from my cheek. "I guess my signals are still a little crossed. You can't blame a brother, Ari."

My brain was scrambled like an old TV signal as I struggled to find the words. "Why?"

"Because, despite vowing to be on my best behavior, kissing you again is all I can think about."

I leaned back in the chair as Porter eased his chair next to me, his eyes piercing me with longing and need.

I knew that look. I *invented* that look. Porter wanted me. Bad.

Damn.

"Weeks? Really?" I stroked the back of my neck, my fingers twirling damp coils at the nape with nervous energy.

"Mhmm. Do you know how hard it is to be near you and not want to close the door and kiss you for hours?" Porter's teeth grazed his bottom lip, sending a current of electricity to my clit. He looked over his shoulder. "You do realize the door is closed right now, don't you?"

My eyes darted past Porter. *Shit. It was.* "Porter, we can't kiss in the office," I asserted. I needed to put an end to any more talk of kissing for the sake of my sanity and my vagina. "We can't. Period."

"I know we said we'd keep it professional. And that we both said that we don't date coworkers." Porter's voice lowered to a seductive rumble that I felt in my belly. "But I really like you, Ari. I do. I can't turn my feelings off like a faucet."

Porter reached out for my hand. I pulled my hand back, looking into his eyes. They were bright and dancing, excitedly expecting another kiss. Another touch. Another answer. I wanted him to touch me all over until I was a putty in his hands. But I couldn't. I wouldn't.

"Porter, seriously. I can't."

"I know. I'll wait until you can."

I looked at Porter, a level beyond shock registering in my brain. "Are you serious?"

Porter rolled his eyes and put his hands in his very fitted slacks pocket. "Yep. I'm serious. I'll wait for you. And when the time comes, I'm going to show you off. I'm not going to treat you like some dirty secret. I'd be honored to be your man. But…for right now. I'm your friend."

This man was unreal. I rubbed my temples. "Porter, that's ridiculous! You can't just wait for me to change my mind. What if I don't change my mind? Then you've wasted your time."

"I can and I will. I'm a grown ass man. It's a risk I'm willing to take. Besides, you'll never be a waste of time to me."

"Grown ass man or not," I sighed. "You really aren't making it easy, but I really want to just be friends…for now."

A smile slowly returned to Porter's face. "Fine. Like I said, I'm your friend."

I looked around my office. "In the meantime, are you going to continue to shower me with more flowers or what? Because that would really make it weird!"

Porter laughed, then waved his hand. "Nah, girl. You closed the door on any more showering. Trust me, I was going to shower the hell out of you."

I reached for Porter's hand, gently stroking the tops of his knuckles. "Well, I'm going to relish it for now."

Porter took his other hand, placing it on top of mine. "You should. Because this is the stuff you deserve. Every damn day. Not just from me. From anyone who adores you."

Oh my God. This man was like a walking greeting card.

Just then, there was a knock at the door. Porter and I quickly released hands and stood up.

"Come in," I said, leaning against the table attempting to look normal.

The door slowly opened as Ms. Gayle peered around its massive frame.

"Hey, I was looking for the two of you! Porter, did Ari tell you who sent the flowers?"

Porter smirked. "No. I think she's being coy with me about her secret admirer. Dude spent a few paychecks on these flowers." Porter let out a whistle in faux appreciation.

"It's just a guy trying to get my attention. It was over the top, but it worked. You can take one or two vases to the front desk if you'd like, Ms. Gayle. Liven up the space."

I saw Porter roll his eyes out of the corner of my eye, and it took everything in me not to laugh.

"Oh, my! I appreciate that, Ari," said Ms. Gayle, reaching for two lovely yellow bouquets. "Well, I hope you give him a chance. The onboarding meeting for the new client is about to start in ten minutes. I printed out the reports for all the associates. They're on the table in Boardroom A."

"We will be there shortly. Porter and I were just going over some last-minute talking points."

Ms. Gayle nodded and closed the door with a sly smile on her face.

Porter smiled. "I'm over the top, huh?"

I folded my arms, giving him my best homegirl neck roll. "You know you are, Porter!"

Porter nodded with a grin. "I better leave. I'll see you in the boardroom."

As he turned to exit, I put a hand on his shoulder to stop him.

"Porter?"

Porter turned to me with concern. "Yes, Ari?"

"My favorite color is pink. Roses are cool, but next time, if you were to get me flowers, you know, *as a friend*, get stargazer lilies. Those are my favorite."

Porter smiled, then nodded with a wink. "Duly noted, Ms. James."

Chapter Fifteen

Ari

"I'll wait for you."

Despite those words being forever burned in my psyche, I knew where I stood with Porter. We were solid in our friendship. There had been no more vases of flowers. No declaration of feelings. Yet, every time I was alone with Porter, I found myself staring at him, losing track of time in his eyes. I'd memorized every line on his face and was keenly aware of the smell of a new cologne. When he spoke, I paid more attention to the movement of his mouth, than his words. I had to remind myself that I was the one that wanted to be friends. I was the one who had more to lose in going there with him. *Would he really wait for me? Would I ever be ready?*

The week after our botched presentation, Porter and I remained focused enough to create an exquisite layout for the LED display. One that could rival the Dallas stadium, creating an immersive soccer experience. Porter left room for there to be a standing-room only fan area which had a magnificent view of the screen. During the end-of-week meeting, the partners along with the Serrano Group representative, nodded their heads in approval. We were back on track.

September was here with fall around the corner. We were reminded that the Serranos' primary focus in the fall months was the harvesting of grapes for their wine production, therefore, they wanted to see more designs that we could take from the conceptual phase to design phase by the end of harvest. Greer and Jacobi had already presented the Serrano Group with several options that seemed to meet some of the Serranos' exacting standards. They liked some of our design ideas as well. Some wasn't good enough. Porter and I were working at a breakneck pace to get our designs to the Serranos up to par. We were going over every detail with a fine-toothed comb. We had calls and conferences all day, mostly with representatives of the Serrano Group who had questions or suggestions about several design choices. It was arduous but nothing we couldn't handle. Porter and I didn't take lunch away from our desks instead of taking a break to try some new restaurant Porter had no doubt salivated over on Instagram. Instead, it was takeout from some quick, casual spot Ms. Gayle chose at random. I'd never eaten standing up so much in all my life. I was starting to believe that if I ate standing up, it burned calories faster.

As we pored over the owner's suite layout in my office, Ms. Gayle knocked on the door.

"You two have a call. It's from the Serrano Group."

Porter and I stared at each other, a little confused. "We just talked to them earlier this morning. Why would they want to talk to us again?" asked Porter.

"She didn't say," said Ms. Gayle. "I'll patch the call

in, but since it's unexpected, I thought I'd give you a heads-up."

"Thanks, Ms. Gayle," I said.

Porter and I looked at each other, puzzled. We weren't due to meet again for a few weeks, so phone calls out of the blue, directly to us, could only mean a few things: they had radical changes or complaints. Or worse, they wanted to fire us. The phone line rang. Nervously, I put it on speaker.

"Ari James here."

"And Porter Harrison," Porter chimed in.

"Ms. James. Mr. Harrison," the familiar female voice of Paulo Serrano's assistant said in a soothing Spanish accent. "Mr. Serrano has asked you all to join him and his wife tonight for dinner. At Bacchanalia. 7:00 p.m. Are you available?"

Porter and I looked at each other. It was almost six. In midtown traffic, it would be damn near impossible to get there on time. Plus, my attire wasn't exactly five-star restaurant appropriate. I was shaking my head with a vehement "no," but Porter panicked.

"Sure," he blurted out with a shrug. I hit him on the arm, and he winced playfully.

"Great. Mr. and Mrs. Serrano will see you then. We will send a car shortly," said the assistant, who then hung up without saying goodbye.

"What in the…" I said with exasperation in my voice. "Dinner? Do clients normally take you all out to dinner?"

Porter rubbed his beard. "No. Clients may take Riddle and Robinson out once a project is over. But never the associates who are doing all the work."

I looked at myself in the full-length mirror which

hung on my small coat closet door in the office. I had on a silk shantung floral shirt, black pencil skirt, and heels. My coordinating blazer was on the chair. I didn't look bad, but I certainly didn't look ready for a dinner at one of Atlanta's most exclusive restaurants. Porter stood behind me as I looked in the mirror.

"Well, I like what I'm seeing back here," Porter said as he playfully bit down on his bottom lip. We were doing a great job of keeping it aboveboard at work, but Porter sometimes couldn't help himself with a compliment here or thinly veiled innuendo there. I didn't mind. If he knew the thoughts that crossed my mind, I'd be in trouble, too.

I put my hands on my hips, exasperated. "Porter! Come on! Be serious. I look like a librarian!"

"A sexy librarian?"

I shot Porter a look, and he threw up his hands. "I joke. You look fine, Ari. You look very chic and conservative. Luckily, I just threw this on."

Porter had on brown slacks, a burgundy tie and blue pinstriped shirt. I deduced it was probably from Brooks Brothers or Zegna. If that was his version of "I just threw this on," I hated him. He looked like a *GQ* model. He could wear a burlap sack and still look amazing.

"Well, do you think they want to dump us?" I asked.

"After the glowing reviews from his team these past weeks? Why would you think that?"

Porter folded his arms, looking at me confused.

"You know how a guy will take a girl out on a nice dinner, only to dump her at the end of the date? I'm just wondering if this is what this is. Ever done that?"

Porter replied, stone-faced. "I'll neither confirm nor deny that I've used the dinner-and-dump tactic."

"You've definitely done it."

Porter's face turned faintly red as he cleared his throat. "I highly doubt the Serranos are asking us to a four-course, prix fixe dinner to dump us ceremoniously. Maybe they just have questions or like what we're doing. Shit, maybe it's a tax write-off business dinner."

"Or" I interrupted. "They want to dump us." My eyes widened into two giant saucers full of terror. I needed this job. I needed this project. It was one thing to be sacked by the firm, it was another to be sacked by the client. I'd never work in architecture again.

"Do you need me to kiss you again to calm you down?" asked Porter as he inched closer to me. I caught a whiff of his cologne and my stomach clenched.

I recoiled with a shriek. "No! God no! I'm fine." Although, kissing and maybe a little more *would* calm me down. Orgasms have been scientifically proven to reduce stress. Porter, by all accounts, seemed like the type of man who *really* appreciated scientific inquiry.

"James, I'm not going to kiss you," Porter laughed, putting a comforting arm around my shoulder. "You're cute when you worry. I'll get our coats."

The darkly tinted Escalade pulled into the Star Provisions complex which housed the James Beard award-winning Bacchanalia. I knew this because it was all Porter the foodie could talk about on the drive over. He wanted to distract me with something, anything, other than worrying about the Serranos firing us. After hearing about their menu offerings for thirty minutes straight, I was regretting not asking for that kiss just to shut him up.

Porter opened the door to the dimly lit restaurant. We looked around. The hostess, bartender and some waitstaff were scurrying around like ants, clearly trying to take care of their high-profile patrons. Other than the employees, the place was empty.

"You've got to be kidding me," I whispered to Porter. "Private dining at this restaurant?!" I clutched my handbag close to my side. This was some super baller shit.

"Yeah," said Porter. "Luckily, it's a weeknight. So, not too pricey, I'm sure." Porter wasn't that impressed. He must be used to dining this extravagantly. *Trust Fund indeed.*

We followed the hostess to a private room. As we entered, Paulo and his wife stood, the gorgeous brunette reaching out for a handshake. Porter obviously did not remember that Paulo Serrano was married, probably confusing him with his womanizing older brother, Marco. However, I'd learned in my research that Paulo had been married for eight years to his beautiful wife, Marina. Together, they had two small children, ages six and three.

Porter reached to get my chair, but a waiter seemingly out of nowhere, did it for him. Porter frowned. I slid into the chair, amused at Porter's annoyance at the waiter for doing something he always did for me when we dined.

"I ordered wine. From our vineyards, of course," said Paulo, motioning for the sommelier who poured us all glasses of the full-bodied tempranillo. Paulo raised his glass, "Salud!" We all took a sip. I wasn't a big fan of red wine, but as soon as the first notes hit my palate, I swooned. It was so smooth and rich, with hints of vanilla. The Serranos may have just made me a fan of red wine.

"I'm sure you both are wondering why I asked you to dinner," said Paulo. "Let me cut to the chase, as you all say. I wanted to just get to know the people who are going to be handling this project. It is so special to me. I want everything perfect. It is our baby."

"Yes, he loves this stadium like he does his sons!" chimed his wife, Marina. "But yes, I too wanted to meet the team responsible for the design of the stadium. It surprised me to learn that one of them was a woman. It is a pleasure to meet you, Ari. I looked up some of your past projects. I was highly impressed."

"Thank you, Mrs. Serrano." The lighting was dim, but anyone with eyes could see that I was flush with nervousness. I'd never been around this much money in one room in my whole life. Their net worth was the GNP of a developing nation. And they liked *my* work. It was unbelievable.

"Please. It's Marina!" continued Marina. "And although I love design, my main concern is cost. Marco doesn't concern himself with those things, but Paulo and I do."

Paulo smiled. "That's her degree in economics from Cambridge. It is always about the money."

Despite my thorough research, I'd forgotten one minor detail—Marina Serrano wasn't just some former beauty queen, she was brilliant. Marina was an economics genius responsible for crafting policy for the Spanish government. I admired the fact Marina's beauty, and her intelligence were things that Paulo equally admired about his wife. *I wondered if Porter felt the same about me.*

The chef brought out the first course himself. He and Paulo laughed like old friends, slapping each other firmly on the back. Marina and I eased into conversation, with Marina showing me pictures of her sons and talking about the unpredictable weather here in Atlanta.

I smiled and laughed, the nervousness eventually dissipating. I felt so much warmth from the Serranos. Porter looked at me, giving me a reassuring nudge. I smiled.

As they served the second course, the four of us eased into casual conversation. I could easily blame the different Serrano wines we had with each course, but Paulo and Marina were easy to talk to. They didn't come across as stuffy, despite their net worth. The Serranos were charming, down-to-earth billionaires that seemed to enjoy having a great meal with regular folks.

"So, whose idea was the fan experience area? I loved it!" said Marina.

"Oh, it was Ari's," Porter said. "Ari's design eye is exceptional. You know she lived in Florence for a while." My chest bloomed at his words.

"And London," I chimed in, the wine giving me a boost of confidence. "I thought about Wimbledon and the lawn. It is literally the best experience in sports I've ever had, and I thought I could bring that experience to the stadium. Combine it with the feel of your vineyards. I know you're all about sustainability. So, no space wasted. And hopefully, built as green as possible."

As Porter and I talked about the design of the stadium, we would finish each other's sentences. Paulo smiled as Marina nodded, looking at her husband. Without thinking, Porter put his hand on the small of my back, making small circles. I wanted to melt just like the chocolate flan on the menu.

"She's as smart as she's sex—" stammered Porter. "I mean, self-confident." I looked at Porter, admiring the profile of his face as he continued to speak. His face beamed with an incredible sense of pride.

There was my answer.

By the time the fourth and final course came, Porter and I had the Serranos eating out the palm of our hand. I talked more about my time in Florence, making them laugh at my stories of a supposed Medici "prince" who wanted to marry me. Porter and Paulo talked about their shared love of vinyl records, each of them comparing what they owned in their vast collections.

With the wine flowing, a cotton-candy-like softness swirled around me and the thought of someone slipping me out of this librarian skirt was becoming more appealing. It had been months since I'd had sex with anyone. No booty calls to my "stand-ins." No trips around home base with Big Papi could satisfy what I wanted right now. And what I wanted right now, the touch and feel of the one man that, even though I knew it was wrong, could satisfy me.

After Paulo and Marina gave their kudos to the chef, we ended the night with hugs, more kisses on the cheek and an open invitation from the couple to come yachting in Marbella.

"You two are a great team. My secret weapon, no?" He enthusiastically patted Porter's shoulder and kissed my cheeks fervently.

We waited outside for the car service. We were both full and extremely buzzed. Porter, just a few inches taller than me, had the perfect shoulder to rest my head. As I rested on his shoulder, I felt him lean down, his cheek resting against my temple.

"Private dining? Drinking $800 bottles of wine? I feel like Jay-Z and Beyoncé," I whispered to Porter.

"You're prettier," Porter said, without a hint of sarcasm.

"Now, I know you're lying." Porter laughed and squeezed my hand.

"You were amazing back there. It was as if you dined with billionaires all the time," Porter remarked, his nose grazing the side of my forehead. I heard him inhale deeply. The feeling, so small, so intimate, ignited tiny electric sparks against my skin.

"I could say the same for you," I chided.

Porter laughed, a deep soulful rumble. "Well, a few. My grandfather and his pals shut down a place a time or two. But…that stuff doesn't impress me. The way you treat people is what matters. You treat people like they matter, Ari. I love that about you."

I shook my head, trying to fight off the heat that was quickening my pulse. "You're right. People are people. And I love people. Besides, to quote Maya Angelou, I'm a sista who laughs like I have gold mines in my backyard."

Porter took my face into his hands and looked into my eyes. "And you're a phenomenal woman."

I tried to hold in my snicker but failed, erupting in full-blown laughter. "That's sweet. I appreciate the sentiment but that's the wrong poem."

Porter shrugged, sheepishly tucking his hands back into his pockets. "You know what I mean. I was never one for poetry, which is why I got a C in English Lit in college."

I began laughing, then wrapped my arms around Porter's neck, pulling him into a deep kiss. At first it was slow, as our tongues got reacquainted with each other, then sped up rapidly. His tongue met mine stroke for stroke. A tingle tickled the underside of my jawline as we kissed.

"What are you doing, Ari?" Porter whispered against my lips.

"It's called kissing," I replied. "I'm very good at it. Remember?"

Porter withdrew his warm, berry tasting lips. "I thought we both agreed to…"

I put a finger against his lips. "Shh. You talk too much, Harrison." Then we found each other's lips again.

We both pulled back from the scorching kiss just as the Escalade pulled up. The driver, an older blond gentleman, swiftly opened the door, and we both slid into the back seat.

Porter placed a hand on my thigh, the heat of his palm coursing through my skin. I could see the erection in his dress pants becoming increasingly uncomfortable. I buried my lips in the curve of Porter's neck, kissing it softly. His moan quickly evolved into a low growl as my lips traced a pathway from his neck to his lips, and back again. Porter's hands found their way under my shirt, feeling my nipples, stiff to the touch. It had been so long since someone touched me, my body responded hungrily. My panties dampened with each stroke of his thumb across my nipples. I moaned into Porter's mouth, which encouraged his hands to dip from my nipples to the folds of my waist. I felt his fingers slip between the band of my skirt, inching closer to my pelvis. We were giving the driver a show, not bothering to care about the partition that was down. Between our kisses, the trippy jazz music the driver streamed were the only sounds we heard.

I pulled Porter's hands out of my skirt. "Don't go home, Porter."

Surprised, Porter licked his lips slowly, as if to savor our moment. "Are you sure? Because it won't upset me if you change your mind. I won't do this…not if you're not ready for this. I meant it when I said I would wait for you."

Admittedly, all that tempranillo had made me bold as hell. "I want you to come home with me. Can you do that? Can we just focus on tonight and we think about the rest later?"

I gave the driver my address and watched as he input the information into his navigation system.

"With traffic, we will be there in twenty-five minutes, sir, ma'am," he said with a slight grin as he finally rolled up the partition.

"Can you wait twenty-five minutes?" Porter asked, with a smile so sexy that I wanted to jump his bones immediately.

With my lips to his ears, I nibbled and replied, "The question is, can you?"

Porter pulled away, then stared at me. "Twenty-five minutes, Ari. We have twenty-five minutes to think about this. To think about something that's going to change who we are to each other for the rest of our lives."

Fuck. I adjusted my skirt, sat back, and stared out the window. "Okay. Twenty-five minutes."

I chewed the inside of my jaw. *Should we do this? Could I blame it on the wine and abject touch-starvation? How would everything change?*

"Twenty-four minutes." Porter shook his head. "Whatever we decide, trust me, I'm not going anywhere."

I felt Porter reach for my hand and interlock his fingers with mine. I closed my eyes and leaned my head on his shoulder. Porter pressed a kiss to my forehead.

Chapter Sixteen

Porter

Twenty-five minutes later, Ari was tugging on my belt, which was a hassle to unbuckle, as she led me up the steps to her door.

We'd taken the full twenty-five-minute ride to think about this. I meant what I said: no matter what, I wasn't going anywhere. I'd still wait. But before I could say anything, Ari turned to me and whispered, "Come inside."

She could barely get the key into the door when I began kissing her, unzipping her skirt, and pulling it down. Ari loosened my tie and threw it on the floor as she kicked off her heels. I was already out of my jacket, quickly unbuttoning my shirt before throwing it to the ground. My chest rose deeply with each yearning breath. I began kissing Ari's neck, following the hollow between her breasts as I unbuttoned her shirt.

"You have on way too many clothes," I said, growling hungrily into her decolletage, the faint scent of her perfume still lingering.

"And you have on a belt that's way too complicated to unbuckle." I laughed as I finished unbuckling my belt, sliding it gingerly out of the belt loops. Ari unbuttoned the fly of my pants, pulling me close to her as her fingers pulled down the zipper. Finally, I shimmied out of the heavily starched pants, standing there in my black boxer briefs and maroon, pink, and brown argyle socks. Ari giggled.

"What?" I asked, looking down at my socks. "You hate my socks, don't you?"

"No! They're adorable," she said, trying to hold in her laughter. I thought they were a whimsical pop of color. I guess she begged to differ.

"Fuck that. I'm not about to do this, standing in these socks like a grandpa." I hopped on alternating feet as I took off my socks, which was entirely too difficult to do after several bottles of premium wine.

We stood in silence, trying not to salivate. I had imagined Ari naked thousands of times and the real thing was a lot to take in. Ari stood there, skin the color of dusk, in sky-blue lace bra and boy short with amazingly impressive calf muscles. As she turned, her ass was a firm, high peach-shaped bubble that was begging me to take a bite.

"Wow," I said, looking her up and down. "You're beautiful."

"Really?" she asked. With her hair tousled and makeup dewy, Ari was the total picture of seduction.

"Yes, really. But you know that." I turned her shoulders toward the mirror that was in the foyer. "Look at you, Ari. You're gorgeous, girl."

I stood behind her, my body pressed up against her still suppleness. Feeling the rigidity of my dick grazing against her backside, I wondered if she would have objected to being bent over and fucked in her foyer. But I didn't want her there. Not for the first time. I needed to feel her in a bed. Her bed.

I pushed her hair to one side, kissing her neck. I stared

at the two of us in the mirror. In the low light of the foyer lamps, we cast an amazing glow from our two striking complexions. I was fair, muscular, and taut. She was shorter, ruddy-brown, and curvier. Perhaps to others, we looked like a bit of an odd pairing. I thought we couldn't be more beautiful together. My breathing was heavy yet steady, the excitement building. *God, this was really happening.* Ari turned to face me, her back against the small table. I looked at her, deliberately not breaking our gaze. Looking at me, her hands on my chest, trailing a finger down toward the top of my boxer briefs, Ari leaned in closer.

"Do you want me, Porter? Do you still want to do this?"

I pushed a wayward, kinky coil behind her ear. "Do I want you? More than you know, sweetheart. Do *you* want to do this?"

Ari traced a finger against my jawline. "Yes, Porter. I do."

With that, I lifted her in one fell swoop. Her eyes grew wide, surprised that a guy with my build could pick up a girl of significant weight so easily. I could have carried her one thousand miles if she wanted me to. Besides, I benched three hundred and fifty pounds on the regular. Ari was as light as a feather in my arms.

"Which way is your bedroom?"

Ari pointed down the hall. I carried her across the mahogany-colored floors, the coolness of the hardwood against my bare feet.

"Which door?" I asked, breathing the words into her neck.

"Left."

The bedroom door was already open. Its centerpiece was a massive California king bed with a tufted headboard. I placed Ari in the middle of the bed. The room was dark, but I could make out Ari's body in the shadows, illuminated by the light of the early fall moon through the window.

Ari moved up the bed and turned on the low lights of her reading lamp on her nightstand. She hurried back to the middle of the bed as if she heard me beckoning her back. The bed was a dark navy with a cream-and-navy floral comforter. Ari, lying there in her striking sky-blue bra and panties, looked like a summer sky above a field of flowers. Did this woman have any idea how goddamn beautiful she was?

Ari's breathing was shallow. Her hands gripped the edge of the bed as she looked at me standing in front of her.

"What now?" she asked. Her hands were moving to take off her panties. I held up my hand. She froze, her eyes confused.

I leaned back, allowing my eyes to roam over Ari's body. "Baby, stop. Let me just drink you all in. Just the sight of you like this is too much. Just let me have this moment. I may not have it again."

I admired Ari, starting with her toenails, which were a soft pink color. Her legs were thick, smooth, and gorgeous. The low light of the room reflected her skin's golden undertones which made her radiant. Her blue panties stopped right under her navel, and I could see faint traces of her bikini line. Her stomach wasn't flat but round, soft and inviting, with a deep, cavernous navel. I looked at the slight stretch marks on the sides of her hips and moved my eyes up toward her breasts, which were spilling out of her bra. She had a few moles right on her rib cage, in the shape of an unknown constellation.

Her deep brown areolas peeking out from the top of her bra, with an errant nipple poking through the lace, made my dick stiffen even more in my boxer briefs. Her hair, which had been a low bun, was now loose and all over the place, creating an alluring, dark halo round her face. Lines. Curves. Constellations. Peaks, Valleys. Caverns. She was a map of heavenly beauty that I had to travel.

There was a tufted upholstered bench in front of her bed. I used it for leverage as I climbed toward Ari. On my knees, I slowly spread her legs with a gentle push of my hands, cradling myself between them.

"Ari, I'm asking you again. Are you sure?"

"Yes," she said, her breath rapid and voice uneven.

I bent down, kissing her with intense thirst. It was like I had been in the desert, and she was the coldest, freshest drink of water.

I devoured her lips, sucking in her tongue hard. I slowly released her and focused on her bottom lip and bit it slowly, but firmly. Ari let out a satisfied moan. I could feel the sticky barrier between my dick and my briefs. I had to get them off. But first, I had to get her off.

I kissed Ari's neck, trailing my way down into her ample cleavage. I could taste the faintest trace of her perfume. Oranges, mangoes. Roses. She was a garden in bloom. I felt Ari's fingers run through my hair, which was curlier and longer than usual. She twirled a single curl around her finger and tugged. Playfully, I nibbled her shoulder. She let out a low, sultry giggle. It was the sexiest laugh ever.

"So, you want to play?" I asked, looking into her big brown eyes.

Ari's long black eyelashes fluttered as she bit her full

bottom lip, which still had traces of coral colored lip-stick.

"Of course, I want to play. But this isn't about to be a game, is it?"

"Oh. It's definitely not a game, Ms. James."

I slid my hands underneath her torso and moved them to the clasps at the back of her bra. I unhooked the bra, slowly removing it as her ample breasts spilled out. Her areolas were dark brown against the honey brown of her skin, with nipples the shape of chocolate kisses. They instantly made my mouth water, and I had to take one into my mouth. I gently leaned down and sucked, running the rough pad of my tongue over her nipples over and over until they were stiff peaks. I pulled one nipple slightly between my teeth before sucking it all over again. Ari squirmed underneath me and moaned. I positioned myself firmly over her. I felt her nails gently dig into my shoulders as I alternated between each breast with my mouth.

"Jesus, Porter." Ari's voice broke as she tried to gather herself. Her back arched as I lifted her breast and ran my tongue at the spot where her breast and torso met.

"Do you want me to stop?" I asked, looking up at her as my hands massaged her, my fingers gently pinching the hardened coffee beans that were her nipples.

"Don't. Fucking. Stop," Ari responded, moaning each word, each syllable, softly.

I moved from her breasts down to her stomach, placing butterfly kisses all over every inch, in between every curve. Lingering my tongue around her navel made her back arch further. I could feel her underneath, her stomach muscles tensing. It was as if she was restraining herself, limiting her enjoyment of pleasure.

"No, don't do that…" I whispered, looking up at her with my head positioned at the top of her panty line.

"Do what?"

"Don't hold back with me. Let go with me. Let it all go."

Instantly I felt her abdomen relax, the tension subsiding. I moved my lips down, tasting small beads of sweet sweat on her skin. My hands, nervous and anxious, pulled her panties down. Ari lifted her hips up to allow me to get them totally off. I looked at her, totally naked. She had a slight landing strip of hair on her otherwise clean-shaven pussy. Not knowing what to expect, the sight of her pussy, glistening with wetness, made me ravenous for her.

I took my fingers and parted her wet folds, moving my fingers slowly inside her and slightly over her taut clit. Slipping one finger inside, I teased her G-spot as my thumb circled her clitoris. Ari moaned, fisting the sheets of the bed. I removed my drenched fingers, slowly placing each digit in my mouth. Her intake of sharp breath at the sight of me licking her taste off my fingers made me want to have a deeper, more fulfilling drink of her.

I bent my head down and lapped my tongue on her plump little clit. I moved in small, quick circles, alternating my tongue between her wet slit and her exposed bud. When I could feel her legs begin to clamp down, I pushed back, using my hands to expose more of her clit from underneath its hood, moaning and sucking faster, deeper. I could feel Ari take her hands to my head and bury me in her. If I was going to suffocate and die, dammit, it would be worth it.

"Fuck, Porter. Fuck!" she yelled with primal yearning. I would not stop until she came, tasting her juices flowing into my mouth. And she tasted divine.

Once the wave of her orgasm passed, I kissed her, letting her taste her own arousal. She moaned in deep satisfaction. I moved off the bed to remove my boxers. My untamed erection leaped out of my shorts and was standing at curved attention. Ari looked over and immediately sat up.

"Wow," Ari said. "I mean…damn." As she tilted her head to the side in admiration, a coy smile crossed her face.

I smiled, feeling my cheeks flush as I looked down at my dick, then back at Ari.

"Is it to your satisfaction?"

Ari put her elbow on her knees, head in hands, and chuckled. "Hmm. Oh yeah, definitely."

I looked around her bedroom floor for my pants to get a condom, but realized they were in the foyer. Sensing the panic on my face, Ari smiled and slowly opened the top of her nightstand. I peered inside. There was a cornucopia of condoms in every imaginable brand, size, and color, lube, a couple of vibrators (including an enormous black one), and… *Were those anal beads?* I raised a brow.

"Ari James, you surprise me," I remarked under my breath as I searched for an appropriate condom.

"Well, a single woman has to be prepared," Ari retorted. "And uhm… I've been single a long fucking time."

I looked in the drawer at the rainbow assortment of condoms. (And made a mental note to ask about the anal beads.) I could have gone for a Magnum like most brothers with supposed big dick energy, but I wasn't trying to embarrass myself. I mean, I was a well-equipped brother. I never had complaints. But I also didn't want to seem like, well…a dick about my dick.

Before I could grab a condom, Ari sat up, dangling her thick, gorgeous legs off the side of the bed. Her thighs were touching, looking warm and inviting under the low light of the lamp. I held the blue packet in my hand and looked at Ari curiously.

"What? What is it? If you don't want to do this…" She held up a hand and smiled slyly.

"The thing is, Porter. I believe in reciprocity. And I think it's only fair that I return the favor."

I blinked quickly, realizing what she meant. *Oh.* I wasn't a man that "needed" that. I wasn't a selfish lover. For me, it was all about a woman's pleasure. I got off on making my woman get off. Sure. I had imagined Ari's lips wrapped around my dick plenty of times. Okay. A lot of times. But tonight, I guess I wasn't expecting it our first time having sex.

"Return the favor? Oh, Ari…you don't have to…"

"Shhh," Ari said as she put her hands on my waist and pulled me closer to her. "But I want to. I have to make a proper introduction."

Before I could object, I felt her take me into her warm mouth. Her lips encircling my shaft with such ease. She moved her lips up and down, her tongue circling the head of my manhood. I felt her tongue move up and down until it hit the juncture of my heavy sac. At one point, her lips clamped down on the head, creating such a force of suction that my knees buckled. Constellations. Moons. Stars. I was in heaven. I could feel my breathing become ragged and my heart raced. All the blood draining from me and stiffened my dick until it hurt in a good way. I gripped the condom between my fingers while I put my hands in her hair and she moved up and down on me. Ari used her hands and lifted my shaft, running her tongue down the base before grabbing my ass, pushing me deeper into her mouth.

"Goddamn, Ari! Why are you doing this to me, baby?"

Ari paused for a moment and looked at me with the most devilish grin. "Because…reciprocity," she said before taking me into her mouth again. I felt my eyes roll to the back of my head and I was getting light-headed. The pressure was building, as I was so close to coming. There was absolutely no way that I'd come like this. Not this soon. No, I wanted to come inside her. I wanted our bodies to meet. I had to feel her. All of her.

I pulled back from her quickly and tore open the condom, sliding it on in record time. It was all I could do to keep myself from passing out or coming into my hands. In the moment, I had the anticipation of a horny teenager, not an over-forty-year-old man.

Ari leaned back on the bed; one leg lifted slightly. Her pussy was still wet and glistening. The sight of her womanhood made me hungry for her. I climbed between her legs and leaned down to meet Ari's lips. Instead of kissing her, I felt the heat radiate from her lips between her deep, slow breaths. I tried to slow down my anticipation, but it was like unwrapping a Christmas present on Christmas day. And indeed, Ari was a gift.

"Are you sure you want this, Ari?" I asked again, while I planted a kiss on her cheek, then on the curve of her jawline. She shuddered underneath my touch. "If you don't want this. I can stop. I'll stop. No questions asked."

"Yes. God, yes," she said, breathlessly. "I want this. I want you."

I lifted myself and pulled her hips toward me, easing myself between her thighs. My gaze with Ari didn't break as I guided my throbbing dick inside Ari's tight, wet pussy. She let out a quick gasp, adjusting to my size.

I could not take my eyes off Ari. I couldn't take my mouth off Ari, either. My lips found a home on her neck, then on her clavicle. I had to taste some part of flesh as I entered her. She grabbed my lower back and pushed me deeper inside her, taking the full weight of my body on top of her. Her thighs wrapped around me as her moans evolved into panting.

"Porter…oh God… Porter. Fuck me."

"Yes, baby. I'm here, baby… Fuck! You feel so good."

I could barely get the words out. My pulse was racing with each stroke. I felt her pussy clench down on me, harder with each entry inside her. I took my hands and grabbed her breasts, slightly pinching the nipples between my fingers with each movement of my hips. Ari's hair was sticking to her face with perspiration, and I was so turned on by her uninhibitedness. Tonight, I got Ari, wild and free. Wild. Free. And mine.

"Porter, turn me over," begged Ari. I kept moving and didn't immediately do as she asked. I wanted to look into her eyes and that beautiful face of hers. It wasn't until her voice cracked and she asked again, begged again, that I stopped, lifted her hips, and turned her over.

I pulled her legs toward the edge of the bed and grabbed hold of her ample, round ass. As I entered her from behind, she let out a deep, long moan. With her back arched, her face was down, her ass moved in lush, rhythmic waves against my pelvis. I could hardly focus. I'd thought of having Ari at least seven hundred ways, and even still, this was all too much.

I pushed into her faster, harder. She was so wet and

so ready for me. The feel of me entering her repeatedly reminded me of swimming in the thickest, warmest jar of Tupelo honey. It was as if her body was made for me. I gripped the edges of the bed, and I could see from her reflection in the dresser mirror she was biting the sheets. She was trying to talk, but she was barely coherent. So was I. Some semblances of words and phrases spilled out my mouth, but in the moment, it all sounded like gibberish.

As I kept pace from behind, I took a free hand and stroked her clit as I worked deep inside her. The hard bud responded as did her pussy, as my hand was flooded with an ample amount of wetness. Ari's head snapped back, and she looked back at me with raw, carnal desire in her eyes. It turned me on even more. I kept stroking her clit until she screamed and collapsed in climax. Soon after, I felt my own body shudder as I came with sweet relief.

I rolled the full condom off and grabbed a tissue from Ari's nightstand, throwing it into the wastebasket next to the bed. Ari leaned back on her pillows, staring up at the ceiling, her hands on her chest. I eased next to her, kissing her damp shoulder, enjoying the saltiness of her skin, and pulled her closer to me. She turned to face me with a smile, taking a free hand to wipe my very sweaty brow.

"You made me put in some work, girl," I said with a grin.

Ari's brows bunched. "Aren't I worth it? Besides, hard work hurt no one."

I kissed her lips, tracing my tongue along her lush bottom lip. "You're worth it. So worth it."

We had fought this hunger for each other for so long. Tonight, with the passion building, we gave in. I knew as soon as my body shivered, releasing every fiber of my need for her, that this had changed everything. I couldn't go back to being friends. This woman had woven herself in my DNA.

Ari wrapped her leg over me, staring into my eyes until we were fast asleep. I knew before I closed my eyes that this was just round one. I had to have her again before sunrise.

I wanted more of Ari. In every way.

Chapter Seventeen

Ari

The sun was peeking through my blinds, softened by the chiffon curtains. I wasn't sure what time it was, but I knew it was early. Porter's head, his curls a bit tousled, rested on my chest and the European pillows supported my back. Even after sex, he smelled so good. Maybe even better. How the hell was that possible?

I can't believe I'd just had sex with Porter.

I looked around my room. Condom wrappers were on the nightstand and floor. Condoms were in the wastebasket.

Correction: I had sex with Porter multiple times.

Our bodies were wrapped in sheets that were barely on the bed. Porter was sleeping like a baby in my arms. His soft breathing warmed my collarbone. I wanted to pat myself on the back and do my congratulatory "you put it on him" dance until a feeling of dread pricked at corners of my mind.

Oh. My. God. I had sex with Porter. Multiple times!

I felt his chest rise as his eyes opened. I closed my eyes quickly, so he wouldn't suspect that I'd been staring at him most of the morning.

"Good morning, Mon Coeur," said Porter in a very husky voice. His morning voice made something tingle deep inside me. Okay. He made my pussy tingle if I was being honest.

I opened my eyes slowly, feigning sleepiness. "Morning, Porter." I added an exaggerated yawn for good measure. "And I'm sorry but my French is rusty."

Porter stretched. "It means *my heart*. My dad called my mom that sometimes. Also, that's the only French I know. Much to my grandmother's dismay."

"Oh," I responded, surprised. *Had we reached pet name level? Damn, I must have really put it on him.*

Porter looked up, worry making his nose scrunch up. "That didn't freak you out, did it?"

I smiled. "Not at all. My dad called my mom *juicy*. Now that I think about it, it was probably code for something dirty." I bent down and kissed the top of his head. Porter rose up, his face meeting mine.

"Good." He kissed me on my lips, hard and deep. He must really like me because, Jesus, I hadn't even brushed my teeth and my morning breath had been known to make my own eyes water.

Porter got up from bed, and I watched him walk to my unfinished master bathroom. The sunlight hit his very muscular, warm fawn-colored ass just right. I giggled. He looked back at me and winked, continuing into the en suite bathroom. I tried to peek my head to see him, but from my angle on the bed, I couldn't.

"So, what's up with the unfinished shower?" Porter yelled out as he used the bathroom.

Ugh. Mr. George. I bit my lip, thinking of the plastic and unfinished tiles where the shower should be. Damn, had I been more decisive, we could have used that shower this morning. Together. I imagined all the hot shower sex we could have had when I heard Porter rustling with the plastic. I snapped out of it.

"Well, Mr. George, my contractor, and I are having a disagreement about what to do in that space," I shouted back. "I have one idea and he has another."

"Well, it's your house so what do you want to do, Ari? By the way, this tile in here is amazing."

Porter came around the corner, holding one of my fluffy bath sheets. The morning sunlight was doing something amazing to his skin. His chest was smooth, defined, and nearly hairless. The tufts of hair above his manhood were softly light brown and curly. I strangely wanted to twirl my fingers between its softness. I looked down at his masterpiece. God curved it in that "I'm a human G-spot finder" kind of way. I made a mental note to thank God for it in my daily prayers. I glanced up at Porter, whose lips turned up in a devilish grin.

"What do you want to do? I mean, regarding the bathroom," he said, wrapping the towel around his waist.

I laughed and shook my head, pulling the sheets up to my neck. "Well, I want a very massive shower. Big enough to fit two or three people comfortably."

Porter raised an eyebrow. "Three people? Ari, what type of freaky stuff are you into? I mean first the sex drawer and now an orgy shower?"

I playfully threw a pillow at him as he laid across my bed on his stomach. "No… I mean well… Yeah, I must admit. I've always wanted a shower big enough for me and my future…" I paused. *Partner? Lover? HomieLoverFriend?* "Resell," I continued. "But Mr. George thinks if I want to get more bang for my buck in the future, I should probably install a fancy claw-foot tub or some sort of jet tub contraption. I'm not here for it. I'm also not looking to sell anytime soon. I'm already tired of the vultures calling me every week."

Porter propped his elbows up and his hands on his chin. "Well. What about a compromise? You know, the homes I've seen now have the large tub inside the shower. So then, you don't have water everywhere from your bath. The drainage system is already there. Maybe you can also add some nice rain showerheads as well. And then, you have choices. See, a compromise."

"Wow. I hadn't even thought about that. Funny, with as many home improvement shows as I watch, I didn't think of that idea at all. I'll have to run that by Mr. George."

"See, what would you do without me? Partner-in-design," Porter said, smiling widely. He gently stroked my exposed leg, peeking out from under the sheets. He slid one finger up and down my shin, and then past my thigh. I felt a shiver each time his touch reached the bend of my knee.

"I don't know. I've been asking myself that a lot lately," I mumbled.

I felt the warmth of his hand move past my knee, under the sheets, and toward my inner thigh. Porter was now on his knees, his hands inching closer toward the growing primal aching that he was causing. He slipped a finger inside me, and I let out a moan. Fuck, I was already wet. It was as if my body instinctively responded to his touch. After last night, he had already claimed his spot forever. I knew it and apparently, so did my pussy.

"Could you do this without me?" he asked in a husky, low voice.

I moaned and arched my back a bit. "Yes, but it

wouldn't be as fun," I replied, my voice laced and dripping with anticipation. He was such a tease, but I loved it.

I looked over at the clock. Shit. It was almost a quarter past eight. We had to be in the office by nine for morning briefings with the partners.

"Do you want to be late for work?" Porter asked, his voice heavy and thick with lust. "I know your boss. I'm sure he wouldn't mind. But only if you had a valid reason."

"Would you like me to give you a valid reason?"

Porter increased the movement of his fingers, the wetness between my thighs ramping up. "Hmm… I'm sure I can think of something. I can say you had engine trouble, and I came to give you a jump."

I snapped my head at Porter. He'd pressed a thumb against my clit at the same time, bringing me to the edge of having yet another orgasm. *God, he was good.* "You've got five minutes," I said breathlessly. "And my car takes time to warm up."

Porter grinned. "Just your car, huh?"

Porter slowly unwrapped the towel from around his waist. He licked his bottom lip, plump and peachy. I looked down at his Adonis belt and the hardness of his obliques. My eyes slowly began making my way down every inch of him, finally landing on his G-spot loving dick. He returned his hand to the spot where he was stroking me to near ecstasy.

"Okay. Make that ten minutes."

Porter crawled closer. "I need more than ten minutes. You know that Ari."

My breath hitched as he continued to stroke me. His touch scrambled my mind and thoughts like old-school television. "Porter, seriously, we need to talk…"

Porter's lips were near my neck, nibbling as he followed the curve of my throat to my shoulder. "We are talking, Mon Coeur."

I leaned back. "No. Porter. About us." I bit my lip, trying not to scream as my clit was responding to his touch. I had to focus. "Seriously…"

Porter groaned, removing his lips and tongue as they left their slick imprint on my skin. He leaned back on his knees, reluctantly removing his hands. "Okay. What about us, Ari?"

I looked up into Porter's eyes, which were soft mint and sweet, like pistachio ice cream. "Porter, you know I like you, right?"

Porter wasn't sure if he should smile or frown. So, his face did something in between. "Okay? I'm pretty sure I know that."

"And I want to keep liking you…"

Porter narrowed his eyes. "Ari, what is this about?"

I chewed my bottom lip. "We can't be a thing, Porter. I don't care how bomb the sex was…"

Porter smirked. "So, the sex was good, eh?"

I playfully pinched his nipple and he laughed. "I'm serious. Porter, we can't."

"And I told you I'd never hurt you. This is not that. I'm not *him*. I'm Porter. Porter Etienne Harrison, Junior."

"Your middle name is Etienne?"

"Yep."

"That's kind of…bourgeois. Maybe a touch pretentious."

"Uhm. That's rude. It's a family name. And you're getting off topic, Ari."

I took a deep breath and rubbed my temples. Porter reached for my hands, placing them inside his large, warm palms. He was right about one thing; he certainly wasn't Maurice. Maurice had never been this damn good in bed. Or this considerate of my feelings. *Or orgasms.*

"Porter, you're amazing," I blurted out.

"As are you, Ari." Porter leaned closer to me, placing a chaste kiss on my forehead. "I'll take your lead. No pressure."

"No pressure?"

"No pressure."

I traced my tongue against my teeth. "No expectations?"

Porter nodded. "No expectations."

I turned and looked at Porter. "Just sex. No…relationship?"

Porter looked at me, puzzled. "Is that what you want? Ari, I don't want you to feel like I'd be sexing you, and *only* sexing you, in secret. Didn't you say Maurice…"

I cut him off. "You're not like Maurice."

"Right, but…"

"We can't be together."

We sat in silence. I pulled the sheets off my body and stepped onto the floor. Before I could get out the bed, Porter grabbed my arm.

"Ari?"

"Yeah?"

"I care about you. Last night wasn't a mistake. It wasn't us just being horny and blowing off steam. You know this, right?"

"I know that, Porter." I more than knew that. Last night differed from anything I'd experienced. But for the sake of everything, we couldn't be anything more.

"So, is this what you want?" Porter asked, his voice heavy with dejection. "What you *truly* want?"

I nodded. "It's what we have to do, Porter." I sat on the edge of the bed, my feet dangling as I thought about it.

Porter turned my chin toward his face, a small smirk forming at the corners of his lips. "Fine, but I was in the middle of starting something. And I'd hate to leave a job half-finished."

I looked over my shoulder at Porter and smiled. "Well, if you insist, you have five minutes."

Porter pulled me into the bed, pillows tumbling to the floor. I laughed as he whispered into my ear, his teeth tugging at my earlobe.

"Make that twenty."

Chapter Eighteen

Porter

Twenty minutes turned into an hour. Every morning and a few afternoons. For a month straight.

We hustled upstairs to make the last of the morning briefing. Given that everyone knew Ari drove a clunker of a car, they seemed to buy our excuse that Ari's car had clunked out on her again and she needed a ride. Again. *And ride she did...*

After settling into my office, I searched for my tortoiseshell reading glasses. I'd tossed my dry contacts in the trash at Ari's and was operating blind. Just as I was reviewing new drafts of a cross section of the stadium, there was a knock at the door. Ari stood at the door wearing the hell out of the form-fitting dark green dress and heels she picked out this morning. It took everything in me this morning not to unzip that dress and have my way with her again. The fact that I knew this woman intimately felt like my perfect little secret. A secret that now, was starting to make my dick hard as concrete. *Porter, have you no shame?*

I got up from my desk and strolled over to Ari, whose thighs rested on the arm of my couch. Thighs that, less than an hour ago, I was wearing like earmuffs. Thighs that I wanted to touch under her dress at the spot that I knew made her whimper and moan. Just sex with her wasn't going to be enough. I knew it and she knew it. Not when I'd had a taste of her. It was like trying to put toothpaste back in the container. Impossible.

"I feel like I should give you a proper good morning kiss," I said, standing next to her. I could feel the heat of her body next to me. She smelled like the soap from her bath, perfume, and the lotion I'd helped apply all over her body, taking extra time with her gorgeous calves. It was the right mix of everything. I wished I could bottle that smell up and sell it.

"But you gave me a proper kiss, well, more than a few kisses, this morning." Ari grinned. "And those were good morning kisses, right? As in, no more kisses until we're out of the office?"

"Do they have to be?" I put my hands around her waist and pulled Ari in closer. I nuzzled my nose into her neck, inhaling her. She eased my hand from around my waist, out of my grasp and turned to face me. I looked into her eyes, searching for the look she'd given me last night and this morning. The look that said "I want you. I want this."

"I think we should get to work," she whispered as she maneuvered around me. "I'd actually like to look at a few of the cross sections of the left embankment of the stadium."

Fuck.

"Oh, yeah. Sorry." I cleared my throat, letting out a sigh. The feel of her hand brushing past me sent electric ripples against the exposed skin of my forearm. It reminded me of the feeling of her breath against my naked body as she said my name. *Over and over and over.* I shook my head, trying not to think about us in any more compromising positions.

I met Ari at my desk and watched as she looked at the drawings and frowned. "I don't know, Porter. Don't you think this seems a bit…"

"Yeah. Wack," I said flatly. "It's not what I had in mind. It's definitely not building off the idea we had last week. I feel like I got lost somewhere."

Ari nodded in agreement. "I didn't want to say that, but the Serranos are all about sustainability and functionality. I'm loving the front facade we designed last week. But this doesn't seem…"

"Harmonious," we said at the same time. I smiled. We had gotten to where we were finishing each other's sentences. Working together had created our own rhythm. *Bumping uglies probably also helped to create an even better rhythm, but I digress.*

"We need to think." When we got stuck on a design issue, this was always my cue for putting on what I called "thinking music." I thumbed through my office collection of vinyl and put on some Lionel Hampton. The familiar first notes made me sway.

"Stardust?" Ari asked, joining me in her own gentle sway.

"You know it?" I asked, genuinely surprised. I knew Ari loved old school R&B, but I didn't take her for someone who liked jazz. The laugh lines around her sparkling cocoa eyes crinkled with pleasure, making my heart beat in time with the song. If there wasn't a risk of being caught, I'd spin her around and dance right in the office.

"Oh yeah. My dad, he loved some jazz. Saturday mornings, he'd play big band music or some soulful vocals. Dinah or Sarah. And after a long week with the gas company, he'd sit back with his scotch in his La-Z-Boy and tap his foot."

I smiled. "The more you talk about him, the more I wish I could have met him." I wished my dad could have met Ari, too. He would have loved her. I was sure of it.

"Yeah, he was great," she said. "With Thanksgiving coming up in about a month, he's been on my mind a lot. After the football games, Daddy would put on some jazz, sip some bourbon, and relax for the night. The day won't be the same without him."

I nodded. "My dad had his Thanksgiving rituals, too. Flag football with us was one of them. I missed that."

"Our dads were pretty special dudes, huh?" Ari's eyes dipped into sadness.

I reached out and touched Ari's hand. "Yeah, they were."

Just then, the door to my office flew open. We both looked back, and it was Greer. Quickly, I withdrew my hand from Ari's.

Greer looked at me and then at Ari. "Am I interrupting something? You got the jazz going, Harrison. Are you setting the mood or something?"

"No," I began. "Just...looking over these elevations for the second floor of the stadium."

"Well, if you don't mind, Ari, I'd like to steal Porter away for a minute. I need to ask his opinion on the Buckhead Events Center remodel that I'm overseeing. Not that I need it. But I'm trying amicably to resolve a dispute with Jacobi, and I need an impartial opinion."

"Sure," I said. "I'll be there in a second. Ari, can you pull up the 3D model from last week we worked on?"

"Of course," she said. She turned to Greer. "Oh, and Greer, I'd be happy to look at the remodel plans, too."

I looked at Greer, waiting for a response. I knew the answer but part of me hoped he'd surprise me for a change. Greer folded his arms. "Thanks, but no thanks. I think I'd trust the eye of the most senior architect here. No offense."

Ari shrugged. "None taken." But one look at Ari's face made it clear she was highly offended. She'd designed entire convention centers for goodness' sakes.

I interjected. "She really has a good eye, Greer. You should take her up on her offer." *Because your dumbass isn't as good as you think, I thought to myself.*

Ignoring my suggestion, Greer continued. "So, Porter, if you're not too…preoccupied…see you in about 5." Before I could object, Greer turned to walk out the door.

"Well, he's a delight as always," Ari said under her breath.

I laughed. "I heard that. Let me go see what this fool wants. He's probably wrong, by the way."

I gathered my iPad and a legal pad as I headed out the door to Greer's office. Before heading into the hallway, I paused. *We can be friends, right? I mean, nowhere in the rule book of platonic friends who happen to be co-workers does it say friends can't hang out on the holiday, right?*

I turned, clearing my throat. "Since you mentioned Thanksgiving being around the corner, do you have any plans?"

Without looking up from her sketches, Ari answered. "Probably not. Bella is heading to Martha's Vineyard with her in-laws. My mom is going to the casino with her girlfriends and going to hit the Turkey Day buffet with them. I'll probably be home watching football and eating whatever I can find in the fridge. Maybe I'll order takeout."

That seemed totally sacrilegious. Thanksgiving was about the four *F*s: family, food, football, and fellowship. Ari didn't need to be alone with thoughts of her dad looming.

She looked up, clearly bothered by the horrified look on my face. "Hey! Don't look like that. Trust me, it's no big deal."

"Takeout on Thanksgiving? Sounds depressing."

Ari laughed. "I assure you; it is not depressing. It's cool. Just another day. It'll be me, a marathon of *Flip or Flop*, and some Mongolian beef."

"So, do you like gumbo?"

Ari smiled, widely. "Absolutely. Are we ordering that for lunch?"

I smiled, pushing up my reading glasses. "No. I'm just checking. I'll make sure my mom knows I'll be bringing a guest to Thanksgiving, so she needs to make extra. Be forewarned: My family can be a lot." I took a pause then sighed. "Especially my little brother." Holidays made Todd outrageous and sometimes unbearable. He was a half-time show unto himself. Maybe with company present, he'd think twice about showing his ass.

Ari narrowed her eyes. "How's your brother a lot?" She was an only child and didn't have a clue about sibling relationships. She knew that Todd and I were close. I talked about him all the time, but she had no clue how contentious our relationship could be.

I waved my hands, dismissively. "It's nothing. Sometimes he's just…forget it. So, will you come?"

Ari looked at me, her lips a bit twisted as she thought it over. "I don't know. You sure? I don't want to impose."

Instead of whining about us being in relationship limbo, I decided being her friend was what she needed most right now. "Hey! You said you like gumbo. And we always make Senior's gumbo every Thanksgiving. It's tradition."

Ari shrugged and I knew then what she was thinking: It was a date. One where she was meeting my entire family. Calmly, I assured her that it was all good but internally my brain was yelling *"Just say yes. God, just give being a normal couple a freaking chance."*

"It's not what you think. Listen, this is one friend looking out for another. It's Thanksgiving and you don't need to be alone. Besides, my mama would love to meet the woman who's been my rock at work. Don't break my mama's heart, Ari James!"

I could feel Ari watch me as I left the office and rounded the corner toward Greer's office. I stopped midstride to face her. Worry was etched all over that pretty face of hers.

"It's just dinner, Ari. Trust me, it'll be fun." I gave her a wink as I headed down the hall.

Chapter Nineteen

Ari

I handed Bella her favorite cup of pumpkin spice latte as I sat next to her on the bench at the park. She smiled, grateful for a cup of warmth as she watched the girls and her husband playing on the playground. At three years old, the twins were fast as lightning, and Zach was having a hard time keeping up. The October air was crisp, swirling the orange and yellow leaves all around them. It looked perfect, as if Bella had staged the outing. I looked around, waiting for a camera crew to pop out from the bushes. They all had on various shades of designer plaid prints and looked like an ad for laundry detergent or something. Bella, coordinated in a Burberry print poncho, dressed as the chicest mom of toddlers that I'd ever seen. I swear, the woman didn't know the meaning of the word *casual*.

"Malia! Sasha! Slow down, loves!" yelled Bella, peering over her copy of *Harper's Bazaar*.

I smiled. "You know, I still can't get over the fact that you named your girls after the former First Daughters."

Bella turned to me, pulling her shades onto her nose

with a quizzical expression. "Name a greater duo of sisters? I dare you."

"Hmm. Venus and Serena? Beyoncé and Solange? Debbie and Phylicia? Oh! I know! Tia and Tamera?"

Bella turned to me with folded arms. "Okay. Fine! I get the point!" We both let out a laugh as Bella nudged me playfully.

"So, what made you join us on a Saturday afternoon? Don't you have a social life, girl? Work? Renovations?" asked Bella, taking a long sip of her latte. "Or some fresh man to get under? Didn't I tell you to find a man to get under?"

"Can't I just want to see my best friend and my gorgeous goddaughters? They're getting so big. Maybe I'll push them on the swings. Give Zach a break."

Bella put her shades on top of her head and furrowed her brow. "Cut the shit, Ari. You hate playgrounds. You'd rather take the girls shopping and get them sick off Pinkberry. So…what is this about?"

I pulled the zipper of my insulated vest up and took a deep breath as it all came out like word vomit. "Maybe I willed this to happen. You did tell me to get under a man. Then I did. And I didn't stop even though I said I would. It was, well *is*, so damn good. We probably, no, definitely, shouldn't be doing this. And I…"

"Wait! What are you talking about?" Bella interrupted. Her face was obviously full of confusion at my rambling. Hell, my own ramblings confused me.

"I slept with Porter, Bella. Well. I take that back. Because slept with implies one time and well…there have been multiple times. So, I'm sleeping with him, I guess."

Bella turned to look at me, silent as a stone. Bella's

mouth normally moved a mile a minute so clearly, she was beside herself.

"Bella! Say something! Anything. I made a mistake, didn't I? I mean, I should have learned my lesson with Maurice. But…"

Bella's lips turned up into a sly smile. "It was good, wasn't it? Dick this good tends to make a chick ramble."

Exasperated, I let out a sigh. "Oh my God, Bella. I lost count of how many orgasms I've had. But it's just sex. Good sex, but just sex. He knows this. I mean, I told him I can't be in a relationship. I'm not getting caught up like last time. He knows about Maurice and the shit in Chicago. He knows I can't do it again."

Bella took a sip of her latte. "But?"

"But my God, the man has skills. Girl, the things he did with his mouth are probably illegal in a few of the red states. And God, he can go nonstop rounds like a prize fighter."

"Damn!" yelled Bella. The girls immediately paused in the middle of a rousing game of tag. Malia wagged a finger in her mom's direction. Zach threw up his hands in confusion.

Bella held up her hand, apologetically. "Sorry, girls! Mama said a bad word! I'll put a dollar in the swear jar."

Bella scooted closer to me and began whispering at toddler-and-husband-proof levels. "Now, I need details, bitch. After I met Porter at Dunn's River, I did some digging via the alumni networks. Nothing major. No real red flags. His family is loaded, though. Seems like his grandfather was a US senator from Louisiana. Very old money. Other than his very impressive pedigree, I have nothing to report. Porter was a couple of classes ahead of us at Hampton, so I don't have any dick reports. Which is surprising because, man, do I know some hoes. Well, reformed hoes."

I glared at Bella. "Dick reports? Really, Bella? We hadn't done that since we were in our twenties. I'm forty. I don't care about dick reports."

"Yes, girl! Dick reports! At our age, that's even more critical. You have to wonder why a man that rich, accomplished, and fine is over forty, single, and not an ex-wife or baby mother in sight. Besides, you never know what girls we know that may have been with him! As soon as I learned who he was, you know I asked around. And the HU gossip networks were surprisingly dry. Seems like despite being a frat boy, Porter didn't get around like that. Maybe he's the real deal, Ari."

I rolled my eyes. "Bella, I don't care about, nor do I want to hear about his so-called dick reports. My report is the only one that matters."

"Okay so, give me your report, heifer! Is he big? Is he small? Does he have any special skills? He's a little on the light side, so... Is it all the same color? What?" Bella was squirming in her seat like an eager teenager at a slumber party.

My eyes nearly bulged out of my head in shock. "Is it all the same color? Jesus, Bella, have you no shame! All I'm going to say is, I feel like it was perfectly crafted for me." I put my hand over my chest, thinking about last night and early this morning. *And meeting up later that afternoon.*

Bella raised a brow. "And by *it* you mean his dick, right?"

"YES! BELLA! HIS DICK!" I said, loudly. This time it was Sasha who yelled, "Oh, Auntie Ari said a bad word! Is *dick* a bad word, Daddy?"

Zach rolled his eyes as he yelled in our direction. "I swear to God I'm going to have to ban the two of you from being within earshot of the girls! Save that talk for brunch and mimosas or whatever the hell!"

Malia wagged her tiny finger at Zach. "Daddy! You said a bad word! A dollar for the swear jar!"

Zach shook his head and placed a frustrated hand on his forehead. We were going to give the man a stroke.

Trying not to laugh, I yelled across the playground. "I'm sorry, Zach. Bella just doesn't understand context clues."

"I understand context clues just fine," said Bella through tight veneers. "What I want to know is how you ended up in his bed in the first place?"

"My bed. We were in my bed. We had gone out to meet the clients of our project and $800 wine was flowing. We got a little handsy on the ride back to my place. One thing led to another. And when I woke up…"

"Wait…he spent the night? Because you never let dudes spend the night!"

Groaning, I shook my head. "I'm breaking all my cardinal rules, but yes, he spent the night. We were late for work the next day because we had to get one more round in. Make that two more rounds in. Again, it is just sex. Just us getting our frustrations out. You know we've been working nonstop on this soccer stadium design. It's stressful as hell."

Bella fanned herself. "Jesus. I can't remember the last time I had twenty-four hours of sex without some little person interrupting us with 'Mama, I need this!' or 'Daddy, I need that!', 'Sasha hit me with a sippy cup!'"

I smiled and looked at the girls. "Yeah, but those two are too precious! It's all worth it in the end, right?" I'd

thought about having kids a time or two, and Bella's relationship with the twins made it look so fun and easy.
They were the sweetest and kindest kids. *I wondered if
Porter wanted kids.* I swiftly popped that thought like
a soap bubble.

"Yeah, they're the best, but Mama needs to get some
too!" complained Bella with an uneasy chuckle. "I can't
remember the last time Zach went down on me. I had
to sneak and give him some head in the butler's pantry
while they napped. Two licks and it was over because I
heard tapping at the door. I'm telling you, those two are
some cock-blockers!"

I patted her knee. "Oh, girl. You will get you some
real soon."

"Hmpf. I don't know when. Time isn't on our side."

"Plus, you're getting the event planning business off
the ground. Zach is in the middle of his plastic surgery
residency. The girls are a lot, and you have tons of re-
sponsibilities. Trust me. Things will get better."

Bella smiled and put her head on my shoulder. "You
always know what to say, Ari. How'd I get so lucky to
have a best friend like you?"

I laughed. "Because we were two lost and anxious
freshmen at college and clung to each other like mold
on cheese."

"You say that like it was a bad thing!"

"It's not. You don't always find a best friend like that.
Don't tell Zach, but you're my soul mate."

I could feel Bella wiping away a tear. I rolled my eyes.
She was always the emotional one. I patted her shoulder.
"There, there. No crying, La Croix."

Bella sat up. "You're right. No crying. Especially when

I'm still waiting on all the details from your night…excuse me…nights and mornings of sexing with Porter."

"I'm not sure I have the words to describe it. Trust me, it's amazing, Bella. When we're together, I feel things I've never felt before. It's as if he pays attention to every single inch of me. We just get lost in each other. It's the same way at work. We get lost in talking about the project for hours sometimes. Often, we're just talking about everything but the project. It's different. I'm not comparing sex to work, but the man is very detail oriented."

Bella's neck craned in shock. "Well, well, Ari James. Sounds like you've met your match."

I bit my lip and shook my head. "No way. It's just hot, secretive sex with my coworker. I've been there before. Only this time, I don't think he'll screw me over…job wise, that is."

Bella folded her arms, taking the last sip of her coffee. "Hmpf. Keep telling yourself that. And you'll end up like me—married and pregnant."

I laughed. "And what's so bad about that?"

"Is that what you want?"

I shrugged. "I don't know what I want. Right now, I like the idea of a secret, brief affair with a sexy guy. You know? No strings attached. I'm not sure that guy should be Porter. But then again, maybe it should."

Bella held my hand. "I want you to have fun, but I also don't want you to get hurt, Ari. Okay? By all accounts, Porter seems like a good dude. He's not a dick like Maurice."

I squeezed her hand reassuringly. "I won't. It's just casual sex. Not a relationship, for real." I wasn't sure I believed what I was saying. Bella gave me a knowing look.

"Really? So, does *he* know the sex is a casual, no-strings-attached deal? If the sex is the way you say it is. That hot and that intense. I highly doubt the two of you can keep it casual for long. Sexual chemistry like that isn't something you can control. It's not a faucet you can turn off and on. Besides, sex that hot can't stay cooped up in the friend zone. Your coochie is going to be mad with you. How dare you dust her off only to pack it up again? Traitorous!"

I tapped the fingertips of my free hand on my thigh. Bella looked at me with a wary expression. "Okay. What is it now, Ari?"

"Well… Is it casual if he asks me to come to Thanksgiving?"

"Seriously, Ari! Thanksgiving? Men don't bring just any old woman to Thanksgiving."

"Maybe he's just inviting me as his coworker," I retorted. "He knows I'm alone for the holiday. He knows how the holiday makes me feel about my dad. Porter assured me that it wasn't a big deal."

"Don't be daft, Ari!"

"Bella, people invite coworkers to Thanksgiving all the time."

"Is that right? Fine, let's ask Zach!"

"Fine." I shrugged. It was casual to me. That was what mattered most. I'd had my heart stomped on and I wasn't about to have that happen again. I can separate my feelings from the sex. That was exactly what I was doing and needed to do. Besides, there wasn't going to be any chance of it becoming more than sex. At least that was what I kept telling myself.

Just then, Zach and the girls approached the park bench. The twins, all bundled up in their hoodies, jumped into Bella's lap. She somehow miraculously balanced them both like a circus artist.

"Zach, I have a question: do men casually invite friends to Thanksgiving?" asked Bella, still balancing the twins with all the dexterity of an Olympic weightlifter. "Lady friends, that is?"

Zach looked at Bella and then at me. "Not usually. Why?"

"Because a man has asked Ari to come over for Thanksgiving with his entire family present. Yet, she insists they're friends. *She* says they have a casual arrangement. *She* says this is no big deal." Bella put the emphasis on *she* because the broad didn't believe a word I'd said.

"We are! We do! It's not!" I threw my hands up in exasperation. Bella rolled her eyes, then chuckled. The nerve. I mean, Thanksgiving wasn't that big a deal. At least I didn't think it was. And given that I haven't really celebrated a proper Thanksgiving since my dad died, I really saw it as just another day.

Zach laughed as he wiped the twins' hands down with a sanitizer. "Ari, guys rarely invite platonic *female* friends, shoot, not even female coworkers, to Thanksgiving. Too many questions and assumptions. If he invited you for Thanksgiving without batting an eye? Yeah, that dude likes you, Ari."

Nervousness settled in my stomach like a boulder. It felt as if I had ocean-liner-level motion sickness even though I was sitting down.

Bella took one look at me and laughed as she did her best Whoopi Goldberg impression. "Ari, you're in danger, girl."

Chapter Twenty

Ari

After changing clothes three times, I'd settled on a casual black turtleneck, a tan cardigan, and jeans with leopard flats. Since I didn't want to show up empty-handed like an improper Southern belle, I decided to bake my mama's famous lemon pound cake with caramel glaze. It had been so long since I'd been to a proper, sit-down Thanksgiving dinner. Porter had offered to come and pick me up, but I opted to drive. Just in case I wanted to make a run for it, I could. Meeting a guy's parents made me nervous, which was why I rarely did it. Porter spoke so highly about his mother; I expected Clair Huxtable in the flesh. But again, this wasn't a big deal. We weren't a couple. It was just dinner. With his entire family. *Fuck*. Maybe I should make a run for it, head to Kroger, get some ice cream to go with this cake and go home.

As soon as I was about to put the car back in drive to book it, Porter was knocking at my window. He stood outside, grinning widely. I rolled down my window, feeling an early winter chill in the air.

"Hey. Is everything okay? You've been outside a minute," he asked. With a brief gust of wind, I could smell his familiar cologne. Porter wore a denim shirt, his sleeves rolled up to show his strong, muscular forearms. *And had he shaved for the occasion*? I bit my lip. It just made no sense for him to be this fine. Maybe I should just go inside to thank his mother for making him.

"Is that a cake on the front seat? Looks amazing," Porter said, practically drooling in the window.

"It sure is. My mama's recipe." I smiled tightly and handed him the cake through the window. He held the cake with one hand and opened my car door with another. I took a deep breath and grabbed my purse. Porter extended his free hand and helped me out of the driver's side.

"It's going to be fine. My family is totally normal," said Porter. "Well, except my brother Todd. I'm pretty sure he's an alien." We both chuckled, walking up the sidewalk toward the house. As we approached the door, I felt Porter's hand on the small of my back. As he leaned toward me, I felt the tickle of his breath on my ear.

"You look amazing," he whispered. His thumb made small circles on the small of my back. I felt goose bumps down my spine. It was less like goose bumps and more like deep reverberations. I looked at his hazel-green eyes dazzling in the midday sun. He looked so happy to have me here that I couldn't help but smile.

He opened the door, beckoning me inside. The foyer to the home was covered with colorful, floor-to-ceiling paintings. They were remarkable. I stopped to admire them. I gently fingered the canvas, feeling the brushstrokes of thick, oil-based paint on the canvas. You could tell whoever created them really was passionate about their work.

"This is my stepdad Desmond's work. Pretty amazing, huh?" he said. I was almost speechless at how vibrant they were. Aside from pretentious dudes who proclaimed to be artists and just sold T-shirts, I'd never met a real, live visual artist before. Desmond was a genuine artist. It was masterful.

"They're breathtaking, Porter," I said, turning to look at him.

"Now, don't ask me what any of it means. I'm sure there is some deep, esoteric meaning that I'm just not able to wrap my head around. I'm no art critic. You'll have to ask him yourself."

"There she is!" said a voice out of nowhere.

Porter's mother came around the corner. A slim, dark-skinned woman with closely cropped relaxed hair, she wore cat-eye frames and a Kente cloth patchwork apron that said, World's Best Grandma. The pictures in Porter's office didn't do her beauty any justice. She looked more like his sister than mother; clearly her black was not cracking. She quickly wiped her hands on the hem of her apron. "Hello, Ari! I'm Porter's mom, Eloise." I extended my hand for a shake, but Eloise pulled me in for a hug. She smelled like all the spices of the season, warm and inviting. She smelled like memories of home.

"Nice to meet you, Dr. Harrison," I said. She frowned and looked at Porter. He shrugged.

"Did Porter tell you to call me that? Oh, you don't have to be so formal, dear! Eloise is fine. Now, come on in. This cake looks divine! Do you make it? Porter, take that cake and put it on the dessert table. Take the girl's sweater and hang it up. Boy, I raised you better than that. Let me introduce you to my husband, Desmond." Eloise spoke so fast, taking me by the arm before I could object.

I looked over at Porter. He gave me a sympathetic smile as he hung my sweater up in the coat closet.

Locked arm in arm with Eloise, I was given a quick tour of her home, starting with the foyer. She explained how Desmond was an abstract artist, with much of his work being influenced by his Caribbean heritage. Even she didn't understand his work sometimes, but she found it beautiful. We stood in front of a painting near the powder room of what appeared to be a woman on a beach. It gave me Romare Bearden vibes.

"He says this is me," said Eloise with a smile. "I don't see it." Her head tilted to the side as she examined a piece. I was sure she looked at it 1000 times a day. Yet, her eyes still were in wonderment.

I stood back a bit. "I can see it. It has your energy."

Eloise looked at me and smiled. "You think so? Oh, that's very sweet." She patted my arm in tender, appreciative acknowledgment.

Finally, we entered the large family room. It looked like something out of *Town and Country* magazine. I quickly realized Porter's idea of "just family" extended to friends of his parents and an abundance of laughing, teenage girls. His mother explained she'd also invited her students who didn't have stable homes or were food insecure. It seemed as if Porter's kindness and generosity was the byproduct of amazing parents.

The incredibly large television was blasting football while calypso music was simultaneously playing. I recognized the man in the recliner as Porter's stepfather, Desmond. He was talking to a guy balancing two toddlers, a boy and girl, on his knee. I assumed that the man was Porter's brother, Todd. They looked like they were having a bit of a spirited argument. I felt nervous, as if I was intruding. I looked down and in front of Todd were several beer bottles and an empty rocks glass.

"Everyone," announced Eloise. "This is Ari. Porter's... coworker. They're working on the soccer stadium project together."

Everyone turned around to look at me. I heard a couple of coughs and felt a few uneasy stares. The teenage girls were whispering and giggling. I wanted to run and hide, but I felt Porter's hand on my shoulder. I quickly scanned the room and landed upon Porter's brother Todd. His brother's expression was blank, maybe a little confused. After Eloise's introduction, Desmond got out of his seat and approached us. He hugged me and kissed me on the cheek.

"Eh eh! Porter never say he coworker was so beautiful!" he said in a very thick accent.

"And Porter never mentioned that his stepfather was so talented. I love all the paintings." I extended my hand toward his and he kissed the top of it.

"Thank you, dahlin!"

I smiled. He reminded me of my father, who was also smooth as silk at charming people.

Eloise shook her head and laughed. "You know how to get on his good side, Ari! Gold star for you!"

Desmond's booming laugh rose above the noise of the living area. Just then, a woman who could have been a carbon copy of Halle Berry, carrying a tray of charcuterie, entered the room. She placed the tray down on the ottoman between the guests and walked over to extend her hand toward me.

"Hi, Ari! Porter's told us so much about you! I'm Kim, Todd's wife. Must be odd to be in that weird environment of all-men. Girl, I know how that is. I'm the lead prosecutor in my district. Only Black girl, too. I'm sure we could trade war stories." Kim spoke just as fast as Eloise. Before she could say anything else, her children jumped off Todd's lap and were beckoning her to play with them. "Sorry. The munchkins want me! Nice to meet you! We'll talk soon!" She smiled and excused herself. Even in that brief exchange, I knew I liked Kim.

"Come with me," said Eloise quietly. "You'll have enough time to meet everyone and have them give you the third degree."

She led me into an immaculate kitchen that rivaled that of a five-star restaurant with its sparkling stainless steel, copper pots that hung down, and granite countertops. But the smells! It was heavenly. The massive island was covered with cuisine representing the entire diaspora. From rice and peas to corn bread dressing and tamales, Eloise had it all covered. She waved me over to a massive cast iron pot on her Viking stove. She opened it and the fragrant smell of gumbo wafted in the air. My stomach growled in response.

"It looks amazing, Eloise," I said. "And smells incredible."

Eloise smiled as she picked up a wooden spoon and stirred. "My first husband, Senior. He taught me how to make gumbo. He was a New Orleans boy through and through. And he told me if I wanted to be with him, I had to know what a roux was. I was a country, west Texas girl. Living in my little town of Armonia, which was full of Black and Brown folks, I could make tamales just as easily as I could a pot of greens. But learning Creole cooking was something else entirely. He was so patient with me. In this very pot, I burned every roux I made at first until I got it just right. The perfect roux is a science. It takes time and patience. You can't turn your back on it."

Eloise stopped stirring and looked at me wistfully. "I remember the first time I went to New Orleans to meet his family. It was also the first time I had gumbo. It was fall break at Hampton Institute, as they called it back then. You went to Hampton too, right?" She barely waited for my nod before continuing. "Anyway, Senior was so proud to show me off. He got dressed in his Navy ROTC uniform. He looked so handsome. Like a movie star in uniform. I wore the best dress I had, a little yellow shift dress my mama had made. It was a little tight because I was a few months pregnant with Porter. I had pressed my massive afro with a hot comb, and it was barely brushing my shoulders. I was this scared, pregnant, almost twenty-year-old college junior trying to present my best self, just like my parents taught me. When I got to the door of this big mansion near the French Quarter, their maid, without even looking at Senior or batting an eye, said, 'Miss, if you're here for the catering job, you're late.' Shock ripped through me. Senior had grossly downplayed his family's wealth. I was a dark-skinned, gangly country girl who grew up on a cattle ranch in Texas, working side by side with Mexican immigrants. Didn't know a thing about high society Black folks. First off, they had a maid. I did not know Black folks had maids. That was some new stuff to me!"

We both laughed. She motioned for one of the staff to take over stirring the gumbo. Eloise put her arm around my shoulder and led me to the plush, white leather barstools in front of the kitchen island.

She continued. "Senior said, 'No, Tilly, this is Eloise. My fiancée.' The absolute look of horror on that woman's face, which was, ironically, *my* complexion. Those looks of horror didn't stop because, child, the good Senator Armand Pierre Honoré Harrison, and his wife looked like they wanted to pass out. I was 'unrefined,' his mother said. They were literally blue-veined, aristocratic folks whose ancestors were free people of color. I was a girl who knew how to steer a bull better than I knew my salad fork from my dinner fork. Mother Harrison said I was 'sullying their legacy.'"

I felt sick to my stomach hearing how Eloise was treated. Porter told me his grandfather was still alive and healthy, nearing ninety. Would his grandfather feel the same way about me, too? Would he think Porter was sullying his legacy with a fat, Black girl?

Eloise continued. "During dinner, I think I saw the old bat wipe away tears. I kept quiet and continued eating that gumbo, which was one of the few things my pregnant hormones could handle. So, I sat there, eating delicious gumbo, and answering their questions with 'yes sir' or 'no ma'am.' His father was livid but had the good decency to show his anger in private with Senior. Senator told his oldest son that he'd disown him if he married me. Senior stood his ground. He said I was the smartest, prettiest girl he'd ever met. He would not give me or his baby up and he didn't need their money. We were getting married, with or without their blessing."

Tears pricked the corners of my eyes. "Wow, Senior sounds like a pretty brave man, standing up to his father like that."

"Indeed, he was." Eloise moved closer to me and sat two wineglasses in front of us. She poured me a generous glass of chardonnay, and then one for herself. "He lost a lot of respect for his family the day he chose to marry me. But that wasn't even the worst part."

"It wasn't?" My eyes widened in disbelief, unable to imagine how the story could get worse.

"Do you know they even invited his beautillion escort to dinner?" Eloise continued. "I'll never forget her name: Mary Lafayette. They thought for sure he'd marry that girl. She was the right pedigree, went to the right schools, was in the right organizations. Above all else, she was the right shade of Black. I had to sit through that dinner with this girl making googly eyes at my man, talking around me like I was invisible. I was sitting up there with a baby in my belly. I couldn't exactly hide it."

I swirled my glass of wine around. "That must have been tough."

Eloise nodded. "It was, but Senior ignored the noise and still chose me. Sometimes it amazed me. We got a lot of stares on campus because of how we looked together. He was so, so fair. And rich to boot! I was so, so dark and poor as dirt. It was the seventies. So, most folks thought he was just 'getting his Black thing together.' You know, going for the darkest girl to prove how 'down for the cause' he was. A lot of the fair-skinned brothers who were conscious did that. But that wasn't Porter. He wasn't into all of that. I mean, he was aware of what was going down with Black Power and all. He just happened to fall in love with me. And I loved him. He told me I made him better. We made each other better and wanted to make a life for us. There wasn't any deeper motivation behind us being together except love. By the way, Mary Lafayette and her husband ended up in jail for running a Ponzi scheme."

"Like Madoff?" I chuckled at that revelation.

"Yes, honey, like Madoff! Serves her right."

I took a slow sip of the wine. "Did things ever get better with your late husband's parents?"

Eloise scoffed and shook her head. "You know, I thought when we had the boys, it would make our relationship with his parents easier. Grandkids usually ease tensions but that didn't help. They barely talked to Senior, and they damn sure didn't talk to me. But every summer, they sent for the boys to come to New Orleans no matter where the Navy stationed Senior. They paid for their college educations, although they were sore with Todd for choosing Howard over Hampton. His parents adored their grandsons, especially PJ, because he was the spitting image of his father and grandfather. They were thanking God that genetics had benefited them, I guess. They'd do anything for that boy. Both of our sons, really. Although Todd probably didn't see it that way. He says they played favorites. I'm sure they did, if not deliberately, but in subtle ways. Yet, there was nothing that those old, snooty Harrisons wouldn't do for them. In the end, Senior didn't care about any of it. If he had us and his parents didn't hurt the boys, filling their heads with too much nonsense, he was happy."

Eloise paused and stared at me. "Do you know why I'm telling you all of this, Ari?"

I shook my head, taking a gulping sip of the wine. "Not entirely, ma'am. I mean, Eloise."

Eloise pushed her wineglass away and put her hand on top of mine, squeezing it gently. "Because sometimes what's good for us isn't always in the package that folks expect for us. Even now, my marriage to Desmond shocked a lot of folks. They thought after Senior's death, I'd marry a man just like him and in the same social circles. Especially Todd. He certainly inherited the Harrison snobbish attitude. But I didn't. I've always listened to my heart. Desmond is different. He's artsy. He's spontaneous. But he makes me happy. When I first looked at you, I saw a piece of myself. The way my PJ looks at you, it is the way his father looked at me. All starry-eyed and blissful. I knew you were good for him. He's done nothing but brag about you before you walked in the door."

Panic came over me as heat rose in my cheeks. "I'm sorry. He talked about me? I don't…we aren't…"

Eloise leaned her head back and laughed. "Oh, let's not play coy, Ari. A mother knows. It isn't every day that Porter invites a woman, or even a coworker, to Thanksgiving with us. My son is in love with you, Ari. Don't you realize that, dear?"

Shit. Bella and Zach had been right. My throat felt dry and heavy, like I swallowed a pack of marbles. I downed the last of my wine without a pause. So much for keeping it casual.

I put down the glass on the counter, finally exhaling. "We work together, Eloise."

Eloise raised her brow at me and smirked. "That isn't an answer to my question, darling."

"I don't want to complicate things. We don't want to complicate things. It's a long story."

Eloise let out a sigh. "I think Porter could use some complication in his life. The boy is so straitlaced sometimes. If you insist you're nothing more than friends, I'll leave it alone." She uncorked another wine bottle, quickly refilling her glass and mine. "But sometimes… love is like a good roux. It takes time and patience. You can't turn your back on it."

I didn't say a word. I understood her perfectly.

Eloise patted my cheek, gently. "Come along, pretty girl. I've interrogated you long enough! Let's eat."

We walked back into the family room as Eloise announced that dinner was ready. Everyone walked toward the massive dining room that looked like it was decked out for heads of state, with seating for well over twelve. Porter walked over to me, gently putting a hand on my shoulder. I turned to face him and smiled.

"What were you and my mother talking about in the kitchen? She really had you hostage for a while," he laughed. "Should I have rescued you? Once she gets going, Eloise can talk!"

"Oh, she was just fine…showing me how to make gumbo."

Oblivious, Porter raised an eyebrow. "And did you get any good tips?"

"I learned that the secret is in the roux. Sometimes you have to burn a few batches to get it just right."

Porter shook his head with a smile. "Actually, that sounds like something my dad would say."

I smiled. "Smart man."

Porter pulled out a seat for me at the massive table directly across from his brother Todd and Kim. Todd looked up from his drink and smirked. Either Todd didn't like me, or he was really feeling his bourbon. A small waitstaff brought out portions of the food to be served at the table. Eloise said she had everything catered, except the gumbo. She couldn't bring herself to have someone else handle that. Everyone laughed as Desmond proclaimed he didn't care who cooked the food just as long as there was plenty of curry goat.

After Desmond said grace, everyone passed around the myriad of dishes. I was so overwhelmed that I decided I would simply just try a little of everything. I mean, everything looked so delicious. Plus, I had to make room for Eloise's gumbo. Just as I was scooping out a small portion of the curry goat and passing the bowl to one young lady, I felt Porter's hand on my knee. I looked over at him and smiled.

"So, you two, how is the design for the soccer stadium coming?" Eloise asked. She passed the rice and peas to her husband, who greedily piled his plate high.

"Oh yes, real football deserves a real stadium," chimed Desmond with a smile. "I can finally enjoy a game instead of that nonsense you all call football." Everyone laughed. Well, everyone except Todd.

"It's going really well," said Porter. "Ari has an amazing design eye. She added these vineyard-type slopes to the fan experience. I think her designs have pleased the Serrano brothers." I could feel myself blushing. No one had bragged so much about my work, especially not a colleague. It felt amazing.

"Yes," I echoed. "I think that the Serrano brothers really like what we're doing. Porter is adding some really nice, high-concept design touches as well."

Eloise looked at both of us and smiled. "You two seem to work together well."

"We're finding our groove," said Porter. I felt his hand once again on my knee.

The waitstaff brought out small bowls of gumbo topped with beds of rice. Eloise smiled. "Everyone eat up. It's Senior's recipe!" Porter smiled at his brother. Todd raised his replenished glass of bourbon in silent tribute. I tasted the gumbo. The spices danced on my tongue. It was literally the best I had ever had in my entire life.

"Amazing, Eloise," I whispered to her.

She smiled and patted my hand. "Thanks, sweetheart. But all the credit belongs to Senior."

As the waitstaff served more gumbo, everyone sat at the table, enjoying each other's conversation. I learned about how Kim and Todd met as law students and the pressures of her job in the district attorney's office. She said it was an "old boys' club" and there was no room for a Black woman at the top. I nodded, feeling empathetic. It was part of the reason I left Chicago. Even if Maurice hadn't sabotaged me, the old guard would only let me go so far before I hit that glass ceiling. I had hope that I could grow at Riddle and Robinson. No glass ceiling in sight.

"Porter, I'm really proud of you, son!" said Desmond. "After this stadium, partnership is within reach for you."

"Ughhhh!" groaned Todd. "All fucking day! Porter this! Porter that! Porter's building a soccer stadium. Porter's bringing a friend to Thanksgiving. You've all been ass-kissing and fawning over your precious Porter! Who gives a shit!"

The entire dining room was so quiet, you could hear folks' thoughts. I looked at Porter whose eyes were shooting flaming hot daggers in his brother's direction. His nostrils flared. "Dude, what the entire fuck is wrong with you!"

"Hey!" Eloise yelled. "Have the two of you lost your ever-loving minds to think you can curse in my house! Do you think you're that grown?"

"No, ma'am. Sorry," said Porter apologetically to his mother.

"Todd, what is wrong with you?" questioned Eloise. "You need to apologize to the table right now."

"For what? The truth?" Todd continued sipping his bourbon.

"Bro, you need to fucking chill. Shit's embarrassing!" Porter yelled, reaching across the table at Todd's drink. Todd, despite being tossed, snatched the drink from Porter, sloshing the brown liquid all over the ivory table linens that I was sure cost a fortune.

Eloise let out a horrified gasp. "The two of you! Stop this!"

The table had gone still. Even the teenage girls had stopped gossiping . I feared that they were going to broadcast this entire fight on TikTok.

A hesitant member of the waitstaff brought out what appeared to be slices of my caramel pound cake to the table. I should have been happy that Eloise chose to share my cake with everyone but in that moment, I was hurt that she had to see her sons having what seemed to be a cyclical fight.

"I think I'll take my cake to the other room. Ari, pleasure meeting you." I watched as Todd snatched the dessert plate from the table, along with a fork, and tramped out of the dining room.

A few folks began murmuring about Todd's behavior, embarrassing his "legacy," but Eloise clapped her hands together, like the seasoned teacher she was, bringing the chatter to a halt. "Everyone, I'm sorry for that. Please, enjoy the cake that Ari so graciously baked for us." Eventually, everyone began to dig into dessert and resumed their previous conversations.

Porter finally sat down, then turned to me, his voice low. "I'm so sorry you had to see that, Ari."

"Hey, my family has had some lively Thanksgivings.

You should see when we get the spades table going." I
chuckled, uncomfortably.

Porter shook his head. "Todd is...listen, I'll understand if you want to leave."

"Porter, don't apologize. Seems like Todd has some
things he's going through."

"Thanks for understanding. We're trying to get him
under control. It's been tough."

"I get it." I smiled, squeezing Porter's knee. "But I'm
not leaving. Besides, after eating all this good food, I
think it may be physically impossible for me to leave.
That gumbo was serious! I probably could use a nap."

"Word?" Porter chuckled. "I got the perfect place to
chill post-dinner. Let's head to the sunroom. There's a
TV there. We can wrap up under the blanket, light the
fire pit, and see who loses the games. Neither one of us
has a dog in the fight."

I smiled. "That sounds wonderful."

As we rose from the table, I noticed a look of worry
etched across Eloise's face as Des held her hand. I
stopped, placing a hand on her shoulder. "Are you okay?"

Eloise looked up with a soft smile and patted my hand
resting on her shoulder. "Oh, my dear. I'm fine. Embarrassment never killed anyone. Drama is par for the course
it seems in this family. It's nothing we can't handle. We'll
talk to Todd. Don't let this run you off, now."

I looked at Porter, who stood waiting for me at the
doorway to the hall. A genuine smile finally on his face.

"I'm not going anywhere."

Chapter Twenty-One

Porter

The intro music to the evening news was just beginning as I woke up, buried under another thicker plaid blanket. I smiled, know that it had to have been my mother that added the extra layer of warmth. Ari was still napping, her head resting on my shoulder. She looked so at peace, so comfortable here with me. I buried my nose in her hair, smelling the familiar scent of her tropical conditioner. The gas fire pit was low, providing an amber glow in the dim sunroom. As I moved my arm, Ari stirred.

"Hey, sleeping beauty."

Ari looked up with a smile. "Jesus, how long were we out? I guess the effects of tryptophan in turkey are real."

I looked at my watch, then the television. "Well, we slept through the second game, that's for sure. You up for something else?"

Ari stretched and pulled the blanket over her. "Sure. What do you have in mind? Des did mention playing dominoes."

I turned toward Ari. "Listen, I know Thanksgiving didn't go as planned, but I had something planned for us after dinner. So, will you go with me? I'd hate for my surprise to go to waste."

"A surprise? On Thanksgiving? Just about everything is closed."

My lips quirked up into a knowing smile. "Trust me. It's going to be worth it. I hope you have a coat in that Honda. You're going to need it."

Given that it was a holiday, no one was on the roads. At least not at this time of night or in this general direction. A complete anomaly for Atlanta, with its notoriously terrible traffic. I put on a nice mix of jazz, ranging from Billy Eckstine to...

"Carmen McRae," said Ari. "My dad used to love some Carmen McRae. He said her voice sounded like she made love to the notes. Caressed them. Made them breakfast in the morning."

I laughed. "Your dad really had a way with words. You're sure he was a utility worker and not a poet?"

"Nope, totally and truly a blue-collar guy," Ari assured me. "But blue-collar guys can be poetic too."

Typically, Thanksgiving in Atlanta is mild, but this year an arctic blast had taken over at sundown. The windows of my Porsche were struggling to stay defrosted. I looked over at Ari and saw that she was making hearts and circles on the misty fog of my window. That made my heart beat a little faster than usual. Maybe I childishly hoped one of those hearts were meant for me.

We exited the highway, and I eased into the lane that led directly to Truist Park. Ari turned to me, confused. I tried to hide my smile as best as I could.

"Where are we going?" she asked.

"You'll see," I said. "Do you trust me?"

"Of course." She put her hand on my knee. Even

through my jeans, I felt the warmth of her touch. I wanted it to stay there. Make a home there.

I parked the car in the massive stadium parking lot. Ari looked around, confused. "What are we doing here? Season's over. There's no game."

"I know."

Ari put on her warm down coat, pulling the hood over her curly poof, and I laughed because the hood and her hair made her look a little cone-headed. But she was still beautiful, regardless.

We walked toward the stadium, where my buddy Sean was standing outside.

"Dude. I'm sitting here freezing my ass off! I thought you'd never show up." Sean was frail, pale, and a fiery redhead. Originally from Boston, he should have been used to the cold.

"Sean, when have I ever stood you up?" We hugged and shook hands. "Ari, this is Sean O'Malley. He helped build this stadium with his construction firm. We've worked on a lot of projects in the city together. Sean, this is Ari, my…" I hesitated, trying to find the right words, and settled on, "She's my partner on the soccer stadium."

Sean looked at me and smirked. He extended his hand toward Ari, and she shook it.

"And the girl who's been to almost every classic stadium in the MLB. Impressive."

Ari looked over at me. If it weren't so cold and she wasn't so brown, I'd have assumed she was blushing. She put her head down and smiled. "Porter told you that. Well, yes. All the classic ones."

"Fenway? Astrodome? Wrigley?" asked Sean, playfully quizzing Ari.

Ari shook her head. "Of course. We even went over

to Toronto to see the SkyDome after a trip to Shea Stadium."

"Wow, Porter. Marry this one!" said Sean, his accent still thick even after all these years down south. "Even though you don't know dick about baseball."

I smiled and scratched my head. The thought of Ari as a bride flashed in my head for a millisecond. *She'd be a beauty.* I brushed it off.

"Ah, let's just get inside, Sean. I'm freezing my nuts off."

"Well. Porter tells me you haven't had a chance to see Truist Park. You're not one of those 'Fuck Cobb' enthusiasts, are you?" Sean asked Ari as we walked through the eerily quiet corridors.

"Well, I must admit," Ari began, "maybe slightly. I mean, I grew up in the West End. The old stadium was a stone's throw away. I was sad when it moved. Folks like me, and die-hard fans, didn't get it."

"I hear you," said Sean. "But I hope this all-access private tour, courtesy of Porter, makes up for it. You can add Truist Park to your list of stadiums." He winked at me.

Ari looked over at me and whispered, "When did you set this all up?"

I smiled. "A man has his secrets. Besides, this could be pretty good recon for our own stadium design, right?"

Ari took my hand in hers and squeezed it. I interlaced my fingers in hers and felt a pulsating rhythm between us. It felt as if my heart was literally in her hands.

"Hey! I heard that," said Sean. "Don't go stealing these designs for your fancy, Spanish-wine-drinking soccer fans." We all laughed, the sound echoing in the empty lower atrium.

Sean gave us the grand tour. Ari got to sit in the owner's private box. She got to see the home- and visiting-team locker rooms, and she squealed when she touched Ronald Acuña's locker. She looked up in amazement at the rows and rows of pennants the Braves had won. I laughed as she pulled out her cell phone and took a selfie with a 1995 World Series trophy encased in glass.

"May I?" Sean asked Ari for her phone, motioning me to join her for a few candid shots near the trophy, and then near the Hank Aaron statue. After posing for several shots, I watched as Ari stood in front of the bronze statue of Hank Aaron and stared in amazement.

"It's really cool when the waterfalls are running," whispered Sean, careful not to disrupt Ari's admiration.

"Man, you all did an amazing job here. I never really admired the work before."

Sean turned to me and smiled. "Thanks. And you're doing an amazing job pretending that you're not into this girl. 'Colleague' my left nut! Dude, whatever!"

I shushed him as Ari came closer to where we were standing.

"Gosh, if my daddy was here, he would love this!" Ari said, running her fingers across the large 755. She pivoted her head, trying to prevent me from seeing her wipe a tear from her eye. I walked over to Ari and placed my hand on top of hers. As she turned to face me, I tucked the lone curl that was on her forehead neatly back under her hood.

Ari's mouth parted slightly, as if she wanted to say something. I focused on the fullness of her bottom lip, still berry stained from her lip gloss. Cupping my hand against her waist, I pulled her closer and felt her softness, even under her bubble coat. I leaned in, anticipating the feel of her lips.

Just then, I heard a cough. I had forgotten that Sean was standing there.

"Uh. Hey, guys. We got to make this quick, but I haven't shown you the pièce de résistance!" he said.

I leaned away from Ari and scratched my head in embarrassment. Ari's face was flushed with warmth. We looked like two caught teenagers as we followed Sean down a long corridor. There weren't many lights on this part of the stadium. It was as if we were walking into the abyss. As we approached a nondescript door, Sean stopped us.

"You guys, this is my little secret passageway. You do the honors, Ari. Go on, open it," he said, coaxingly.

Ari looked at me, hesitating to move an inch further. I shrugged. I did not know where this secret door led, but I put my hand on the small of her back, reassuring her I'd be there for her. *I'd be there for her. Always.*

Ari eventually pushed the door open and audibly gasped. I followed behind and instantly understood Ari's amazement. We were standing in the middle of center field, above the rocks of the roman waterfall. Ari looked around as the stadium lights came on one panel at a time. It was blinding. Ari twirled around and laughed with infectious deliciousness. In her bubble coat, she looked like a little kid excitedly experiencing a fresh winter snowfall for the first time in the south. I looked over at Sean, who winked at me and mouthed a "Dude, you're in there" and gave me a thumbs-up for good measure.

"I can't believe I'm standing in center field. This is crazy. How many people can say they have stood here!" Ari said in amazement.

"Yeah, this is great. Thanks, Sean," I said, giving him a hearty handshake and a pat on the back.

"You're my dude. No problem, anything for you and your girlfriend," Sean said. I looked at him wide-eyed. Even though it was cold as a brick outside, I could feel heat rising in my chest.

"What?" he asked, playfully. "Not girlfriend? Fiancée, then? Wife? Did you elope?" He gasped. "Eloise is going to kill you!"

Now he was being a deliberate ass.

Ari turned to him, laughing. "I'm not his girlfriend or wife. He's telling the truth, Sean. We're just friends." I couldn't help but feel a bit of a sting in how she said *friends. We could be more. So much more if she'd allow it. Lord knows I wanted it.*

"Uh-huh." Sean, whose nose was turning as red as his hair, laughed. "Well, Porter, this was one hell of a nice thing you did for your…*friend.* But my balls are probably going to freeze off out here! Temps are dropping. Come on, you guys, we better get out of here before I get fired."

Ari and I laughed. As I turned to enter the little hidden door, Ari grabbed my hand. "You think you'd ever want to come and see a game with me…you know… When it isn't so cold?" she asked.

I took her hand and looked at her eyes, cola-colored and sparkling. "I'll even sit through a double-header. Beer and dogs on me," I said. I hated hot dogs. I hated baseball even more. But I'd suffer through both for Ari.

Ari squeezed my hand and smiled. "Awesome."

We made our way out of the stadium, walking hand in hand, along the bridge toward the parking lot. Ari stopped abruptly.

"Be honest. How much did this cost you? How rich are you, Trust Fund?"

I laughed, then made a gesture with my index finger

and thumb. "Just a little bit. But tonight, wasn't about money. I just so happen to know a guy that could break into a multimillion-dollar stadium at night. That's priceless."

She pulled me closer, grabbed me by the shoulders, and kissed me. Ari deepened her kiss, finding my tongue eager and wanting. It was cold outside, but that kiss could have melted an iceberg. "Thank you for this. All of it."

I smiled, tucking that loose curl under her hood. "It was nothing."

When we finally reached my car, Ari sighed, turning to me. "Listen, if you did all this to... I don't know, convince me to be with you or something. Porter, I still don't think we should. We can't risk it. I can't risk it."

I exhaled a plume of cloudy air against the cold stillness. My frustration with her apprehensions dug into me like thumbtacks in my palms. "Ari, do you really think I'm that manipulative? Seriously?"

"So, why'd you do all this?"

The wind began to pick up, the unseasonably cold chill making my eyes water. At least that was the excuse I had because they were tears. Tears at the fact that she still didn't get it. She didn't get me. "You were sad about your dad. And I thought instead of a sad memory, you could have a happy memory about Thanksgiving. I know he couldn't see Truist when it was done but, you could. For him. Keep the tradition alive. There's no ulterior motive here."

Before I could say anything else, Ari clasped her hands around my face and kissed me so soft, so deep. I grabbed her waist and moved my lips in time with hers. I'd missed them so much. When she pulled back, my lips felt betrayed by the interruption. I looked at her eyes, red-rimmed and brimming with tears.

"You're unreal, you know that?"

I didn't respond. Instead, I opened the car door and waited for Ari to get in. I leaned down, staring into her face. "Do you know what I could go for right now?"

Ari looked up at me, blinking rapidly. "Uhm…what's that? Don't tell me you want…"

Before she could finish that thought, I narrowed my eyes. "Some more of your caramel pound cake."

"Oh."

"Oh, wait? You thought I was going to say sex, didn't you? If I have to fight Des for the last piece, I will. I saw him eyeing it."

Ari let out a riotous laugh that echoed all around us. "After tonight, I'll bake your weight in caramel pound cake if you want."

Chapter Twenty-Two

Porter

I looked over my notes from Serrano Group regarding the corporate skyboxes for the stadium. I had put on a vinyl of Ella Fitzgerald doing Christmas standards as I pored over each detail. I needed something to put me in a good mood. Marco, the older playboy brother, had exacting tastes, sending over samples of Corinthian leather that he wanted for the seats to make sure our designs fit his aesthetic. I wanted to get this right before the holiday break. With the constant barrage of holiday parties, shopping for my family, and the upcoming construction bids looming, the final touches of this design had to get done.

As I hummed along to Ella's voice, I heard a knock at my door. I looked up to see Todd standing in the doorway along with Ms. Gayle.

"Your brother is here to see you. I thought I'd walk him back myself."

I groaned. It had been a week since his outburst at Thanksgiving and we hadn't spoken. My voice mail was full of messages from my mother asking me to "put Todd out of his misery and call him back." She'd also asked me to participate in an intervention that Kim was facilitating with a counselor. I agreed to do that; however, I refused to talk to him, the hurt still raw and palpable. He had embarrassed the shit out of me, in front of Ari no less. That was unforgivable.

"It's fine." I nodded toward Ms. Gayle, who left me alone with Todd.

"Still playing stuffy jazz as you work, huh? No Uncle Luke Christmas jams?" Todd said, trying to break the ice.

"What do you want?" My jaw tensed at the sight of him. I didn't know whether I wanted to punch him or hug him.

"Let me come in, PJ. I need to talk to you," Todd begged. "To apologize."

I motioned for him to take a seat in front of my desk. "Spit it out. I don't have time to waste. On a deadline, here." Todd loosened his coat and exhaled. I watched as he picked at nonexistent lint on his pants. His eyes were tired, his body just as worn down. My anger was quickly replaced by pity. Todd had aged before my eyes in a matter of months. I regretted that my response came out as harsh as it had.

Todd rubbed his hands over his bald head. "Look. I'm sorry, PJ. Not sure what came over me. I was a real asshole in front of Ari and a dick to you too, man. I'm going through some heavy shit right now. Plus, Thanksgiving always has me missing Senior. You know that."

"So instead of talking to me, or Mama, you felt the need to put on a show, brother? What's really going on?" I eased back into my chair, studying my baby brother's face.

"I know it's not an excuse, but shit gets hazy, especially around the holidays. You know that, PJ. I miss Senior so much."

I stared at Todd. I may have had his name and looks, but Todd was Senior's favorite son. They'd had a special bond that was severed far too soon when Dad died. Now, Todd was trying to heal the hurt at the bottom of a liquor bottle.

Todd scratched his moustache. "And then there is the thing with the job."

I raised a brow. "What thing with the job?"

"They're trying to tank a big case that I worked my ass off to bring it to the firm. I don't get it, PJ. I play their games. I go to their golf clubs. Host the poker nights. And what do they do? Tank my case on the word of some new guy because he's the partner's godson. I swear I work ten times harder for nothing. Nothing, man."

I had no clue he was going through any of this. "Sorry, Todd. I did not know. Why didn't you talk to me?"

"Yeah, I didn't want you to worry. Plus, this stadium is a big deal for you."

"Todd, I'm your brother. It's my job to worry about you. But, T, you know the drinking isn't helping things."

Todd fell silent, eyes focused on the floor. "I know. Kim told me I needed to get help or…she was out. I don't want to lose my family, PJ. I can't. They're the only real thing I have." He rested his elbows on his knees, cradling his head as he wept. The last time I'd seen Todd cry like this was Senior's funeral. He was a sixteen-year-old boy who had lost his whole world. He was on the brink of losing it again.

I sighed, trying to hold back my own tears. "Well? Do you want to lose your family, Todd? Do you want liver failure or cancer like…?"

"Like Senior," Todd said. "You can say it, PJ. Cancer like Senior."

The pain of remembering Senior's final days twisted my insides. All the chemo that took out his curls. All the sores on his skin as he aged rapidly. "Yes, Todd. Like Senior. I know his death was hard on you. But seriously... I can't lose you too, man. You're the only brother I have. You're my best friend."

Todd sniffed, wiping tears on his shirtsleeve. "I know. Sorry. I guess I was just...projecting my stuff on to you. In some ways I envied your life."

My eyes widened in disbelief. "My *life?* I work too much and go home to an empty loft. You have a home that includes wife and kids who, despite your shit, love you. I should envy you."

Todd chuckled uncomfortably. "I know but the reason I was working so hard was to prove that I was just as perfect as you. Hell, that I was better. To Granddaddy Senator, the sun rose and set on you. You never had to work for anything."

I threw my pen on the desk, frustrated. "Todd, why do you keep saying that as if despite the connections, I haven't worked my ass off to show that I'm actually good at what I do?"

"I know that now, man. I do. And Ari. I'm sorry about that. Embarrassing you in front of your coworker. You like her, don't you? More than a friend or coworker. I could tell."

I looked over at Ari's office door, which was closed. "Ari is amazing, inside, and out. We work well together. We have a lot in common and she makes me laugh. I'm not her man, but all I want to do is make her happy. Weird, right?"

Todd stared at me in disbelief. "Wow. I've never heard

you talk about a woman like that. So, I take it the no dating coworkers thing is off the table."

I took a deep breath and scratched my beard. "That's the thing. This is new for me. I'm not a person who goes against their principles but what have principles gotten me? Nothing. I want what you and Kim have. What Mom and Senior had. Hell, what Mom and Des have. I think I can have that with Ari. The only thing is…"

"You work together," said Todd, scratching his head. "Yeah, that's probably tough."

"Right. She doesn't want a relationship and I don't want to date in secret. Ari doesn't deserve that. She's had some shady dealings with a dude she's worked with in the past. If an asshole like Greer found out about us, who knows what he'll do. This could put our project at risk. I don't think us dating is a big deal, but Ari is the first woman to last this long in our firm. I don't want them to think I took advantage of a situation. I don't want this to be an HR nightmare. But I love Ari…"

I love Ari.

I sat there frozen. It was the first time I had said it out loud to someone.

Todd smiled, then nodded. "If you love her, y'all will figure it out. Ari seems like an exceptional woman, truly. She's smart. She's pretty. And I won't lie, she makes a mean caramel pound cake."

With a slight grin, I walked over to Todd, who stood up. He hugged me, hard and long. I held on to him tightly, my grip firm. I hadn't hugged him in forever. Today, we both needed it.

"I love you, Big Bro," said Todd. "And again, I'm sorry."

"Thanks," I said. "But you need to make it up to Ari."

"I will. I might need your help though."

I nodded, smiling. "I got your back."

A couple of hours later, Ari knocked at my door. She folded her arms and stood in front of my desk. "Please tell your brother I said thank you. I'm assuming you told him that stargazer lilies were my favorite."

I walked toward her. Her hair was down and coily, pulled back with a simple black band. I placed my hands to my side, resisting the urge to run my fingers through her hair. "Yeah, I didn't want another Harrison man making the same mistake twice with the flower thing."

Ari smiled and sat at the table. "Wow, you Harrison men are smooth. How is your brother, by the way?"

I pulled out a chair and joined Ari. "I'm not sure. I think he's better. Thanks for asking." I put my hand on top of hers. "I appreciate that."

Ari smiled as she eased her hand away from mine. "No problem. We're friends. So…"

I chewed the inside of my lip, thinking about what I'd just told Todd. "Right. Friends."

Friends didn't kiss like we had. Friends certainly didn't fuck like we had. If I thought about that any longer, I'd probably break out into hives from the stress of it all.

Instead, I hooked a thumb over my shoulder, motioning toward my computer. "Let me show you what I've been working on. I think you're going to dig it."

Chapter Twenty-Three

Ari

Saturday morning, I pulled up to a little Inman Park bungalow, which had been converted into a fitness studio for Atlanta's newest fitness crazy, Soul Pilates. It was just Pilates set to R&B music, but Bella insisted that we try it. I parked on a dodgy-looking side street to wait for Bella and cautiously rolled down the windows to feel the warm breeze. The running joke about Atlanta is, if you want a change in weather, wait fifteen minutes. It had been nearly freezing Thanksgiving night and now, weeks before Christmas, it was in the 70s. For a minute, I thought back to how cold it was Thanksgiving night at the baseball stadium. And how kissing Porter warmed every part of me. I probably shouldn't have kissed him. But in the moment, it seemed like the appropriate response. He'd broken into a major league stadium for me, for goodness' sakes.

I watched all the women walk into the studio, some barely wearing anything more than their designer workout clothes. I recognized a few reality stars, famous housewives of other celebs, B-list celebrities and social-media influencers. How on earth had Bella scored us entry into this exclusive exercise session? What the hell was I doing here? I wanted to turn and eat a warm croissant at the French bakery I passed on the way over.

In my driver's side mirror, I saw Bella parking her obnoxiously large SUV on the opposite side of the street and putting on a pair of Dior shades, her hair up in a super tight bun. She ran up to my car door, more than enthusiastic for so early in the morning.

"Are you ready to sweat your man problems away?" she asked with a grin.

I rolled my eyes and grabbed my bag. Bella opened the car door for me to get out. "Can't have man problems, Bella, if I don't have a man," I retorted.

"Hmpf," snorted Bella. "Whatever. Did you see anyone go into the studio? I heard it's a hot ticket. Even the mayor's side piece goes here! Thank God I could snag entry to this Saturday's session. I planned a birthday party for the owner's daughter. Do you know how hard it is to find ponies to dress and dye as unicorns?"

"Ahh. I was wondering how you could get into this place. I'm certainly no Celebrity Housewife."

Bella jokingly hip bumped me. "You could be. What happened to Korey? He's been on CNN and everything. Rubbing elbows with all the political intellectuals."

I groaned. "Dear God. He bored me to tears. Do you know all he does is talk about himself? And name-drops. I don't think in the two years I've known him, that he has asked a single question about me. Not to mention, the sex was subpar."

Bella frowned. "That's unfortunate. I hate men like that. You can't be boring and with bad dick. Pick a struggle, dude. Come on. Let's go in and get us a good spot so we can people watch."

"I thought we came here to work out. Destress?"

"We can do both. Plus, I can hand out business cards." Bella smiled as she curled her arm around mine. "I heard they give you CBD warmed towels at the end." I shook my head, walking along the sidewalk into the studio.

The studio was large, with about twenty-five Pilates reformer machines. Bella and I entered and signed in, hanging up our coat and cardigan. We went to the machines toward the back of the room. As I walked in, I felt eyes staring at us. Well. Not us. *Mostly me.* It felt like a high school cafeteria with all the cool kids in one corner. I wasn't all dolled up in Lululemon. In my Old Navy yoga gear with a curly, messy high ponytail, I certainly wasn't chic.

The instructor was a Black woman, who was very tall, dark, and elegantly appointed. She looked like a statue. Except, it was clear she was faking a British accent, which was layered over a very real Southern one.

"I'm Folashade. Welcome to Soul Pilates, where we stretch yourself and your soul mentally and physically. All with our culture in mind," said the woman as she flailed her arms around. "Be at ease as we take this soulful journey together."

I rolled my eyes. This chick used the word *soul* far too many times. "How much is this class?" I whispered to Bella. "And you know her mama ain't name her Folashade! It's probably Sadie."

"Shhh! It's normally…like $200 a session but totally worth it," whispered Bella.

"What!" I whisper-yelled. A few eyes turned to look in my direction. Our distraction visibly annoyed the Real Housewives of Fulton County. I mouthed my most apologetic "Sorry" and turned to listen to the instructor.

The speakers in the studio played classic John Legend. The lights lowered, and I smelled lavender being pumped into the air. Bella was more than excited, and she clapped her hands in anticipation. This all seemed like an overpriced, overhyped gimmick.

We went to our machines and began with single leg stretches. The instructor walked around, making sure everyone was in proper position. The music moved from John Legend to Silk's "Meeting in my Bedroom." *Dear God. Seriously?* The music took me back to the night of the first kiss between Porter and me. My stomach flipped in knots.

"You look tense?" said Folashade as she looked at me on the machine. "Try to relax your pelvic floor."

"I'm fine," I said. The more the song played and echoed throughout the room, the more I thought of Porter. His touch. His hands. His lips. His…

Folashade leaned down, her head tilted a bit. "Ms. James, listen, there is no shame in admitting if this is strenuous. A woman your size…you know. Just take your time!"

I spun my head and through gritted teeth, I repeated, "I said I was fine."

"Okay!" she said defensively, as she moved along the row of machines to the group of athlete's wives, each one carbon copies of the other.

"What was that?" whispered Bella as her legs moved midair in a hundred positions.

"Nothing," I said as I attempted to do the same. My mind could not focus. The smell of the lavender became stronger and was almost dizzying. The speakers boomed with the bass of Ginuwine's "So Anxious." *Anxious.*

That's exactly how I felt that first night. His hands all over my body set me on fire.

"That's it. Damn this." I unhooked my legs from the Pilates machine. "Bella, I'll wait for you in the lobby."

"Oh," said Bella. "Sure." She furrowed her brow in confusion but kept on with her exercises.

I grabbed the towel, my purse and cardigan and sat in the plush chairs that lined the narrow corridor. I scrolled through my phone, looking at photos of Porter and me at Truist Park. Porter was all bright smiles and eyes. We looked so happy. Like a *happy couple*. I bit my lip as I sucked in a breath. What the hell was I doing?

Time passed swiftly, and soon the class was ending. I put on my cardigan and watched as Bella passed out her business cards to several of the women in the room. The last woman I recognized from the reality show *Doctors and Wives: Atlanta*. She was in her early fifties and wore a sleek, low chignon and matching bright yellow and orange yoga wear that looked more runway than workout.

Bella and the woman were walking toward me. I stood up and smoothed out my clothes.

"And this is my friend Ari I was telling you about. She's an architect at Riddle and Robinson. Ari, this is Dr. Misha Babineaux."

I reached out and shook her hand. "Yes. I recognize you from the show." Dr. Misha was an icy-tempered plastic surgeon to all the stars in Atlanta. Some of whom had gone under her knife many times. Let the blogs tell it, all their assets were God given. Lies. It was the patented Babineaux Butt Lift.

"Yes," said Misha. "I hope for all the good parts!" Bella and the woman shared a forced laugh. I tried to smile.

"Bella tells me you're the only woman over there. I

know Riddle. I'm going to have to call him. He must do better."

"I'm sure I won't be the last woman there," I said hastily. Dr. Misha nodded fervently.

"Well, it was nice to meet you. Ari and I have some other appointments. And you have my card," said Bella. Bella could always sense my unease in social settings and always had a lie ready in her back pocket for us to get out of Dodge.

As Bella and I walked toward the door, I heard the woman call my name.

"Excuse me, Ari," Dr. Misha said. I turned around and felt her press a glossy laminated card into my hand. It had her name, office number, and information on it. I raised an eyebrow.

"I just noticed you walked out of the class. I do bariatric surgery as well. If you're interested. You're a gorgeous girl. With my help, you'd be stunning."

I folded my arms. I could hear Bella say "oh shit" under her breath. She knew when I folded my arms like an irritated grandmother, it was trouble.

I took the card and handed it back to the good doctor. "I'm good. But thanks anyway."

Dr. Misha grabbed my hand, pushing the card into my palm. "Oh, it doesn't have to be for bariatric. I mean, even if it's for a little lipo or…"

"I said I'm good!" I yelled. The other women who had been chatting got silent.

"Listen, no need to get snippy," Misha said, as if I was the one who offended her. "Just trying to help."

I clutched my purse and threw the chamomile-scented towel down in the chair. "Who said I needed your help? Did I ask for your help? So, you know what you can do?

You can fuck off, Dr. Misha. Keep doing your tummy tucks and Babineaux butt lifts for the Instagram chicks who need them."

I crumpled the business card and threw it at Dr. Misha's feet, pushing past Bella and slamming the door of the Pilates studio. I walked down the sidewalk and only turned when I heard Bella yelling for me to slow down.

I stomped toward Bella. "Is this why you took me here, Bella? So, I could get a consult by Atlanta's premiere fake butt surgeon?"

"Of course not! I brought you here because I needed a wing woman while I tried to get these rich hussies to hire me. Besides, I didn't think she'd do something like that!"

"Of course, you didn't, Bella! You never think! You think the world revolves around little, perfect you!"

Bella's brow knit, confused. "What's that supposed to mean, Ari?"

"Just forget it. You were too busy giving out your business cards and rubbing elbows to care!"

Bella shook her head and put on her shades. "You're tripping. I'm going to ignore this. Misha was rude and you need someone to take it out on. That's fine. I get it. We'll talk later."

I stood next to my car and watched Bella throw her hand up in disgust and get into her SUV.

I felt the tears roll down my face, and I wiped them with the back of my cardigan.

I put my key into the ignition, deciding to treat myself to a big French breakfast.

I turned the key. Nothing.

Fuck me! Fuck this entire morning!

The engine turned over several times, sputtering and squealing. That wasn't a good sign. I reached into my glove compartment for my AAA card, only to see that I had failed to renew it. Not to mention, I'd left my wallet with my debit and credit card at home. My head banged on the steering wheel. I couldn't call Bella. Not after our fight.

I called my mother. It was Saturday, and there was no telling what my mother was doing or where she was.

"MA!" I yelled. I could barely hear her with all the noise in the background.

"Honey? What is it?"

"My car won't start. I'm in Inman Park near this bougie Pilates studio. Can you come and get me? I'll get the car towed later."

"Oh, honey. I wish I could. But I'm in Birmingham for the day with the Senior Olympics swim team. We're in the quarterfinals."

I sighed and held the phone, frustration percolating. "Okay. I'll…try to call someone else."

I scrolled through my phone and looked at numbers. My house-arrest uncle. Unreliable cousins. Guys I knew from high school. Guys that were booty calls. I stopped at Korey's name.

A voice mail. Thank God! I hung up without leaving a message, but I was back to square one. I kept scrolling and ended up with the last name in my phone: Porter.

Since our kiss on Thanksgiving, I'd been a little skittish. I was avoiding him. Better yet, I was avoiding having any further conversations about what we were to each other. We both knew it.

I bit my lip and tapped my fingers on the steering wheel. I looked at my car, which was now slightly smoking.

Fine.

Desperate, I dialed his number. Just when I was about to hang up, he answered.

"Ari? Hey… What's up?" Porter's voice had a thick, lazy drawl that signaled that he'd just woken up. I loved that voice.

"Sorry to wake you. But… I…my car…"

"It finally died, huh? Where are you?"

"In Inman Park? At this Soul Pilates spot? Off Euclid. I… I'm sorry to bother you, but everyone else is busy and my AAA card isn't current. I don't have my debit or credit card. I said off Euclid, right?"

I could hear Porter rustling around. I bit my lip. *Ari, you probably sounded neurotic, calling him like this.* I imagined him pulling back the sheets, rubbing his head, and stretching out on his bed just before getting up. I'd seen that scene play out so many times. The thought pulled at my heart's longing for him for a millisecond.

"Okay. I'll be there in about 15 minutes. Hold tight. And I'll call you a tow truck. Text me the address."

"Okay. And thanks, Porter."

"Of course. Anything for you."

I leaned back against the headrest of my now defunct jalopy and tucked my hands into my cardigan. I took a deep breath and pulled up the streaming service on my phone to play some smooth jazz. There was no way that I could handle any more R&B lyrics. I closed my eyes, and eventually the sound of Boney James lulled me to sleep.

A knock on my window startled me out of a nearly drool-inducing nap. In front of me were gray sweatpants that showed just the right amount of dick print without being sleazy. The gray sweats eventually leaned back, and there stood Porter, with a sheepish grin. I rolled down my window.

Men did not know how much gray sweatpants turned women into horny teenagers. And by the looks of it, the sweats, Dunks, and hoodie had knocked at least fifteen years off Porter's age. He looked more college co-ed than forty-two-year-old elder millennial.

"Sorry to wake you from your nap, but the tow truck is here."

I looked at my smart watch. "Wow. That was fast. Thanks."

"It's nothing. I know a guy," said Porter with a grin. He "knew a guy" for every scenario, it seemed.

I grabbed my purse and tossed my cell phone and keys inside. "Thanks, Porter. I guess you can take me home. I'll figure out the car situation another day. This one is junk at this point."

"I know it's hard to part with it."

I nodded slowly. Porter scratched his beard, which was a lot fuller these days. I liked it.

"Or—" Porter suggested excitedly with a raised brow "—we can just go look for a new car. I mean, you know I love looking at new whips. Besides, I know a guy…"

I laughed. "Of course, you do. Fine. I'll look. No promises on if I'll purchase."

"That's fair. But right now, let's get you some breakfast. There is a cute little French bakery around the corner. And I know how much you love madeleines. So… want to go? My treat?"

I scratched my head and looked around. The tow truck driver was hooking my car up, dragging it onto the back. Bella had pulled off ages ago. And I was just there. With Porter. And his gray sweats. *Shit.*

I pursed my lips, then relaxed them. "Fine. You had me at madeleines."

"Cool." Porter clapped his hands in victory.

I shook my head. *Ari. It's just breakfast. No harm in that*. "Cool," I repeated.

I rolled my eyes and walked beside him to his car, peeking over at him.

"I know. I look like a bum. But in all fairness, when you called, I was in bed," Porter said.

"Uh-huh," I replied as I stood next to the passenger side of the car. Porter came up close to me, putting his hand on the door handle. He smelled simultaneously like soap and sleep. He leaned over, grazing my breast. It made my nipple hard like muscle memory. My body hadn't forgotten what his touch did to me.

"I was alone. Just so you know," said Porter as he opened the car door.

"Okay. I didn't ask but…okay."

"I know you didn't. But just in case you were wondering."

"I wasn't," I said sharply, as I eased into the passenger seat. That was a lie. I was wondering. A little.

"Uh-huh," said Porter. He pulled his hoodie over his head and leaned back against the headrest, turning toward me. Every part of me resisted looking at him until, finally, I looked over and his green eyes twinkled with a devilish sparkle. I felt a twinge in my undercarriage.

Fuck. Fuck this ridiculously gorgeous bastard.

The smell of espresso and sweetness filled the air of the quaint Emile's Patisserie.

Only Porter and I would notice such a nondescript spot hidden in the middle of a neighborhood known more for its funky eclectic style than traditional fare.

Porter and I waited as a perky blonde with bangs

and a bun tied back with a red bandana showed us to our table. Typical French musette was pumping through the speakers.

The server pulled out a pencil from her apron. "Madame, Monsieur, can I take your order?" said the blonde whose French accent took both Porter and me aback. We were expecting something and someone entirely Southern.

"The lady will have an order of madeleines and café au lait," said Porter. "And I'll have an espresso and a small spinach quiche."

"Very well! I'll be back shortly with your order, okay?" she said, as she bounced toward the back of the house to put our order in.

Porter pulled down his hoodie. His hair was a mess. His normally tamed, curly fade was fluffy and askew. My instinct was to put my hands through his hair, smoothing it down gently. Instead, I tapped my fingers on the table nervously.

"What's wrong, Ari? It's just…two people, friends, having breakfast," said Porter. He unzipped his hoodie a bit, showing the top of his smooth chest hair. My body quivered.

"I'm not nervous. Just…just thinking about my car," I lied.

"I know. You loved that car, Ari."

Porter reached out and took my hands. I looked up at him. His eyes were soft and longing. I knew that look. It was his "please, talk to me" look. I diverted my eyes and pulled my hands away just as the server brought our coffees and food. Thank God for a distraction.

I took a bite into the pillowy madeleine and closed my eyes, savoring the lemon vanilla flavors. It was amazing.

When I opened my eyes, Porter was looking at me over his cup, smiling.

"I love when you enjoy something you love," said Porter, softly. "The look on your face is priceless."

I took a deep breath. "Porter, let's not even do this."

"Do what?"

"We cannot fall back into…whatever that was, Porter. Now, I appreciate you picking me up. Taking me to breakfast, but…"

"There is no but, Ari," said Porter. "There is no but when you care about someone." He took his fork and stabbed at his quiche, quickly putting a piece in his mouth.

I adjusted the napkin on my lap. "I appreciate that, Porter, I've clarified that we need to just…be friends. And I know the position we're in at work. So, let's just be friends. Partners-in-design, remember?"

Porter put his fork down and sat back. He stared out the window. "It's not that simple. I'm not trying to pressure you into anything. I also can't be near you without wanting to be with you. You can't expect me to sleep with someone without feelings being involved. I'm sure a lot of men can do that, but that's not how *I* work."

I took a sip of my coffee. "I know. That's not fair. It also wasn't fair for me to kiss you Thanksgiving night. That was dangerous territory."

"Right. But it's not like I stopped you from kissing me. I could never reject you. Rejection hurts. Rejecting someone you love hurts even more. You…"

"Porter, don't say that," I said, interrupting his sentence.

"Say what?"

"That you love me."

"Why not? It's true. I can't help it. I'm passionate about you, Ari. About the possibility of an us."

I folded my arms. "Trust me, I've heard this all before. Passion isn't love. I'm too old for passion. It burns bright and then what? You'll get bored. You'll move on."

Porter wiped his mouth with a napkin, balling it up. "I don't get you, Ari. One minute, you're ready to rip my clothes off. Fuck me into a coma. Kiss me until I can't breathe without you. Then you want to keep me at arm's length. You're so hot and cold. And when we get close to solidifying our feelings, you push me away. How am I supposed to feel? This is unfair. Don't break my heart this way, Ari."

"It's not my intention, Porter. I also don't want to mess up this project. This feels like my last opportunity to prove myself. Besides, I'd hate to be the reason you don't get this promotion."

Porter rubbed the back of his neck. "If I make partner…if I don't make partner. That has nothing to do with you. Right now, I'm talking about us. What are we doing here?"

I looked out the window. An older couple with gray hair and stooped backs held hands as they walked down the sidewalk. A fleeting thought about Porter and me being that old crossed my mind. *Would he have flecks of silver in his curls? Would he hold my hand as I walked beside him, back hunched over with old age?* Porter reached across the table, pushing a stray coil of hair back behind my ear. I allowed his warm, gentle hand to cup my cheek gently, until he let go.

As if he could read my mind, Porter whispered, "I know what you're thinking, and the answer is of course."

I smiled, slightly. "You know what your mother told me at Thanksgiving?"

Porter raised his eyebrow, cocking his head to one side. "Other than Senior's gumbo recipe? No."

"Eloise said when she met your father, she knew she wasn't who people, his people, expected him to marry. But your father knew she was good for him. Your mom said she saw the same thing in me, for you. It's a new feeling for me. Someone thinking that I'm good for them. Because I know I'm amazing. It's about time someone else recognized that."

Porter's mouth was parted. For a second, he was at a loss for words. "Of course, you're good for me, Ari. You're amazing. You're the woman of my dreams."

"I am?" I asked, eyes widening with disbelief.

Porter laughed a bit. "Yes, ma'am. One day, you'll know just how true that is."

I furrowed my brow, confused.

Porter pushed his coffee cup away, looking into my eyes. "Listen, I know you want to be friends. I'm respecting your wishes. But I need a favor."

"Sure. It's the least I can do after today."

Porter scratched the back of his scruffy neck. "Well, I'm without a date next weekend to the Hampton Atlanta Alumni Gala. Will you go with me? As friends?"

I raised my eyebrow. "Seriously?"

"Seriously. I mean, my mom and Desmond will be there. And now that I know she's such a huge fan of yours, how can I disappoint her? So, is it a date? I mean, as friends? Alums? I know my mom would love to see you again."

I dipped my madeleine into my coffee as I pondered the invitation. "Bella's always begging me to go. I never do. I guess I can make an exception. I'd hate for you to be all dateless in your tux. Wait, is it black tie?"

I hadn't worn a formal dress since Bella's wedding. The anxiety of sequins, control top garments, and back zippers made me sweat. The one downfall of being single is not having someone to zip up your dress. Zippers in the back should be banned.

Porter nodded. "Of course, it's black tie. But before you start worrying about your outfit, can we finish breakfast?"

As Porter reached over for a madeleine, I smoothed his hair down, running my fingers through the short curls. He closed his eyes, allowing my hand to tame a stray hair. His lashes fluttered against the palm of my hand as he turned his lips inward, grazing the inside of my wrist.

"You had a piece of lint from your sweatshirt in your hair," I lied, embarrassed at my need to touch him. To feel him. *Dammit, Ari. You're not making it easier.*

"Thanks, Ari. These wild curls, you know," Porter said, slightly above a whisper, his lips dangerously close to my wrist. His faint, heated breath tickled my skin and hastened my pulse. I sat perfectly still, trying to gather my words.

I pulled my hand back. "Truthfully, I don't know how to react when you tell me how you feel about me. This is new for me. Someone who wants me this way."

Porter frowned. "What way is that?"

"Honestly. With so much confidence, it spills over. It's too much to handle, PJ."

"You deserve that level of honesty for a change."

I blinked back tears, turning to look out of the window. The older couple were no longer there, replaced by skateboarders in oversized shorts. I looked back at my tablemate. Porter's eyes were transfixed. His green eyes seemed to twinkle with amusement.

"What's so funny?"

"You called me 'PJ.' I don't think I've ever heard you call me that."

"Oh… Wait. Is that what you took from my entire spiel here?"

Porter laughed. "Of course not, woman. But it's good to know you're comfortable enough with me now to call me PJ. And I heard you. I hope you heard me too."

I nodded. "Yes, I did."

"Since we're prioritizing honesty, can I be frank?" Porter exhaled deeply, then continued. "Ari, you challenge me. You're so sure of yourself in ways that I'm not. You're sexy and smart. Sometimes I just marvel at your ability to just exist and be. Nothing rattles you. The partners. Other people. Assholes like Greer. I've never met someone who just knows who they are. Whether it is work or anything else. I realize I can be myself with you, Ari, because you see right through my bullshit and call me on it. That is scary and new for me."

Porter's fingers fiddled with his zipper. "I've just been in relationships that work because we never got deeper than surface level. Never have to work at it. And I liked it that way. I could just put on the suits, go to the dinners, and just leave it at that. You've opened yourself up to me, and I'm opening myself up to you in ways that I never have with anyone. You don't want a relationship right now. Cool. I'm a patient man, Ari. I'll wait for you forever if you'll allow it, but I'm not going anywhere. But if I had the opportunity to make you mine, I wouldn't dare fuck this up."

I sat back and looked at Porter with astonishment. "What do you mean, I'm confident in ways that you're not? Porter, I've had years of building myself up all because people want to tear me down because of the way I look. Being a big woman is difficult. Being a big Black woman is ridiculously challenging, especially in the industry we work."

Porter folded his arms. "And do you think things are easy for me?"

My mouth parted in bewilderment. "PJ, what does that mean?"

Porter rubbed his forehead. "I know what it feels like for folks to make assumptions based on how you look. I have the great misfortune of looking exactly like my late father and my grandfather. You know, amongst certain groups of our people, a light complexion is still a hot commodity that comes with a lot of unspoken privileges. People assume—with the eyes, the complexion, the hair—that I'm this arrogant pretty-boy who knows it all. Everyone thinks that I'm skating by because of my looks and connections. I'm a Harrison, the great senator's grandson. Even Greer hints at that any chance he gets. That couldn't be farther from the truth. I'm an insecure, shy nerdy guy who just played the role people expected of me. A people-pleaser who went to the right college, picked the right major, joined the legacy of a frat, had the girls, drove the fancy cars—all because that's what's expected of a guy like me. Ari, I hate fancy suits. Maintenance on my car is a beast. I live in an overpriced loft. I'd much rather be painting than doing 3D renderings. Deep down, it's all a facade. It feels like a life someone else designed for me."

My madeleine was now soggy, lying on a napkin. I

stared at Porter. His eyes were softer. Sadder. "I didn't know…" I breathed.

"It's cool. No one really does. I keep so much stuff to myself."

"Porter, you don't have to keep stuff to yourself. I'm here for you."

The small table felt like an ocean separating us. I leaned across the table, my index finger tracing the faint lines on the palm of his hand.

Porter clutched my hand, intertwining our fingers. "Ari, are we good?"

I nodded. "We're good."

Porter smiled, then clapped his hands. "Good! Because right now, we need to get you a new car, homegirl. Pronto."

I stubbornly folded my arms. "I guess I'll let you help me find a new car. Under one condition."

"Sure. What's that?"

My lips quirked up into a teasing smile. "Don't put me in anything as pretentious as your Porsche."

Porter indeed knew someone at a luxury dealership who got me a great deal on a new car—a fully loaded, steel-gray BMW 740i. He laughed when I told him that BMWs were basically taxis in Europe. Porter said, "Ari, this is no taxi. You're a grown woman with a grown woman's job. You need a grown woman's car."

Afterward, we said goodbye to Honey. I sold Honey the Honda to his friend Craig for parts. As Craig was writing the bill of sale and looking over the title, Porter squeezed my hand and said, "It's going to be okay. Your dad knows you love that car. And him." I nodded. When Porter asked where the first stop in the new ride would be, I told him I had to see Bella and apologize. I'd blown up at her for no reason other than my own frustrations.

During my drive over to Bella's, I put on the old school R&B station that was playing "Cruisin'" by D'Angelo. I took it as a sign. The original version had been one of my dad's favorite songs. It was the fitting farewell to Honey.

With the promise of margaritas and tapas, Bella was more than happy to accept my apology and take a ride in my new car. More than anything, it was an escape from the twins who had been driving her crazy. Before getting hammered on Don Julio, Bella insisted we head to the cosmetic store because my new car called for a mini makeover to celebrate. The bright lights of the cosmetic store made me looked washed-out and ashy. I looked at myself in the mirror and winced. Had I not been taking care of myself? Maybe Bella was right. I needed a skin-care routine.

I picked up a shopping basket, headed toward the skin-care aisle, and watched as Bella twirled around, asking the sales associate what shade of lipstick would go best with her new caramel brown hair color.

After picking up an ample amount of toner and moisturizer, I perused the fragrance area. The first bottle I picked up absolutely reeked, smelling of verbena, and what I could only presume was onions. I gagged and looked at the price tag of $200! They were out of their ever-loving mind.

I moved over to the men's fragrance section and ran my fingers over the brightly colored bottles. Finally, I paused, recognizing the bottle instantly. I picked up the frosty blue glass bottle and smelled. It flooded my mind with images. The smell of Porter's chest against my nose.

His body on top of mine. Brushing up against me and feeling the end of his tie against my hand. I shuddered and held the bottle to my chest. I dropped the bottle of cologne in my shopping basket, deciding to purchase it as a thank-you gift for Porter. For rescuing me, in more ways than one.

Bella stood in line ahead of me, going on and on about how she was so glad to find a particular shade of lipstick and how she wasn't sure if she'd even have an occasion to wear it. Suddenly, I felt my phone vibrate in my purse. I looked down, and it was Porter. My eyes darted to the bottle of cologne, and I smiled.

"I was just thinking about you," I said cheerily as I answered the phone.

There was silence. Then, soft crying.

I looked at the phone, making sure that it was the right number. "Porter?" I repeated. My heart raced, the beats thrumming louder in my ears. Bella was waving at me to head toward the sales counter, but I held up a finger, asking her to give me a second. "Porter? Is everything alright?"

"Ari. It's Todd. He's…he's hurt."

I dropped the basket.

"Bella, I have to go."

Chapter Twenty-Four

Porter

Desmond took a deep breath, put his hands on my shoulders.

"They took him down for X-rays and a CT scan. Kim with him now. Porter, it's by Jah's grace that he ain't kill heself or nobody else. He drove pon a busy sidewalk and hit a utility pole. We ain't sure, but there may be some internal damage. Your brother is bad off. He wasn't responsive."

I felt nauseous. My head was spinning like a top. I leaned up against the wall, bracing myself.

"But he just called me. He wanted me to come to the bar, but I was too tired. I should have gone. I should have driven him home."

Todd had called me, totally smashed, asking me to come hang with him at the bar with some of his law school buddies. I'd just left Ari and told him I didn't feel like it. He called me a "pussy" and hung up on me. And that was the last I'd heard from him. Now, guilt was eating me alive that those could have been my last words to him.

My mother finally lifted her head as she clutched her

rosary. "Oh, Porter, darling. Don't blame yourself. This is no fault of yours. Todd got behind the wheel on his own."

We were still waiting on Kim to come back with news on Todd's condition. Desmond cradled my mother in his arms. I looked at them. There was a twinge of envy. Even at this moment, I wished I had what they had. The comfort. That person to lean on. I didn't know where I stood with Ari. Yet, she was the first person I'd called.

I was pacing the emergency waiting room so much that I was sure I was putting a hole in the carpet.

"Honey, why don't you sit?" implored my mom again. She motioned toward an empty spot on the sofa next to her.

"Mom. I'm fine. Really." I stuffed my hands in the pocket of my sweats. I moved my fingers frantically. Not sure what I was searching for. Lint? An old gum wrapper? Something to hold on to.

There was a soft knock at the door. I looked up, and it was Ari. Her curls were loose, framing her face like a soft, brown cotton candy cloud. She still wore her leggings from Pilates with a cardigan tied around her waist, with just a hint of her fleshy, soft stomach peeking out. She clutched her tote close to her body, moving closer with hesitation.

"Hello, Eloise. Desmond," Ari said softly in the direction of my parents.

Without thinking, I got up and threw my arms around her as if it hadn't been just hours since seeing her. I buried Ari's head into my chest, smelling the familiar tropical scent of her hair. My fingers clutched her curls as I felt the tears run down my cheeks.

"Ari… I…" I barely could get it out.

"I know." She hugged me around the waist, burying

her head just a little deeper into me. She exhaled, and I felt the warmth of her breath through my T-shirt. I had to pull away to look at her face, to see if she was really in front of me. *She'd come. Without a second thought, she'd come.*

"What's happening?" Ari asked.

My mom got up and hugged Ari. "Thank you for coming, dear. It's Todd. He's been in a nasty car accident."

"And I should have been with him," I interrupted.

Ari looked at me, confused. "Why should you have been there?"

"Because he called me. And I told him I wouldn't come to the bar. I should have gone. I should have driven him home."

My mother shook her head and put her hand on my shoulder. "Stop it, Porter."

"Ari. I'm sorry for calling. I just…"

"Don't be. I'm here for you. You know that."

We sat on the sofa opposite my parents. I rested my head on Ari's shoulder. I felt her fingers run through my hair, reminding me I desperately needed a fade. *Why the fuck was I thinking about my hair at a time like this?* My legs were shaking uncontrollably. Ari placed a hand on my knee, instantly suppressing the shaking.

"Ari, I'm a terrible brother. I should have been there. I'm just not understanding why he'd drive!"

"He'll be okay. I know he will."

I looked up at Ari. "I hope I wasn't taking you away from anything important."

Ari smiled. "I was at the cosmetic store with Bella. We had a ride in my new car. When you called, I was in line about to buy your favorite cologne."

I smiled. "Really. My cologne?"

"Yes. It was a thank-you gift for helping with the car."

My heart swelled at the thought of my scent being something she loved. I put my hand on top of hers, giving her an apologetic squeeze. "No gift necessary. But I'm so sorry I took you away from time with Bella."

Ari shrugged. "She understood, Porter."

Just then, Kim walked in. Her eyes were bloodshot as she clasped her hands in front of her. Her hair was stuffed under a ratty, Howard baseball cap.

We all stood up, anticipating the worst. I held Ari's hand tightly. She put her right hand over mine and rubbed it.

"He's okay. He has a few broken ribs, wrist fracture, and a concussion," said Kim, slowly. "But he's going to be fine. The police were here, too. Todd is being charged with a DUI and possibly a few other things. He just…" Kim cried, choking on each syllable. "I'd organized the intervention and I thought it worked. I don't know what to do."

My mother went to Kim, hugging her. "You're not alone, sweetheart. We will get through this. Don't worry."

"I'm sorry, Kim," I said. "I should have been there."

Kim looked at me, her brow furrowed. "Porter, oh my God. Please don't do this. Don't blame yourself. Trust me, I've done it too. We've done all that we can. Like the counselor said, alcoholism is a disease. This isn't on any of us. You're not his father. Todd is a grown man."

You're not his father. The words hit me hard, like a kick to the chest. I knew I wasn't Senior, but I was his older brother. His only brother. The man of the family. I ignored every sign that it was getting bad. I should have known.

"How did this happen, Kim? I mean, why?" *Fuck.*

What was I saying? It was a dumb question, one that I wasn't sure I knew the answer to, nor did Kim.

Kim rubbed her temples. "It's the job. He'd been working on an important case. You heard of Templeton Tobacco? They had been polluting the homes of minorities of the Georgia Sea Islands—many folks got cancer from the runoff in the water and land. Todd was fighting on behalf of the plaintiffs. Well, his partner's godson, Kyle, that asshole got wind of it because his daddy and others in the firm had some financial interest in Templeton. He purposely tanked his case. That's when the drinking got worse. Four years of work down the drain. The people won't get a dime. They've been trying to find a reason to fire him. Now with this accident, Todd's job status is…uncertain."

My face heated with anger for my brother. "Todd told me about the guy at work, but I had no idea it was over a case this major." I wanted to punch a wall, find this Kyle dude and dust him up. Ari squeezed my hand.

"Well, it is." Kim continued, turning to address the rest of the family. "I want you all to go home and get some rest. Todd's going to stay here overnight. Make sure nothing else is wrong. We will meet with the social worker to get him some help. Weigh our options. Not to mention, I need to call our attorney and the insurance company. It's all such a mess. Mom, can you take the kids home with you and Daddy Des? They're still at soccer practice."

My mother nodded and then kissed Kim on her forehead. "Of course. We can keep the kids for as long as you need us to. We will work it out." My mother looked at me and Ari, our hands still intertwined. I couldn't let her go. I feared if I did, I'd pass out on the hospital floor.

"Ari, can you please look after my PJ? Make sure he gets home, okay? Get something to eat? I can tell by the way he's shaking that he hasn't eaten."

Ari nodded her head. "Yes, Eloise. I can."

Mom put her hand on Ari's cheek. "Thank you, my sweet Ari."

I looked at Ari. "Ari, it's cool. I can drive. Trust me, I'm fine."

Ari's lips turned up into a smirk. "Didn't Eloise ask me to make sure you were okay? Then I'm going to make sure you're okay. Besides, I have a new car, remember? I'll whip us up some dinner at home."

I looked at Ari, repeating the word. "Home?" The word sounded both familiar and foreign from my lips. But when Ari said home, it felt warm. Safe.

Ari shrugged. "Sure. Unless you don't want to."

I looked over at my mom, attending to Kim, who smiled gently in my direction. I think it would give my mom some peace knowing I was in Ari's hands.

"Yeah. Let's go home."

Chapter Twenty-Five

Ari

I leaned against the kitchen counter, watching Porter push arroz con pollo around on his plate.

"Not hungry?" I asked, gently, removing his plate and wrapping it with plastic wrap to place in the fridge. The situation with Todd had him worried; he was never one without an appetite. His glass of water was untouched, and his eyes were blank and empty.

"No," he said, squeaking out the word in a gravelly voice.

Finally, after several minutes of silence, he continued. "It looked great, Ari. But... I can't eat."

"Do you want something stronger than water? I mean, I hate to ask but..." My voice trailed off. That was probably a dumb thing to ask. Given the circumstances.

Porter sat up straight, his hands folded in his lap. "Can I get some black coffee? That's about as strong as I can handle right now."

I nodded, quickly placing a single serve pod of coffee in the machine, which brewed within minutes. Porter stared down at the inky cup of espresso in front of him. I watched as his lips blew and he gingerly took the hot cup to his lips. He closed his eyes and took a deep breath, letting the warmth of the hot elixir soothe him.

Finally able to move my feet, I sat next to him, rubbing his shoulder. "Better?"

He rolled his neck, leaning into the feel of my hands. "Yeah. Thanks. And thanks for coming today. It's crazy. You're the first person I called. I couldn't have faced that without you."

I felt my heart crack open. "I was just out with Bella, at the cosmetics store. You don't have to thank me, Porter. I'm your friend."

Porter turned and looked at me. "We're more than friends, Ari. We're…just more than that. You know that."

My lips tightened. "I know. Partners-in-design, too." I playfully punched his arm. Trying to defuse tense situations with humor was not my strongest attribute.

Porter didn't smile. He reached up and twirled my hair between his fingers. "I love your hair like this."

I frowned with a raised brow. "Messy? Kinky?"

Porter shook his head, his bottom lip edged between his teeth. "No. Just free. It reminds me of…" His voice trailed off. "The last time we…"

"Oh." I felt my chest and neck burn with the thought of us together. The closer his hands moved, his fingers inches from my cheek, the more I could feel my pussy tighten from the memory.

I coughed, moving my head slowly, trying not to think of my body's reactions.

Porter let the curl unravel out of his fingers. "I'm a terrible brother. A terrible son. My dad would be so pissed. I'm my brother's keeper, he would say. I should have been there for Todd. The signs were there, but I made excuses. I thought, hey, he works a lot. Or you know, he needs a break. He's just unwinding. No, Todd is an alcoholic. We should have intervened years ago. Like, right after my dad died. He was sixteen years old, drinking Johnny Walker Black from my granddaddy's study like it was nothing."

I put my hand on Porter's thigh, muscular and firm even in well-worn sweats. "You can't torture yourself. Sometimes, things like this are hard to pinpoint."

Porter put his face in his hands. I could see tears drop through his fingers and onto the kitchen island. When he lifted his head, Porter's nose was red, and his eyes were bloodshot.

"I should have been there today. He could have died. All because I was just too annoyed to leave my house. Ari, my brother could have died."

"But thank God he did not. He's bruised but not broken."

"Thank God indeed."

I bit my lip and tapped my fingers on the kitchen island. Porter grabbed my hand. "What's wrong?"

I felt a crushing agony in my chest. "I'm just…sad for you. Anxious for you. And I can't do anything to help you feel better."

Porter moved his hand up my arm, his index finger leading the way. Goose bumps appeared wherever he touched. He moved in closer, putting his lips on my neck. I leaned into it, allowing myself the pleasure of feeling the warmth of his lips and wetness of his tongue as it glided up and down my neck. His lips reached my earlobes, his tongue circling the skin near my earring. If this was what he needed, I'd give it to him. Maybe this was what I needed too.

"Who says you aren't making me feel better?" he said in a husky whisper.

I sighed, enjoying the familiarity of his lips against my skin. "Your mom wanted me to look after you. You didn't even eat."

"I don't need to eat. I'm with you. I'm fine." Porter's kisses traced along my jawline, then across the bridge of my nose. "I love your nose."

"My nose?" I repeated, puzzled at his random thought. I never really found my wide, upturned nose interesting.

"Yep. It just fits your face. Plus, the freckles. Very fucking cute."

I giggled like a teenager. "Cute? Oh, really? Freckles are a turn-on now."

"Hmm. Really," said Porter as he kissed the tip of my nose. "Everything about you turns me on. You know this."

I felt my breathing become uneasy. Porter took my hand, leading me toward my bedroom. I sat on the edge of the bed and waited with anticipation. If the reason he couldn't eat was because he had an appetite for sex, I was all for being on the menu. I felt an electric throbbing in my abdomen that seemed to travel to the tips of my toes.

Porter pulled his shirt over his head. I watched, my eyes roaming all over his body. Every sinewy muscle in his abdomen flexed with fluidity. It's not like I hadn't seen Porter naked a ton of times. But it seemed like he enjoyed getting naked for me. Enjoyed the buildup. It was like opening a present on my birthday every time.

Porter slowly pulled down his sweats, revealing royal blue Calvin Klein boxers. I thought about Marky Mark and the classic Calvin ads. Porter could have given him a run for his money. He sat on the bench on the end of my bed and took off his socks. He then stood in front of me, in just his boxers. And with an erection that was hard to miss. No pun intended.

We hadn't had sex in a couple of weeks, and I needed it. Wanted it. Missed it. I moved to take off my own pants and Porter bent down, putting his hands on my thighs.

"Ari, stop. Just wait…"

I froze. "What? What is it?"

"I don't want to have sex tonight."

I ignored my clitoris beatboxing all over the place, like Doug E. Fresh, choosing to think like a rational adult. As much as I wanted to sex this man like crazy, given the circumstances, maybe now wasn't the time.

"It's totally fine. We don't have to."

Porter groaned. "Trust me, I want to. I just… I don't want you to think all we do is… Or all I want is… I'm not trying to violate your boundaries."

I laughed. "Porter, you've never violated my boundaries. I'm not worried about that."

Porter bit his lower lip, the color in his cheeks blush pink. "I know. It's just. Right now, we don't know where we are. I don't need the confusion. I just want to touch you. Hold you. Lie with you. Be intimate without being… well…intimate. Just let me hold you, Ari. Can we do that?"

I sat back on my elbows and looked at Porter. I smiled. He stood there in his boxers asking me to allow him to be something a lot of men hadn't—vulnerable.

"Sure."

Porter smiled. "Okay. But first, let me undress you."

Suspicions rising, I gave him a piercing look. "Undress me? And you don't want to have sex?"

Porter shook his head. "No sex. I'm not lying. When have I ever lied to you?"

I thought about it. Porter truly had never lied to me. Ever.

Porter bent down and softly peeled down my leggings. I lifted my hips, and they slid down easily over my thighs and bare feet. Then I remembered...

Oh, fucking hell.

"Are those Wonder Woman underwear?" said Porter, trying hard to suppress a chuckle.

Shit.

My faced warmed with embarrassment. "Yeah. I mean, it's the weekend. I need to do laundry."

Porter let out a laugh deep from his belly. "You were serious about being a DC girl." He put his hands on the soft folds of my belly, his thumbs making those slow, soft circles that he always did. Porter's touch alone was enough to make me come.

"Yep. A DC girl." I breathed out.

Porter moved his hands up my torso and removed my cropped sweatshirt over my head. Luckily, the tank-like bra matched the panties, with Wonder Woman crests right over the nipples. Porter pulled the covers back, and we both slid into bed. Warm and safe under the covers in just our underwear, we could hear the soft whirring of the central heat coming on. I looked at Porter and he moved me into the cradle of his arm. I felt his lips on my forehead, the familiar smell of his cologne all around me.

"Thank you for being there for me today, Ari," said Porter.

"Again, you don't have to thank me. Besides, you were there for me today, too."

Porter brushed my hair against the coolness of the pillow, then wrapped my thigh over his leg. I laughed.

Porter kissed my shoulder. "I just love this part of snuggling with you. When your legs wrap around me."

"Well, you know what they say, thick thighs save lives."

Porter erupted into laughter. "I suppose so. I guess in a way you saved my life, Ari."

I looked up, directly into his face. Porter's green eyes looked like mossy ocean water, inviting me to take a dip. "How did I save your life?"

Porter twirled his index finger in my hair. "Before I met you, I was just existing. Work and life were just routine. Now, I get excited going to work. Because I know you will be there. I never know what I'll experience with you, Ari. You make me passionate about so many things now. I mean, look at the progress we've made in designing the stadium. And today, Jesus, where would I have been without you by my side."

I bit my lip, holding back tears. My hands rubbed Porter's sandy brown curls. I lifted my face toward Porter, kissing him softly and slowly until we both fell asleep. Our lips still touching and breathing words unspoken into each other.

Chapter Twenty-Six

Porter

I blinked a few times as my eyes adjusted to the image of Ari straddling me. The sun shone brightly through the blinds and sheer curtains, signaling midmorning. We'd cuddled in her bed all weekend and I preempted the last-minute choice of us playing hooky from work Monday by emailing Ms. Gayle to tell her that Ari and I were working remote. Truth was, I didn't want to leave Ari. *Or her bed. Or her thighs.*

Right now, I was enjoying the view.

I peeked up at Ari with one eye slightly closed. "Well, good morning, Mon Coeur. To what do I owe this lovely set of thighs on top of me?"

Ari folded her arms and poked out her lips. With her hair all wild, she looked like one of those Bratz dolls my niece liked to play with. She pouted playfully. "I mean, I loved the cuddling and all. But I want…"

I started laughing, adjusting myself underneath Ari. "You want what, Ari? You need to use your words."

I could feel my dick growing harder as she shifted around on my lap. Ari's eyes narrowed and her lips curled up in a knowing, sexy grin. I shifted her Wonder Woman panties to the side with the crook of my finger and stroked between the folds of her pussy until her wetness made my fingers slippery. As much as I wanted to just bend her over and fuck her into a coma, I slowed down.

Ari moaned slightly as she ground her clit against my hand. "Can't you just make me cum?"

I smiled, looking at the lust-filled expression on her face. I felt my finger become slick with the writhing of Ari's hips. There was no joy greater than making Ari beg for it.

"I could...if you say please. Say please, Ari."

I sat up, wrapping her legs around my waist. Ari moved my fingers out of her panties. She took my wet finger and licked it, savoring her own taste. I felt my dick quiver in excitement, reminding me it had been weeks since I'd been inside of her. Ari leaned back on her hands, the strap of her tank bra falling on her shoulders. Her still berry-stained lips parted, and she let out a breathy sigh.

"Please, PJ?"

I put my hands between Ari's core and my body, feeling the heat between us. I pulled out my dick from my shorts and stroked until I was hard. Ari licked her lips and put her hand on top of mine, following the motion of my hand against my dick. If our hands moved any faster, I would probably explode.

Ari lifted a bit, and once again, moved her panties to the side. She slowly lowered herself down and the heat of her pussy against my dick, which was harder than concrete, radiated throughout my body. I reached quickly for a condom in Ari's nightstand, grabbing one and putting it on in record time.

No sooner than I could get on protection, Ari lowered herself on me, and she let out an aching, alto-infused moan that struggled to escape from her throat. I watched as she leaned back, allowing her body to ease into the familiar movement of us. I moved my hand up her stomach toward her neck and firmly took hold. Even through the condom, I could feel her tightness taking hold of me, taking all that I offered her.

"God, I've missed you…missed this," Ari said through sporadic breaths.

"Then show me," I said, now holding on to her hips.

Ari's hips moved faster and faster. I loved the view of her on top, riding me. The crests of her Wonder Woman top covered hardened nipples that had me mesmerized.

"Ari? Ari? You here, baby?"

"Baby, I'm not there yet," I responded.

Ari looked down at me, puzzled. "What?"

"I said I'm not there yet?" I grunted between strokes.

Then the unfamiliar voice repeated. "Ari? Honey? You here? I just let myself in! I brought something called a cronut. I think Mr. George may enjoy these."

"Shit! It's my fucking mama!" Ari yelled. She practically leaped off my throbbing dick like a pogo stick, which wasn't a pleasant feeling at all. *Ten out of ten. Do not recommend.*

Ari ran around her room, throwing my sweats at my head and trying to locate her own pants. I stood up, hopping on alternating feet to get dressed.

"Where the fuck are my pants?" said Ari. Outside of sex, I'd never heard her curse this much in a five-minute period. She was bending over, looking under the bed. I was enjoying the view of her ass perched high in the air with Wonder Woman emblems dancing about. I was hoping she wouldn't find pants at all.

"Ari, just grab some shorts out of your dresser," I said, cocking my head to one side, mesmerized by the bobbing *W*s over a perfectly ripe peach.

The sound of someone clearing their throat interrupted all of that.

Ari's mother was standing in the doorway. She folded her arms and behind her glasses, her brows crinkled in an expression that was something between amusement and annoyance. Her short, cropped hair was a coppery red, which seemed to match her tartan print wrap. I felt like a horny teenager caught sneaking out of his girlfriend's bedroom.

Her mom cleared her throat. "Ari, I'm sure whatever you're looking for isn't under the bed." Then she looked over at me. "Or in the bed it seems."

Startled, Ari bumped her head on the metal frame as she slid from underneath the bed.

Ari looked like she wanted to pee herself. I walked up to her mother, wiping my hands on my pants, and extending it toward her for a shake.

"Hi, I'm…"

"Porter," she said, finishing my introduction, smiling as she shook my hand. "I'm Doris, sweetie. Call me Doris. Or Miss Doris. Hell, call me Ma. Especially now that I've seen you half-naked." She pointed toward Ari. "And I gave birth to this one, so her sitting here in her superhero drawers ain't nothing. I thought you grew out of wearing Underoos, girl!"

"Ma! Seriously, what are you doing here? And why are you using your spare key! It's for emergencies!" squealed Ari, still rubbing her head. I tried to suppress my laughter. Ari was acting like Doris caught her red-handed for skipping school to fuck.

"Well, I called your job, and they said you were working remote. So, I figured you were at home. I didn't know that you weren't home…alone," Doris said, with all the innuendo her voice could muster.

Ari finally scrambled to find a Guns N' Roses T-shirt and some sweatpants. "Ma, this is Porter."

"Honey, we've already made introductions. Now, y'all come to the kitchen. I'll put on some coffee to go with these cronuts. Or do you two need something stronger? Sex makes me thirsty for a gin and tonic." Doris trotted down the hallway, her mules clicking along the hardwood.

I began laughing. "Well, that was a hell of a way to meet your mom. I was hoping I'd meet her for brunch. Not shirtless in my drawers. Well, you were in drawers."

Ari rolled her eyes and punched me in the arm. "I can't stand you. Listen, let's just get this over with."

I put my hand on the small of Ari's back. She relaxed against the palm of my hand. I kissed her forehead. "Come on, it's going to be fine. Besides, like she said, she's already seen me half-naked. What's the worst that could happen at this point?"

Doris looked at us over her coffee cup as Ari and I ate our cronuts in relative silence. Ari tapped her fingers nervously against the kitchen island and her mother shook her head with a slight smirk.

"So…what was so important that the two of you skipped work?" asked Doris as she put a cronut on her saucer. "You know what? Don't answer that."

I cleared my throat. "The truth of the matter is, Miss Doris, is that, well, Ari and I… Well, I had a rough weekend. My brother was in an accident. And Ari was keeping me company. Being a friend."

Doris's eyes enlarged. "Oh my. I'm so sorry, honey. Is he okay?"

I nodded. "Yeah. I think so. I'm glad Ari was there for me. She was my rock."

Ari blushed. "We just needed some time away from work. Away from the project."

Doris smiled. "Seems like you two needed a break. And needed each other." Doris grabbed our empty coffee cups and refilled them both with ease and grace, carrying them like a professional waitress. She placed them in front of us, without a drop spilled. Impressive.

Doris folded her arms and leaned back, looking at us. "And by the way, Ari. I know you said your co-worker was good-looking, but honey, you grossly downplayed this boy's looks. The boy looks like a young Smokey Robinson! And you know I loved me some Smokey! Come to think of it, we conceived you to some Smokey, Ari. Maybe."

Ari coughed, nearly choking on her cronut. "Jesus, Ma!"

I rested my fist on my chin to keep myself from laughing. "Well, I appreciate it, Miss Doris. I like Smokey, too." I liked Doris. She was hilariously raunchy. I instantly realized that Ari inherited her sense of humor.

Doris asked about the project, and we filled her in on the progress. I bragged about Ari's design capabilities. Ari kept talking about how I was about to make partner after this stadium project. I rested my hand on her knee, drawing circles with my index finger. Ari looked over at me and winked.

Doris reached into her pocket and pulled out a key,

laying it on the counter with a dramatic thud. The clink rang throughout the kitchen. "Well, it looks like I don't need this anymore. Seems like Porter may need this more than I do."

Ari looked at me and then back at her mom. "Ah. I wouldn't go that far, Mama. You know, we're friends."

"Well, you know, just in case. Besides. You already know I have like four more copies."

Ari threw up her hands. "Of course, you do, Doris James!"

Doris smiled, reaching for her purse on the opposite end of the counter. Its bright red color also matched her hair. Doris was a whiz at coordination and had a flair for style. I wondered if Ari would be just as fly at her age.

"Well," Doris declared with a florid swoosh of her Burberry cape. "I'm going to leave you two to your hooky day from work. Get back to…you know…whatever it was you all were doing before I came in. I wouldn't mind if you made me a grandbaby. Ari, are you on the pill?"

"Goodbye, Mama," Ari huffed.

Doris kissed Ari on the cheek and stretched her hands out to me for a hug. I hugged her, and she squeezed tightly.

"Treat my baby right, Smokey," Doris whispered in my ear. "Even if she resists!"

"I will," I said.

I watched as Doris threw her hand up and switched her hips out of the door. I turned to Ari with a smile. "Your mom is something else."

Ari, still reeling from embarrassment, put her hands in her hair. "Ugh. I know. My mama is just…a lot. Listen, about the key thing. When the time is right, we will talk about it. Until then…"

Before I knew it, I pulled out my key ring and located my extra key. I slid it across the counter toward Ari. Her bright brown eyes widened. I didn't know why, but it felt right.

"Only if you want to," I said. "No pressure. We don't even know what we are. But I'd rather you find me before my cats ate my remains in my loft. Also, clear my search history."

"Clear out search engine for *Big Booty Judy 3*. Got it. Wait." Ari squinted. "You have a cat? Multiple cats?"

I snorted. "God no. But if I had cats, that would be my worst nightmare."

Ari slid my key toward her, placing it in her pocket. She handed me her key that Doris left on the counter. "No pressure either. But you make a compelling argument with the cats."

"So, what does this mean?" I asked, hesitantly.

Ari sighed, stared up at the ceiling, and then looked at me. "This means I'm willing to try. If you'd like."

"I'd like that. Can I ask you something?"

"Sure?"

"Are you still going to be my date at the gala?"

Ari smiled, leaned over the kitchen counter, and placed a kiss on my cheek. "I'd be delighted to escort you, Mr. Harrison."

I beamed. "It's a date. An official date."

Ari frowned. "Wait, so all the other times we've gone out for lunch? Or drinks after work? Or sex? Those weren't dates?"

I shook my head. "Nope. We were just friends. Friends who had scx but friends."

"Okay, then what are we now?"

I scratched my chin. "Lovers and friends?"

Ari laughed, then started dancing to some unheard beat. "Okay Usher…"

I laughed too. "Listen, let's not think about it. No pressure, remember? When the time is right, we'll know. Okay?"

"Okay. No pressure."

I winked as I took Ari's hand in mine, pulling her into my lap. "Okay. Now, let's get back to the lovers' part, you know, before your mama saw you in your Underoos."

"I hope a dozen cats eat those pretty eyeballs!" laughed Ari as she pressed her lips against mine.

Chapter Twenty-Seven

Ari

I couldn't breathe.

No, I literally couldn't breathe because I had on at least two pairs of Spanx under this dress. I was nervous. This Hampton Atlanta Alumni's Blue and White gala would be our first truly public outing as a couple. And this was a hell of a public place to debut. A fundraiser gala with some of who's who in Atlanta. Were we a couple? I mean, I wasn't entirely sure. Yes, we spent time together. Since helping me find my new car, and coming to the hospital, Porter and I literally saw each other 24/7. We hadn't really defined what this was. We were still at a crossroads. But it felt nice. Natural. Like Porter had always been a part of my life.

I wasn't driving my new car tonight. Porter had insisted on picking me up. For the gala, I decided on a gold, low-cut sequin dress that had a small train. It hugged every single curve. My hair was half up/half down and I threw on a very expensive red liquid lipstick that I had been saving for special occasions. I looked at myself in the full-length mirror and attempted to take a breath. I was second-guessing the choice to wear false eyelashes when the doorbell rang.

I grabbed my purse and my heavy winter wrap and opened the door. Standing in front of me was Porter, who looked every bit the part of Black James Bond. Damn, he looked good. And knowing Porter, that tux was custom-made. Instantly, I wanted to unravel his bow tie slowly, feeling the delicate silk run through my fingers, and use it to blindfold him. Or tie him up. All the dirty thoughts were running through my head.

"Wow. That dress! You look amazing, Ari," said Porter as he bit his lip slightly. He was holding a corsage. I looked at him, a bit puzzled.

"A corsage, Porter?"

"I remembered you saying you didn't go to the prom in high school. So, I thought I'd make up for lost time. You look amazing. Did I say that already?" Porter rubbed his hand over his softer, shorter curls.

It was cute. Porter was nervous and extremely flustered. I suppose this dress was doing its job.

I extended my arm toward Porter, who was blushing slightly as he put the corsage on my arm. He then held my hand and pulled me close to him, kissing me on the cheek.

"I don't want to ruin your makeup," Porter whispered as his lips traced up to my ear, landing butterfly kisses all along my jawline. I shivered.

"Don't worry. This $40 lipstick is kiss-proof," I said, as I melted into him. He smelled so good, but unfamiliar. The cologne had to be new for the occasion. I liked it, but it wasn't the usual smell of Porter I'd grown accustomed to.

"Wait? Forty dollars? For lipstick?"

I looked at him and matched his raised eyebrow. "Says the man who clearly has on new cologne that I'm sure wasn't cheap."

He smiled and laughed. "You have a good nose. Touché."

The Botanical Garden was magical, adorned with elaborate light installations among the flora and fauna of the garden, signaling the beginning of the holiday season. I had never seen anything so beautiful and so artistic. After valet parking, we entered the Great Hall to a live band playing some jazz standards. Porter handed over my wrap for coat check. I stood still, looking at the sea of beautiful, well-appointed varying shades of brown skin. The decor was elaborate. Flowers were everywhere, and they'd decked the tables and chairs out in the school colors. There was a bevy of tables for corporate sponsors, including a prominent Atlanta movie studio owner. I felt slightly intimidated. I worked for a well-respected architectural firm. But in the grand scheme of things, I wasn't important enough to shell out $200 a plate for a table. Suddenly, I felt Porter's hand on the small of my back, making those small, reassuring circles with his thumb. I leaned into him.

"I hope you don't mind. But we're sitting with my mother and Desmond," Porter said.

We made our way through the crowds when suddenly we crossed paths with Jamal Faulk. We hadn't seen him since the night that Porter and I had burgers and played pool. His stylist dressed him in a very elaborate brocade patterned tuxedo jacket. On his arm was a girl whose expression said it all. She was just there for the photos.

"Oh snap! Porter and Ari. Good to see you again," he

said. Porter gave Jamal a close, secret, fraternal hand-shake. Jamal hugged me quickly, then took a step back.

"Damn, Ari. You're looking good, girl!" said Jamal. His date rolled her eyes and pulled him in closer. I rolled my eyes so hard that they practically hit my skull. Trust and believe, no one was checking for Jamal. Certainly not me. I had the finest date in the room.

"Thanks," I replied. "You both look great."

Jamal turned to introduce his date. "Y'all, this is Fiona. She's a beauty influencer. She has like six million followers."

"Cool," said Porter, who was clearly feigning interest. I could tell he wanted to get away from Jamal as fast as possible. Porter probably did not know what an "influencer" was or did. The man could barely navigate Instagram.

"Yeah. I'm getting a shade of LaTrixie lipstick. Fiery Fiona," she chimed in, her head still buried in her phone.

"Oh, how lovely," I said. "I'll look for it in the stores," I lied.

"Jamal, I need a drink, dear. Lead me to the bar," Fiona said. Her phony accent was somewhere between Paris, France, and Paris, Texas. Just floating aimlessly and not really landing anywhere.

"Right. Good to see you guys. I'm going to go mingle and see if I can pass out some real estate cards. Houses won't sell themselves," said Jamal. "Remember, I handle all matters of real estate. Commercial and residential. Leasing and owning." Without thinking, Jamal handed me another flashy gold business card to add to my growing collection. Before Jamal left, I saw him whisper something to Porter and hit him on the shoulder.

"What was that about?" I asked, curiously.

"It's just Jamal being Jamal."

I looked at him and tilted my head to the side. "Is that right?"

Porter smiled. "He just said 'about damn time.'"

"About time? As in 'about time' we started dating?"

"I guess. Maybe he saw something between us that night at Hemingway's." Porter drew me close to him, putting his hand around my waist.

"And what was that?" I asked as I leaned back into him, his beard soft against my forehead.

"Kismet," he coolly responded.

I waited for him to elaborate, but he didn't. He just stood there with this devilish smile on his face, knowing that I wasn't in on his secret.

We made our way through the crowd and found our table. Eloise and Desmond both rose from their chairs when they saw us approach. Eloise kissed me warmly on the cheek. Desmond hugged me gently, squeezing my bare shoulders reassuringly.

"My dear, you're simply radiant in this dress," said Eloise.

"Indeed," agreed Desmond. "A vision. A golden goddess, eh, PJ?"

Porter nodded. "Yes, a vision." Porter pulled out my chair, and I sat down. I wiggled a bit, trying to catch a breath, but the double Spanx wasn't letting up. It had a vise grip on my fupa.

"I'll go grab us some drinks. Any requests?" Porter asked the table.

"I'll take whatever white wine is available," I said. Although truthfully, I wanted something stronger to calm my nerves. I'd been to plenty of fancy events. Some even with Korey. Truth be told, I'd usually agreed to go because I was there for the free booze and food. But this time, I was on the arm of someone I truly liked and cared about.

"You know me, son. A rum on the rocks," said Desmond. Eloise shook her head, forgoing anything to drink.

She leaned over to me. "One of us must be sober and drive us home. Plus, with Todd, I'm too shaken up to drink."

"I understand." I smiled. I don't think the nervousness had completely left my face because Eloise patted my hand.

"It'll be fine. And again, thank you for taking care of PJ that night."

"Oh please, don't thank me. He's my...friend."

Eloise looked at me with a knowing smile. "Uh-huh. Friend," she repeated.

"I hope Todd's doing well," I asked, eager to change the subject.

Eloise gave a small smile. "He is, dear. Physical therapy is going well. He's taking it day by day. I think he's going to be alright."

I smiled. "I'm really glad."

Our table slowly filled up with Eloise's guests: the dean of the library and her husband. A couple of professors. One of Eloise's college roommates. An art historian. Just like Thanksgiving, it was a very erudite table. Once everyone was seated, Eloise introduced me.

"Everyone. This is my son Porter's colleague and girlfriend, Ari."

Girlfriend? And here I was afraid to say "boyfriend." Porter returned to the table with drinks in hand.

"What did I miss?" he whispered.

"Your mother introducing me as your girlfriend to her friends."

Porter's green eyes widened as he stammered. "Seriously? I can tell her that's not cool. I just… But I mean… is that what you want?"

I tried my best to suppress a laugh but failed. Porter sounded like a nervous teenager, not a man in his forties.

"Porter. It's fine. Really."

Porter looked at me. His cheeks were flush, but his eyes danced in the soft candlelight of the room. "But you being my girlfriend does have a nice ring to it."

I felt my hands shake and my breathing hasten. Before I could answer, I heard my name.

"Ari! I thought that was you! Why didn't you tell me you were coming! You look fucking fabulous. Doesn't she, Zach?"

It was Bella, who was at the table next to me with her husband, Zach, who was tugging at his bow tie uncomfortably. As a person who was on the homecoming court, Bella wore a modern off-the-shoulder ball gown in the school colors. With her hair in a tight chignon, she looked like Cinderella.

"Hi, Bella. Hi, Zach. This is Porter. My date for the evening," I said, quickly running through introductions.

"Good to see you again, Porter," said Bella. "Looking like you stepped off Savile Row!" She nodded her approval.

Porter blushed a bit as he nodded a quick thanks. I thought it was cute how Porter easily got embarrassed. I absolutely loved that about him.

Wait? Loved?

Zach and Porter shook hands. "So, you and Ari work together. That's how you met, right?" I stared at Bella as she drank her glass of champagne and shrugged. So much for secrets between girlfriends.

"Yeah," replied Porter. "We've grown closer these past few months." I took a gulp of my white wine. *Closer* didn't seem like the right word. It felt too small. I'd say we had grown more intimate. But you can't just say "intimate" to your best friend and her husband without the sexual connotation. I suppose *closer* would have to do.

Bella interrupted. "Well, Porter, thank you for getting Ari to come to this. I've been trying to get her to come for years, and she just refuses. I guess you've given her a reason."

"You know this isn't my thing, Bella," I said. "But this year, I have a good excuse to come. You know. The stadium project and all. Get the firm's name out there." I felt Porter's hand move to the center of my back, where he traced what felt like hearts on my skin. I instantly felt warmth tugging at the deepest, most private center of myself.

"Cool," said Zach. "Well, Bella dragged me to this thing. I don't know why she insists on coming every year. It's the same tired crowd. Old money alums berating new money ones and new money alums wishing they were old money."

"I think it's great networking! I can grow my event planning business and you can get new clients when you open your private practice. You know good and well half of this room needs a little nip and tuck," chided Bella as she grabbed a glass of champagne as a waiter passed by. "Now, come on, Zach. I must find those wonderful mini crab cakes Lakitha was going on and on about. We will see you all later! I'll text you later, girl!"

Bella grabbed Zach's arm and winked at me. As much

as I loved seeing Bella, I was glad that her insatiable need to network gave her an excuse to leave. I could have Porter all to myself and try to focus on these feelings that were tugging at me. It was like pulling the string of a rug. I was unraveling, but in a good way.

I turned to him. "Now, where were we?" As soon as I asked, the band struck up a jazzy, instrumental version of Anthony Hamilton's "The Point of It All." My heart leaped. I absolutely adored that song. Porter extended his hand.

"Ms. James? Would you do me the honor of taking a spin on the dance floor with me?" I looked at Porter.

"It would be a sin not to dance to this song," I said. "Of course, I would, Mr. Harrison."

We swayed to the rhythm of the band as if we were in our own world. It felt as if there were only the two of us on the dance floor. I looked up at Porter. He was staring directly at me. Tonight, his eyes looked and felt different. There with a passion and yearning I hadn't seen before. I put my head on his chest and he bent down, kissing the top of my head.

"So, the whole girlfriend thing," I said, hoping he could hear me as I almost buried myself in his chest. I inhaled and exhaled the unfamiliar scent of him. I'd have to get used to it.

"I wanted to know… If you wanted that. If you wanted there to be an us," he asked softly. "I know it's complicated with work, but…"

I stepped back a bit and put a finger up to his lips. I had to say this before the moment was over and I lost my nerve.

"I'm scared," I confessed, in disbelief those words had left my lips, but it was true. "I've been fighting my feelings because I'm scared. The past, like you said, was haunting me. I'm ready to move forward with you, Porter. I don't want you to pay for some other man's mistakes. I know you're not Maurice. You've been nothing less than amazing. A gentleman. I had a wall up with a moat around it, not allowing anyone to get close to me. But all my defenses come crashing down when I'm with you."

Porter's voice cracked slightly as he responded. "That's…that's good. I'm glad you feel that way around me. Tonight, seeing you with my family, it just felt right. Everything just felt like it fell into place. You know, my mama loves you!"

I laughed. "And my mama loves you… Smokey."

"I guess the nickname is sticking, huh?"

I put my arms around his neck, audaciousness replacing my nervousness. "From the moment I saw you, I wanted you."

Porter's eyes narrowed, the green gleaming in the soft light of the dance floor. "You don't know how long I've wanted you."

I laughed. "I have a pretty good idea."

"And you'd still be wrong." Porter leaned down and kissed me. At first, the kiss was tender. Then, quickly, the level of heat and intensity increased. He pulled me in closer, his hands still on my waist. I moved my hands to his chest, trying to allow space for hands to roam freely. His lips drew me in as his tongue met and danced intimately with mine. I felt his hands grasp my face as his kisses became faster, harder. He sucked my bottom lip, grazing it slightly with his teeth before finally letting me go.

"Wow," I said breathlessly. I looked at him and

laughed. Amazingly, my $40 lipstick was worth every penny. There wasn't a trace on his face at all.

Porter wiped the corners of his mouth with his index finger and laughed. "Wow, is an understatement."

I looked around and realized the music had stopped. The dance floor had cleared out, and it was just me and Porter standing there. I looked over his shoulder to see Eloise with her hand to her chest, smiling. I could not suppress my smile, either.

The band began to play an instrumental version of "The Wobble." Every elderly Black person in the house ran or hobbled to the dance floor, including Des and Eloise. A geriatric line-dance stampede.

Porter whispered in my ear. "Maybe we should get out of here?"

I looked at him, puzzled. "Porter? You want to leave? Now? We haven't even had dinner and I know you don't want to waste $500 of your hard-earned cash."

"What would be a waste is not getting you out of that dress fast enough. You're coming home with me, Ari."

My stomach muscles clenched at the husky, primal tone of his voice.

"Are you sure?" I asked. My voice trembled with excitement and nervousness. We were going at what seemed like warp speed.

Porter moved a strand of hair stuck to my face. "Before this night is over, I'm trying to make you come a record number of times."

A devilish grin was plastered on my face. "Oh yeah? How many?"

"However many the woman I love wants."

I looked up at Porter. The look on his face was all lust,

joy and want. It was all too much for me. I closed my eyes, taking in a deep breath. "You love me?"

"Yes, Ari. I love you. If you don't love me, you don't have to say it if you don't…"

"I love you," I softly whispered, interrupting in a voice that was barely audible, unsure if Porter had heard me. But he had.

Without another word, hand in hand, we ran out of the ballroom.

As soon as we entered the elevator to his loft, Porter wasted no time claiming me. He leaned into me against the wall. His tongue was uncontrollable, and his hands were all over me. First in my hair, pulling me deeper into his kiss, then along my waist. His hands glided between the split in my dress, palming my thighs. I moaned and bit my lip. I wanted him. Badly. I had never fucked in an elevator, but I'd give it a shot.

"I want you," he whispered as he kissed along my jawline. "I want you right now."

"I want you, too," I said, barely able to breathe between kisses.

The elevator stopped on Porter's floor. He opened the door with one hand and led me inside with the other. His loft building used to be an old sugar mill. Porter's loft was on the top floor of the building, which had the most amazing view of the Atlanta skyline. The building was a U shape with his windows facing another set of loft windows. I walked over to his large, expansive windows and looked at the rain falling. I traced my fingers along the cold window, making a heart out of the condensation.

I felt Porter come behind me. He moved my damp hair from my shoulders and slowly zipped down my dress. He took his time, kissing along the way as the zipper slowly moved down. I felt his tongue follow my spine, and a shiver overcame me. I closed my eyes and leaned into the amazing feeling of his lips.

That was until I remembered the two layers of control top shapewear I was wearing.

"Stop," I said in horror as I turned to face Porter.

A look of confusion replaced Porter's previously hungry eyes. "What's wrong?"

"I…uh… Need to…go to the bathroom."

"Okay. I'll be waiting right here," he said as he eased himself onto his long, black leather sectional. I smiled and held the back of my dress together, running into his bathroom down the hall. Quickly, I took out the hairpins holding my topknot together, letting it fall into the rest of my hair, which had curled from the rain. I pulled up my dress and wiggled out of the first pair of Spanx. Huffing, I tried to get out of the second pair, but I forgot I bought it one size smaller on purpose. It wasn't budging. I sat on the toilet to catch my breath. Sweat trickled down the side of my face as I pulled at the material sucking the life out of me. I grabbed a hand towel, wiping away beads of sweat. I looked at the crisp white hand towel and felt terrible for putting my makeup on it. For a guy, Porter kept an immaculate bathroom. It was like a hotel and the man had high-quality bath linen.

A soft knock interrupted my admiration. "Everything okay?" Porter asked softly.

"Uhm yeah…" I said, still breathing like an asthmatic.

"Are you lying?" I could hear the concern in his voice.

I leaned back and looked at myself in the mirror. What was I doing? Why was I acting like I was a woman, a grown woman, who didn't have on shapewear? And if

Porter was going to be with me, he had to deal with the real me. I stood up and slid the bathroom door open.

Porter looked at me up and down, confused. The perspiration was still on my brow.

He looked around the bathroom at the towel and Spanx on the floor. "Is something wrong? What happened here?"

I took a deep breath, resting a hand against the sink. "Listen. I have…well…had on two pairs of Spanx. And well… One is stuck to me. I wasn't trying to get sexy with you in double-layers of Spanx."

Porter walked into the bathroom, picking up the first pair of Spanx, gently folding them and placing them on the counter.

"Turn around," he demanded.

I turned and faced the bathroom mirror. Porter stood behind me with a slight smirk on his face.

"Do you think this is funny?" I asked. I could feel my face getting hot with embarrassment. Jesus, this wasn't how I wanted this night to go.

"Shh…" he admonished.

He finished unzipping my dress. I felt his index finger trace a path along my back. His fingers made the hairs on my arm stand on end. He pulled the straps of my dress off my shoulders and, as if by magic or command, my dress fell to the bathroom floor. I stood there in my strapless bra and too-tight Spanx. It was unclear if the Spanx or excitement were cutting off my circulation. Uncomfortable, I shifted my weight.

"Be still, Ari," Porter scolded. He reached next to me and opened a drawer on his vanity. He pulled out a sleek pair of woodgrain-handled scissors. I froze.

"What are you going to do with those?" I said in a panic. I clearly didn't want to end up on the news at 11.

Woman dies as boyfriend accidentally hits an artery try-ing to cut her out of her Spanx.

"Shh. Be still."

I felt Porter's fingers tease the top of the Spanx away from my waist. The cold steel of the scissors against my skin made me jump, forgetting to stand still and not get maimed. Porter put his hand against my waist to steady me. I felt the scissors move down my hips, along my thighs as he snipped away. First, on the right side and then on the left. The shredded Spanx fell to my heels. Porter lifted my foot and removed them, tossing them in the wastebasket by his sink. The entire ordeal should have embarrassed me. But having a man armed with cold steel scissors, cutting me out of my undergarments, was the sexiest thing I had ever experienced. Porter stood behind me. His eyes still with the same hunger that he had before.

"Better?" he asked as he kissed my exposed shoulders.

"Yes," I whispered, feeling less sheepish with each kiss.

Porter unfastened the hooks of my bra and gently cupped it in his hands. Aside from my heels, I was totally naked. Turning to face him, I loosened his tie, slowly letting it slide through my fingers and onto the floor. He watched as it floated along the tiles.

"That's a $200 tie," he said.

"Those were $100 Spanx," I retorted.

"I'll buy you more if you want me to. But honestly, you never needed it in the first place."

Porter's body relaxed as he let me unbutton his tux-edo shirt, including its delicate French cuffs. I pulled it off his muscular, broad shoulders, tossing it on the sink. He undid the button of his tuxedo pants, stepping out of them with ease, standing there in Tom Ford boxers and trouser socks. I giggled as I thought of the first time we had sex and his affinity for argyle, grandpa socks. Porter, with a sly, remembering grin, coolly slid off his socks, then his boxers, where an eager dick leaped out without provocation. Women wouldn't normally describe a man's penis as beautiful but there was no other way to describe Porter's dick. It was indeed beautiful: even-toned, heavy, and carved to guarantee orgasms. I likened it to Ken Griffey Jr.'s bat—it always found the sweet spot.

I leaned against the vanity and opened my legs, anticipating whatever it was he was going to give me. Porter bent down, grabbing his tie. I was open and ready. Seeing this, Porter licked his bottom lip and shook his head as he planted a kiss on my thigh.

"Impatient, are we? Well, you're going to have to wait."

He took my hand and led me out of the bathroom and back into the open, expansive living room. All the lights were on. The rain was coming down harder. We walked back over to the massive windows. Porter positioned himself behind me. I could see our reflection in the window.

"I want them to see what I see," Porter whispered.

"Them?" I questioned.

"Yes, the neighbors that I know are watching us."

As he talked, Porter moved one hand between my legs and the other cupped my breasts, which were spilling over between his fingers. His thumb and index finger held on to my nipple, alternating between stroking and squeezing them. With each touch of his fingers, I wanted to climax. I groaned. He needed to fuck me. Now.

Porter continued, his voice heavy and dripping with desire. "I want them to watch. I want them to watch me make love to the most beautiful woman in this city. In this world. Is that alright? I'll do whatever you want, Ari. Whatever."

I was always adventurous as a lover, but I'd never had an audience when I had sex. I was so turned-on Porter could have asked me to let a bus full of monks watch, and I would have said yes. The pressure of his fingers on my pussy became harder, moving faster as his thumb pressed slightly against my clitoris. I could hear the wetness gliding against his fingers with each stroke.

"Yes," I answered between the strokes of his hand. "God, yes." More than anything, I wanted Porter to stop teasing me and just fuck me. This was becoming too much.

Porter stopped stroking. "Widen your stance," he said firmly. I did as I was told.

Porter kneeled and cupped my ass. His tongue, hot and wet, slithered along my cheeks and then dipped between, finding my clitoris from the back. It felt so good, I could barely hold on. I gripped the exposed brick wall, my fingertips touching the cold, wet window. A flicker of lights from the opposite lofts shone through the window. I let out a moan that echoed throughout Porter's expansive loft.

Porter came up for air. His beard was glistening with my arousal. The lights from the windows cast him in an amber glow. "Did you like that, Ari?"

"Yes," I said. I was dizzy from the erratic breathing that my orgasm created. Turning around, I faced him and leaned against the brick wall. He didn't need the validation, but I was glad to give it.

He reached down on the floor and picked up his tie.

"I saw you admiring this when I picked you up. Again. This is a $200 tie." Porter slyly smiled.

"I was admiring your tie, wasn't I."

"I want you to know they're watching us without you watching them."

"What does that mean?"

"Let me show you."

Porter held both of my hands. "May I?" he asked. I nodded affirmatively. Turning me around to face the window again, he slid the tie across my shoulders, then around my face. He placed the tie in front of my face and finally, across my eyes. The tightness of the tie around my eyes made my nipples harden with excitement. The sound of a condom wrapper opening sent wetness pooling. His hand ran down the length of my back. Instinctively, I bent over. Porter grabbed me by my waist and slowly entered me from behind, filling me up completely. I bit my lip hard, leaving faint indentations in my lower lip from trying not to scream. He was stretching me, filling me deeply with every inch of him. I was more than willing to accommodate him. I wanted him. All of him.

As the rain pounded the windows, Porter met the rhythm of the early winter storm with every stroke. He interchangeably held my waist, then grabbed a fistful of my hair. I could see nothing and hear everything. Panting and gasping, the coldness of the windows beating against my splayed fingers made me wetter. I wasn't sure if anyone was watching us through the floor-to-ceiling windows, but the thought turned me on even more. It was sexy as all fuck.

Eventually, when we met each other's threshold, we collapsed onto each other. Porter, supporting my weight, pulled me down to the floor and loosened my makeshift blindfold. He grabbed a blanket off his couch and wrapped it around our naked bodies. We sat facing the windows. As I rested my head against Porter's chest, he bent down and kissed my sweat-drenched forehead.

"Sex with you is my cardio," I chided. "I'm spent!"

A low, rumbling laugh trickled from Porter's lips. "Good. But this is a break. I promised multiple orgasms. I'm not done."

I smiled. "I love a man who keeps his word."

Porter hummed softly into my wild, tousled hair. "I love you too, Ari."

I turned to face Porter. I ran a finger along the outline of his strong, chiseled jawline, feeling the faint prickle of his soft beard. His normally green eyes were now deepened pools of hazel. They devoured every inch of me. I wished I could have taken a photo at that precise moment to capture his face.

"I love you too, Porter."

Porter sighed. "My mom is right. We make all the sense in the world, Ari. We don't have to make sense to anyone else."

"Why is that?"

"That's simple: You're my person."

I could feel my heart swelling three times bigger at his words. I pressed a chaste kiss against his lips, then leaned against his shoulder as he ran his finger through my tangled mass of hair.

We sat there on the floor of the loft, in front of the windows, and listened to the rain play us a private concerto.

Chapter Twenty-Eight

Ari

Porter and I sat dumbfounded in Conference Room B as the partners relayed the news.

"February?" I repeated, still unable to wrap my brain around it. "The Serranos want to break ground in February? Final designs were supposed to be due in late spring. What happened to the May/June start date for construction?" It was a week and a half before Christmas. Our offices would be closed soon for the holidays. I could feel beads of sweat dampening my hands. How the hell would we be ready before February? A design project of this scope usually took a year, sometimes more. Right now, we were squarely in the conceptual phase, with the Serranos having seen a number of designs from the firm. Were they ready to decide right now?

"Yeah. Paulo Serrano said he wants to break ground on the stadium as a gift to his wife. Or something foolish of that nature. I'm guessing this is more of a publicity stunt than anything. I don't understand these billionaires," said Robinson, who wore his usual expressionless countenance. "It's foolish if you ask me. I think you'd both benefit with more time. You haven't even had a chance to talk to the engineers, for goodness' sakes!"

Porter put his hands on the table. "Look, this is a shock. I mean, Ari and I are more than ready. It's just…" Robinson held his hand up. He looked over at Mr. Riddle, who sighed, then nodded.

"This isn't how we normally operate," finished Riddle. "But we must listen to our client. If he wants to break ground in February, then so be it. We'll just have to rush the request for tender. Although it's going to take well over a year and a half to complete, beginning construction in the cooler months would be ideal for this climate. I've seen what you've come up with thus far, and it's brilliant. You two have pleased the Serranos with your work. Your work has pleased us as well. Naturally, if your design is chosen, you two will still be involved. But I believe you two are more than ready. I wouldn't have agreed to this rushed timeline if I didn't think so."

"What about submittals?" asked Porter, his eyes crinkling with worry.

Robinson waved a hand. "We can let some junior associates handle that. They'd be more than happy to do the grunt work."

I let out a breath and looked at Porter, who smiled warily. "That is great, Mr. Riddle. But when do we need to present our final design? After the New Year is pushing it."

"Well," chimed in Robinson. "I suggested next week."

"Next week?" I squealed, uncharacteristically. My heart felt like it was beating outside of my chest. I felt like I was in an episode of some reality show where the host was throwing in a monkey wrench to see who could stand the heat. It was risky. We were catapulting from conceptual phase to final design in record time.

Robinson looked over his glasses. "Is that going to be a problem, Ms. James? Riddle here seems to have faith in the two of you."

I shook my head. "No, sir."

Riddle cleared his throat. "Good. In the meantime, get your best stuff together. Over the past few weeks, you've presented some amazing work. You two will be presenting after Greer and Jacobi."

Internally, I groaned. I was sick and tired of playing this game with Greer, being subjected to his criticism every time we presented our designs. Our designs were getting better every week. Greer's designs hadn't been the greatest but nevertheless, he had convinced the partners that this was some sort of pissing contest between him and Porter to sew up the partnership. We couldn't let that happen.

"Very well. You'll be ready. Both of you will, I'm sure." Mr. Riddle smiled.

"We will," we said in unison, rising from our seats. The partners looked at us and gave us cautiously optimistic smiles.

Porter and I walked down the hall toward his office, passing a leering Greer and Jacobi as they talked in hushed tones with other associates. I ignored Greer's impending scowl and turned toward Porter.

"A week? Porter, I don't know about this. There is too much room for error. We cannot fuck this up," I whispered.

"We won't. We got this," Porter whispered, leaning in so close I could feel the heat of his breath. "We'll knock this out. I'll get this partnership. You'll be a senior associate in no time. Especially if I have anything to do with it."

I smiled. "Wouldn't that be a conflict of interest? Given that we're, you know…"

Porter looked over at me with a smirk. "Why would it? Your talent alone proves you have a place here at the firm. Besides, by that time, Ari, we'll disclose our relationship to the partners, right?" Porter's eyes skirted over my face. "I told you, no secrets."

"Of course," I said, reassuring him. "But I want to earn my place here. Not because of our relationship."

"I understand. Now let's go in here and lock this thing up, partner!" He extended his fist for a bump. At that moment, I realized I didn't have my iPad with me.

"Oh shit. I need to go back to the boardroom. I don't have my iPad."

I hurried down the hall, giving Ms. Gayle a warm smile as she passed by. As I was about to enter the boardroom, I heard the voices of Riddle and Robinson…and my name.

"Ari is no doubt talented," said Robinson. "I can see she's really pushed Porter to do some of his best work yet. He's giving Greer a run for his money."

"I agree," said Riddle. "These past six months he's done some out of the box thinking. They work well together, Earnest."

"So, you understand my reservations."

"I understand your reservations, but…"

Reservations? I leaned in closer to the slightly open door, my heart thumping in my ears.

"There is no 'but,' Douglas," said Robinson. "I know you hiring her after her scandal at Leland was a risky move. One that has seemed to pay off. But you did it behind my back and I can't risk her pulling a stunt like the one she pulled on that young associate. I don't need her costing us hundreds of thousands, too."

Oh god. *Leland. Chicago. Maurice.* My head rattled like a speaker in an old Chevy. The memories of that time crashed into me like a glacier, all at once, shattering the thin amount of security I'd felt. I braced myself against the wall and tried to catch my breath. *No. This wasn't happening. Not now. No. No.*

Riddle sighed. "Earnest, we don't know the full story there. Surely, you don't think Ms. James lied about…"

Robinson scoffed, interrupting Riddle again. "I don't know, nor do I want to know. What I know is that Leland wouldn't have let her go without just cause. They have a reputation for excellence, as do we. But firms talk. This industry is insular, Douglas. You know this. Especially for a minority firm like ours. She's a goddamn HR nightmare waiting to happen. We don't need that kind of heat again. Thank our lucky stars that Greer had the foresight to come to me and tell me all about the whole payout and sexual harassment fiasco. You surely wouldn't have."

Greer? You have got to be fucking kidding me. But how? Anger pulsed through me, unsure if I wanted to punch something or cry.

I could hear Riddle shuffling around before responding. "Listen, I'm quite appreciative of Greer looking into this. Since his prior missteps, he's had the firm's best interest in mind. That's something to consider in terms of the partnership."

Robinson laughed. "Well, that's a given."

The two men quieted down for a moment until Robinson spoke again. "I know you want to keep Ari. After this stadium is over, maybe we can move her to some lesser projects, letting her work in the background. Eventually, we can phase her out. Give her another generous severance if we have to. We'd give her an excellent recommendation, naturally. We got what we wanted out of her."

Phase me out? I dropped my head. I thought Chicago, Maurice and his lies were the past. Instead, they were haunting me like ghosts, circling me until I'd eventually give in to them. All because of one ambitious fuck.

"I see. I'll say she's doing a damn good job of making Porter look good. Polishing him right up," Riddle said. "He was a diamond in the rough before."

"More like a lump of coal. But women do that, you know," Robinson said. "Being nurturers and all that jazz. Ari looks like she has that motherly vibe, you know, that a lot of women like her have."

Riddle chuckled, lowly. "That's true. Porter ought to thank his lucky stars I hired Ari. I love the boy like my son but he's not exceptionally talented. He's lucky that I was friends with his grandfather. I owed him one."

Robinson laughed. "Finally, you realize that. Well, it was nice having a woman around while it lasted. And it was nice to see a nice, round ass around here. Gayle has passed her prime."

They laughed. Two men, old enough to be my father, *laughed.* I felt bile rise in my throat as two men that I respected, instead of talking about my work, were talking about my ass. Bella was right. Misogynistic to a fault. I wasn't here to bring my design skills to the firm or my perspective. They brought here me to make Porter look good and polish him up in time for the partnership and in front of the Serranos. I thought I was here to redeem myself, to show that I had what it took in this industry.

To show that Maurice and his lies would not stick and
that I was a damn good architect with vision, depth, and
a clear point of view.

I guess I was wrong. Dead wrong.

Slowly, I put my hand on the door of the conference
room and entered. Riddle and Robinson, like deer caught
in headlights, quieted their laughs, and stiffened their
bodies as their gaze moved from questioning to lightly
horrified. Their faces were clearly wondering what I had
heard. Trust me, I'd heard enough.

"Excuse me, gentlemen. My iPad." I pointed as I
grabbed it. The two of them nodded as I moved between
the two of them to retrieve my tablet. My heart was
beating so fast that I feared my rib cage would shatter.
I turned on my heels and left the boardroom as fast as I
could, the words repeated in my head like the chorus to
a terrible pop song. *Liability. Reputation. Phase me out*.

Before I knew it, I was in front of Greer's door. Without warning, I threw it open, slamming it into the wall.
Greer looked up from his computer and smirked, his
face the picture of unashamed arrogance.

"You're a grimy son-of-a-bitch! You had no right to
go digging into my past! Who the fuck do you think
you are!" I could feel my blood pressure rising, making me dizzy. I held on to the chair in front of Greer's
desk to steady myself. He wasn't going to get rid of me
that easily.

Greer folded his arms. "I absolutely had every right
to investigate you. I mean, what person up and leaves
one of the nation's most prestigious firms to come work
for this place? It's like moving from the penthouse to the
ghetto. Especially when they had been doing so well. It
had to be something major."

"Who told you?" My voice was shaky. "No one at the firm knew what was going on. LSB would never let that happen. It would ruin them." We had all signed NDAs which was a condition of my severance package. No one would risk being fired.

"Oh dear," said Greer in the most patronizing way possible. "Money makes anyone talk. A little green, a little gift of gab, and I was able to get all the information I needed. Didn't take much to get them to open up. By the way, Maurice says hello."

I wanted to crumble at the mention of his name. "Maurice? He's a liar and a thief. Greer, you can't believe him. Even you can't be that stupid."

Greer gave a flippant wave. "Oh yeah, I'm sure he's lying. But that doesn't matter. What matters is that he's believable, Ari. His story is convincing. And just convincing enough for the partners to believe."

"You're pathetic!" I yelled, not caring who in the office heard me. I was seething. "You know you're not going to get this stadium design, so you sink this fucking low. Such a coward!"

With that, Greer rose from his seat and closed his door. He inched closer to me, his stifling cologne nearly choking me. "Baby girl, you think this is about the stadium. I could give a shit about that stadium for a second-rate soccer team and slick-haired Spaniards who make shit wine. This is about *my* partnership. It's clear that Porter isn't fit to take this firm to the next level. And you're part of the reason. You're a good designer, Ari, no doubt. But you don't belong here. You're a distraction to the firm. Especially to Porter."

I furrowed my brow. "A distraction? To Porter?"

Greer chuckled, dryly. "Yeah. We aren't blind, Ari.

If Porter became partner, he'd promote you to senior associate in no time. Give you the better projects. Maybe even a corner office. How would that look to the partners?" He paused, looking me up and down. "Especially since you're fucking him."

I felt my heart sink into the pit of my stomach. "You have no idea what you're talking about."

"Right," said Greer, unconvinced. "The long lunches. The 'remote' working. The way he looks at you. Touches you when you think no one is looking. I guess Maurice was right about one thing. You'll fuck anything that moves. Had I known it was that easy…" Greer reached, squeezing my wrist with a firm grip. "Maybe I would have taken you for a ride. So, this is how we're going to play this. You're going to say absolutely nothing. Not a word from that pudgy face of yours or I'll make damn sure you're out on your ass again and not a single firm will be willing to hire you."

I twisted my wrist away from him. "You wouldn't. You don't scare me."

Greer moved back. "Don't test me, bitch. You don't know what connections I have. Now get out of my fucking office."

The way Greer said those words made my blood run cold. I hurried to my office, closed my door, and then the blinds. I leaned against the wall next to the door as tears wet the collar of my blouse. *I knew this would happen.* I looked over at my desk. There had been fresh bouquets of stargazer lilies delivered every day to my office since the night of the gala. Once pleasant, the scent began to turn my stomach.

Dear God. What had we done?

Chapter Twenty-Nine

Porter

This evening, I walked into my loft to find Ari, dressed in sweatpants and a tee, seated at the kitchen island. Her hair was in a ponytail, and she looked like a sexy college coed. I placed two greasy brown paper bags in front of Ari, whose head was buried in her laptop. When the scent of the delicious food didn't move Ari, I cleared my throat.

"Ms. James, I went all the way to Doraville, in thirty-degree weather, for these birria tacos from El Taco Veloz. They're the best in the city. This consommé smells like heaven. You know I wouldn't steer you wrong. Dig in, babe!"

Ari barely looked up from her laptop, her reading glasses perched on her nose. "Oh. Thanks, but I'm not hungry."

I folded my arms, leaning against my kitchen counter. "Ari, what's going on? You barely ate anything at lunch. When have you ever turned down tacos of any sort? Need I remind you of the ownership of a shirt that says tacos are life?"

Ari huffed, then mumbled, "Well, there's a first time for everything."

I stared at Ari, confused. Ari's sarcasm usually wasn't a turnoff for me, but today it was annoying. Combined with her aloofness, it made me ready to blow a gasket. We'd been working nonstop on our presentation, trying to sew up the final design. Not to mention, due to our crazy work schedule, we hadn't had sex in days, so there may have been some pent-up angst. I was man enough to admit that.

I moved behind her, lifting her ponytail away from her neck, kissing along the curve of her neck. "Come on, Mon Coeur. I even have that Belgian pale ale in the fridge you like. The one with the long ass name I can't pronounce. Let's have a drink, eat these tacos, and admire my poorly decorated Christmas tree. Take a break, baby girl."

Ari sighed, moving her neck away from the feel of my lips. A feeling of icy dread swept over me. "Porter, I said I wasn't hungry. This may come as a shock to you, but sometimes I don't feel like eating. Now is one of them."

I backed away, raising my hands. "Whoa. I'm sorry. I wasn't thinking that at all." I sat on the barstool and looked at Ari. Her eyes were tired, and her energy was low. *Not low, sad.* I placed my hand on her leg, massaging her thick sweatpants-clad thigh. "Ari. What's going on? Talk to me. Ever since we met with the partners today, you've been acting weird. Did I do something?"

Ari closed her eyes, inhaling deeply before removing my hand. "No, Porter. You did nothing. Not that I'm aware of."

"What does this mean?"

"Nothing."

"Are you sure? Because it doesn't feel like it." I pushed up the sleeves of my henley and leaned against the island, watching, and waiting for Ari to respond. Silence filled the space between us. Ari was never one to mince words. Her unusual quietness was unnerving and made the hairs on my neck stand up.

This wasn't a good sign.

Ari removed her glasses, pinching the bridge of her nose. "Porter, I.... What are we doing?"

I laughed. "Uh, until a few minutes ago we were about to eat tacos and then I was going to convince you to take a break and join me on the couch for a *Property Brothers* marathon. You know I love when you try to guess which twin is which. You're never right, by the way."

Ari didn't laugh. She didn't even crack a smile. Damn, even my corny jokes weren't landing. My heart sunk a little lower. Ari turned toward me on the barstool. "No, Porter, I mean, what are *we* doing?"

I scratched my beard and let out an exasperated sigh. "Ari, not this again."

"Really? You're going to tell the partners we're together? Is that wise?"

I leaned back. "Ari, we talked about this. After we finish the stadium, when they name partner, I'll disclose our relationship. After your situation in Chicago, I thought maybe it'll make things easier. For both of us."

Ari scoffed. "Yeah right."

"Ari, I said that I would. When have I ever lied to you? Broken a promise to you? I don't want this to be a secret. Is this why you're mad? Because I haven't told the partners about us?"

"No. But it's probably not going to be a good look when they find out that you were dating me."

"Ari, I'm sure they wouldn't care."

Ari rolled her eyes. "Then you don't know them."

I folded my arms. "What's that supposed to mean? I've worked there for fifteen years, Ari. Clearly, I know the type of men they are. Riddle and Robinson are good men. Progressive guys. Trust me, they wouldn't care."

Ari laughed. "Porter, you're so naïve."

"Naive? Ari, where the fuck is any of this coming from? It seems out of left field right now. What do you have against Riddle or Robinson? I mean, they hired you, right?"

Ari chewed her bottom lip. "Did you ever stop to think about why they hired me? Seriously? Especially after everything I'd gone through at Leland. You said yourself you all hadn't been successful in retaining female talent. Why hire such a risk?"

My head throbbed. "Because you're a fucking amazing architect. Your talent speaks for itself. They were singing your praises, Ari."

Ari smirked, her smile bitterly cold. "Really? And what was *your* talent like before I got there? Seems like they weren't totally singing your praises at all."

Heat pricked at my neck, anger bubbling at the surface of my skin. "What are you insinuating? That I was shit before you got here? I mean, I'll admit, I'd had some misses. But I've worked my ass off to get where I am. I'm a damn good designer."

"Good, but not the best."

"Ari, that's fucking hurtful."

"Hurtful, but the truth," Ari interrupted. "Then along comes Ari, to prop you up and make you save face. Shine you up. Over seventy percent of the ideas for this new stadium are mine, but your name is going to be all over this."

Confusion clouded my brain. "Is this a credit thing?

Do you want credit? Fine, you can have it! If you want top billing on this, cool. If that's going to make you happy. Is that what you want?"

"Yes…no… Ugh. It doesn't matter what I want!" Ari threw her hands up.

I paced across the kitchen floor. "It matters to me! What matters to me isn't the ultimate design or recognition. Not anymore. What matters to me is you, Ari!"

"No! Just stop it!" yelled Ari. She slammed her laptop case and yanked the adapter out of the outlet. I reached out for her hand, and she pulled back.

"Ari? What the hell! Why are you so mad? What did I do? All this anger. I don't understand… I don't."

Ari's lip quivered, tears glossing over her coffee-dark eyes. "Of course, you don't. You don't get it. I don't think you ever did."

I searched Ari's face, as tears glossed her brown skin. I didn't understand any of this. I couldn't read between these cryptic lines. I reached out to wipe a tear, but Ari stepped back.

"Baby…please. Talk to me."

Ari began to gather her things, not bothering to look up. "Porter, you and I are over. This isn't going to work. It never was. After this presentation Monday, we can pretend that *this* never happened." I watched as Ari pulled on her winter coat and hat, grabbed her tote, and walked out of the door.

I stood in the middle of my kitchen, the thrum of the slamming door still reverberating in my ears. What was that? I ran through every scenario in my head, trying to place where I made a misstep. Did I say something to her? We were all good this morning. And now, our relationship had disintegrated into a pile of ash, burned by the flame of her words.

I looked down at the birria tacos on the counter. The brown bag was now layered with a cold, oily sheen.

I picked it up and tossed it in the trash.

Chapter Thirty

Porter

Greer tugged at his cuff links, agitated. "I understand your frustration. But just think about the maximized use of space. And if you look here..."

Greer and Jacobi were bombing. Their design seemed devoid of anything that the Serrano Group had specified. Hell, it was lacking anything Jacobi had contributed from earlier designs. Instead, it was Greer's arrogant attempt at showing everyone that he knew better than they did. It wasn't going over well.

Paulo Serrano held up his hand. "Mr. Greer. We've seen enough." With a frown, Paulo turned to his older brother Marco, who sported the darkest aviator shades known to man, and spoke in whispered tones. The tension was thick in the boardroom crowded with junior associates and the Serranos' large entourage.

At the head of the boardroom table, Riddle and Robinson flanked both sides of the Serrano men, respectively. Marco rattled off some choice words in Spanish, the only one I could understand was "basura." Riddle seemed skittish, something I never had seen in him before. Robinson had his usual cool, aloof demeanor as he tapped away on his smartphone. After a peek at his watch, Riddle nodded. "Mr. Harrison. Ms. James. I think you should probably begin."

I passed out notes as Ari gave a brief introduction, talking about our design aesthetic and our direction. She stood next to me, wearing a simple black shift dress and heels, her hair back in a tight bun reminiscent of her first day at R&R. I willed my eyes to focus on the monitor because Ari looked so damn good that it was hard to focus. It had been a week since she'd called things off. It felt like an eternity. As she pulled up the design on the computer, I sat back down. I shifted a few times in my seat as her hips were parallel to my face. My twitching dick was being signaled by my brain. To think we've had the pleasure of seeing this woman naked. Those hips were on top of us. I moved my eyes down to my notes, willing my penis to behave itself. Now wasn't the time. But dear God, I missed her.

As Ari pulled up her laptop to connect to the larger screen at the head of the boardroom, images flickered. A look of panic came across Ari's face. I jumped up.

I leaned close to her. "You okay?"

"Not this shit again," Ari whispered.

My eyes widened. "It's probably a glitch. Don't worry."

Just as Ari was about to speak, we heard a collective gasp from the audience, and then claps. We both looked at the screen as our images came up. My heart finally slowed down to a normal beat.

"See, it's all good," I whispered to Ari.

Ari nodded curtly. Assured that everything was fine, we proceeded with our presentation. We kept the idea for functional gardens and green space, including suites that included Mediterranean inspired terraces. Ari's final version of the fan experience, complete with what would be the largest outdoor screen in major league soccer, received many nods of approval. I looked over at the Serrano team for some sign of approval. They were nodding their heads. Even Marco was taking notes.

Once we concluded, the boardroom was so quiet you could hear a mouse piss on cotton. We sat in our seats, waiting with bated breath for some type of decision. My mind was all over the place. I wanted this over with.

Paulo Serrano sat in his chair, whispering to his assistant, who nodded and spoke rapid Spanish. After a few minutes of his assistant taking notes, Paulo cleared his throat and began. "We both appreciated the hard work each team brought to the design of this stadium. I appreciated the options presented. For us, soccer is a passion. It is a sport that shows the heart and humanity of people. It is a sport whose emphasis on teamwork is at its core. For that reason, we picked the team whose design had heart and passion, who clearly valued teamwork and our principles. For them, it was a labor of love. So, congratulations to Mr. Harrison and Ms. James. We will move forward with your design."

The boardroom erupted into applause. Ari reached out for a fist bump, but I quickly pulled her in for a hug—a hug that seemed to go on for an inappropriate amount of time. I didn't care. I held on to the moment, to the smell, to the feeling of her in my arms again. My hands found the small of her back like muscle memory. I heard Riddle clear his throat, and we broke apart quickly.

"Congratulations, you two. Ms. James. Mr. Harrison. This is an amazing accomplishment for the two of you." Riddle patted me on the back.

"Yes, it is." Ari attempted to respond calmly, her excitement still radiating.

"Yes. I couldn't have done this without Ms. James." I turned to smile at Ari, whose smile barely reached her eyes.

"Good, now can we go? I have a flight to Milan to catch," quipped Marco, who was already back in his dark shades and typing away on his phone.

Ari and I looked at each other and smiled. Paulo approached us, shaking both of our hands. "Excellent, you two. I knew it! My secret weapon! I was right, no?"

I looked over at Ari and then Paulo. "Indeed, you were."

Mr. Robinson approached as the Serranos and their team were leaving the boardroom. "Porter, we'd like to have a word with you. Ms. James, if you'll excuse us."

Ari nodded, gathered her notes, and quickly exited along with the rest of the associates. Before she left, Ari turned and gave me a thumbs-up. The first sign of warmth from Ari I'd had in a week. I smiled.

I swallowed, closing my eyes to take in a deep breath. *This is it. This is the moment. Riddle, Robinson, and Harrison.* Riddle motioned for me to take a seat and I did, with Robinson sitting directly in front of me.

Robinson smoothed out his tie. "You and Ms. James seem to have a good working relationship."

I nodded. "We do. She's amazing. Not sure I could have pulled this off without her."

Riddle nodded. "Yes. She's seemed to be a positive influence on you. Design wise, that is."

"Yeah, she's been great to work with. Ari, I mean, Ms. James was integral, really."

Maybe I was laying it on a little thick, but I wanted

them to know that Ari had more than done her fair share with this stadium project. If it was credit that Ari wanted, I wanted to make sure she got it.

Riddle and Robinson quieted and stared at me. Riddle uncomfortably rubbed the back of his neck. The temperature in the room suddenly changed. *Was this not the promotion?* I stared between the two men until Robinson leaned across the table.

"And how well do you know Ms. James, Mr. Harrison?" he asked, his tone curiously suspicious.

I scrunched my forehead and leaned back. "I know her well. It's been nearly four intense months of working together. And…"

I hesitated. Although my partnership was on the line, I had no idea where Ari and I stood. Up until a week ago, I would have been ready to disclose our relationship.

"And" I continued, "we've begun seeing each other's…vision and design aesthetic." I swallowed the last words.

Robinson shook his head while Riddle scratched his temple. I waited a few seconds before responding. "As a potential partner, I can be impartial when it comes to new projects or clients. Although Ari and I have a close working relationship, I'd show no favoritism at all."

Robinson huffed under his breath, his disdain apparent and stinking up what was a joyous boardroom like three-day-old shit. What was going on?

Riddle frowned. "Porter, I hate to ask but is anything else going on between you and Ms. James?"

A wave of coldness hit me like a ton of bricks. "No. Why?"

Riddle gestured wildly with his arms. "Porter, I'm glad to hear it's just work between the two of you. I'm going to be honest. I hate to disclose such matters, but Ms. James left Leland due to her close working relationship with a colleague. It seems like she has a pattern of getting involved with coworkers, and when things go south, she begins harassing them and defaming their character, making outlandish claims about their work ethic. Glad to hear that Ms. James is keeping it above board."

The hairs on the back of my neck stood up. "Mr. Riddle, Ari has told me all about what happened. It was awful. Seems like the only person harmed in the situation was Ari. Surely, you're not taking their word for it. Have you talked to Ari? Heard her side of things?"

Robinson scoffed, "Porter, are you questioning the honesty and integrity of a firm like Leland, Stokes, and Brandies? Those were serious allegations she slung toward a promising young architect."

Promising? I felt sick at the thought of Maurice characterized as anything beyond a lowlife. "No, but even a firm like LBS can get it wrong. You and I both know this industry can be savage. People do anything to get to the top. Ari was just an example of the many people who've been used and hurt in this industry because of someone else's ambitions."

Riddle folded his arms across his chest. "You don't get it, son."

Robinson nodded in agreement. "Yes. While we certainly think Ari has elevated your work and that she's a talented architect, we can see now that your friendship has clouded your judgment. And if you want to make partner, you don't need that distraction."

Distraction? The words swirled around my head until it registered: They were going to fire her. They had used her to get the stadium project and now, they were going to let her go.

I leaned across the table, anger flaring my nostrils. "Ari isn't distracting me, sirs."

"Do you want to make partner or not, Porter? That's the real question," countered Robinson.

I looked between the two men, bewildered. "Of course, I do. I also don't want the firm to lose a good architect like Ari either. I mean, why did you hire her in the first place? Do you want her to sue you all?" I was hoping the threat of a lawsuit would take some of the wind out of their sails. My mind raced; I could call Todd. Even if he couldn't take this case, Todd knew plenty of high-powered attorneys that would be biting at the chance to get a large settlement due to wrongful termination. Ari could beat this.

Riddle shifted uncomfortably in his seat, his glasses sliding down the bridge of his pointy nose. "Son, let's not talk lawsuits. Besides, Porter, it's no secret that your work lately had been, how shall I put this, uninspired. I thought someone as talented as Ms. James could bring something out of you design wise. And look! She did. Be thankful she's elevated you to the top of your game. You're a genuine contender for partner. This stadium on your résumé is the crown jewel."

Then along comes Ari, to prop you up and make you save face. Shine you up...

My mouth went dry as I thought about Ari's words. The vein in my neck throbbed as my fingers dug into the boardroom table. Basically, they hired Ari to be my "work fluffer" so they could seal this deal with the Serranos. They didn't believe in my talent. They didn't think I was good enough to do this on my own.

Robinson shifted in his seat, interrupting my thoughts. "Porter? Are you with us?"

I nodded, still in a haze of thoughts. "Is that all?"

Robinson scratched his receding hairline. "Porter, we think it's best that you and Ms. James discontinue working together. It'll give the appearance of impartiality if you become a partner. We'll put her on other projects until we figure things out."

Shit. They were going to ice her out. This was Riddle and Robinson's tried-and-true tactic if they wanted to fire someone. They put those deemed unworthy on bullshit projects or gave them very little to do until the person quit or made the slightest mistake, which resulted in their termination. I didn't want that for Ari.

I rose from my chair, having heard enough. "Sirs, Ari is a damn good architect. It would be a shame for this firm to lose her."

"One that you're willing to bet your career on?" asked Robinson.

I stood erect, buttoning my suit jacket, and smoothing out my tie. "I would."

"Very well," said Robinson. "We'll be announcing the partnership decision at the groundbreaking. In the meantime, evaluate what's important to you, Mr. Harrison. Women come and go, trust me. I'm working on wife number four." He and Riddle let out dry chuckles. I felt my stomach working itself into knots. Ari was right all along. Men in our industry were colder, more callous than I could ever imagine they were. I was naïve to think Riddle and Robinson would be any different.

I made my way toward the boardroom door, slamming it closed behind me. I walked the halls in a stupor, not sure of what I'd just heard or experienced back there. First

Ari, and now this from the partners. It felt like the world as I knew it was fracturing. As I went to open my office door, Greer's face appeared out of nowhere.

"Shit, man! What the fuck!" I yelled, startled at the hazy figure in a deep purple suit. Greer looked like a ridiculously tall walking eggplant.

Greer threw up his hands. "Sorry. I just came by to congratulate you."

My eyes widened in disbelief. In the fifteen years working here, Greer had never congratulated me on a damn thing. "Wow, thanks, Greer. I appreciate that."

Greer huffed. "I guess the Serranos were looking for something more…pedestrian."

And there it was. The backhanded compliment. "Well, thanks anyway. I need to go talk to Ari." I moved past Greer to go across the hall.

"By the way," Greer chirped. "I hope you got more out of Ari than some design inspiration."

I froze as my brain slowly processed Greer's words. "What did you just say?"

Greer stepped closer, leaning down to whisper. "I heard she likes to give her design partners a little congratulatory sloppy top, if you know what I mean?" He dryly chuckled as he motioned a lazy blow job with his hand. "So how was it?"

My mind went black as I pushed him up against the wall, anger searing my lungs. Greer had at least twenty pounds and two inches on me. At that moment, logic was out of the window.

"Don't fucking talk about her that way!" I hissed, my eye twitching with rage.

"Yo! Chill, Porter, it was a joke! Let me go!"

I held on to the lapel of his jacket. "Keep on fucking with me! I dare you!"

"Porter!" a female voice yelled. I turned to face Ari, who had one hand on my arm. A crowd of associates had stepped into the hallway. I let go of Greer as Ari led me into her office.

Ari closed the door and pointed at a chair, instructing me to sit. I couldn't. I was too charged up, opting to move about in circles in her office.

"I swear, I'm going to kill him!"

"Porter, stop! Greer isn't worth it."

"Did you hear him? He disrespected you, Ari!"

Ari frowned, then shrugged. "I did and who cares!"

I stopped pacing. "What do you mean, who cares? Ari, he's making you out to be some kind of...whore."

Ari closed her eyes, then sighed. "I don't care what he thinks about me. Or what he's heard about me, Porter. Your outburst, however, wasn't warranted."

"I was defending you, Ari," I yelled.

"I don't need defending, Porter. I've told you repeatedly, I'm a grown woman. I've heard worse. Trust me."

I sat in the chair next to Ari's desk. Ari sat behind her desk, her hand on her chin. "Porter, do you want to be partner?"

"Of course, I do!"

"Do you care about my career?"

I squinted, then frowned. "Of course, I do, Ari. That's a dumb question."

"Then why are you making things harder for the both of us? There are only about five hundred Black architects in the world. How many of them are women?"

"I..." I didn't know the exact number, but it was small. Ari interrupted. "Listen, Porter, I don't know how long

I'll be here at the firm. I don't need my time here made worse by the immature actions of a man."

"I'm sorry," I whispered, ashamed that I'd given her secondhand embarrassment. I thought I was doing what any man would do...what *her* man would do.

"It's fine. It's just... I don't need another reason for the partners to want to axe me."

"What do you mean? Did the partners say something to you?"

Ari blinked. "No. Did they say something to you?"

I swallowed, and it felt like razor blades were in my throat. "Well, sort of. They were just saying I was in the running for partner." I took a deep breath and looked up at the ceiling. "They thought it best that we don't work together anymore so I can appear impartial moving forward in the process. And..." I hesitated.

Ari stared at me. "And what?"

"Ari, I think they're up to something. I think the partners want to ice you out until you either walk or..."

"They fire me," finished Ari.

"Wait, did you know? How?"

Ari narrowed her eyes. "That's not important. The real question is why would you want to jeopardize everything we've done by fighting Greer? Over rumors?"

I shook my head, unable to understand why Ari was being so nonchalant over this. "It wasn't nothing. It was about you. Ari, I love you. Your reputation is important. We can fight this. I can call my brother. And..."

Ari scoffed. "Porter, it's pointless. As for my reputation? Trust me, that ship has sailed, it seems."

"What are you talking about?"

Ari waved her hands dismissively. "Nothing. Just forget it."

We sat in silence for several minutes. I was scrambling, replaying the events of the morning. It couldn't go down like this. What could I do? It was clear that Ari didn't have the energy to fight this.

"Porter?" Ari was looking at my face, her brow furrowed in consternation.

My eyes reluctantly met hers. "Let's just get back to work. Do a little post-presentation analysis. Maybe anticipate any changes the Serranos may have for us with the overall design?"

Ari nodded as she pulled out her laptop. "Great. Let me pull up my notes."

I leaned against the chair and internally cursed myself for letting the bullshit of this office get the best of me.

Chapter Thirty-One

Ari

My meeting with the partners came days after our stadium presentation, just before the holiday break. I nodded my head and smiled an achingly saccharine smile, thanking them for the opportunity to work on something new. I should have gotten a fucking Oscar for my performance. *Best Docile Female in an Office.* Immediately, they put me on some smaller projects in the office, the projects other associates didn't want to touch. I guess their strategy was to bore me to fucking death until I left. Too bad that would not work. I found pleasure in anything. I was going to make the best of this until I left on my accord. Quitting a job before the new year wasn't the wisest thing to do. Besides, I hadn't spent Christmas with my mother in ages. I couldn't let my mother spend another holiday season alone.

Porter and I were cordial, but we kept our distance. It hurt. Knowing that Greer was willing to use our relationship against us was reason enough to not be seen together. I worked late most nights, avoiding everyone in the office, especially Porter.

As I looked over sketches for a dorm at a private Lutheran college, stuffing my face with takeout Chinese, there was a knock at my door. It was well past eight and I assumed it could only be the janitor doing their usual rounds. Without looking up, I called for whomever to come in.

"Ms. James. I hope I'm not disturbing you," said a voice in a soft, musical accent.

To my surprise, standing there was Paulo Serrano. I choked, attempting to swallow the last of the chicken lo mein I'd been eating.

"Do you mind if I come in?" Paulo asked, already inside my office. I motioned for him to take a seat in front of my desk, hoping he didn't take notice of my shaking legs. Had he changed his mind on the design? I couldn't take any more losses for the year.

"Mr. Serrano. What can I do for you at this hour?" I asked, as I tried to temper the nervousness in my voice and swallow the remaining lo mein in the process.

"Ms. James. I came once again to congratulate you and Mr. Harrison on your design for the stadium. It was phenomenal. You two really work well together. Mr. Riddle told me you two are moving on to other projects individually. That is a shame, Ms. James. Sometimes the best partners are those we work with. I saw the chemistry you two exuded when my wife and I had dinner with you. You two are in love, no?"

Stunned, I smoothed down my gray silk blouse and adjusted myself in my seat. "Well, Mr. Serrano, that would be inappropriate. We were just partners on this project. That is all," I concluded.

Paulo nodded with a knowing smile. "Ms. James. Ari, if I may. I'm no fool. What the two of you had, just worked. The chemistry. It flowed into the designs you gave us: passionate, creative, full of life. Not that sterile, reductive nonsense Greer presented to us. That's why we chose your design. I know Mr. Harrison contributed, but I know you were the heart and soul of the design. I've seen your previous work. You carry that heart everywhere you go."

My heart swelled at the compliment. "I appreciate it."

"Yes. So glad the firm could accommodate the modified timeline. I know us breaking ground on Valentine's Day is a bit of a stretch. I had to do some negotiating, but permits are in place. Construction is secured. I just cannot wait to see the smile on Marina's face. Maybe I'll name it after her. The Marina Center." Paulo gestured, his hand dancing across the air.

I smiled. Only billionaires could give entire stadiums to their spouses as gifts. "I'm sure she's going to be thrilled."

"But I'm not here to talk about the stadium. I have a proposition. So, I'll cut to the chase, as they say. My brother and I are interested in opening a few resorts on the coast of Spain and Portugal. They would be small, intimate, high-end luxury resorts. I spoke about you with a friend in Madrid. Do you know Claudio Velez?"

I nearly fell out of my chair. "Claudio Velez? Of Velez Design Group? Of course, I do. Well, I know *of* him, of course." I was grossly downplaying my love of Claudio Velez. His designs were inspirational. Velez was head of one of the top architectural firms in the world, working on a variety of notable buildings that ranged from museums to the homes of the rich and famous. And now, Claudio Velez knew who the hell I was. I could die.

"Good. Well, I told him about your fabulous eye for design. He wants to meet you. You two would work together in Madrid on our next venture: Serrano Resorts. Here is his card." Paulo pulled out a sleek black-and-gold business card and slid it across my desk. "He'll be expecting your call next week. After you finish our project, of course. Have you ever been to Madrid, Ari?"

I shook my head, staring at the embossed card. "No. I haven't, actually."

Paulo smiled. "You're going to love it. The work of Antonio Palacios is exquisite. A true master in your field." He looked down at his Rolex. "I apologize. I must run. I look forward to working with you. Talent like yours doesn't need to be squandered. You're bigger than this stadium. Start brushing up on your Spanish, señorita." Paulo excused himself and left my office.

You're bigger than this stadium.

I stared at the card, twirling it through my fingers. Claudio Velez. CEO. Velez Design Group. Madrid. My grandmother used to say when God closes one door, God will open a window. This was more than a window. It was a goddamn retractable roof.

I looked around my office. My heart ached. I thought I had felt at home again—at a job I love, in a house I wanted to keep for generations, in love with someone who cared for me. But I had been wrong about one thing: Riddle and Robinson would never feel like home.

An offer like Paulo Serrano's was a once-in-a-lifetime thing. Especially for women like me. I put my heels up on my desk, threw my head back, letting out a tremendous sigh. Working with Claudio Velez would make everyone who ever doubted me eat their words. It would be the sweetest revenge and I'd relish in that fact. They could all kiss my ass.

Well, not all of them.

Would I tell Porter? Would it even matter? As a friend and colleague, he'd be happy for me. He'd want me to spread my wings. As the man who loved me more than my heart could take; this would crush him even more than my meltdown had weeks before.

I held the card up to the light, admiring the glint of the gold lettering. The opportunity to design with Claudio Velez for the Serranos seemed to be part of God's perfect timing.

So why was I feeling like crap?

Chapter Thirty-Two

Porter

I fucking *hate Valentine's Day.*

The press, local and national, crowded the front of the stage, out in full force for the groundbreaking of the stadium. The crowd of other spectators was also rather sizable. My mom, Desmond, and Todd showed up as my guests to the groundbreaking. My mom, in her bright yellow suit, gave me a big thumbs-up and blew a kiss. Todd was biting his nails, trying to hide his nervousness.

Today was a monumental day for the firm and possibly for me. Despite me nearly beating Greer down in the hallway, I was still in the running for partner. As weeks went by, I became more indifferent. The thought of being affiliated with the likes of Riddle and Robinson left a sour taste in my mouth. This relentless pursuit of becoming a partner had cost me the one thing I wanted most—Ari. I wanted Ari standing next to me. This was our baby. Without her, it was pointless to be here.

I stood on stage in the unusually early spring heat, in my tailored suit and hard hat. Riddle and Robinson were all smiles with the Serrano brothers, shaking hands furiously. Of course, Greer was there, smiling like a schem-

ing comic supervillain as if he had done all the work.
As soon as we'd arrived at the groundbreaking, Greer
had said it was "on." I rolled my eyes. He was far too
confident for a guy who was always coming in second.
Today was going to be no different.

Paulo and his wife were there, dressed immaculately
as if they were the King and Queen of Spain. They
smiled warmly at me, and I nodded politely. Marco Serrano was also there, with his new model of the week on
his arm and in his signature dark aviators. I admired the
man's commitment to his playboy image.

Suddenly, I felt Sean's firm hand on my shoulder. I
looked at him, dressed in a suit, which was unusual for
him. I looked down at his feet and laughed. Yep, still in
black Timberland work boots. Sean's firm had won the
bid for construction of the stadium, which was a lucky
break for everyone.

"Good to be working with you again, buddy," said
Sean, his wild red hair sticking out of his O'MALLEY
BROS. emblazoned hard hat. We both turned and plastered on fake smiles as a photographer motioned for us
to get closer for a photo.

"Thanks, dude. This is going to be fun," I said through
my smiling teeth.

"Yeah, I saw the designs. You and Ari did a bang-up
job, man! That fan experience. Sustainable and functional gardens? Wow. What an innovative approach,"
said Sean, as he strained to do the same.

The mention of her name was like twisting a knife in
what remained of my broken heart. I took a deep breath.
"Yeah, she did a great job."

Sean looked around, confused. "Where is she, by the

way? I wanted to say hello. I got tickets for opening day. Thought you two would enjoy going."

I looked out at the crowd with a blank expression. "She's not with the firm anymore."

Sean chuckled. "What'd you do, man? Run the lady off."

When we returned to the office in the new year, Ari's office was dark, completely cleared out. I had to learn from Greer that Ari resigned to take a position with Claudio Velez, effective immediately. She'd put her notice in a few days before we returned back in the office without telling me a word. Not a call or even text which hurt like hell. Had things gotten that bad between us? Of course, I wouldn't have told her not to take the job. It was a huge opportunity. Nevertheless, she'd left, closing the book on the possibility of us.

The news station aimed another camera in my direction as I continued to talk through my teeth, an artificial smile plastered across my face. "Maybe. She leaves for Madrid today."

"Madrid? As in Spain? Dude, you fucked it up that badly that she had to go all the way to Europe to get away from you?"

I looked at him, expressionless. He abruptly stopped chuckling, sensing my annoyance. "I'm sorry, dude. Why Madrid?"

I looked down at the red clay under my feet. "She got an offer that she couldn't refuse. Claudio Velez? Ever heard of him?"

Sean's jaw dropped. "Claudio Velez? That did the huge Dubai hotel? *That* Claudio Velez?"

"Yep. She's on to bigger and better." I wasn't sure I

was talking about Claudio Velez's firm anymore. Neither was Sean.

"Aww, buddy! Alright, let me go over here and get some shots with my foreman. And rub elbows with the Serranos. Maybe some rich people's vibes will rub off on me!" Sean patted my shoulder, giving it a bit of a squeeze. "She'll be back before you know it. You two can't stay away from each other." I appreciated his hopefulness.

As cameras flashed, Greer stood next to me. "Missing your girl?"

A flash of heat crawled up my collar. "Why the fuck do you care?"

Greer adjusted his cuff links. "She wasn't a good fit at this firm, anyway. I don't get what you saw in her."

I turned to Greer. His hard hat was nearly at the top of my forehead. "Greer, keep Ari's name out your mouth."

Greer laughed. "Someone should have been telling you to keep your mouth off Ari. The way you stood up for her, I should have known it was something more. You lack focus. That's not the makings of a partner. I thought you had better sense than that."

I clenched my jaw. "After today, never speak to me again, you conniving, back-stabbing motherfucker. You're strutting like a peacock like this was your project. This was my project. Mine and Ari's. You came in, thinking you were going to be the closer. Dude, we won. Get over it."

I smiled a bit to myself. Ari would be proud that I used a baseball metaphor. *Even if I don't think I used it correctly.*

Greer huffed. "Winning? I'm not the one pouting because they lost their girl. See, that's your problem, Harrison. Instead of reveling in the fact that you designed this monstrosity of a stadium, you're crying over some bitch. A bitch who apparently lets her partners hit. Glad I got her up out of here. Just a worthless excuse for an architect."

"What the fuck did you just say?" I stepped to Greer even closer, the smell of his overbearing cologne simultaneously making me sick and enraged. Greer tried to back up, but I met him pace for pace. "Say that shit again. I dare you to."

"You heard me. She had to go. I told the partners about her Chicago days, and they agreed. She was a liability. Both of you...worthless." Greer turned his back, attempting to walk away.

I grabbed his arm, turning him around to face me. "And you're one step below Clarence Thomas, thinking your Harvard degree makes you better than everyone. You're from Compton, my dude! Cut the bullshit."

As soon as I stepped an inch closer, I saw Riddle out of the corner of my eye coming to swiftly maneuver between us. A photographer was in tow, standing at attention, ready to snap a few shots.

"Ah. Yes...can you get a picture of me with my seniormost designers here?" Riddle was grabbing my shoulder with a death grip as he turned us around to face the camera.

"You two, cool it," he said under his breath to us. "Even after our announcement, the two of you still must work together. Understand? We're a team."

"Yes, sir," I said through my teeth which were clenched so hard I was sure I was cracking a crown.

"Of course, Mr. Riddle," said Greer, his tone saccharine like a scolded child.

"Good," Riddle said as he patted both of our shoulders, hard. I winced. For a rather small man, his hands packed a punch.

I let out a deep breath and tried to release the anger that was tightly wound in my jaws. I looked out into the crowd and focused on my family. Under ideal circumstances, Ari would have been my center of calm. Luckily, they hadn't seen me almost coming to blows with Greer in front of hundreds of people. *Stay cool, Harrison.*

A tap on the microphone quieted the crowd. Mr. Robinson was at the podium, flanked by most of the firm, the mayor, and, of course, the Serranos and their entourage. In front was a long, red ribbon, embossed with the Serrano Group logo, readied for the cutting. I stood reluctantly next to Jacobi, who eyed me with a combination of pity and disgust.

"Greetings," began Robinson. "We want to thank the City of Atlanta for joining us on this momentous occasion. The Serrano Group and the firm of Riddle and Robinson are proud to bring the city one of the most state-of-the-art soccer stadiums in all Major League Soccer. But first, I'd like to thank the team here at Riddle and Robinson who made it possible. In almost forty years of existence, we haven't had a finer lot of designers."

The crowd clapped. My mother was beaming, taking a photo with her phone. I'm sure it would be blurry, and Desmond would have to fix it. I smiled at the thought.

Robinson continued. "I'd like to thank the leadership of my founding partner, Douglas Riddle, for guiding the ship and cultivating a new talent. I'd like to thank the hard work of our senior designer, Porter Harrison, Jr., as well as the talent of our former junior associate and his partner on this massive undertaking, Ms. Ari James.

Ms. James is no longer with the firm. We wish her well as she joins the design team at Claudio Velez, Madrid. We wish her the best and are thankful for her vision on this stadium."

The audience clapped. I tried my best not to roll my eyes. Surely, they didn't wish her the best. They couldn't care less where Ari landed. I'm just thankful that Paulo saw something in her that Riddle and Robinson didn't. She wouldn't have to deal with the crap of her past anymore. Her future was so bright. *Finally.*

Once the applause died down, Robinson continued. "Riddle and Robinson are moving into the future. As we break ground on The Marina Center, we break new ground in terms of leadership at our firm. Without further ado, the firm is delighted and honored to name Darius Greer, our newest partner. We're proud of his tenacity and hard work, always putting the firm first. Darius, if you'd like to say a few words…"

Darius?

My ears began to ring like a church bell. My vision went blurry as the crowd appeared to clap in slow motion. I looked out toward the crowd, my eyes instantly locking on my mother, who covered her mouth with her hands in disbelief. Todd looked as if he wanted to vomit. Desmond's lips were moving furiously as he gestured toward the stage. I looked over at the Serranos, who were clapping as well. Paulo gave me a sympathetic smile.

I stood frozen. Darius brushed past me with a smug expression and said a few words at the podium. My head was pounding, as if Art Blakely were drumming on a continuous loop. I zoned out during Darius's self-aggrandizing speech, only snapping out of it as he turned the mic over to the Serrano Group PR team. I took off my hard hat, smoothing my curls down into submission.

Dazed, I turned to Sean. He patted my shoulder. "Dude! This is so fucked up."

I was numb. Fifteen years of busting my ass late nights and early mornings were pointless. I tried so hard to prove my worth for nothing. I had co-designed an amazing feat of architecture. For what? Nothing. None of it had been worth it. I didn't have a partnership with the firm. I didn't have the respect of my peers. And I didn't have Ari.

I could change that.

I looked at my watch. It was close to 12:00 p.m. I moved through the crowd on the stage, past the partners and toward Paulo Serrano. Paulo turned to me with a sympathetic smile.

"Porter. I'm sorry about the partnership, my friend."

"What time is she leaving?" I said, the words falling out of my mouth heavy like stones.

"Aye. Who is leaving?" Paulo asked, confused at my line of questioning.

"Ari! Do you know what time she leaves for Madrid?" I was yelling and had to catch myself.

With a slight smile, Paulo looked at me, then turned to his assistant. He spoke in rapid Spanish. Confused, the assistant reluctantly opened her iPad and scrolled for what seemed like ages. Then she responded to Mr. Serrano in Spanish. He nodded, giving her permission to relay the information.

"Ms. James's flight is at 2:30 p.m., señor."

I groaned. "Fuck. Thanks."

Just as the mayor was about to cut the ribbon for a photo op, I ran, pushing past everyone onstage, including her security. Riddle grabbed my arm.

"Porter, son? Where are you going? We still have some photos to take. Questions to answer."

Mr. Robinson joined Riddle at his side, his face creased with anger. "Don't make a scene, Porter. I know things didn't go as planned but…"

I snatched my arm away from Riddle. I looked between the two men, disappointed at them. I shoved my hard hat into Mr. Robinson's chest and he took a little stumble backward.

"I'm not your fucking son. I quit."

"Porter, you don't mean…"

"I said I quit!"

Before I could leave the podium, Greer stepped in front of me.

"No hard feelings, Porter? I had to let the partners know about Ari's shit in Chicago. It's just business. Okay?" He extended his hand.

Before I knew it, I'd pulled back and punched him square in the jaw. Greer stumbled backward on impact, nearly landing on Jacobi.

"I'm suing you!" Greer yelled, clearly rocked by the punch, rubbing his jaw. "Better yet, you're fired! As named partner, I'm firing you!"

"You can't fire me, asshole!" I yelled. "I don't work here anymore!"

I ran down the steps, pushing through the throngs of reporters to find my family. Their faces were in shock. And rightfully so. I'd just punched a guy on national TV. I was sure I'd be on TMZ before long with the headline Crazy Architect Breaks Ground and Jaw on Live TV.

"Oh, honey!" My mom stretched her arms out for a hug but I stepped back. Naturally, she was confused. I looked toward Todd, desperate for my little brother's help. Todd's sobriety had been unwavering these past months. But I had to be sure.

"Todd? You good?" I asked.

Reluctant to answer, Todd looked at mom, then responded. "Uhm. Yeah. Why?"

"Because I need you, brother. You're taking me to the international terminal. I'm going to get Ari."

"But… I…" began Todd, his faced etched with worry. "I don't know, PJ. I really shouldn't… I'm on a provisional license. I can't fuck things up. You understand. I would if I could—"

In that moment, I felt a hand on my back. "I got you, buddy," said Sean, his face bright with a smile. "I'll drive. Besides, your hand is in no condition after landing that Tyson-level punch!"

My mother grabbed my face, kissing my cheeks until they burned. Desmond patted my back hard and said, "Me proud of ya, son!"

I looked at my parents. "Mom. Desmond. I don't want you to worry but, if you couldn't tell back there, I don't have a job anymore. I'll be fine. And…"

"Boy, hush! Go get that girl," interrupted my mother, still kissing my reddening cheeks.

I tossed my keys to Sean. "My car is faster."

"Dude, I got a new BMW!" scoffed Sean. "My knees will be to my chest in that matchbox of a car!"

"Sean!" my mother yelled. "Now is not the time to have a pissing contest about the goddamn car. Get my son to that terminal!"

Chapter Thirty-Three

Ari

Every television in the airport terminal was tuned to the news, whose top story was the groundbreaking of the state-of-the-art Marina Center in Atlanta. One reporter called it an "ambitious feat of design that was going to wow soccer fans for years to come." I beamed with pride, knowing that my hard work was being praised. My time at Riddle and Robinson wasn't a total waste. As the camera panned out, my heart stopped as soon as I saw Porter's face, solemn and serious. He looked uncomfortable in the hideous yellow hard hat that concealed what I'm sure was a neat fade topped with curls. I felt a twinge of regret. I ignored his every call and text, trying to save myself from the heartache. In true Ari fashion, I'd left without a word. It would have been entirely too painful, and I didn't do painful goodbyes.

The gate agent signaled that boarding would begin in ten minutes. I looked at my first-class ticket, thankful that Claudio Velez had allowed me to come a few weeks early to Spain to get settled. The irony of my flight being on Valentine's Day wasn't lost on me. Everything and everyone I'd loved was here in Atlanta. My mother. Bella. My beautiful house. Porter. Especially Porter.

I was leaving them all behind; once again I'd fallen in love and once again, it cost me everything.

I headed toward the gate as the agent called for first-class seating. I took a quick look inside my bag, making sure my passport was there. As I handed the agent my boarding pass, I heard a familiar voice.

"Ari! Ari Marie James!"

I turned to see Porter, running toward me. His tie was loosened, the sleeves of his gray button-down messily rolled up. The sunlight from the massive windows shone directly on him like a spotlight. By the time he reached the gate agent, Porter was out of breath. Shocked, I excused myself and stepped out of line.

"Porter? What on earth are you doing here? Aren't you supposed to be at the groundbreaking for the stadium?"

"Ari, I quit."

My mouth dropped open. "You did what? Porter, why?"

"I quit because… Let's be honest. I'm not that great of an architect. Besides, working there every day is pointless if you won't be there."

"Porter! Are you serious!" Travelers near the gate stared at me, annoyed. I lowered my voice, apologetically.

"I'm dead ass serious."

My jaw went slack. "I'm about to board a flight to Madrid! As in…now!"

Porter ran a hand down his face. "Ari, listen to me. I've been in love with you from the moment I saw you."

My lips curled up into a smile. "When you saw me in a virtual state of undress in the middle of my office?"

Porter put his hands in his pocket, taking a deep breath. "No. From when I saw you on the train, heading to your first day. And the lady with the tiny dog…and the coffee cup…"

I looked at him, totally bewildered. "Say what?"

"I was on the train that morning. My car was at the mechanic's, remember? The moment I saw you, my heart stopped. Then you were in my office. It was fate."

I felt faint, as if I was going to do a ballroom style death drop to the floor. "You… You saw me earlier that morning? Why didn't you say this before?"

Porter shrugged. "I don't know. I guess I was waiting for a more romantic moment. Like, when I proposed. Or on our fiftieth wedding anniversary."

The gate agent began her last calls for the final boarding zones. I looked at Porter, panic-stricken. The last of the passengers were slowly making their way onto the plane.

Porter grabbed both my hands. "Ari, I have a ticket for the next flight to Madrid. If you want me, if you love me, I'll come with you. If you don't, I'll turn around and go home with a broken heart and a non-refundable plane ticket. I'll try to move on with my life, but I'm telling you now, I won't be able to because my life means nothing without you. Ari, you're my destiny. Since day one."

What the entire fuck was happening? When had my life become a rom-com? Was I secretly Queen Latifah?

As Porter held my hands, I felt the prickly heat between his hand and my own. The sensation pulsed through my veins. *No. I can't do this.* I let his hands go.

"Did you make partner?" I asked, hesitantly. "I mean, before you quit."

Porter looked at me, then pinched the bridge of his

nose. "No. They gave it to Greer. They were never going to make me a partner. Even if they offered it to me, I wasn't going to take it."

Stunned, I put a sympathetic hand against his cheek. Porter gently removed it, kissing my palm, pressing his warm lips into my hand. Tears pricked my eyes.

"Baby, listen to me. All your career you've sacrificed yourself. Let someone else sacrifice for once. Just say the word."

Slowly, I inched my hand away. "I'm sorry, Porter, but I have to go."

I turned and walked toward the gate agent who was doing last calls for the flight, handing her my boarding pass again. The agent, giving me an annoyed side-eye, took it and swiftly scanned it. As I walked toward the gangway, my feet felt as if they were filling with lead. I tugged my hands on the sides of my skirt. I mean, I was heading to Spain. Without Porter. Was I making a mistake?

I stood frozen, halfway between the airplane and the door to the gate. Late passengers pushed past me as I stood like a statue in a garden.

"Ma'am? Ma'am? Is something wrong?" said the flight attendant, peering at me from the door of the plane. "Do you need assistance?"

"It's all wrong…" I said out loud to no one. "I got to go…"

I ran back toward the door, lugging my oversized tote bag. I made it to the door just before the agent was closing. I could hear the woman cursing just as I made it back to the terminal. I scanned the gate, looking for Porter over the crowds making their way through the busy airport. I finally found him standing next to the coffee kiosk, scrolling dejectedly on his phone.

I walked behind him, holding my tote close to me. "I mean, I guess my luggage will get there before I will."

Porter turned around, eyes wide in disbelief. "But... I thought I saw you get on the plane?"

"I got halfway down the ramp and turned around. I sprinted back before they closed the door. The agent was calling out to me, but I didn't care. You made me run. You know I hate running."

Porter put his hands on my face, pulling me closer to him. Our lips met and we kissed without regard to the crowds around us. I'd missed his kisses, the warmth of his breath, the fullness of his lips against mine. Porter deepened the kiss, moving his hands to my hips and me into him, where I was fully aware of his erection, growing slowly in the airport. I pulled back, the taste of his lips lingering. Porter let out a satisfied moan.

"You're stuck with me," I whispered.

"And I'll follow you to the moon and back. Or in this case, Madrid."

Porter kissed me, pushing his body closer to me, and gripping my ass through the fabric of my skirt. The firm grip of his hands made me smile against his lips.

"I'll pay for the ticket change for both of us," Porter whispered into my ear, finally coming up for air.

I threw my head back, laughing. "Oh, I know you will, Trust Fund! And it better be first class. I'm not flying to Madrid in coach."

We kissed again, deeper and with more urgency. We pulled back, desperate for air. Yet, wanted to still drown in each other.

"I love you, Ari."

I looked into his seafoam eyes. They were pooling with tears. Wetness rolled down my own cheeks. Porter took an index finger, sweeping the tears away.

"And I love you too, PJ. But I have a question?"

"Ask me anything, baby?"

"So, when did you kick Greer in the balls? Before or after you quit?"

Porter smiled. "You know me so well, Mon Coeur. But it was more like a punch to the face. My knuckles are still sore."

My face slowly crept into a smile as I looked down at Porter's swollen knuckles. I lifted his hand and kissed the deep purple bruise. "Well, you'll have to tell me all about it on the flight over to Madrid. In the meantime, let's get some ice for that hand, Champ."

Porter laughed. "I will but right now, I'm starving. The flight to Spain is going to be long and I need one last hit of soul food before we go."

"Come on. Let's get you something to eat. I hear they have gumbo on this concourse. I mean, it won't be like Senior's. But—"

Porter kissed me midsentence. After several sweltering kisses, I pulled back, gently pressing the tip of my nose against his. He smiled. "That'll be perfect."

Epilogue

Ari

3 Years Later

We watched as Desmond hung the large mural across the wall of the office foyer. Porter supervised while Eloise, my mom, and I all stood back with our heads cocked to one side in curiosity. Porter had his hands on my back, and as always, was rubbing it in small, reassuring circles.

"Well… What is it?" asked my mother, as she put the temple of her glasses between her teeth.

"Can't you see it?" asked Desmond. "It's a train. You know, where Porter first saw Ari. Porter's the artist. He can explain it better."

"Well," said Porter. "It's my interpretation of that."

My mother shrugged with squinted eyes. "I guess. I don't see it. But if you say so."

Todd walked in, carrying a large box, followed by Kim, holding two gorgeous lamps. Todd was doing great, having been sober for almost three years, and practicing civil rights law at a smaller firm. Todd shifted the box to one hand, giving me a one-arm hug. Kim balanced a lamp on each hip. Both stood in front of the painting, transfixed, trying to figure out what it was.

Todd scrunched his lips in confusion. "Des, what is this? A worm?"

"Yes, a worm! Through a sunset, maybe?" speculated Kim.

Desmond threw his hands up, kissing his teeth. "And you all call yourselves cultured! You all have no eye fuh good art, you know! Rich folks pay good money fuh art like this!"

We all erupted into laughter.

"Well, I think it's nice, honey," said Eloise as she kissed Desmond on the cheek. "This is really going to brighten up the spot for the kids. Look at them! Their first office!"

James-Harrison Designs was a small fine art and architectural firm in the historic Sweet Auburn district. Porter didn't win the bet on calling it "Harrison Squared." Luckily for us, Jamal was now one of the most popular real estate agents in the city. He wasted no time finding us an exceptional building in a glorious, refurbished warehouse space. It was large enough to house a full-size studio for Porter's art as well.

After spending almost three years in Spain, Porter and I knew it was time to go home.

Living in Spain gave Porter the clarity he needed, realizing that architecture hadn't truly made him happy. Porter spent much of the time in Spain working on his art, exhibiting his work in several small, well-respected galleries, and selling pieces. He was truly at peace and happy to have found his calling, without the Harrison name behind him.

My time at the Claudio Velez Firm was amazing. Velez and I had designed four award-winning resorts for the Serranos. All housing James Beard-award-winning chefs, much to Porter's greedy delight. When I resigned, Mr. Velez begged me to stay, enticing me by raising my salary by almost double. He even said he'd hire Porter if it would make me happy. "He's okay," he said. "But I like you much better." I laughed. I told Velez that I appreciated the opportunity, but we were both homesick. He understood.

I watched as Mr. George put the finishing touches on the logo on the door. My mother walked over, deliberately sauntering, swaying her ample hips to bring him a bottle of water from the makeshift cooler. He smiled widely in eager anticipation. A lot had changed in the three years since we had been away—like my mom and Mr. George dating. She said it started with her asking him to help her with some small renovations in her condo. The next thing you know, he asked her to dinner every weekend. I couldn't believe it. Mom assured me she wasn't trying to be the next Mrs. Flores, but she was happy. Mom had even met his kids, and they adored her. She was learning Spanish for an upcoming trip to Ecuador. It wasn't going so well. Beyond learning "agua" and asking where the "baño" was, Doris was hopeless.

Just then, a streak of green and blue tulle swished past, almost knocking me down as they grabbed my legs.

"Sasha! Malia! Get off your Auntie Ari!" yelled Bella as she carried in a box of cupcakes and a thick notebook that I knew was her event planning bible. As usual, she was deliberately overdressed for move-in day in heels, a cardigan, and jeans. She was more invested in planning the welcome party for our new clients than moving boxes. When we opened our firm, we had no problem finding clients, including some former clients of Riddle and Robinson. The endorsement by the Serrano brothers and Claudio Velez certainly helped.

Bella put the cupcakes and the notebook on the receptionist's desk. I had a tinge of sadness looking at the still vacant area. Ms. Gayle had turned down our offer to be our new office manager, saying she'd rather "monitor the old men" and retire with them. Ms. Gayle promised she would visit us from time to time to make sure that we were doing alright.

The twins released me and ran into the arms of my mother, who gave them kisses on each cheek, and then to Porter, who picked both girls up and allowed them to give him a big bear hug. Porter had instantly become Sasha and Malia's favorite new person.

Bella turned to the notebook and began talking a mile a minute. "Listen, I know you don't want to think about it, but I need to know your decision for the open bar. Are we doing a champagne toast at the end? Any particular brand? Also, we need to pick high-boy linen colors. I was thinking gold. I brought cupcakes from the baker to taste. Also, centerpieces…"

I put my hands on Bella's shoulders. "Relax, Bella. It's okay. Whatever you decide, I'm here for it. I know it's going to be beautiful."

Bella took a deep breath and smirked. "I mean, I want to make sure this is perfect for you. This is a major event. Besides, it isn't like I helped plan your *wedding*."

I looked down at my ring and bit my lip, feeling just a little guilty that my best friend wasn't there at one of the biggest moments of my life. Porter and I eloped in Spain six months after our arrival. Despite not having family there, our wedding day was perfect. We were married early morning in a small, village Catholic church. We

signed the registry, and that was it. My mother almost
had an AME-holy-ghost-fit when she learned it was in
Catholic church. Eventually, Doris forgave us. Since dating Mr. George, she'd learned to appreciate a few "Hail
Mary and we out of here" church services.

I felt a tap on my shoulder and turned to face my in-
tern Justina, who wore a Georgia Tech sweatshirt and
sneakers. Her partner Lakshmi, a cute, petite dark-haired
beauty, was by her side, holding a box.

"Welcome to your new home, Justina! I hope you
found your office up to par. I'm still getting used to the
massive layout," I said as I hugged her with a smile.

"Of course, Ari. It's beautiful. I can't thank you
enough. This is going to be amazing," Justina said as
she squeezed Lakshmi's hand. We were lucky one of the
top firms hadn't snagged Justina. After winning several
design awards in undergrad, Justina was a rising star in
architecture in the city. After graduation, she worked a
bit at Riddle and Robinson but left when she and Greer
butted heads. No surprise there. Since making partner,
word on the street was that Greer had become even more
of a raging egomaniac. Even Jacobi left the firm to pursue one of his hidden passions: drag performance. He
was a contestant on *America's Top Drag Superstar*. He
looked amazing but was terrible at lip syncing, though.
He was eliminated on the second episode.

Lakshmi shifted the box in her hand. "It is very gorgeous. And is that a picture of a roller coaster in the
foyer?"

"It be a train! Da boy painted a blasted train!" yelled
Desmond from the foyer as he repositioned the painting
for the hundredth time.

I watched Porter as he walked toward me, wearing

jeans, sneakers, and a fitted gray V-neck shirt. He was still so sexy, even now with a little gray around his temples. He handed me a bottle of water and took a cupcake from Bella, who slapped his hand away playfully.

"Are you sure you don't want to call the firm Harrison Squared, Mrs. Harrison?" said Porter, sinking his teeth into a tower of mint-colored frosting.

I kissed him on the cheek, wiping a little frosting at the corner of his mouth with my finger. "Honey, we've had this conversation. I'm Ari James at work. Besides, James-Harrison Designs sounds…"

"Like an old white dude," said Todd in passing with a wink.

I shook my head. "I was going to say *astute*," yelling in Todd's direction. "Besides, everyone knows I'm your wife. And if you change it now, Mr. George is going to kill you. He just spent an hour putting that logo on the entrance. If he doesn't kill you, my mama will on his behalf."

Porter looked at me, a sly grin on his face. "Girl, you know your mama loves me."

I folded my arms. "Yes, PJ. Everyone loves you. Or will love you."

Porter looked at me quizzically. "Will?"

"Yes, Porter." I reached in my bag and handed Porter a small box. "Will."

Porter sat on the lobby sofa, still covered in plastic. Slowly, he opened the box and pulled out a blue-and-white "Future Hampton Pirates" baby onesie.

Porter's eyes grew large as two Granny Smith apples. "Are you serious right now? Don't play with me, Ari! Am I going to be a daddy?" The word *daddy* echoed in the empty offices. Everyone stopped and turned to look at us. Porter and I had been trying for three years straight with no luck. We went to every specialist in Spain. We completed several rounds of IVF. I winced as I remembered Porter gently administering my shots in the morning. When IVF failed for the final round, I gave up. I was nearing forty-five and thought I was too old. I thought that parenthood wasn't in the cards.

Porter had never given up hope. "Just relax and it'll happen. It'll be easier once we go back home to the States."

He was right. Once we stopped scheduling sex and shots, it happened. I guess we needed to be where we could feel love. And a comfortable mattress. I hate to say it, but European mattresses felt like sleeping in a tomb. Imagine trying to get busy on one.

Porter held up the onesie, yelling with joy. Desmond almost knocked the painting off the foyer wall. Bella put her hands over her mouth, trying to contain her screams and tears. Eloise and Doris hugged each other so tightly, singing a made-up song about becoming grandmas. Todd, Desmond, and Mr. George came over and gave Porter hearty pats on the back. Todd joked that the baby "needs a Howard onesie instead," which resulted in Porter playfully putting his brother in a headlock. Justina and Lakshmi hugged me tightly, too.

Justina eased up, releasing me from her arms. "I don't know how this works. I don't want to hurt the baby!"

I laughed. "It's fine, Justina. Right now, the baby is only the size of a marble."

After the excitement died down, Porter took my hands and stared at me. His face was full of emotions that I knew he couldn't quite articulate. I pushed a stray curl out of my face and leaned in to kiss him. I felt Porter's hands wrap around my waist and then creep around to the front of my T-shirt. He gently rubbed and laughed with amazement to himself. Porter leaned down in front of me and whispered, "Hey, my love! Can you hear me? This is your daddy! I'm going to teach you how to make gumbo, how to tie your shoes, and all about Paul Williams and Augusta Savage. You'll be Porter Harrison, III."

I laughed. "Porter, I'm not sure the baby has ears yet at this point. Also, let's table the third talk for now. One Porter Etienne is one too many. Besides, the baby could be a girl."

"You're right. Maybe her name can be Porsche."

"After your car? You've got to be kidding."

"Yeah. You're right."

Porter eventually got off his knees. "You've made every dream in my life come true, Ari. Who knew that girl on the train would be my destiny?"

Porter spun me around with one hand as giggles escaped me. I smiled, leaning my head on Porter's shoulder. "I think you did."

"I did. That reminds me. We should get some superglue for the new office. For any shoe accidents? Scratch that. You can't be walking around in heels carrying *my* baby. Flats from now on!"

I punched Porter in the shoulder in jest. He pretended to wince. "I'm carrying *our* baby, you jerk! You need to be nice to me."

He pulled me close and with a low voice said, "Oh, I promise to be nice to you. All over this office. Our office…especially back in that boardroom over there. Bending you over that table has been on my mind all day. I mean, when you're the boss married to the other boss, there's no conflict of interest there."

I raised my brow and shook my head. "Porter Harrison, you're something else." *Honestly, I had thought about that table too.*

"And, Ari James Harrison, you're perfect. Always have been and always will be."

I smiled. "Partners-in-design?" I extended my fist.

Porter fist bumped me back, then bent down to kiss my lips, then my belly. "Partners-in-design. For the rest of our lives."

We looked out the window at the city skyline, the gorgeous stadium we designed within view. Porter's hand was firmly around my waist, encircling my growing tummy. Our friends and family were bustling around us, laughing and excited about this new chapter of our lives.

Faintly, in the distance, you could hear the train pulling out of the station.

* * * * *

Acknowledgments

I would be a poor excuse for a Missionary Baptist-raised kid if I did not start these acknowledgments by giving honor to God who is the head of my life. Without God, nothing is possible in my life. Thank you to my spiritual consultant, Pastor D. Danyelle Thomas. You have no idea how much your guidance helped me.

To Kate Marope, thank you so much for seeing something in me and my writing. When I had given up on the dream to have this book out in the world, you fought for it. I thank you from the bottom of my heart.

To Kerri Buckley, at Carina Press. Thank you for making me stretch and grow, breathing new life into my manuscript and me as a writer. I really appreciate everything you've done in making *The Build Up* what it is.

To my writing communities: Inclusive Romance Project, founded by the wonderful Kharma Kelly and Wordmakers, founded by Tasha L. Harrison. Thank you so much for lifting me up, believing in me, and giving me confidence when I needed it most.

To my mentor, Kilby Blades. Your time working with me to polish this manuscript and get it right was invaluable. You are not only a mentor, but a dear friend. I adore you.

Thanks to the writers/critique partners I've met and befriended along the way: Cat, Terri, Noreen, Fortune, Grace, Katherine, Noué, Kwana, Catherine, Dr. Margot, Ruthie, Mimi, AH, Mia T, Lisa, Karmen, Charish, Kelly, Mia H., RM, Ro, Gigi, Piper, Jeannette, Sri…your friendship has been invaluable. Thanks for helping me squash my imposter syndrome.

To my podcast partner, Dr. Yakini Etheridge. You've been there since day one, cheering me on. Thank you for being with me to start our podcast which has afforded me so many opportunities, including this book. It's been an adventure. With a friendship over twenty years strong, we will ride this thing until the wheels fall off.

To my bestie and earliest beta reader, Candace. You have heard me cry, scream, and shout with joy. You never ignore a text message or FaceTime. You don't know what your encouragement has meant to me. I really love you, girl.

To my other besties and forever beta readers, Adana, Yvonne, Taheerah, Angie, Tanisha, Peaches, Jackie, Rita, and Nisha. I love you to the moon and back.

To my HU consultant, Chris Hammond. Thank you all so much for giving me insight into the world of Hampton University, answering silly questions about minute things. You are my brother for life, despite me going to CAU (lol). It's all HBCU love.

To my architectural consultants, Dr. L. David Stewart, and R. Denise Everson. Thank you for giving me insight into the world of Black architects. From jargon to issues, you answered all my questions. Romesha, you showed me how hard it was for sisters to make it in the field. I hope I did you proud with my honest portrayal of Ari.

To my family, especially my dad Ronald, and brother,

Michael. Thank you for encouraging me and making sure that I never gave up. Daddy, thanks for pulling out things I wrote at eight years old to remind me to keep going. Thank you to my mother-in-law, Pat, sister-in-law Janelle, and members of the extended Richardson/Mathews/Chaney clan. There are too many to name, so I thank you and love you.

To Teagan, my little miracle. You pulled me out of a dark place and gave me hope. I hope mommy makes you proud. You are too young to read this book but one day you will. Let's stick to Pete the Cat for now.

Finally, to my husband, Jay. Thanks for supporting me through the nights, early mornings, and tears. You are the cinnamon roll hero of my dreams. My muse. My love. My life has been better than any rom-com I could write. I love you 5-eva.

About the Author

Tati Richardson is co-founder of the Romance in Colour Podcast. A higher education professional for two decades, Tati holds degrees in English from Clark Atlanta University and University of North Carolina-Greensboro. A native of Atlanta, Tati lives in the suburbs with her husband and daughter. She collects red lipstick, Wonder Woman memorabilia, and unique eyewear. The Build Up is Tati's debut novel.

Tati's podcast, Romance in Colour, is available on Spotify, Apple Podcast, Google, and most podcast platforms.

Tati Richardson is represented by Keisha Mennefee, Literary Manager at Honey Magnolia Media. For more information, contact: info@honeymagnolia.co.

Learn more about Tati by visiting her website www.tatiannarichardson.com.

A tour manager determined to revitalize her career.
The client she can't stop thinking about.

Don't miss In Tune *by JN Welsh*

Luke Anderson needs a manager—fast. His last one quit, leaving his tour and his future in jeopardy. Now instead of focusing on his career, he's forced to concentrate on damage control. Powerhouse manager Leona Sable is the full package—smart and talented, not to mention sexy as hell—but her past makes her impossible to trust.

When opportunity knocks in the form of talented EDM DJ Luke "The Musical Prophet" Anderson, Leona is ready to answer. But salvation doesn't come cheap. Luke won't sign until Leona agrees to his outrageous terms—including a no-sex-while-on-tour clause.

Dictating what she does in her personal life crosses a line. But Leona's never been one to back down from a challenge.

One thing is for sure: if she has to suffer, so will he.

Chapter One

If Leona Sable had known how this day was going to turn out, she would have stayed in bed, nestled against her boyfriend pillow with the covers pulled over her head.

How the fuck did I get here? A conversation with her boss and mentor, Abraham Wallace, that started with "The client only wants you" and ended with "Meet me at the Metro Hotel this evening at seven and be dressed for a night out." That's how.

Ever since that conversation a few short hours ago, Leona had been collecting intel on Electronic Dance Music DJ Luke "The Musical Prophet" Anderson.

Had Abe not looked so stressed and hell-bent on acquiring said potential client, she'd still be in hiding, paper-pushing due diligence forms.

Leona sat in the hairdresser's chair in Midtown Manhattan. Her tight corkscrew curls dripped wet onto the towel draped over her shoulders, while she pressed the cell phone to her ear.

"Dale, sweetie, you're telling me that Luke's manager left his tour? Just like that? Why?" Leona strained to hear above the light music playing in the salon.

Dale, her fabulous, long-time source swam in the know while others simply dipped their toe into the pool.

"Allegedly, there was a mash-up of problems. Money issues and fraternization," he whispered into the phone.

Leona wasn't a gossip but she sometimes had to play the role of one to get the information she needed.

"They were dating? Was it serious?"

"Who knows in this industry? But I will say that hearts were broken. And…"

Leona couldn't believe the next words that came out of Dale's mouth, and neither would Abe when she briefed him. "No!"

"Yes, but you won't find a lick about it in the rags. The family is wealthy and adamant about her privacy. They keep paying out."

"Then why would she do that?"

"I don't know, girl. Money got these people like…whoa!"

"Stop." Leona laughed, assessing her milk chocolate brown image in the mirror. "Thanks, D. You gave me a lot to work with. I appreciate it."

"Listen, love. Please don't ever go underground again. I need my concert tickets."

"I promise." Leona hung up.

Her hairdresser started to work. "Let me get started on your twists."

"Change of plan, Kim. Geisha bun. Sleek and sexy."

Kim stilled with wide-toothed comb in hand. "You haven't had that style in a while. Does this mean you're back?"

Kim's excitement surprised her. "No." Leona's raised voice carried above the music.

"Okay, okay. Just asking." Kim's grin reflected in the mirror.

Leona surveyed the room and tapped her left earlobe. "The last thing I need is that rumor getting out."

Kim readied her tools—complete with blow-dryer and brush—for Leona's hair. "Maybe after tonight it won't be a rumor."

For the past year, Leona had stayed out of the spotlight. Lately, she had to admit that the administrative role Abe allowed her to perform was a snore fest, and she'd thought about waging a comeback and once again doing the work she loved. Though she was an experienced personal manager, with production and tour experience, the entertainment industry was fickle and would make her pay for her absence. More importantly, a nagging question remained.

Am I ready?

Leona checked her messages and returned a call to Tracy Ruiz, one of the resident lawyers at Wallace Entertainment. "Hey, Tracy. Got anything on Mr. Wonderful?"

"He doesn't have any priors, but there have been some disturbances of the peace. Mr. Anderson has had a string of episodes involving angry outbursts, but no one was hurt. Only a couple of scuffles here and there."

"This just gets more interesting by the hour. Okay, Tracy. Thanks."

What the hell did Abe get me into? A client with a shady business past and anger management issues... Seriously? A shiver scuttled up her back and her shoulders shimmied in release. *Just get him in the door, Leo, and you'll be done.*

Kim took a brief break from pulling at Leona's kinky curls. "You cold, girl?"

"Oh, no, I'm good. Just some old ghosts trying to bully me."

Kim patted her shoulders.

Leona was tempted to contact Luke's family members for more information, but her experience with her ex-boyfriend gave her pause. The media craziness had adversely affected the Sable family. And though she only sought information—it was a line she was unwilling to cross.

With her hair completed, Leona thanked Kim and headed home. In her walk-in closet, Leona chose her outfit while she listened to one of Luke's interviews. He mentioned a fondness for animal crackers and she chuckled. "And not just any kind either." She loved researching potential clients. Sometimes their quirks and preferences were predictable, other times quite unexpected.

Her phone rang. She picked up when she saw it was Abe.

"Leo? I'm on my way to the hotel. What'd you find out, darlin'?" he asked. Though from Scottish and Spanish stock, Abe had been born and raised in North Carolina. He used the touch of Southern twang in his voice to sweet-talk anyone into doing his bidding.

"He's very into his fans. In fact, that's why this guy is all over the place and not just in the States." She put Abe on speaker and scrolled through some notes on her phone. "Yeah, Brazil, Australia, United Arab Emirates… Yikes. The list of worldwide appearances goes on for pages. What a treacherous schedule."

"Hard worker. What else?"

"He's passionate about his music and active on all social media outlets. We like passion."

"We?"

"Wallace Entertainment," Leona clarified. "People have nice things to say about him. But, Abe? There's a bit of controversy around his last management. His ex-manager stole some astronomical amount of money from him and—"

"That's an unfounded rumor. We need him, Leo."

There's that desperation again. "I get that you want him, but…"

"No, Leo. The company needs him."

"The company? Okay, Abe. What's really going on here?"

Abe was silent. "I'm in a cab, coming up on 14th Street. We'll talk later. See you in a bit."

"Abe…" she called to a dead line. *Damn it. What the hell?* She breathed deep.

She dressed in snug off-white leather bootleg pants and a fitted black shirt with capped sleeves. Sexy black lace accented the top of the shirt—from above her bust to her neck—and covered her back. It was the perfect day-to-night outfit, yet still professional. Too much time had passed since her life required such attire. The outfit felt foreign at first, until the old familiar part of her began to stir.

A sheer off-white shawl draped over her shoulders allowed the light material to pop off of her brown skin. Black peep-toe booties added four inches to her five-foot-four frame. She quickly evaluated her image in the mirror and extended her arm to the reflection, as if offering a handshake to see how her outfit moved. She hadn't done that in years. *You're nervous.* She wiggled her shoulders. *Shake it off. This is old hat, Leo.*

She didn't know what situation awaited her at the Metro Hotel but she was as ready as she'd ever be.

In Tune *by JN Welsh*
Available now wherever eBooks are sold
www.carinapress.com